THE DARK WEDDING DUET

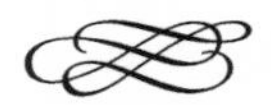

KITTY THOMAS

BURLESQUE PRESS

THE DARK *Wedding* DUET

Kitty Thomas

Burlesque Press

The Dark Wedding Duet

Printed in the United States of America

ISBN-13: 978-1-960480-44-6

Wholesale orders can be placed through the author.

Published by Burlesque Press

Contact the author at kittythomas.com Please use the "licensing" link in the top menu bar.

The Proposal

Kitty Thomas

Burlesque Press

CHAPTER ONE: LIVIA

THE PROPOSAL

I stand at the back of the enormous church. The stained glass windows mute the over bright sun outside on this unassuming summer Saturday at half past four. The string quartet begins to play Pachelbel's Canon in D. Two hundred and fifty guests stand. I take a deep breath and walk down the aisle clutching the bouquet of pale pink roses which hide my shaking hands. I'm wearing a stunning white Valentino gown which I'm convinced has seven thousand buttons down the back. It's a true white, but it's a soft, elegant white.

You don't realize the variety of white until you shop for your wedding gown. The color palette of white goes all the way from the harsh tacky bright white of office supply copy paper to off-white, into beige and blush barely-there pinks and lavender. Occasionally there is the most subtle mint green which you are sure must be a trick of the light.

And even though they aren't all really the same color, lined up on the racks they seem like they all belong together. Like family. I'd considered going a little less traditional with a pale lavender or pink gown, or even that daring pale fairy green, but in the end I went with tradition —anything else feels like half measures with a man who doesn't know the meaning of that word.

I chose to walk down the aisle by myself. I've never liked the idea of giving the bride away or what it represents. Besides, I don't want to bring my father into this; it feels wrong. He's here, on my side with the rest of my family and friends who admittedly take up a much smaller portion of the guest count than the groom's side and business associates. His business associates are seated on my side, so everything looks more even and normal for the pictures.

I am twenty-nine, and to everyone here my story is the story of Disney Princesses—the story every seven-year-old girl fantasizes about until she's long grown out of such fantasies. But I'm not walking down this aisle to my prince. I'm walking down this aisle to the most ruthless man I know.

I feel as though I'm being kidnapped in the middle of a crowded room, but I can't scream. It's like a dream where everyone acts as though everything is fine even though an evil killer clown is sawing my hand off. But still, everyone smiles politely and makes small talk—or in this case, everyone stands and murmurs complimentary things they don't think I can hear as I drift down the aisle like a fairy tale princess.

They think this is the part of the story where the princess gets the prince, where they get married and live happily ever after. But this is the part where she gets locked in the tower.

When I reach the altar, he takes my hand in his, helping me up the two small steps to stand in front of him. The collective sitting of two hundred and fifty people is the last thing I consciously hear as his intense, searing gaze holds mine hostage. His thumb strokes over the back of my hand, and I don't even know anymore if the gesture is meant to comfort or control me.

We stand there, staring at each other. Words fall over me like gentle rain. Vows are spoken. Rings are exchanged. The announcement that we are now husband and wife moves through the air like a cool breeze.

His hand snakes behind my neck pulling me possessively toward him as he claims my mouth as his property. Later he will claim everything else.

I've never had sex with this man. I'm not an innocent. I'm not a virgin, but right now I feel like one—off balance and unsure of what's in store for me behind the closed doors of our suite in only a few short hours. I want to run as far and as fast as I can, but I know he would catch me. Right now the reception is the only thing that buffers me from his dark intentions.

We take what feels like a thousand wedding photos, each one more intimate and romantic than the last. His hands and mouth suddenly feel foreign on me as though he's a stranger and not a man I've been seeing for the past year. The reception is being held at the swank nearby 5-star hotel called The Fremont, where we'll spend the night before taking his jet to our honeymoon in Costa Rica. Our jet. Is it *our* jet now? Or am I merely an indefinite extra on his stage? I'm not really sure anymore.

We don't speak during the limo ride to the reception. I don't know what to say to him. Suddenly, for the first time ever, I have no words. All I can think about is what will happen later when there are no longer hordes of unassuming guests to protect me from his attentions. I feel more and more uncertain about this devil's bargain I've made—like I ever had a choice.

He would have destroyed me. At least this way there's a veneer of love and respectability. At least this way it looks like he is giving me the world instead of taking it all away.

I glance up to find his triumphant gaze locked on mine. It scares me as much as it thrills me, and then his thumb is stroking the back of my hand again. I find the courage to speak, but the words fly out of my mind as soon as they appear as the limo comes to a stop in front of the hotel.

The door is opened for us and my husband guides me out, helping me so that my dress doesn't get dirty. Husband. That word feels so strange to me. So wrong and somehow scandalous. This can't be real.

His grip on my hand tightens as he leads me up the stairs and through the hotel lobby back to where our reception is starting. The guests are already seated and being served their dinner. We're led to our own private table at the front of everything. Some people come by and talk to him. He's so polite to everyone, so normal, so different from the man I've come to know.

As we eat, silverware clinks against glasses, and each time we kiss as expected. Before the first dance, he rises from his chair, takes the microphone that is handed to him, and addresses our crowd of guests. And he is *so* charming. So smooth. The perfect beautiful lie.

"Livia and I would like to thank you all so much for coming to share this special day with us and supporting us as we start our life together. Don't get too creeped out, but I filmed the proposal. If she'd said no, I would have burned the evidence."

Obligatory laughter. He continues.

"But it occurred to me that probably many women wish

they had a video of the proposal. And so now she does. With Livia's permission I'd like to share that video with you now."

Our guests are very excited about this prospect. No one knew they'd be seeing this. A large projector is rolled out along with a screen and a few minutes later a video begins to play.

He and I are on his boat in the middle of the ocean. I'm lying in the sun in a red bikini and oversized dark sunglasses. He approaches with a wrapped gift. It's large—about the size of a Labrador puppy.

"Livia, I have something for you."

My eyes light up on the screen. "A present? Is it a pony?"

He chuckles. "Not a pony."

"A Ferrari?"

"Nope."

Our guests laugh at my antics, their anticipation growing, knowing somehow inside that giant box is a ring.

"Open it," he says.

I dutifully open it, only to find another gift wrapped box, then another, then another as I go through about five boxes, each time, the gift getting smaller and smaller.

"Is it an empty box?"

He chuckles again. "No. There's something in there."

I open the final box to find a blue box. Yes, *that* blue box. A box from Tiffany in just the right size.

The me on the video screen looks up at him and says playfully, "Is it a clown pin?"

He laughs again. "No."

I open it and start to cry when I see the ring.

He gets down on one knee and says, "Livia Fairchild, will you be my person?"

I'm blubbering and crying and say, "Yes, I will be your person." We kiss. He puts the ring on me. It's all so perfect.

Our guests say a collective, "Awwww" as the screen goes black. Then they're back to clinking their silverware against their glasses, and he leans over and kisses me again.

Before he pulls away, his mouth brushes my ear. "Time's up. You're mine tonight." His words are a growl so different from the version of himself that everyone else in this ballroom sees. It's jarring the way he can go from this charming facade to something so dark and menacing in an eye blink—the way he can transform only feet from our guests. Yet only I can see the monster. Everyone else sees the man.

I swallow hard at this proclamation and twist the wedding band on my finger. There are three words engraved on the inside of the band. Those three words seal my fate.

The rest of the reception goes by in a blur. The first dance. The dances with the parents. The cake. The bouquet. The garter. All the well wishes that come from guests as they each take turns wishing us a long and happy marriage. We go through a tunnel of sparklers created by our guests, riding off in the limo with the *just married* sign on the back and the cans dragging along the road behind us, only to circle back into the parking garage so we can go up to our suite for the night.

My hand is trembling as he takes it in his, leading me back inside the hotel and up the elevator to our room. He carries me over the threshold. Inside are candles and champagne and fancy chocolate and rose petals everywhere.

Two men in tuxedos step out of the shadows, looking me up and down with an appreciative once-over.

"It's about time," one of them says.

My husband guides me over to the other two men, and then all three of them are touching me.

The words inscribed on the inside of my wedding band are their names:

Griffin. Dayne. Soren.

CHAPTER TWO: LIVIA

THE REAL PROPOSAL

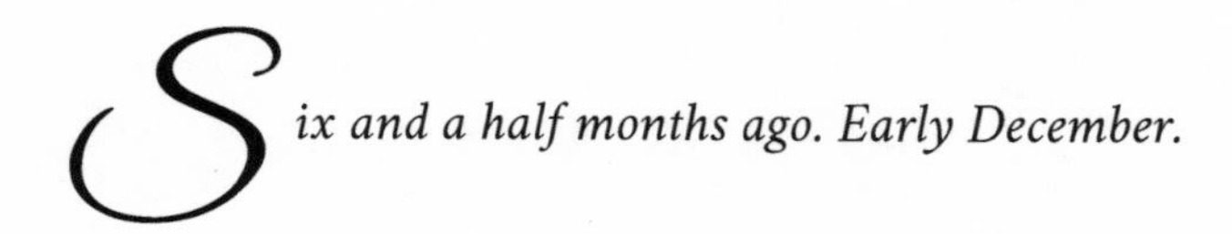

S*ix and a half months ago. Early December.*

I WALK into Capri Bella fifteen minutes late, my heart thundering in my chest. I have a dinner date but because of my schedule and his, we had to meet tonight instead of him picking me up. He did send his driver to collect me, though. I try to seem cool and collected about that but a driver *collecting me* is still a relatively new thing in my world.

I take a slow measured breath as I take in my surroundings. It's not that Griffin doesn't take me to nice restaurants. He does. But this isn't just a nice restaurant. It's a nice *romantic* restaurant with marriage proposal stats. And he said he had something very important to talk to me about. So what else could it be?

A part of me feels like I've won, but another part of me wonders, is this the man I want? Can I give up all others for him? Can I really do lifelong monogamy now that it may be upon me?

I smooth down the siren red dress. It's sexy but not slutty, reaching a few inches below my knees, showing just enough leg to get the sexy-in-heels benefit. I approach the reservation desk.

A refined older gentleman looks up at me over glasses which could probably more accurately be called spectacles. "Can I help you, Miss?"

I give him my date's name and say I'm meeting him here.

"Oh yes, Ms. Fairchild, your party is already seated. Let me show you to the table."

I expect to be led to a small out of the way intimate table set for two, candlelight, maybe a nice view of the city, or maybe a table out on the private balcony. Instead, I'm taken to a larger round table with three men seated at it, and one seat left vacant for me.

The three men are Griffin, Dayne, and Soren. I've been dating all three of them. I never made it a secret that I wasn't exclusive with anyone, but I was discreet and didn't expect them to ever meet each other.

All three men stand.

The man who brought me to my table has disappeared, and I'm left alone to face them. But I don't fall apart. I haven't done anything wrong. They *knew* we weren't exclusive. And I never acted like a jealous girlfriend. I never told them they couldn't see other women or fuck other women. I don't care. It's not my business. We aren't exclusive. If the price of my freedom from dead-end relationships is the men I see being allowed to fuck who they want, as long as it's not me they're fucking over, fine.

They all knew my terms. They all agreed to my terms.

No one at this table has any right to be upset. If they wanted me, they should have locked me down with a ring and something real.

I meet each of their gazes in turn, a challenge in mine, daring them to speak first.

"Which one of you is getting my chair?" I say when it's clear we might all stand here in a death stare forever.

If they think after months of them opening doors and pulling out chairs that it's ending now, they are sadly mistaken.

Dayne stands closest to me on my right; he comes around and pulls out my chair.

"Thank you."

I sit, and they sit. The staring contest commences again. I take a sip of my water and look down at the menu, unwilling to be the first person to speak or act as though I've done anything wrong when they knew my terms from the beginning. They don't get to turn this around on me now. How on earth do they know each other? I try to imagine how the subject even came up, and I find I'm not that imaginative.

This is one of those restaurants where only the man's menu has prices. About a year ago, there was a giant freak-out and pressure about the *misogyny* of the menus with hysterical demands that they put prices on all of them, presumably because empowered women want to split the bill. *Empowered women* are ruining life for the rest of us.

The restaurant, being very upscale and determined to preserve a certain elegant atmosphere and old traditions, held firm and waited for the shitstorm to blow over. Their popularity more than doubled after that, and it's been next to impossible to get a reservation ever since. But Griffin got one.

I wonder which of the three men sitting at the table with me has the menu with the prices, or if they all do. I wonder what the man at the reservations desk thought about a dinner in a romantic restaurant that obviously isn't a business dinner but has one woman and three men claiming a single table.

"So," Griffin says.

But he's interrupted by a waiter who takes first my order, then theirs. I order the Penne Bolognese and Merlot. I don't notice what they order because I swear I'm about to hyperventilate. I'm left hanging onto a thin thread of hope that they won't make a scene. Surely if they planned to say or do anything dramatic they would have met me some place else.

The waiter takes their menus then has to pry mine from my unconsciously tight-fisted grip. Then he departs.

"So," Griffin begins again. "I've had some interesting conversations recently."

"Oh?" I say, taking another sip of water. The water has two lime slices in it, exactly the way I like it, and I wonder which one of them put in that request.

"Did you know we knew each other?" he asks, not betraying any emotion about any of this.

"Of course not."

And I didn't. What are the odds? I admit that as I leveled up the quality of the men on my roster, I had the concern in the back of my mind that they might run in the same social circles. Once you reach the top echelon in a city, everybody seems to know each other. But it's a big city, I was discreet and thought that was enough. Obviously not.

"Well, we do," he says as if this clarification were necessary and will somehow spark off some deep tearful confession on my part—which it does not.

So far Griffin is the only one who has spoken. The other two have been watching me shrewdly, observing all my reactions as if they are human polygraphs determined to spot the lie.

"And?" I ask.

I'd like to get this witch burning over with so I can start my lonely cat lady future. There was a grey male cat with only one eye at the clinic last week. He's up for adoption. I could call him Mr. Wednesday.

Griffin continues, oblivious to my insane pet acquisition fantasies. "Imagine our surprise when we found out we all just happened to be dating a wonderful girl named Livia. Did you think we wouldn't find out you'd been playing us? Did you really think we wouldn't know each other?"

"I'm not playing you," I say, leveling a hard glare at him. I can't believe he has the nerve to act as though I've been doing something dirty this whole time.

"Hmmm," is his only response. He takes a sip of his own water. "Are you saying you have *actual* feelings?"

He says this as though I'm some sort of sociopathic robot who has stalked them all like prey. I want to point out that every single one of them approached me.

But instead I just say, "Yes." Though my *actual* feelings in this moment are running more to terror coupled with anger than love. Even so, I'm sure I would pass a polygraph because terror and anger are definitely actual feelings.

"Which one of us do you love?" he demands.

I make eye contact with each of them in turn. "All of you." And it's true. It was the one sticky issue I failed to account for. What if in playing this game to protect myself,

I ended up falling in love with more than one man? I'd decided that was a problem for future Livia. It was a bridge I would cross when I got to it. And here's the bridge, looking far more rickety than I'd originally imagined it would.

None of them betrays any feeling they may have about this proclamation on my part.

"I thought your goal was to date and not be tied down until you found the right man and he proposed. You didn't want to be in the Girlfriend Trap while a man kept you on the hook indefinitely." He recounts this to me as if he's somehow revealing a lie somewhere.

"That's right," I confirm. This feels like the recap of a reality show and part of me wants to look around for a camera crew.

"But you love *all* of us?" he clarifies again. Seriously, is he wearing a wire?

"Yes," I say.

"If one of us proposed marriage, would you accept?"

I only hesitate a moment before I say, "Yes." I can't let my feelings cloud things and cause me to lose sight of my real goals. *One* man that loves and provides for me. But in the past few months in their company I've gotten greedy and haven't wanted the ride to end.

Sitting face-to-face with all three of them it's only now sinking in just how ruthless these men are and what fire I've been carelessly playing with. These aren't college boys or blue collar plumbers. These are powerful men, very used to having a harem of women hanging all over them, but no doubt unused to dating a woman pulling the same power play on them. And suddenly I feel like the checkmate is coming, and it's not me winning the game.

"Okay, so let's say one of us proposes. What about the other two?"

"I'd end it with the other two."

I'm not sure where this is going. Are they going to arm wrestle for me? Such an outcome seems unlikely, especially considering the venue.

"Well," he continues unruffled, "Here's the thing. We don't just all know each other. We pledged the same frat in college in the same year. We've been in some strange and interesting situations together. We've shared many unconventional experiences, and we are quite accustomed to sharing our women."

I've just taken a sip of water when he says this and nearly choke on it.

The predatory way the three of them are looking at me makes me want to get up and flee the restaurant. I glance around to see if guests at nearby tables have heard any of this because I'm certain right now my face is the same color as my dress.

While Griffin is giving this speech, I have the feeling he isn't giving it because he's some agreed-upon de facto leader of the group. It's more because tonight was his date night with me, so it seems only right that he do all the talking. Dayne or Soren could have just as easily carried this speech with the same intensity.

"So here's the deal," he says. "We've decided we're a package deal. You will marry one of us legally—we'll put on the respectable show for all of our friends and family—and you will have binding private contracts with the other two. And then the four of us will live together."

Wait, what?! All three of them? And I notice nobody is *asking* me to marry them. It has been declared. I have been claimed. And instead of competing for one of them to win me, they've decided they'll all enjoy the spoils. How nice for them.

This idea sets my body on fire. The place between my legs flares to life in the most visceral way. It's been a long bout of celibacy—a level of self control I'd deemed mandatory to get my happily ever after without over-attaching too soon to one man and hormonally bonding to some loser while overlooking all his flaws.

I thought I had every angle figured out—every possible way of protecting myself from narcissists, losers, players, commitmentphobes, and general all around dirtbags. But this possible outcome never occurred to me. And while my mind screams no, my neglected body is all in.

I rise on shaking legs. At least half of this shaking is arousal, not fear or anger. But I'm not about to play into their hands. For all I know, they've decided this is the way to win, conquer me, get me to lower my guard in some marathon orgy, then laugh and discard me the next day. If that's their plan it would break me completely.

If they did that I would have just had three players playing the long game on me. No, thank you. No way am I doing all I've done just to have the same ending... Again.

"I most certainly will not!" I practically hiss at them.

I can't do this. It's insane. And even if I could, it would break every pretense I've set up that I'm some kind of classy lady who doesn't just share my body with anyone. I can't give myself to all three of them. It's too fucked-up even for my twisted fantasies.

"Sit!" Griffin says.

People at nearby tables actually turn and stare. I'm torn between fleeing—which will only call more attention to myself—and just sitting back down. I choose to flee.

CHAPTER THREE: LIVIA

WHEN IT RAINS IT POURS

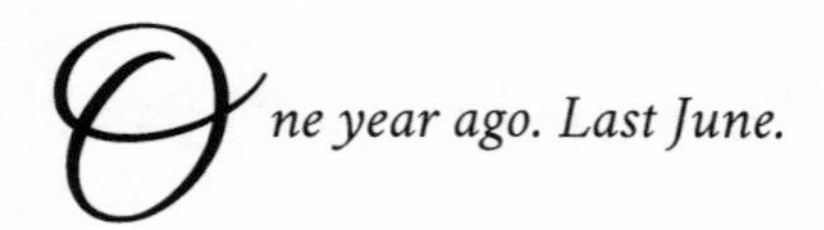

One year ago. Last June.

When I tearfully packed up my stuff and left my boyfriend last year I decided then and there that this would never happen to me again. I'm not completely sure he even *was* my boyfriend. We just sort of moved in together. And stupid me thought that meant something. He wasted two years of my life in this situationship.

Before him, three other men wasted: eight months, a year and a half, and three months respectively. I'd slept with all of these losers because we were exclusive and I thought somehow I was on the road to an engagement ring, the wedding of my dreams, and my happily ever after. I wanted something serious and real, and I'd thought I was doing everything right.

After a couple of weeks crying into pints of ice cream and torturing myself with rom coms, I decided I was done being played and used and kept as a placeholder in some guy's life until something better came along. I started following different dating coaches online until I happened upon what I was sure was the solution to all my problems with men.

Men had game? Well, I now had Lady Game. And it was air tight. No man would ever screw me over again because I had decided instead of focusing all my attention on one man at a time while he waited around and kept me on the hook and made me crazy wondering if he really wanted me like I wanted him and if this was going somewhere, I would date multiple men. Indefinitely.

And I wouldn't sleep with anyone until someone put an engagement ring on my finger. I know that sounds crazy and extreme, but I was fed up and I had about seventeen testimonials of women this had worked for. And if it didn't work, I'd planned to get about five cats and settle into a cranky cat lady future.

I've been keeping a rotating dating roster for the last six blissful low-stress months. I never have to wonder anymore... where is this relationship going? What did he mean by that text message? Why didn't he call me? I just don't care. I don't have to find a way to make it work with the one guy all my focus and energy is on. Because it's not just one guy. I have other options.

And if one treats me poorly or just isn't that into me, I drop him and find someone to replace him. Men have been dating this way forever, and it's fucking brilliant. If men dated like women, honing in and falling into accidental monogamy by the third date we'd have total romantic grid-lock while the whole world lived lives of quiet desperation with the wrong person.

Yes, I am now the CEO of my own life. Since I started

this new strategy I've been taken out on real dates, treated with respect, and wondering why every woman in the world hasn't figured out the magic of keeping several men in rotation. When they know you aren't just seeing them, somehow magically the check gets paid without complaint or making me feel like a supervillain for just wanting to be cared for.

But it does get exhausting. I found out the hard way that five men is just *way* too many. I had to drop a couple of guys I actually liked to make it manageable. But three works. I can handle three.

But tonight is a night off from dating. It's just me at a new opening at the downtown art museum, nobody else. And I find it strangely relaxing to be out for a night in my own company. I meander through the recent exhibits and bump right into probably the most attractive man I've ever seen in real life.

“Excuse me,” I say. I manage to steady my glass of champagne just in time before the contents can escape the elegant flute to assault my new lavender dress.

He isn't nearly so lucky and unscathed.

“I think you owe me a date for the damage,” he says, pointing at the wet stain on his jacket.

Well that's forward. I'm not sure what to say to this. When it rains it pours. Apparently the universe has decided I need another man to date. Oh, that's a fun side effect of dating like this. You never look desperate or hungry, so of course men are intrigued by this uber confident energy you're throwing off. It's almost like I put some kind of pheromone into the air now that men latch onto as I drift breezily past them.

But even though I'm already shuffling things around in my mind to figure out how this could work, the words that come out of my mouth are: "I'm sorry, I couldn't possibly go out..."

"I don't see a ring. Do you have a boyfriend?"

I have a roster.

But I don't say that out loud. "No... but..."

"Ah. I see. You normally date super multi-billionaires, and I just don't make the cut?"

Any other man might make this sound passive aggressive and angry, but he somehow says it in the most endearingly playful tone. Just banter. Nothing serious. He really is nice looking, and he probably does have money. And one of the guys on the roster hasn't called me in a week; maybe he's realized I wasn't kidding about no casual sex and dropped me. It wouldn't be the first guy who's fallen back when he couldn't con his way into my panties.

And if that's the case, there's room for this man who is a definite step up. I'm not saying it's easy being celibate because it isn't. And I've seen this roster dating thing done in such a way where one doesn't have to act like a blushing virgin, but I can't take the risk again of falling for a douchebag, of betting everything on some piece of shit who will just string me along indefinitely wasting my time and all my good years and eggs.

If men think many of us are marriage and baby hungry, it's only because year after year we watch as man after man wastes our time knowing he has all the time in the world, but we don't. If I hear one more smarmy asshole talk about how women are focusing on their careers and waiting too long to settle down and make babies, I might have to punch someone in the throat. That is not why we are "waiting". We aren't waiting. Men are just stringing us along because they can get the pussy for free and see no need to commit to it. It's a free pussy gold mine out there.

The hookup culture is ruining our lives. But we're all pretending it isn't and that we feel empowered by this treatment.

They've figured out they can be our boyfriend for ten years and refuse to settle down, and we have no cards to play.

I look back to this new shiny prospect standing in front of me with a wet champagne stain on his dinner jacket.

"I really do owe you for that damage, don't I?" I say, playing along with this ridiculous date debt. I ignore the voice in my mind that says he's definitely going to want sex by the third date. It's an opportunity to improve the roster —just to have a taste of something a little fancier even if I have to let him go in a few weeks.

He nods gravely. "I'm afraid so."

What the hell? Why not? "I'm Livia," I say, flashing him what I hope is my most demure and charming smile.

"Soren," he replies.

Two minutes later I am somehow on a date with this guy. Right here, right now. I thought he'd get my number and call me later, but nope, he's now squiring me around the art museum as though we planned this in advance. What was supposed to be *me time* has turned into an interview for the position Charlie just vacated. Maybe. We'll see.

CHAPTER FOUR: LIVIA

PERSUASION

S*ix and a half months ago. Early December.*

I DON'T KNOW how I've run three blocks, both because I'm wearing heels and this isn't the best dress to run in, and because I'm not exactly an endurance cardio girl. I duck between two buildings and lean against the wall, trying to get oxygen to circulate properly through my lungs again.

It only takes a couple of minutes for me to realize just how fucking stupid this choice was. I could have and should have hailed a taxi to go home. But I was so flustered I couldn't think straight. I just needed to get away from them. I needed to move. I needed to get somewhere so I could think.

Well, mission successful, I guess.

They are definitely playing me. They're pissed that I've dangled my pussy over them like some virgin being auctioned off to the highest bidder, and you can bet they're all calculating their money and time investments and what they think I owe them. I'm sure they want to lure me in, gang bang me, and dump me—and this time without even the lame girlfriend title that I might otherwise have had if I'd stuck to standard-method *good girl* dating.

I'm about to go back out onto the main road and get that taxi when a broad dark figure fills the opening of the alleyway. This cannot be happening to me.

I start to back away, the heels that allowed me somehow to run three blocks suddenly deciding they don't even want to let me awkwardly stumble backwards now. The alley is a dead end. Nowhere to run. The stranger advances, and I move deeper into the darkness—as if this is a legitimate escape route.

I am going to die in this fucking alley because I couldn't just stay in a nice restaurant and have an uncomfortable conversation. I scream at the top of my lungs before he reaches me. Maybe he'll decide a shrill shrieky screamer isn't worth it. But this stranger who may want to mug me, murder me, rape me, has decided he's good with screaming.

He continues to advance in that slow lumbering horror movie way, and I just continue to scream because short of uselessly beating at his chest, there's not a whole hell of a lot of other options. My purse isn't substantial enough to even pretend to use it as a weapon. It's one of those tiny clutch bags that you can only fit a wad of emergency cash, a cell phone, and a lipstick in.

Just before he can do whatever he's decided he's going to do, someone pulls him away from me and then three men—my three men—are beating and kicking the shit out of him. The mugger/murderer/rapist manages to crawl out of the alleyway and go back to whatever den of iniquity he slunk out of.

Dayne rounds on me, breathing hard. "What in the fuck did you think you were doing? Are you trying to get yourself killed?"

All three of them look livid, and suddenly they seem far scarier than the stranger who almost accosted me.

I want to scream at them, but the tough act has drained out of me, and all I can do is cry and shake like some half-drowned lap dog—even though it isn't even raining.

Soren steps forward.

I instinctively step back. He looks wounded by this, but he removes his suit jacket and wraps it around my trembling form, then without a word leads me out of the alley to the waiting limo with the other two behind me looking like hulking bodyguards. They apparently all traveled together tonight. The four of us get in the back, and the limo lurches forward.

I'm not sure where we're going—probably not back to the restaurant—but I'm wrong about that. The limo stops. The driver gets out and waves off the valet when the man tries to take the keys. Then our driver goes inside the restaurant. Fifteen minutes later he comes out with to-go bags, and we're driving again.

I stare out the window. I'm still quietly crying, huddled in Soren's coat. Nobody speaks. A few minutes later the limo stops to drop us off in front of a high rise. Griffin's penthouse. It makes the most sense. It's the closest. Dayne takes the bags of food from the driver and we all silently go inside.

This is so weird. I should ask the driver to take me home, but I can't bring myself to do it after they just heroically rescued me and got all of our dinner to go like it was fast food drive-thru and no big deal.

"Sit," Griffin says again, when we're standing in his dining room.

I hand the jacket back to Soren and sit awkwardly at the table. I walked into the restaurant tonight feeling sexy and confident and on top of the world. And now I feel like a teenager about to be scolded for sneaking out of the house. They've each got eight years on me and the age difference feels bigger than usual tonight.

The men take the food to the kitchen. When they return, it's on nice plates. Dayne brings in a couple of bottles of wine.

I'm grateful when they fill my glass almost to the top. I need it. My hand is still shaking when I take a sip of the dark red Merlot. The Penne Bolognese is still hot when it's placed in front of me.

"Eat," Griffin says. I wonder how long they've known about each other... how long they've been planning to turn the tables on me?

Nobody speaks as we eat, which is just fine with me. In fact, by this point I'm starting to think what was said at the restaurant was some hysterical hallucination. Maybe we're really only about to have a standard confrontation and break-up. And after everything else that's transpired tonight, I can almost handle that.

In fact, the more I think about it, the more I realize obviously they were just playing a game with me. Maybe the original plan was to con me into bed with all of them, but after what almost happened in the alley we'll probably all have a cordial and mature breakup and that will be that. I can't imagine they'd still try to get me into bed after the almost alley assault.

When we've finished eating, Griffin pours himself another glass of wine, takes a sip, and calmly says to me, "Now, as I was saying back at the restaurant... you will legally marry one of us and the other two..."

"And I said no," I repeat.

He laughs at this. "It wasn't a request. We've decided—"

"You can't just *decide*. That's not how this works. I told each of you when we started dating that if someone proposed and I accepted, I would break things off with anyone else I happened to be dating at the time. So if one of you wants to *ask* me, I may consider the offer."

Though I'm not even sure if that's true anymore after this sudden Neanderthal act—not that I didn't know all three of these men were used to getting their way and how badly that could go for me if I lost control of this situation —which I clearly have.

"No," Griffin says as if trying to reason with a small child about the utility of eating vegetables, "We all want you. We're all taking you."

Again, my body is *all* in with this. And a part of my mind isn't sure about things. Only this afternoon I was in love with all of them and couldn't imagine how I'd ever be able to break up with the others if one decided to call my bluff and propose. And the only thing cooling my ardor is the way they've behaved tonight, but even that is leaving an unexpected and growing trail of wetness between my legs.

Instead of giving in to any of my more primal and uncivilized urges, I stand because realistically there's only one thing I can do now. "Thank you for dinner and for saving me, but this isn't going to work anymore. We're through. All of us." I manage not to start crying again as I make eye contact with each of them so they know I mean it.

They let me walk out of the dining room, and I actually

think I'm going to get out of the building. But before I reach the door, one of them—I'm not sure which—pushes me so that my breasts are pressed against the wall. A hand grips the back of my neck, holding me in place so I can't turn to see who has me. His other hand runs down my dress, and he shoves it roughly up so he can stroke between my thighs. I'm exposed, and I blush as I realize he can feel my arousal and knows how my body has reacted to their indecent proposal.

I don't even care which one of them has me. I feel like a butterfly pinned to a board, wings desperately fluttering, fighting for an escape that isn't possible. Only I'm not moving. I'm not fighting or fluttering. I'm barely even breathing.

I crave the press of his hard chest against my body. A part of me wants to surrender completely, to breach this barrier of enforced celibacy and give my body what it's been screaming for these past long months.

"I want to bend you over the sofa right now and fuck the shit out of you," Dayne hisses in my ear. "You little cock tease."

Dayne is the last one I expected it to be. He's been perhaps the kindest of the three—the most reserved up until tonight. But what happened in the alley earlier has caused a shift in him. The amount of testosterone coming off him right now is intoxicating.

I mean to try to buck him off me, but it ends up being more me grinding my ass against his crotch. I feel his thick hard length straining behind his pants. It's been so long since I've been fucked—since I've had any real passion—since I've been wanted like this. A part of me wants to say screw my whole plan and just do it. Let them all fuck me tonight and who cares what happens tomorrow?

I can take a break from men, eat some ice cream, heal, start again. It's not the end of the world. But isn't it?

"Did you really think you could run this kind of game on us? Who in the fuck did you think you were playing with little girl?" Dayne hisses in my ear.

I'm again shocked by his words. I've always thought of Dayne as the nicest, the least scary and intimidating. But in this moment he is all primal animal and I am reminded in the most stark terms possible that I'm alone in a penthouse with three large men who have been denied entrance into my body for months—three men who've decided they're all *taking* me for no other reason than they all want me.

And yet I can't even be scared about this. I can't force that feeling into my mind or body. I know I should be, but I'm so aroused right now that no common sense thoughts are able to make the long trip up to my brain. Every cell that comes together to form me is consumed with preparing to be *taken,* and there's simply no room for anything but that searing need.

He backs off me for a second, and I turn around, jerking my dress back down to find all three of them staring at me, jackets off, ties loosened, pupils dilated. There's nowhere for me to run, assuming I could convince my mind and body to do that right now, which I'm pretty sure I can't.

"Why?" Dayne growls.

"Why what?" I ask. Did I just black out and miss a whole conversation?

"Why don't you want this? All of us together?" He says it as though my refusal to be their shared meaty bone is beyond his ability to comprehend. Of course they all think I'm a gold digger. So of course the idea of having all three of them fawning over me, buying me things, providing shit for me... that must be worth being their whore. I'm not even sure I could eye roll hard enough if I tried.

It's only now, finally, more than an hour after the suggestion first came out of Griffin's mouth that I realize... they're serious. They aren't playing with me. They've decided instead of dumping me or fighting over me, that they want to share me.

How would it even work? Would they keep discreet mistresses? Because it's definitely not fair for me to get three men and them to only get me.

I don't want that. I want one man who can love me and be faithful to me who will provide and care for me, not three men toying with me while keeping other women on the side. I swipe at the tears which have begun sliding down my cheeks.

Soren speaks. It's the first time he's spoken to me tonight. "I have a very good private investigator, and through some unexpected side trails I happened to find out something very interesting about your past."

I feel the blood drain out of my face. No one knows about this. No one. It can't be what I think. There's no way anyone could know. I was careful. There's *no way* anyone could know. I repeat this thought in my head like a mantra over and over as if just the power of my positive thinking can stop the words from coming out of his mouth.

"Oh, yes. Livia Fairchild killed a man. On spring break. Nine years ago."

My gaze shifts to Griffin and Dayne but neither of them look surprised, which means Soren already told them. They knew about this ambush.

"I don't know what you're talking about." Deny. Deny. Deny. There's no evidence. There can't be any evidence.

There's just no possible way he could know... and yet he does.

Soren just laughs. "You and your friend weren't as careful as you thought. So, you see, you *will* get married, Livia. It's one cage or the other. Prison, or us. Our cage is nicer. Think about it. And it wouldn't just destroy you. Your friend Macy is an accessory. She helped you cover it up."

"I don't know what you're talking about. I didn't kill anyone," I say. Even though I know he can see the truth in my eyes.

"Don't call my bluff, Livia. You won't win."

"It was self defense," I say. "Please you have to believe me. It was self defense." I look again to Dayne and Griffin. Griffin looks pretty tense, but Dayne is calm, leaning against the door frame now, his arms crossed over his chest, just observing me.

"Self defense doesn't require ocean disposal," Soren says.

"It *was* self defense. I was afraid no one would believe me!"

"I can't imagine chopping up a body with a friend is going to make you seem more credible now. So... like I said... you're ours."

I never should have let Macy help me get rid of the evidence. If it was just me to think about maybe it would be different, maybe I'd have a choice, but I can't let my best friend suffer for this.

More tears come, but he isn't moved. "Griffin... Dayne... please... you can't let him do this." But no one is moved by my tears. I wonder how long they've known this, how long Soren has held this card and waited to play it to get what he wants.

I look at the ground unable to meet their eyes anymore. I could continue this melodrama. I could say I don't believe Soren would carry out his threat, but I do. I got just a little too greedy. Not for money—not really—but for men far outside the reach of the rules. Men with too much power. And it was sexy until it was turned on me.

I could have played this game competently with the first three men I'd started dating when the idea of the roster was new and shiny. But every time I dumped one or one fell back, I gained confidence and replaced him with a better guy. Not just better than losers, better than what I was used to dating—men more attractive than I was used to, more moneyed than I was used to. Because I had begun to believe I was worth more than the scraps I'd been accepting from the table of life.

I'd begun to think I didn't want to live like a peasant anymore and that I had every fucking right to go after someone much much higher. After all, I'd worked on myself. I was in a state of constant transformation and self-improvement while most of the men I'd been dating just... weren't. If I'd settled for a man like that, he'd be the crab pulling me back down into the bucket forever.

I needed someone who was *more*. And somehow, that turned into Griffin, Dayne, and Soren. Practically all women are attracted to wealth and power. And not just... we like it... we are *sexually* attracted to it. It turns us on in the way D cups and slutty lingerie turn men on.

But there's a double standard. Nobody says a single word about any man getting any pretty young thing he wants and can manage to acquire, but women... no we should sit pretty and smile and be good little girls gratefully accepting the first nice man who comes along.

Anybody who isn't a serial rapist should "get a chance" because "he's a nice guy."

If we get lucky and this man just happens to live in a mansion, fantastic—that's okay, you're still a good girl. But if he's broke, love is enough and we shouldn't want anything more. We should be the one who believes in his potential whether or not he's ever going to do anything with it. Stand by him, help "build him" as if he's a Build-a-Bear workshop.

To go and intentionally chase wealth and power? Gold digger. Slut. Whore. It doesn't matter if we really do love the guy... we wanted to rise above our station in life and that can't be allowed. People say we live in a classless society. Bullshit. We absolutely have classes and everyone is supposed to stay in their lane.

And I didn't. And now Soren will see to it that I am punished because I made a stupid mistake in college and wasn't as careful as I thought I was.

I know part of this is about the fact that all three of these men must have been convinced because of their wealth and power they could beat out whatever men they might be competing against. It never occurred to them that all my other suitors were just as worthy as they were in that area. They each were sure that eventually they'd break me down and be in my bed—or more likely me in theirs. I'm not sure what would have happened after that, but they've collectively decided to rewrite the entire script, so it hardly matters anymore.

Soren has finally had enough of my crying and hesitating, he backs me against the wall. His mouth is suddenly on mine in a possessing kiss, his tongue tangling with mine as though it's just a new battlefield to conquer me on. He's never kissed me quite this way before, and I want to hate it.

I want to be scared, offended, pissed off. I want to scream at him and push him off me, but all I can do is let my body melt into his as he claims me, every nerve ending on fire while the other two men watch—and maybe in part *because* they watch. I don't want to think about what that says about me.

He pulls away, breathing hard, his dark green gaze locked on me. His voice is low and barely human when he finally speaks. "You belong to us. Now be a good girl and say: yes."

My eyes dart to Griffin and Dayne as if either of them can or will save me from whatever comes next. But each of them is a wall, closed off from me. No mercy.

"Yes," I finally whisper. I have no other choice, and all four of us know it. Soren is ruthless. He isn't bluffing. He isn't the kind of man who makes a threat he has no intention of following through on. If I don't do this, mine and Macy's lives are effectively over. Mine may be over anyway, but this is the only bridge left to cross.

Soren jerks the top of my dress down to my waist and takes one of my breasts in his mouth. My clothes have never come off with any of these men before this moment. I've practically been a nun. It's been so long since I've done anything like this that it feels foreign and shocking like being plunged into a lake in the middle of winter. And tonight it feels far more angry than I remember it ever being with any of the other men I've been with in the past.

I'm crying full on now, the fear finally kicking in as I begin to realize what's about to happen here. "Please. Don't do this..." I whimper, hating myself for sounding so weak and scared, and hating them for making me feel that way after they just rescued me from a different man who may have intended the same fate for me. Somehow this is an even bigger betrayal than all their plans behind my back.

"Soren," Griffin says, putting a hand on his shoulder.

Soren snarls and pulls away, putting my dress back the way it should be. His smoldering gaze holds mine while he does this.

"Fine. You know what? We won't touch you until the wedding night. We know you're not a virgin, but why ruin a good illusion? We'll let *you* sweat it out this time."

I swallow hard at this and look down at the ground, the enormity of tonight somehow engulfing me.

Soren stalks off, and I'm left with Griffin and Dayne.

"I'll drive you home," Griffin says.

I nod shakily and follow him to the parking garage. I still don't know which one of these men I'm supposed to be marrying or what the hell I'm going to say to my family about it. They don't even know I've been dating anyone.

CHAPTER FIVE: SOREN

THE NO GIRLFRIEND SPEECH

Eleven months ago. Last July.

I've been seeing Livia over the past month. She's a strange and unique creature. First, despite my obvious wealth, good looks, and charm—I never said I was modest—she seems somehow unfazed by the *catch* every other woman seems to think I am. Women aren't a challenge for me. Ever.

I can have any woman I want in my bed any time I want. That's not bragging, it's the actual fact of how it plays out. Usually I've got their panties off by the first and often only date. And I've never dated a woman who still turns me down on the third—until Livia—because the third date is the sex date for *good girls who don't want to look too slutty*. On a certain level, though I'd never admit it to another human being, I find this really disappointing—that it's all so easy. Only a century ago no man would expect a respectable lady to fuck a suitor by the third date. It would be expected that he wouldn't get to do that with her until they were married—until he'd offered her a life and safety. How much of this was religion and how much of it was the nature of the male drive to want to *win something*, I'm not entirely sure. I wasn't there. But I could take a guess.

So here we are, on the fourth date with no sex. Other peculiar things about this woman: She hasn't called or texted me once. And when I text her, she doesn't reply. It's infuriating. She only responds to phone calls. I thought she was playing games at first, but she flat out told me she doesn't like texting, she probably won't reply, and it's not the best way to reach her. Oookay. Not once did she worry this would come across as *difficult* or that I wouldn't want to see her again. If the thought ever did cross her mind, she must have decided that would be just fine with her.

This is an unusual situation for me to say the least. I'm equal parts intrigued and annoyed by it.

Women are always trying to win me, earn me, impress me, like I'm a trophy they want to display on their shelf. They want to land a rich eligible bachelor so they can be the envy of all their friends. I'll admit, I preferred when things went the other way around, when it was women who were the prizes. When there was something to live for, fight for, die for. But people tend to overly romanticize the past, and maybe that's what I'm doing now.

There's a part of me that wants to say this woman is too much drama—except that she isn't. She's happy to hear from me when I call. She's fun and flirty when we go out. And she hasn't once asked me "Where is this going?" There is zero pressure. It's like she doesn't care. And I honestly don't know what the hell to do with that. It's so novel that I just keep calling her like a fucking idiot even though part of me is sure she's playing me somehow.

Is she involved in some advanced next-level gold-digging where she gets the man to shell out without ever spreading her legs? Given tonight's extravagant date, that's possible. And well-played, my dear.

I've tried on every date to push things a little, to maneuver her into bed with me... and... nope. She's assured me she's very attracted and feels strong chemistry, but she doesn't do casual sex. I don't normally do the girlfriend thing, partly because I get trapped in vanilla suburban hell where the woman I'm with doesn't have the slightest clue of who I really am or what I'm actually into.

And I rarely feel anymore that I should inflict my sadism and kinks on them for sport. I like to think I've outgrown some of my darker edges, but deep down I know they're only lurking, lying in wait for the right moment and the right woman they can be unleashed upon.

I know I could specifically seek out kinky women to date, but that's often its own brand of drama. Then I not only get the needy clingy girl but I get the needy clingy girl who needs me to order her around 24/7—which is exhausting—and it becomes rote and boring. Then it's like I'm LARPing my own sex life.

Above and beyond the specifics, I miss sharing a woman. I miss passing her around. I miss the joy of watching her get taken by one of my friends.

Tonight's date was a surprise for Livia, and I am definitely raising the stakes. I'm a bastard, but I'm trying to push her buttons so she feels guilty for all I'm spending on her, so she'll give it up—even as I'm intrigued by the bizarre situation of a woman resisting me and wonder how long she can keep it up because I know she's attracted.

I've seen the way her pupil's dilate, the way her breath catches in my presence. I've seen the hungry look in her eyes when our gazes meet, like I'm the very best filet mignon she's ever sunk her teeth into. Except that she hasn't. She's just sitting there, staring at her plate. Metaphorically, of course. We just got to the restaurant.

Tonight, I took her on the jet to an extremely upscale underwater restaurant. It's like an aquarium, all glassed in with the fish swimming around you, and coral reefs and everything. It's pretty impressive, and I can tell she's impressed, the way she looks around, her light blue eyes widening at every new sight. It's like she can't even believe something like this can exist in our world.

I admit I'm kind of charmed by her reaction, this sense of wonder and appreciation she approaches almost everything with. We are seated in a small private dining room at a romantic candlelit table, while sharks swim over our heads—which seems pretty fitting, all things considered.

She's staring at the menu. "Seafood?" she asks wrinkling her nose.

"What else did you think an undersea restaurant would serve? Do you not like seafood?"

She shrugs. "I don't know. I'll feel judged."

"By the marine life?" I ask, incredulous. I can't stop the chuckle.

"Yes. It would be like eating a hamburger while wandering through a field of cows. I feel like I need to cover my plate so they can't see what I'm eating."

Oh Livia, your clothes are coming off when we get back on that jet. The jet has a bedroom, and I have every intention of using it and initiating Livia into the mile-high club—a club I'm somehow convinced she isn't a part of. Fucking thirty-eight thousand feet in the air doesn't seem like her style, which makes me wonder why I'm even pursuing her so hard because I'm sure this girl is just more vanilla suburban hell.

Livia works through her guilt and orders a type of seafood that isn't swimming in her immediate vicinity. When the waiter has taken our menus away, I pull a slim black box out of my suit jacket pocket and slide it across the table.

Those fantastically expressive eyes widen once again. "Soren?" she questions. "What's this?"

"What does it look like? Open it."

She's suspicious now, and I'm sure she can see through all of this. The trip on the jet, the fancy Little Mermaid date, the jewelry. She knows I'm trying to buy her. And in this moment I'm convinced that I've found her price and her legs will be open to me by midnight. A part of me is disappointed it was this easy. She presented the tiniest glimmer of a challenge. Oh well.

She opens the box. "Oh my god, it's beautiful!"

Inside is a platinum diamond tennis bracelet, which looks lovely against the dark plum-colored dress she's wearing.

"Soren, I can't possibly accept this. It's too much."

"Don't be ridiculous. Of course you can and *will* accept it." At first I think she'll fight me on it. Telling her she *will* accept it was possibly too much. But my mind is stuck in the fantasy of telling her she can and *will* accept every inch of my cock. These are actual words I plan to say to her in about an hour.

She doesn't fight me on it, and it seems symbolic of her already-sealed surrender on the trip home. She holds out her wrist to me, and I help her put it on, part of me wishing I was locking something more substantial around her delicate wrist.

I mostly zone out during the rest of dinner. I'm listening and responding but as soon as words are spoken on both sides they seem to dissipate entirely into the air around us. I just want to get her back on that jet. I want to rip that dress off her and throw her down on the bed. I want to hold her down and make her scream my name loud enough for the pilot to hear.

"Thank you for dinner," she says shyly when the check arrives. "This place is amazing."

"You didn't feel too judged by the fish?" I ask.

"I got over it," she replies, smiling. She has a beautiful smile. It inches up a little more on one side of her face than the other. It looks like a sweet smirk, a concept I would have found as credible as Santa Claus until I'd seen it for myself.

I pay the bill and guide her out of the restaurant, my hand on the small of her back. My blood is pulsing and throbbing in my cock as I take her back to the jet. Thirty minutes tops, and I'll be inside her.

But that isn't what happens. I've got her all the way to the bedroom at the back of the plane. I'm about to push her down onto the bed, my hand fumbling for her zipper when she says, "Soren, stop."

I think I may have actually growled. What in the fuck?

This time she leads me back into the main part of the plane as she zips her dress back up. I realize I'd managed to get it halfway down her back. She sits in one of the plush seats, glancing nervously out the window as if she has the option to jump.

I sit in the seat across from her. I'm sure she can see my anger and impatience because she looks genuinely afraid.

Good. She's trapped in the air with me with no one to save her, and I'm growing tired of this prude act. It was cute at first, but I'm just about over it.

She looks down at her hands. "I told you I don't have casual sex," she says quietly.

"Well what the hell does that even mean? Do you want to be exclusive? Do you want to be my girlfriend? Is that what you're angling for?"

She looks up and takes a deep breath. I can see the weight of what she's about to drop on me even before it falls.

"No. I don't do the girlfriend thing. Girlfriend is a fake title for a non-commitment that's just committed enough to fuck but isn't really going anywhere. Trust me, I've gotten that T-shirt. I don't want to sleep with anyone who isn't offering me anything real. And I don't believe in monogamy outside of marriage anymore."

Now I'm gaping at her like one of the fish we just left. She has *got* to be kidding. I want to stop this plane and make her get out and walk. Unfortunately that idea only works on the ground, with a car.

"Excuse me?" I ask. Of all the million things I expected to come out of her mouth, this was never even in the top one hundred. "Wait... are you seeing other men?" I feel somehow weirdly betrayed by this even though I'm usually the one seeing multiple women and keeping them all at arm's length.

We haven't even discussed whether or not we're supposed to only be seeing each other. I just assumed because most women past the second date zero in and focus all their attention on me. So fair or not, it's become an expectation even when I'm not doing the same.

She looks genuinely terrified right now, and still no guilt has arisen over that issue in my mind.

"Yes, I'm seeing other people. And you're free to see other people. We aren't in a committed relationship." She says this like it should be completely obvious. And actually it should be.

"So you're trying to trap me into marriage?" I ask, my voice rising.

She flinches at this, and something dark inside me is pushing at the cage walls to get out. I can hear it growling inside me, claws scraping harshly against metal in the way of fingernails down a chalkboard.

"Of course not," she says. "I didn't say it had to be you. I'm saying I'm not sleeping with any man I'm not engaged to. That's a privilege reserved for the man I love, who loves me, who is committed to me and offering me real security. Whoever that happens to be. And until that man makes that decision and I accept, I will be seeing whoever I want. And you can see or sleep with whoever you want. I'm not asking you to be celibate or putting your dick in a cage."

I'm speechless. For several minutes I just sit there, staring at her, forcing my mind to process the words that just came out of her mouth. It's like she's speaking in a foreign language. I speak five languages, three fluently—Chinese and Japanese I'm only passable in despite doing so much business there. But whatever language she's speaking isn't on the list of the ones I know.

"So what you're saying is, you plan to date other men until you get an engagement ring?"

"Basically," she confirms.

The little con artist.

"And you expect any man to go along with that?"

"The right man will," she replies quietly.

I want to throw things, but everything on the jet is literally nailed down. Or maybe it's bolted down. Either way, there aren't a lot of things I can throw. And I realize that intimidating her in this small enclosed space isn't the smartest idea I've ever had.

I rise from my chair and tower over her.

"Soren..." her voice is small, panicked.

I grip the arm rests and lean down over her. "I could just *take* it," I growl close to her ear as she shudders beneath me.

"You do and you'll never see me again," she whispers.

"What makes you think I even want to see you again after you pulled this shit?" I say. Even though I know if either one of us should want to stop this forever it should be—and probably is—her.

A fire sparks in her eyes and suddenly I'm staring at twin blue flames. "Get. Off. Me," she snarls.

I back off and plop my ass back in the chair across from her, glaring.

"Did you think I was a whore?" she asks. "You know you can pay a prostitute if that's what you want."

"Honey, I can get it for free."

"But not from me," she says.

I don't know why I'm so fucking angry. Only a few hours ago I was thinking about how disappointed I was that no woman was a challenge, and here Livia Fairchild is —a challenge all wrapped up for me. And all I can do is whine like a petulant brat about it.

"Are you some kind of religious fundamentalist?" I ask, because that's the only thing that makes sense to me right now.

"No."

There is a long beat of silence.

"Are you a virgin?"

She looks at me somehow shocked, hurt, and offended all at once. "No." She practically spits the word.

Her voice is a bit stronger when she speaks again. "I have the right to set boundaries. I'm not obligated to fuck someone just because they want to fuck. I want the love and the commitment and the security. Sex means something to me, and if it doesn't mean the same thing to you, I'd rather just not. I'll understand if you don't want to see me anymore, and right now I'm not sure if I want to see you anymore so it might not be your decision to make."

She looks out the window again. We're flying over a city; thousands of lights shine like stars below us.

My mind is racing with all kinds of insane thoughts. I have the money and power, I could make her disappear. I could take her and keep her as my prisoner. I could break her down until she bent sweetly to my will. Fuck vanilla suburban hell. I can lure her into the forest with me and take my time devouring her.

I take a deep breath and say, "I apologize. You caught me off guard."

But I'm just regrouping, just resetting the game board, strategizing, planning ten moves ahead. I will have this woman in my bed if it's the last fucking thing I do. And once I do, she'll be very lucky if I ever let her out of it again. She has no idea who she's playing with.

CHAPTER SIX: LIVIA

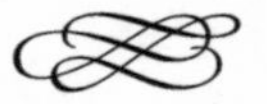

REBOOT

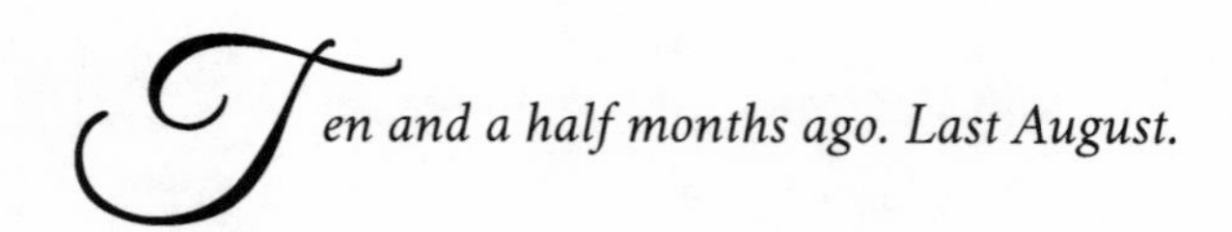

Ten and a half months ago. Last August.

I HAVEN'T SPOKEN to Soren in two weeks, but I can't stop thinking about him. The reality is, the other two men I'm dating are placeholders. They're buffers to keep me from stupidly getting too attached to the wrong man. And I know without any doubt who the wrong man is now. But I haven't seen the others the past two weeks, either. I'm burnt out to be honest.

I need a break from men. I need to think about if any of it is worth it. Dating men one at a time, dating them three at a time... what does it matter? It's still the same stupid bullshit. They won't commit, but they think you owe them your pussy because reasons. I'm so disgusted with this fucked-up dating scene, this instant-gratification culture, inside of which nothing deeper can ever have the hope to grow.

I seriously just want to time travel to when men gave a shit, when they didn't feel so goddamned entitled to fuck by the third date. I realize even as I'm thinking it that I'm being ridiculous. We have this lovely thing called legal and political rights now. I'm pretty sure veterinary assistant wouldn't have been on the menu of career options a few hundred years ago. And I probably would have just been married off to whoever it was *decided* that I should marry, my desires be damned. Still, I stupidly hold onto this romantic notion that there's this great love out there for me, that there is a man who will love and respect me and give me the world, that I can be deliriously happy, have babies, have the fairy tale.

The Disney princess brainwashing runs deep. Those movies get inside us too young. They take root like the vines that grew and twisted around Sleeping Beauty's castle, and we just keep believing that there's a man out there who will fight that dragon and slash through that thorn wall to get to us.

While I've been giving up on men, Soren has tried to call every day. I let the calls go to voice mail, but I foolishly listen to them after the fact. It's apology after apology. He's said all the right things. He's admitted he was horny and stupid and that he would never hurt me. He swears I'm safe with him, that he cares about me and wants to continue seeing me.

I want to believe everything he says, but I know he's dangerous. He's not the good guy. He's not the romance hero who gives me my happily-ever-after. I know he's not. But he's so fucking beautiful, and my body lights up every time he's near me. He smells like cigar smoke and whiskey, and I want to take a bath in that smell. I want to rest for the remainder of my life in the circle of his strong arms, but I know if I agree to see him again he'll be good for a few weeks and then he'll pull something like what happened on the plane again.

I was trapped like an animal high in the air in that aluminum cage. He knew I had nowhere to go and he had all the power. Before that moment I'd been a little turned on by the edge of power and darkness I sensed in him. It wafted off him and enveloped me in its seductive warmth. It had seemed like just a little thrill. Harmless. He'd been the key figure in my twisted sexual fantasies for the month since I'd met him.

And I'm ashamed to admit it, but after that night on the jet, he's been even more prominent in my erotic mental movies. Every night I've gotten off even harder to thoughts of what could have happened, of what he could have done. And this is why I can't possibly see him again. Those feelings are too confusing. And I don't want to be that weak girl who lets a man like that in.

Still, he's called. He's sent flowers, chocolates. Today I received a handwritten letter in the mail from him asking yet again for another chance. It's engraved stationery on cream-colored cotton paper. I know he won't keep this up. There are a few days at the most before he'll stop this pursuit and I will have lost him forever. If I can just be strong for a few more days I can put this and him behind me.

It was only a month. Nothing serious. Soren is not the one.

"I'd ask if I could buy you an ice cream to cheer you up, but that method obviously isn't working."

I look up, wiping the tears off my cheeks to find a very handsome man standing in front of me—as good looking as Soren, in fact. He is an angel to Soren's demon. His looks are light to Soren's dark.

He has a golden tan, sun-streaked blond hair, and some of the bluest eyes I've ever seen—besides my own. And a toothpaste commercial smile with a dimple. A freaking dimple.

He's got that casual Saturday in-the-park preppy look about him like he's just out for a stroll in between a round of golf and walking some pretentious special-edition dog breed. *Settle down, Livia. He's probably got a girlfriend who walks their pretentious special-edition dog.*

I've been sitting on a park bench, reading and re-reading the letter Soren actually put a stamp on and put in the mail to me. And I've been eating a scoop of chocolate chip ice cream out of a disposable bowl from the creamery a block away.

I hurriedly fold the letter and stuff it back in the envelope and stuff it in my bag as though I've just been caught doing something wrong.

"You look like you could use some air," he says.

"We're outside."

He laughs, and it's the most melodic sound I've heard in ages. "That's true, but sometimes even the open air can feel stifling. Sometimes you need to move. I was just going to go for a walk down by the river where it's breezier. Come join me?"

"I don't even know you."

I honestly have no idea what kind of magic I've worked on the universe since I started this roster thing. I thought it was my confidence that was drawing men to me, but obviously not, since this one approached when I was crying and falling apart on a park bench.

"I apologize, where are my manners? I'm Griffin."

"Like the mythological creature?"

He grins. "Indeed. So you know I'm safe."

I laugh in spite of myself. "I'm pretty sure Griffins don't make good house pets."

"So you'll keep me on a leash outside. It'll be fine."

I laugh as that visual swoops through my mind.

I need to stop moping over Soren, and standing right in front of me is my ticket out of this mental spiral. His hand is extended out to me in invitation.

"You're wearing sensible enough shoes for it," he says.

I've already lost track of the conversation and the invitation to walk with him. And I *am* wearing sensible shoes. My ensemble today consists of tennis shoes, soft heather grey shorts with a drawstring waist, and a darker charcoal grey racerback T-shirt. My hair is pulled back into a ponytail, and I look like I'm ready to go for a run.

Finally I sigh and put my hand in his, allowing him to pull me up to stand. This doesn't have to go anywhere. It's not like I'm going to marry him. It's just a walk down by the river.

"I'm Livia," I say finally.

"Beautiful name. Griffin and Livia. I think that'll look just fine on the wedding invitations. Kidding. Relax, it's just a walk."

But my shocked face isn't from the joke. It's the fact that I was just thinking about how it wasn't like I was going to marry him. And all at once my romantic little mind is off to the races again. Maybe... this guy? I know I just met him literally two minutes ago, but don't we often joke about things that have a bit of truth to them? Isn't that the core of a joke? Truth? Could this mean he's at least looking for something real?

We walk for miles, and much longer and farther than

I'd thought we would. I find myself grateful to be wearing such sensible shoes and comfortable clothes. I can't even imagine what it was he saw in me. No makeup—though that's normal for me, workout clothes, and sobbing into ice cream. Nothing says *ask me out on a date* like that combination. Is this a date? Or is he just a nice guy trying to cheer me up? Maybe I remind him of his sister or something. Then again, wedding invitation jokes aren't very brotherly.

We've talked for well over an hour, and I really like him. In the space of a single afternoon he's managed to restore my faith in men.

"Are you hungry?" he asks, suddenly.

I skipped lunch and the ice cream doesn't have quite the staying power of real food.

"Actually... kind of?" I say it like it's a question.

We've found ourselves standing in front of the River Siren. It's a dinner cruise riverboat. I've never actually been on it because it's for the tourists. Griffin looks from the boat to me.

"So, let's go on a dinner cruise."

"I'm really not dressed for it," I say, looking down at my grey cotton workout uniform.

He laughs, gesturing at his khakis and polo shirt. "I'm not much better. But it's fine. You wouldn't believe some of the odd clothes tourists wear on this thing. It's hardly a fancy venue."

I bite my lip. It actually sounds fun, and I could use the cheering up. "Don't you have to have reservations? Tickets bought ahead?"

"Nah. They leave a couple of tables empty in case a VIP shows up."

I arch a brow. "And you're a VIP?"

He winks, and that devastating dimple comes out of

hiding again. “Definitely. I'm friends with the owner of this little tourist trap on the water.”

“Okay. I mean... if you think you can get us in, it sounds like fun.”

He walks up to the outdoor podium where people are showing their pre-bought tickets. Griffin speaks low, so I don't hear him, but I barely catch the words from the man behind the podium. “Of course, Mr. Macdonald, we'd love to accommodate you and your lovely date.”

So I guess it is a date. But I think I already knew that.

The boat serves us Salisbury steak, mashed potatoes, green beans, and dinner rolls along with the best iced tea I've had in a while. It's comfort food—something I definitely needed after my big pity party in the park. After dinner we go up to the top deck where a live band plays swing music. Some of the tourists are already up dancing. Griffin drags me out on to the dance floor. He's a surprisingly good dancer, but I'm terrible.

Still, he's good at leading and keeps me from looking too stupid. Then the music switches to a slow song, and he pulls me in closer to him. I rest my head on his shoulder thinking that for such a shitty start, this day has ended up pretty amazing.

Toward the end of the cruise we're served dessert out on the top deck under the stars: chocolate silk pie and coffee. The boat docks further up the river, closer to where we first started walking. I'm relieved we won't have to walk an hour back to the park we met in. Griffin walks me to my car in a comfortable silence, his fingers threading through mine.

I'm not sure at what point we started holding hands, but it feels natural, not forced. He feels natural—and fun. When we reach my car, he asks for my number. I give it to him, and he kisses me on the cheek and whispers, "I'll call you this week."

I don't know it yet, but this has been the first of many dates with the smooth and charming Griffin Macdonald. And while in the coming week, one man will find himself booted off my roster, it won't be Soren.

CHAPTER SEVEN: DAYNE

THE MARK

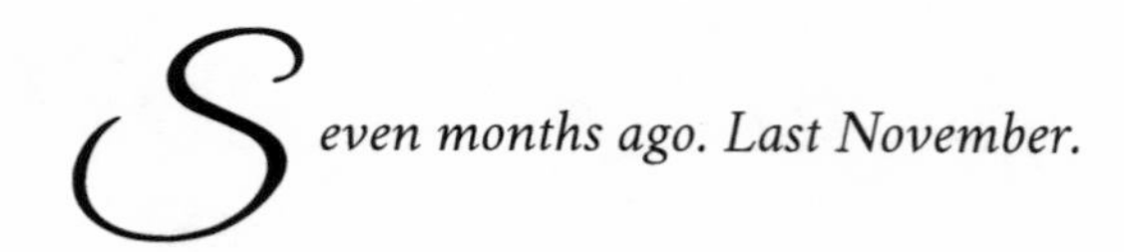

Seven months ago. Last November.

I'VE BEEN FOLLOWING Livia at a distance for the past two weeks, trying to find the right moment to make my move. From the intel I've gathered—including reports from Soren's private investigator—our suspicions are right. She's dating three men: Griffin, Soren, and a guy named Jack.

I've met Jack once. He's kind of a douchebag and definitely not at the same level of success as Griffin, Soren, and myself. My job is to get on her roster and get Jack out. It's tricky business because we all run the risk that she might decide to take me on but drop Griffin or Soren. We've got backup plans for that, but you never know. Then there's the even bigger risk that she'll reject me outright, and there may not be a bounce back from that. Any further attempts after a hard rejection just make me look like a dangerous stalker.

Soren is counting on the gold digger aspect—that she'll go for whoever has the deepest pockets. But I have my doubts about this. It's no question that she's looking to marry up, but does that make her a gold digger? I'm not so sure. She's not asking anyone to buy her a bunch of things or pay any of her bills. She's maintained a certain independence and desire to take care of her own living expenses. Though I'm sure men have bought and paid for things anyway. I know Griffin and Soren have spent money.

And marriage is the big cash out, so she may just be patient enough to wait it out. She *is* remaining chaste with all these men after all, even when it seems clear she wants to go further. So she's not a prude. I will definitely be pushing and testing this button myself at the first available opportunity. Few people in the modern world have this level of self-control, which makes her oddly unpredictable.

I admit, I'm intrigued. When Griffin and Soren first laid out the plan, I wasn't sure I was on board. But just watching her laugh and engage with the world in the sweet uncomplicated way she does these past couple of weeks, and I'm seriously considering it. There's something refreshing about this girl—something untainted and pure, even though I'm sure she isn't a virgin.

And she's beautiful. She has clear light blue eyes like a pristine lake in the mountains and this beachy sun-streaked hair that goes halfway down her back in soft waves I want to slide my fingers through.

Livia doesn't play these cheap silly games of the average gold digger. And she doesn't act entitled. She isn't looking for dumbasses with deep pockets. She wants a smart man that she can respect. It's a dance. It's a game. And I've got the money to burn. I'll play if she will. Plus Soren and

Griffin will kick my ass if I leave them and their grand plan in the lurch.

I'm still not sure I'm prepared to jump into a forever thing with them and this girl. That's why I need to interview her.

Livia is shopping at a high-end boutique today. She has several nice dresses ready for purchase along with a bottle of perfume which I happen to know is Soren's favorite fragrance on a woman. I wonder if she's cataloging all of these preferences for each man she dates. I wonder if she has a list somewhere to keep it all straight or if she truly cares enough to remember.

The sales clerk is ringing up her purchase when I make my move. I have a navy silk tie in my hand from the men's section. I just grabbed the first thing I saw so I could get in line behind her.

I drop my tie on top of her things and pass my black card to the clerk.

"Please, allow me," I say. I'm not sure how I hope she'll react. A rejection of my offer could just mean she wants me to insist, like women who try to go for the check at dinner but really want you to stop them. Or maybe she'll say no flat out. Or maybe she'll say yes with greedy little dollar signs behind her eyes. A foolish part of me hopes she won't do the latter.

She turns to me and smiles. It's a genuine, electrifying and open smile that lights up the entire space. And God help me, but she's already got me. For a moment it's easy to forget she's the mark in a game she doesn't even know she's playing.

"Thank you, that's very kind of you." She steps gracefully aside so I can sign the receipt.

Huh. She knows I can afford it. I *did* just flash my black

card, and this girl is savvy. She knows about black cards. But even though I've been watching her, I didn't expect this reaction. She seems completely unfazed by this gesture but at the same time appreciative of it. She's not ashamed. Not indignant. It's as though I merely opened a door for her. She isn't shocked by this kind of treatment. She's not impressed or overly charmed. But... she's not entitled either. She's not a brat.

I can't put words to how this simple exchange makes me feel.

I sign and wait as the clerk puts our things in two separate bags. Livia looks a bit overburdened by bags already. She's been shopping in the other stores nearby as well. This gives me my next opportunity.

"Let me help you out with your bags," I offer.

She takes a good long look at me. I'm not sure if she's assessing my danger or my dating potential.

In case it's the former I say, "It's broad daylight. I promise I'm not a serial killer."

She smiles and hands over her bags while picking up my small bag containing the tie. "Okay. I'll carry yours if you carry mine. And I know you're not a serial killer. They don't give out black cards to serial killers."

I laugh. She's probably right about that. I like this girl. It's been a long time since I've really liked a woman. Not just been attracted. Not just wanted to sleep with, but genuinely *liked*. And suddenly I'm a teenager worried I'll mess up and the pretty girl at school will turn me down. I'm not sure what to do with this sudden burst of whatever thing it is she's making me feel. It's so foreign, so long forgotten, and suddenly I have zero doubts about this.

There's no guilt. No hesitation. I want this girl. I want this image, this idea, this plan that Soren and Griffin laid out for me. I want us. The four of us. She has no idea the precarious line she walks. I'm determined not to fuck this up.

Even though I'm carrying all the bags, I open the door and let her walk out first, knowing each gallant gesture disarms her and gets me closer to *yes*. Though to be honest she doesn't seem to have a big guard or giant walls around her, which is pretty unusual these days. Part of me is charmed by it and another part of me wants to shake her and ask does she not know the thoughts that go through men's minds? Does she not know the wolves who would eat her alive? Part of me wants to punish her and another part wants to protect her—from men like me and Griffin and Soren.

She pops the trunk when we get out to her car. It's a bit of a walk since she parked on the other end of the lot and was walking store to store. She drives a modest but clean Ford Focus, obviously purchased with her own money.

I put her bags in, and she hands me mine. "Thanks for the rescue," she says, flashing that brilliant smile again. It's so blinding that even the sun overhead can't compete with her.

She's definitely flirting with me which makes me wonder if she's trying to up her man harem to four or if she's already thinking of dropping someone.

"I like you," I say. Maybe it's not the best line in the world, but it's genuinely true, and I'm banking on her sensing it. "Let me take you out to dinner."

She laughs. "He buys me dresses, opens doors, carries my bags, and wants to feed me, too. Is dragon slaying on the agenda, because I want to be sure to get a good seat."

I take her hand in mine. It's a risk, but she's letting me this close into her space and knows I want to date her. And doesn't fortune favor the brave? “Come to dinner with me. I can't let you starve.”

She laughs at this. We both know this girl would never starve in any situation. Men would stumble over their own feet to feed her if she were in true distress. And I would no doubt be one of them.

She sighs. “In all seriousness, my dance card is pretty full right now.”

Shit. Is she really going to keep that Jack douche on the roster? He was a bit of an asshole to her earlier in the week, and I was hoping to play that to my advantage. Even if she says no, this much flirting could buy me another chance if we *bump into each other* in a few weeks. I can wait for Jack to do something stupid and leverage his foolishness in my favor.

“Squeeze me in,” I say. “I'm sure you've got time for one dinner. You have to eat. I'm flexible.”

“Dammit. Okay. Yes. I will go to dinner with you... wait... maybe we should exchange names. I think we're doing this a little out of order.”

I can't believe I didn't remember to introduce myself. I really am behaving like a teenager. “I'm Dayne.”

“Livia.”

“Okay, Livia. You tell me when you can fit me in among all your suitors and I'll take care of the rest.”

CHAPTER EIGHT: LIVIA

MR. BLACK CARD

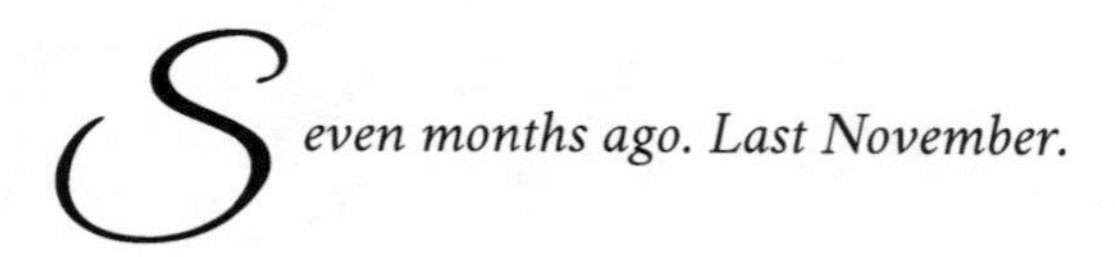

Seven months ago. Last November.

I MEET Dayne at the restaurant. He seems almost relieved by this, and I'm not sure what to make of that. Does he have secrets he doesn't want me to know? Is he borrowing someone else's black card? I sigh. I'll figure him out if he sticks around long enough.

It's a first date, and I don't let men pick me up on the first date for my own safety. It's true that he probably isn't a criminal. The black card joke wasn't entirely a joke. It's a very exclusive card, and while I may not know all the qualifications to have one—except for the poorly kept secret that you have to charge at least a hundred thousand dollars a year just to be considered—I'm pretty sure that a brand like that wouldn't give their card out to a man with any kind of criminal record. Him just having the card is practically a background check all on its own.

Then again, there are knockoffs out there, and it's not as though I could scrutinize the card without seeming tacky.

The restaurant he's chosen is a tiny hole in the wall Italian place. It's not fancy or expensive but it's very romantic, and the food is amazing. I'm wondering if this is a gold digger test. I don't mind it. I mean I am sort of ruthlessly maintaining a roster of men to date until someone proposes. I can hardly blame the guy for seeing how I'll react to this dining choice.

In another situation I might take it as a sign that he's stingy or cheap, but he's already proven that isn't so. He seems like a generous person, and that's what matters because no one wants to be with a man who hoards his money like a dragon guarding a golden egg—someone who keeps a running tally of "all he's done for you".

I'm actually thrilled by the restaurant choice. It shows he's not trying to buy me like a common whore. I might actually like this guy.

Part of me hopes he does something disastrous tonight to give me an excuse not to see him again. I can't date four men. It's too many, logistically. I can't spend my whole life doing nothing but dating.

And I don't really want to drop anyone. I could probably drop Jack, but even though he can be an arrogant prick, I'm not sure if I'm ready to boot him out just yet—though he is the obvious choice for dismissal. A few months ago it would have been Soren, but he's been the perfect gentleman lately.

When I walk inside the restaurant, I spot Dayne at a small candlelit table at the back, but I allow the Maître D to walk me to the table. As we approach, Dayne stands. The Maître D pulls out my chair, and Dayne and I both sit.

I really love that. The standing thing. Part of why I meet men for the first date besides safety is to see if he'll stand when I approach. It's an old-fashioned gesture of respect, and I love chivalry. I love doors opened, checks paid, standing, that hand at the small of my back leading me into a crowded venue. All the things that so many women fight and claw to erase, I savor and enjoy. These things make me feel cherished, and since the roster started, I've dropped any man who doesn't do them. This is how I want to be treated, and a man is never going to get better than the first few dates.

"I love this restaurant," I say.

He seems disappointed by this. "So you've been here?"

"Yes, but it was with girlfriends for lunch. Definitely not the same romantic atmosphere," I say to reassure him that even though I know this place and love the food, he's the first man to bring me here. It really was a good restaurant choice.

When the waiter comes, I'm allowed to order first. I like that Dayne doesn't try to order for me. Telling me what I'm going to eat is a bridge too far. It comes across as controlling rather than chivalrous unless he knows me and what I order—I like it then—but definitely not on a first date. He's just ticking all the boxes. Poor Jack may be on borrowed time.

"You look beautiful," Dayne says when we're alone again.

I smile. "Thank you."

He's pretty beautiful himself. He has dark hair and warm chocolate brown eyes. Kind eyes. And I can tell he's got some serious muscle definition underneath the navy suit he's wearing.

There are several beats of silence, those inevitable

awkward moments of *oh god what are we supposed to talk about now?*

"What do you do for a living?" he asks finally.

I catch him wincing at his own boring standard interview question. And I'm sure he's asking it only because I didn't ask first. I don't do the interview questions. There's plenty of time to get to know a guy. All I care about on the first date is if I'm attracted, if I have fun, and if I feel comfortable with him.

I take a sip of my water before answering. "I'm a lion tamer."

He laughs, "Really?"

"No, I'm messing with you. Guess."

"Hmmm, this is a lot of work for a first date. Is there a prize if I guess right?"

"Yes. A kiss."

"I'd get that at the end of the night anyway," he says, sure of himself.

I laugh. "Well this way it's guaranteed."

"Fair enough. Lady Astronaut?"

"Nope."

"Hairdresser?"

"Nu uh."

He goes through a string of guesses... teacher, dog walker, hotel manager. Finally he gives up.

"Okay, I'll have mercy on you. I'm a veterinary assistant. The clinic I work for works mainly with rescue groups. They get animals out of abusive situations and bring them to us to treat and rehabilitate them so they can find forever homes."

"That's really nice," he says, seeming genuine.

"So what do you do?"

"Guess."

"hmmm, international spy?"

he shakes his head.

My other guesses are oil baron, janitor, firefighter, police chief, and CEO of a startup.

"Good guess," he says after that last one. "You're right."

I lean forward over the table, not missing how his eyes go straight to my cleavage. I grab his tie and pull him to me for a kiss far too sweet for that level of aggression.

"What was that for?" he asks when I pull back.

"Oh, so prizes just flow one way?"

He chuckles.

The ice now broken, we get into a variety of topics that seem safe for a first date. Then the food comes and we have something to occupy us besides nerves and small talk. I'm surprised I still get first date nerves. I should be more afraid of this date going well and how that might disrupt the balance of the roster. I also wonder briefly during dinner if he picked a place he knew I could afford to see if I'd go for the check at the end. The answer to that? Not even if someone dangled him over a cliff.

I've been told if the guy has money I should at least offer to pay part so I don't look like I'm just after his money, but absolutely not. A man that obsessed with the evil of a woman who wants a man who can provide for her is too damaged for me to deal with. If men can excuse their wandering eye with evolution, I can use the same argument for my need to have things paid for. Besides, he invited me. It's rude to invite someone out to dinner and not pay. You can find this rule in any standard etiquette book.

For dessert we share an order of cherries poached in red wine with mascarpone cream, which is just as sexy as it sounds.

After the meal, Dayne stands. "If you'll excuse me for a moment."

He's gone a few minutes, and when he returns he asks if I'm ready to go. It occurs to me as he pulls my chair out that he got up and took care of the bill out of sight so it didn't even touch the table. Damn that's smooth. Jack who?

Dayne walks me to my car and goes for another kiss. I let him because it's not as though I can play the *I don't kiss on the first date* card after I already kissed him in the restaurant.

I thank him and tell him I had a lovely time, and he gracefully disengages and leaves once I'm safely inside my car.

He calls two days later to set up another date. Jack has started running hot and cold on me. I find I can't justify this anymore because I definitely can't juggle four men.

So Dayne is now on the roster taking Jack's place. I'm not sure how I got to this moment of dating three men that are actually serious candidates at the same time. Right now everything is wonderful, perfect. But I can't help my mind moving forward in time.

After all, I can't just rotate men in and out of my life forever. That was never the plan. The idea was that at some point the right man would step up and propose and then this life I was told I was supposed to want, the one that would make me happy would finally get started.

I allow myself for the first time to truly consider the new risk. What if I fall in love with more than one man? My problem is I attach too hard. This dating plan seemed perfect on paper. With three men I could never overattach to one if that one decided to string me along. I didn't truly consider that instead of solving all my problems I might have made them three times worse. Because I've already attached to Griffin and Soren. And I could see myself attaching to Dayne.

What if one of them proposes and I have to break three hearts... the other men I'm dating... and my own? What then?

But my mind remains silent, refusing to offer up an answer to this new dating problem I've created. I'm tempted to call Dayne back and say I can't do it. A love triangle surely is more manageable than a rectangle. But I don't make that call, instead leaving it to fate to untangle.

CHAPTER NINE: GRIFFIN

I MET THIS GREAT GIRL

S*even and a half months ago. Early November.*

I'M at the most boring charity art auction I think I've ever had the displeasure of attending, but my company made a large donation to the museum. My name is in the glossy printed booklet for fuck's sake. So not attending didn't feel like an option. I didn't bring Livia. She already had plans tonight, but she would have made the evening tolerable.

It's one of those black tie events where a date isn't really optional, and I have too much of a playboy reputation to come here alone. So I called an escort agency I've used in the past for things like this—just a pretty girl on my arm for the evening who can get through a night without embarrassing me or expecting anything.

I can tell from the way she's been looking at me since we got here that she is very much hoping this ends up at my place, but that won't be happening. Sharon excuses herself to go to the ladies' room, and I spot a familiar face a few exhibits away.

Soren sees me and crosses the room. "I haven't seen you in a lifetime. I thought you fell off the planet," he says.

I could say the same to him, but I shrug. "Just been busy. Work. You know how it is."

"So how have you been?" Soren asks while he appraises what may be the ugliest sculpture ever created.

"Don't laugh, but I think I found the one. I think I'm going to ask her to marry me."

"That blonde you came here with?" Soren asks. "She looks familiar."

I laugh. Of course she'd look familiar to Soren. He and I have used the same agency in the past. He's probably taken her to an event much like this one.

"No, not Sharon. She's with the agency. Livia had plans tonight."

Soren does a literal spit take of his champagne right onto me. I wipe the back of my face with my hand. "Thanks."

"Sorry. What did you say her name was? The girl you're seeing?"

"Livia."

"Livia, what?" Soren looks like he's seen a ghost.

"Fairchild. Why? Do you know her?"

"I'm *dating* her." He practically spits the words at me.

"You're what?"

"Oh yes," Soren says. "I've been dating that lovely con artist for four and a half months now. How long have *you* been dating her?"

"Three," I say. Part of me is sure Soren is lying or has this girl mixed up with someone else. It can't be the same woman I'm seeing. Livia is so... nice. Fun. She isn't the cheating type.

"Has she slept with you?" Soren asks, almost menacingly.

"I... no... we've been taking things slow. We've been on maybe eight dates. Why? Has she slept with *you*?" I might have to kill him if he's fucked my future wife, our history and friendship be damned.

"No. She has not, in fact. But you seem surprised she's seeing other people. She hasn't given you the *no girlfriend* speech, yet? Because I got it at the end of month one."

"What in the fuck is the *no girlfriend* speech?" We haven't had a conversation about it, but I kind of thought she *was* my girlfriend even though I've dated women for months before while seeing other people. This just felt different. Livia felt different—like it was something real.

Soren's face lights up as if he's thrilled to be the one to drop this bomb on me. Sharon appears at my side then, leaning into me to make it clear she's with me. She may be a professional, but she is more than happy with whose arm she's on tonight. She has the absolute worst timing.

"Soren," she says. "It's good to see you again."

I knew it! I knew he'd taken her out somewhere before. I look back and forth between them, and now I realize the two of us have actually shared this girl. It was a couple of years ago, another boring event like this and we were all drunk off our asses, but it's coming back to me now. It seems like she's looking to have a repeat, and she probably wouldn't even charge us extra for it.

"I'm sorry, Sharon, Soren and I have an important business matter to discuss. We won't be long. If you'll excuse us."

"Sure," she says, but her face falls around her accommodating plastic fake smile.

I grab Soren by the elbow and lead him out to the terrace. He jerks his arm out of my grasp as soon as we're outside. The only reason he didn't do it before was that he didn't want to make a scene.

"Okay, now what in the fuck is the *no girlfriend* speech?"

Soren just smiles at me. At first I think he isn't going to tell me or that he's just making all this up for some reason known only to him, when finally he starts talking.

"She doesn't want to be anybody's girlfriend. She wants the ring. Marriage. Babies, I'm assuming. She wants the whole fucking fairy tale."

"So? I can give her that. I *will* give her that."

"She's seeing other men. She doesn't believe in *monogamy* outside of marriage." He says the word monogamy as if it's a curse word.

"What?!?" My voice is loud enough that people inside the museum are looking up from their conversations. "What in the fuck does that even mean?"

"Exactly," he agrees. Then he adds, "Oh yeah, she intends to keep, I guess a harem of men to date until someone proposes. I guess she plans to eat free and accept presents until someone gives her *real security* as she put it. It's a nice gig if you can get it. And clearly she has."

"Why haven't you proposed?" I ask.

He's been dating her longer, after all. I'm trying hard to imagine a scenario in which a woman has somehow been dating Soren for four and a half months and he hasn't gotten laid. But it probably isn't that different than the scenario where I've somehow been dating a woman for three months without getting laid.

Soren shrugs. "I'm not prepared to give in to the little con artist."

This must be his secret pet name for her. He's called her that twice now.

"Well, say goodbye," I say, "because I'm proposing." Then something occurs to me... "Did you ask her to come with you tonight?"

"Yeah, but she already had plans."

Soren has realized this of course, but it's just now occurring to me that she's probably out on a date with someone who isn't either of us right now. "How many fucking men is she seeing?" I ask, once again nearly shouting.

"Fuck if I know," Soren says. "Though I'm putting a private investigator on her to find out. Part of me thought she was bullshitting about other men—like she was playing hard to get, but now that I know she isn't, I want a full report."

He seems infuriated that she's not *playing* hard to get. Make that two of us.

"Don't bother asking her to marry you," Soren says. "She's *mine*."

I'm about to get into a pissing match with him, but I stop short. I realize I'm enraged right now, but it isn't at Soren. It's at Livia. I've been thinking about marrying this girl and she's been playing both of us, along with whoever she's out with tonight.

Screw this.

Several minutes of tense silence pass. I can't bring myself to go back inside yet because I'm so amped up that I'll only draw attention, and I don't want to deal with Sharon. The whole point of calling the agency was to have someone who wouldn't make demands.

"I should fuck Sharon tonight," I say.

"If you think that will somehow get back at Livia, think again. She explicitly made clear that since we aren't exclusive I can fuck whoever I want. So I assume that rule applies to you as well. We can all do whatever we want until someone gives her a ring, apparently."

"We shouldn't let this screw up our friendship," I say.

Soren appears thoughtful for a moment. "I agree. So why don't we share her? But on *our* terms."

It's been a long time since we've shared a woman in any kind of quasi-serious way.

"Like... forever?" I ask because even when we played this game long term it was a few months at best.

"Yeah, why not? You said you wanted to marry her. That seems pretty committed to me."

"She'd never go for it. She's not the type to go for a triad."

"Really? Because she's doing a great impression of a girl who can handle multiple men. And who says we're *asking* her? She needs to understand who she's been fucking with. We should get Dayne in on this. Is he seeing anyone?"

Every time in the past when we've shared a woman in any sort of serious way, it wasn't just me and Soren. It was me, Soren, and Dayne.

"He's seeing some girl named Rainbow if you can believe it," I say. "It's not serious though."

"Of course not. Nobody seriously dates a Rainbow. Call him. I have a plan. Little Miss Livia Fairchild decided to play the wrong men."

I should tell Soren, no. But there's a dark part of me that's tired of the polished, polite responsible mask I've been wearing recently. And Soren always knew how to coax my inner beast out of the cage. The idea of the three of us together again, sharing a woman in something permanent is too tempting to ignore. The part of me that wants to protect her from Soren is outmaneuvered by the part of me that wants her on her knees.

CHAPTER TEN: LIVIA

THE ANNOUNCEMENT

Six months ago. Christmas Eve.

It's Christmas Eve, and I'm standing on my parents' porch, wondering why I didn't call first to soften the shock. I slip inside the front door by myself, trying to come up with some last minute Hail Mary to make this less of the clusterfuck I'm sure its going to be.

"Livvy!" my mom calls out, rushing toward me. She's got a red Santa Claus apron on, and I know she's just pulled her famous soft gingerbread cookies out of the oven —her yearly tradition for the big family meal.

"You look like you got a tan. Where on earth did you get a tan this time of year? You know how dangerous tanning beds are!" Her rant about the dangers of life-giving sunlight dies suddenly and her eyes nearly fall out of her head when she catches sight of the gleaming rock on my finger.

"You're engaged!?!" she whisper shrieks. "I didn't even know you were dating anyone. Well, where is he?" She's looking past me trying to see out the windows which are too frosted from the cold to see anything but moving shadows.

"He's getting the gifts out of the car."

"Your father is going to lose his shit. You know he doesn't like surprises."

That's the understatement of the century. My father hates surprises so much that you pretty much have to shop for him off a pre-curated list he's created so he knows he's going to like it. Creative deviations are not appreciated.

My mom takes my hand in hers to inspect the ring. "This is a *nice* ring," she says. I swear she's about to pull out one of those things jewelers use to inspect the quality of diamonds. I'm grateful she doesn't actually have one of those things. Nothing would be more embarrassing than my mother appraising my ring in the middle of the foyer.

"It's Tiffany," I say, giddy glee coming out in my voice because this truly is my dream ring and even though I have my doubts about everything else, the ring itself is the one bright spot I have some measure of faith in.

"Really?" She's still whispering. I'm not sure why she's feeling the need to whisper in her own house. Maybe she's afraid my father will hear. "So he's doing pretty well for himself?" she says, fishing.

"He runs a Fortune 500 company," I say, but that's all I say because that's all I know. I don't even know *which* company.

Before I can be grilled further, the doorbell rings. Oh shit, that's him. I feel like the heroine in a horror movie with the killer just outside the door.

"Aren't you going to let him in?" My mother asks.

I'm really not ready to do this but obviously if I'm going to get married, my family has to be made aware of the engagement, and hearing it in person is probably better than finding out when the wedding invitation arrives.

"Honestly, Livvy," my mother says. She flings the door open and smiles brightly when she gets a look at him all handsome and suave and stylish, laden down with Christmas presents like a sophisticated and evil Santa. "Come in, I'm sorry, Livia didn't tell me your name."

He gives me a look like he's disappointed in me and says, "I'm Soren."

"I'm Judith," she says.

"It's lovely to meet you, Judith."

"Harold," she calls... "Livvy brought a man for Christmas." She says this in the same way one might say "Livvy brought a pumpkin pie." And I'm pretty sure my mom thinks both of those things would be equally delicious.

My father appears a moment later. He's smoking a pipe. He has this Christmas Eve thing where he smokes a pipe. I have no idea why he does it. He never at any other point in the year smokes a pipe. This is *his* Christmas Eve tradition. The Fairchild Christmas: Gingerbread cookies and cigar smoke.

He narrows his eyes at Soren.

"Hello," he says, coldly. "And who might you be?" He looks between Soren and me as if Soren is attempting to kidnap me, which is so close to the truth.

"Soren Kingston," he says. Soren can't shake my father's hand—not that my father's offering—because he's still holding the presents.

My father's eyes widen. He actually recognizes Soren's name. I would be willing to bet money he even knows which company he runs.

"Well, that's a name," he says, grimly. "Are you dating my daughter?"

Without missing a beat, Soren says, "I'm *marrying* your daughter. Next year. June 22nd. I hope that date works for you."

My father looks like he might go to the gun safe and commit a felony. But an equal level of malice is rolling off Soren. He's not used to being questioned, and I can tell he isn't loving my father's tone. And I know my father isn't loving Soren's.

This is getting off to a great start.

I hold up my hand, flashing the ring in an attempt to diffuse the situation, which is of course stupid because waving sparkling evidence in front of my father's face of the impending wedding only six months from now is probably not the smartest move. My father's nostrils flare at this visual—like a bull ready to charge. And I am one hundred percent certain that if my father charges, Soren will drop the gifts—breakables be damned—and get into an actual fight with him—like the kind of conflict where neighbors call the cops.

"Harold!" my mother says, finally seeing the situation that may be about to unfold.

"And you think you're good enough for Livia?" he asks, blowing cigar smoke into Soren's face—not accidentally.

I'm surprised when Soren says, "Probably not. But I don't think there were any literal princes on her dating roster, so I'll have to do."

My parents don't know about the roster. Even Macy doesn't know about the roster. She just knew I was dating and keeping it quiet for a while. Of course nobody seems to think this roster talk is anything more than a joke, and my mother is now fully engaged with diffusing the testosterone in the entryway so Soren isn't able to elaborate on my dating hijinx.

"Soren, I'm so sorry, you can put those gifts under the tree. And dinner is ready so if you want to come on back."

Soren offers her a charming smile and brushes past my father to put the gifts under the tree. At the same time, my mom grabs my father by the elbow and drags him back to the dining room.

"Livia's engaged," he announces gruffly to the family, none-to-happy about it.

I'm a bit confused to be honest. I mean yes, this is being sprung on him—did I mention my father hates surprises? But still, I saw the flash of recognition at Soren's name. You'd think he'd be happy to know I'll be so well taken care of. Soren can absolutely provide and protect. And we all knew I wasn't going to ever have a nice lifestyle on a veterinary assistant's salary.

Dinner itself is surprisingly pleasant. My brother, his wife, their three kids, as well as my two sisters and their husbands, and my sole remaining grandmother are all much more friendly to Soren than my father was. There are ooohs and aaahs about the ring, and questions peppered about the wedding and the whirlwind planning that's about to ensue and am I worried about securing a venue? I hadn't thought about that, but now I am.

Soren sits on one side of me and Macy sits on my other. She'll be the maid of honor of course. Macy comes to all my family holiday functions because she has no family of her own—at least none she has contact with.

My two and a half year old niece, Vivie looks like she's half in love with Soren when he cuts her ham into tiny triangles for her.

"Do you think Vivie would want to be my flower girl?" I ask my sister-in-law, Anna.

Anna leans closer to Vivie. "Would you like to be in Aunt Livvy's wedding?"

"Yes!" Vivie shouts through a mouthful of ham, even though I'm pretty sure she isn't clear on what a wedding even is.

After dinner just before everyone gathers in the family room for gift exchanges, my father says, "Livia, I'd like to speak with you alone in my study."

I exchange a glance with Soren, who looks pissed that my father seems to be trying to interfere with his evil plans. But he quickly shifts back to his charming smile as he volunteers to help my mother clear the table. He's at least earning points with her.

Vivie trails behind him with her own plate talking his ear off about flowers and how she's going to be the flower girl, even though I'm sure she has no idea what that is, either—not unless the Disney Princess training has started way early.

I follow my father to his study.

"Shut the door," he says.

I shut the door and sit in the guest chair across from his desk.

"You're not marrying that man," he says flatly.

For a moment I'm speechless. I am, after all, a grown adult woman. And although this whole wedding situation is far more sinister than he could possibly suspect—and my hand was forced—there is a rebellious part of me that wants to flounce off and elope just because I'm being told I *can't* marry Soren.

Something my father and Soren have in common—a controlling streak, which is probably why they got along so famously out in the foyer and had to be seated at opposite far ends of the dinner table with a large centerpiece blocking their view of one another.

"And why is that?" I ask. I don't bother to fall into some over-the-top crying fit or to say *but I love him* like a trashy daytime talk show. My feelings for Soren are very conflicted and confused these days.

"He's a rogue."

"Ummm... This isn't a Regency romance novel. Nobody says *rogue* anymore in that context."

He pierces me with a glare. "He's a player. I've heard some very unsavory things about some of his activities with the opposite sex. And some of the unsavory parties he's been at."

He keeps saying unsavory.

I would ask where he could have possibly heard these things. It's not as though he runs in the same social circles, but my father is a decently paid CPA, and most likely heard some rumor from one of his higher-end business clients. And in order for them to know this about Soren they would have had to have been at those same parties. But I don't bother mentioning this fact.

I'm not even a little shocked by this revelation. I've known Soren wasn't the guy you bring home to your parents almost from the beginning. But my libido staunchly refused to let me remove him from the roster, even when I knew I should—and now it's too late.

"Well? Aren't you going to say anything?" he asks.

I shrug. I'm not sure what there is to say. I actually *am* marrying that man because if I don't he'll destroy me, and my father has no power or pull to stop it. What Soren wants, Soren gets. His unsavory *rogue-ish* ways hardly matter in this scenario.

Finally I say, "Instead of talking behind his back, maybe you should discuss this with Soren and see what he has to say about it. Doesn't it seem a little unfair to convict him without a trial?"

"Fine. Send him in. I'm sure I can persuade him to put a stop to this. The last thing his company needs is another scandal."

I want to ask which company, but now doesn't feel quite like the time. I get up and go into the living room to get Soren.

"My father wants to talk to you in his study," I whisper to Soren, who the rest of my family seems to adore.

He just nods, gets up, and leaves the room. I find myself wondering if my father can actually persuade Soren to leave me alone. And if he does, what does that mean for Griffin and Dayne? Would they leave, too? Do I want them to leave, too? Can I pretend that any of them is pure and clean in all of this, that I could trust them after this?

What will my family think if Soren leaves in the middle of Christmas Eve? Or if the wedding doesn't happen? My adorably clueless niece seems to have really latched onto him and the idea of being in my wedding. *Does* she know what weddings are? I'm trying to remember when I first understood what weddings were in even the most vague way.

A tense silence descends on the room as we all hear shouting—my father's—from down the hall. Then things go quiet in there for a long time, and I'm worried one of them has killed the other. Fifteen minutes later the door opens and there's... laughing? Both of them are engaged in what sounds like a friendly conversation like they have inside jokes... like they've been friends for ages.

I have no idea what Soren could have possibly said to

diffuse my father and win him over, particularly when their initial meeting in the foyer was so tense. The two of them rejoin us in the family room. My father sits next to the fireplace and puts more tobacco in his pipe. Soren joins me without a word, but he seems far more relaxed.

The rest of the Christmas Eve festivities of gifts, gingerbread cookies, and hot cocoa goes off without another cross word from anyone, and I'm left more confused than ever.

CHAPTER ELEVEN: SOREN

THE VIDEO PROPOSAL

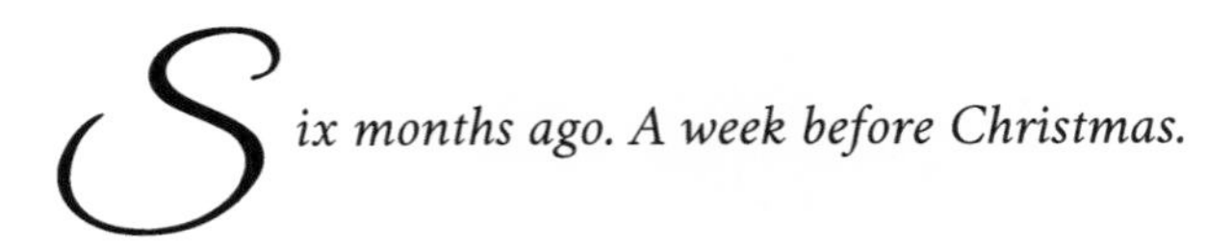

Six months ago. A week before Christmas.

WE'RE out in the middle of the ocean off the coast of Miami. We've taken a short break from the cold just before the holidays. Livia lies on the deck in a skimpy red bikini, the sun licking her bronzed skin in all the places I want to put my own tongue. It seems unfair that the sun should be allowed this intimacy with her. That is *my* body to heat up, consume, and devour. No celestial body should ever get to touch her. The only others who will touch her are Griffin and Dayne, but that's different.

I met the guys during rush week at Dartmouth. It was a period of serious hazing even though it was against the rules. But we weren't the kind of pussy ass little bitches who were going to whine and complain and cry to the administration like little girls. Every generation before us made it through, and we would too. We were fucked with and humiliated to the point I was ready to rip heads off and mail them back to the families in question.

I was livid at the treatment. I shouldn't have to experience it. I had money and power. But so did everyone else. It didn't hold quite the same threat that it did in broader society. At the top, money and power is as common as the Internet. Oh you have an Internet connection? Amazing. Me too.

The things that happened during that period bonded the three of us together not just as brothers, but as lovers. Then once we were in and the pussy was flowing like wine, we started to share women. We didn't think about it, it just seemed like a natural progression at the time. It didn't even occur to us to be jealous because what we had was between us, and the girl was our toy. Nothing more. Our friendship always came out on top against any woman who became our fourth.

But it wasn't a part of my life I shared with anyone outside our circle. Despite how progressive the world seems, it isn't—not beneath the surface. People like to virtue signal so they can get cookies from the wider society to show what good little obedient followers they are.

The average person accepts same sex relationships as long as everyone stays in an identifiable category. You can be with another man, but you can't be an alpha male at the same time—at least not in the eyes of most. People are comfortable with things they can label. Anything else is too scary and makes life too uncertain.

It's black or white. Gay or straight. Alpha or beta. And when someone starts coloring outside the lines, flowing back and forth between one thing and the other, refusing to put labels on things but simply allowing them to be and unfold... that's when people get uncomfortable and their prejudices emerge.

We all knew these things. So when college ended and we entered the real world of business, we pretended to forget all that we'd shared. We still moved in the same circles, attended the same parties, but we stopped fucking each other and taking women to our beds to share between us. Or at least we did it less frequently. Such things were a scandal waiting to happen. Even in this super progressive world we all supposedly live in.

Besides we didn't have time for it. We each had companies to run. Two of us—Griffin and myself—had inherited ours in a sense, each of them Fortune 500 companies everyone knows the name of but no regular person on the street knows who's in charge. It's only a few multi-national companies where the CEO is also a household name—a celebrity almost. Dayne started his own company, not yet as successful. He already owns several properties overseas. So let's be serious, he doesn't have to work. None of us do. We're driven by things greater than money.

"You ready to do this?" Griffin asks, interrupting my thoughts.

Dayne is a few feet away setting up a camera on a tripod, and focusing it on Livia. We want to really sell this story. What we're doing is dangerous. We have families to think of. We have companies. We have status it may seem we were born to, but we've fought and clawed every step of the way to maintain our positions. There is little room at the top for slackers who want to coast on daddy's money. At least there is little respect for it.

We've moved beyond conspicuous consumption to conspicuous production—the new status symbol.

I glance back over at Livia. Her very existence calms

me. She makes my brain stop spinning. She makes the state of *just being* seem so effortless. We work and work and climb and build empires, but we don't have the ability to just sit back and enjoy it, just *sigh* into it. And yet that's Livia's natural state. She's a long deep calming breath from a guided meditation no one had to guide her through.

This girl can never know the power she has. She is the keystone that can hold us all together, but I've seen how she can play.

"Livia, are you ready?"

She looks up at me and raises her sunglasses briefly in acknowledgment, then drops them back down again without a word. This attitude she's starting to develop isn't working for me. I tell myself it's because I'm spoiling her, so naturally she's becoming entitled. But this is her rebellion against my orders that she will be mine. Ours.

I want to flip her over and spank her. I want to pull her bikini bottoms down and leave hand prints on her in the same exact color as the fabric barely covering her ass. But I take that long slow breath and reign it in. There's plenty of time to take deeper control of her. There is plenty of time to teach her not to cross us. For now, I need her to be able to act convincingly. I need her to sell this so any doubt is erased from the minds of any of our friends and associates that this is real, we are in love, we are forever.

"Do you remember what to say?" I ask her.

"Yes, Soren. I'm not a child. I know my lines. We've rehearsed them a thousand times... with feeling," she says exasperated.

Dayne gives me a look like*, are you letting that slide, really?* I sigh and shrug because we need the footage, and we need it to look good. We need parents to laugh, grand-parents to cry, and every bridesmaid in attendance to be jealous. I can't have her looking like a hostage reading lines off a cue card.

So for now, yes, I'm really letting that slide.

Dayne turns on the camera, and we're rolling.

"Livia, I have something for you."

Her eyes light up, and for a moment I believe this act, even though I've seen her do this more times than I can count.

"A present? Is it a pony?"

I chuckle. "Not a pony."

"A Ferrari?"

"Nope."

Griffin gets credit for this script. I wish we could credit him at the end when the screen goes black. The innocent bride-to-be: Livia Fairchild. The happy groom-to be: Soren Kingston. Script written by: Griffin Macdonald. Camera work: Dayne Montgomery.

"Open it," I say.

I watch as she rips through each box in turn. We didn't practice this part because I didn't want to have to wrap things up this many times. Plus, she hasn't seen the ring yet. She doesn't know where I got it from. She doesn't know that her little girl fantasy of getting a blue box is about to come true. And I know it's her little girl fantasy because I got it out of her best friend, the sole person in her life who even knew she was dating.

This part isn't a script. It's the sheer pleasure of watching her face when she understands where that ring came from.

It doesn't matter what diamond may or may not be the most expensive, what brand may be the most valuable in reality or in perception. What matters is that she fantasized about an engagement ring from Tiffany. And that is what she's getting. Griffin, Dayne, and I all went together to pick it out. We got her the best ring they had.

"Is it an empty box?" she says, just like we practiced.

I chuckle again, real anticipation growing this time. It's an odd feeling to be having after so much time of a kind of void inside me. There has been nothing but stark, cold ambition with no soft place to land. Until her. "No. There's something in there," I assure her.

She opens the final package to see the small distinctive blue ring box—a shade of blue that can be mistaken for no other jeweler—a box that even the least brand-aware person just *knows* is something special.

I see the shock in her face, but she doesn't break character. She playfully delivers that final joke. "Is it a clown pin?"

This part comes from a commercial we all saw once. Despite all the social reference points that divide us, that one stupid commercial is something we all share. I can't even remember what they were selling, but the scene is a woman in a romantic restaurant opening what she thinks is an engagement ring. But instead it's this ridiculous clown pin. We thought it would be funny. And it's a reference many of our guests will get because they saw that commercial too.

I laugh again, for once glad the camera is trained on her, not me, because for fuck's sake, I think *I* might tear up here. "No," I say as stoically as I can manage.

She opens the box, and then everything she's held in comes rolling out down her face as she cries. Real tears.

I get down on one knee. "Livia Fairchild, will you be my person?"

It's another cutesy line meant to tug on heartstrings at

the reception when we unveil the premiere of this short Oscar-contending film.

She cries harder "Yes, I will be your person." And in this moment I know she means this and wants every promise contained in that blue box. My mouth claims hers, and I put the ring on her finger. It glints brilliantly in the sun against her tanned skin. It's all so perfect.

CHAPTER TWELVE: SOREN

NEW YEAR'S EVE

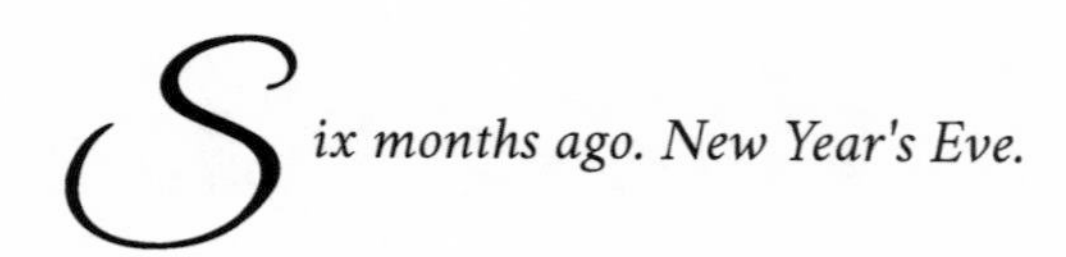

Six months ago. New Year's Eve.

Livia is silent in the passenger side as we drive up the long driveway of my parents' hundred acre estate. She's been to my home, but she's never been to my parents' place. It is admittedly a little stuffy, over-the-top, maybe a bit pretentious, and I can tell she's extremely nervous about this meeting.

"I won't fit in here. Your parents will think I'm a gold digger."

"Aren't you?"

She shoots me a nasty look. "I'm a hostage."

In a few short months she'll learn the price of her smart mouth when she's tied down and begging, calling me *Master*. She has no idea what she's in for with us.

"And tell me, were you a *hostage* during all those months you voluntarily dated me? And Griffin? And Dayne?"

Though admittedly Dayne has been in the grouping a much shorter length of time and by our invitation. But she still said yes to him.

Livia starts to cry, and I feel like the bastard I so clearly am. She flinches when I park the car in the circular drive and wipe her tears away with my thumb.

There's a sick part of me that wants her to always be a little on edge, a little afraid. I get off on it no matter how wrong that may be, but I don't truly want her to hate me. I'm still angry with her even though I know I have no right to be. She wasn't lying. She wasn't cheating. And without her, this relationship quad wouldn't be possible. I know my anger is irrational.

I'm more angry at myself than I am at her, angry that I allowed myself to care, that I became so attached to a woman who so obviously isn't equipped to handle all that I am, who probably doesn't have a kinky bone in her body, and yet I plan to subject her to every dark corner of my psyche, and Griffin's, and Dayne's, for the rest of her natural life.

I still don't know why I haven't let her in to my world. I think I was planning to, but when I learned Griffin was dating her, I had this need to claim her in a permanent way —it was this panicked feeling in my chest. And I had the need to share her in a permanent way. Griffin is probably a better match for her as the public face of the marriage. But I don't care. I want her to have my last name and be seen in public as *mine*. I want all the power, and I want her to know I'm the one who has it.

Griffin wouldn't have had to run interference with her father. He's squeaky clean on paper. But her father was easy enough to manage. I downplayed what he heard, claimed I'd grown a lot since that time, gave a long heartfelt speech about how much I loved his daughter, and then dropped some truth on him about his source—Colin—and just how nasty a piece of work he is, and how nothing out of his mouth should be trusted.

I was smooth, I was calm even in the face of his yelling, and he bought every word because he wanted to buy it. As hostile and gruff as he was, he wants the fairy tale for his daughter. He wants her to be taken care of, loved, provided for, protected, spoiled. And I *can* do all of those things for Livia.

I sigh and soften my tone. "They'll love you. And they won't question my decision like your father. They're just glad I'm finally settling down."

She nods, her lip trembling. I want to hold her right now, but a bigger part of me is unwilling to let her see any weakness. I don't want her to think she can control me with her tears.

I get out of the car and go around to open her door and help her out. She's wearing an elegant black evening gown, adorned in diamonds at her throat, wrist, and ears to go with the rock on her finger. She looks like a princess. I made sure of it. I took her shopping two days after Christmas to make sure she would fit in to my world. And unlike Livia, I called ahead. My parents have known I'm bringing my future bride to the New Year's Eve party since I called them on Christmas day.

I ring the doorbell, expecting Gregor, their butler, to answer the door. But I'm relieved when it's my mother instead.

"Darling!" she says, pulling me into a hug and kissing both sides of my face like I'm a war veteran that just returned from the front lines.

"Mom," I say, trying to extricate myself from her grasp.

Then she turns to Livia. "Oh. My. God. She is just lovely, Soren. You two are going to make the most beautiful babies!"

"Mother!" I say. Though she is right. None of the rest of the world's babies will have a shot in hell against our genetic miracles.

She ignores me and takes Livia by the hand, leading her in to the party. There are too many people for a true sit-down dinner, but there's a nice buffet set-up and tables in the ballroom where they'll do the balloon drop at midnight. There are also some tables outside on the terrace surrounded by giant space heaters.

My mother offered to host the wedding reception here, but even I don't want to spend my wedding night with Livia and two other men under my parents' roof, no matter how large that roof is.

I'm an only child of an only child on my father's side. The only big family is my mom's, but they live five states away, so Livia only has to meet my mother and father tonight. She should be grateful. Dayne is one of five siblings and Griff is one of three. I am by far the shortest gauntlet to run family-wise.

Everyone at the party tonight are friends and business associates, and no one has any strong opinions one way or the other about who I marry.

I trail the two women and hear my mother say, "Oh I'm sorry dear, I'm Lillian." Then she taps my father on the shoulder. "And this is my husband, Stefan."

My father turns from a group of business colleagues, his face lighting up when he sees Livia. He gives me a look that conveys the facial expression version of a thumbs up then turns back to her.

"So this is the bride," my father says. "Have you two set a date yet?" he asks Livia.

"June twenty-second," she says.

"That's a whirlwind. I know how you women get planning weddings. It may just be your full time job."

"She's got a full time job," I say.

"Oh?" my father says. He's got that look on his face as though he's wondering if I'm going to allow her to continue working after the wedding. If she wants to, she can. I would prefer her go to part time, but if she loves her work I'm not willing to become a bigger villain over it.

"And what do you do?" he asks finally when no information is volunteered.

"I'm a veterinary assistant. Our office works mostly with abused rescues."

His face softens at this. He's got a huge soft spot for animals. "That's very fine work to do," he comments, and Livia beams.

Polite conversation is exchanged with my parents for a few more minutes, and then I announce, "We're going to go find Griffin and Dayne."

Livia is caught off guard by this. I guess I failed to tell her they were invited. It won't seem strange to my parents though. They know Griff and Dayne have been my best friends since college and that of course they're in the wedding. The guys have also been present at every New Year's Eve party since college.

I pull Livia away from my parents and toward the buffet. "See? It wasn't bad. That's it. The whole confrontation. Nobody thought you were a gold digger. Nobody asked to see your bank balance. You weren't required to know which fork goes with what or to know which designer bags are fashionable this season."

Despite my parents' lifestyle, they've always been graced with good manners and treat guests graciously, never drawing attention to differences in socio-economic status, which I've always thought makes them far classier than those who try to use etiquette as a weapon against the Emily Post neophyte.

Livia is too relieved by the non-event meeting my parents was to be irritated by my teasing. We get some food off the buffet and take it outside where it's surprisingly warm in spite of the falling snow. Dayne and Griffin wave us over to a table they've claimed in a far corner right next to one of the heaters. They've got a seat saved for her between them closest to the heat source.

She looks at me uncertainly. "Won't it look weird if I sit between them?" she whispers.

I shrug. "Probably not. Not if you don't make it weird."

She sits. Except for the Miami trip, this is the first time the four of us have been alone together since the night we all confronted her a few weeks ago at Capri Bella, and it is as uncomfortable as you might expect. Just like that first night, we eat in complete silence. Prison cafeterias are more joyful than this.

I know she's uncomfortable. She does well enough when she's out with just one of us, but she's clearly still unnerved by the idea of all of us together. And no matter what it may say about me, I like that. In fact, I don't want all of us together at one time again until it's time for the pre-nup, and then the wedding. I don't want her to get too comfortable before that night.

Now that it's been decided that none of us are fucking her until the wedding night, I'm determined to do everything in my power to keep her off balance until it's time to consummate our union. I want to bask in all this delicious nervous energy, this timidity that I've never had the pleasure of experiencing in quite such a potent emotional cocktail.

I've never been the type consumed with virginity nor the type to fantasize about it. I'm not that into purity in a woman. And I know she's been with other men, but it's been long enough that it changes the feel of everything. I want to savor every moment of it. I want to initiate her into my darkness without her having too many glimpses of the light.

After we eat, I pull her up out of her chair and guide her to the dance floor on the terrace. We slow dance together with the snow falling down on us. I watch her watch the table with Griffin and Dayne.

I lean close to her ear. "You can dance with them both at the reception, but not now. Your face gives too much away."

She nods and leans her head against my shoulder.

We're all exhausted by the time midnight gets here, but we dutifully participate in the champagne toast in the ballroom. My father announces our engagement a minute and a half before midnight, which is met with murmurs of approval and applause.

I kiss her a second after midnight as the balloons come down—a sweet, polite public-friendly kiss.

My mother finds her way over to us and kisses me on the cheek and gives Livia a hug and wishes us a happy new year.

When she pulls away, she says, "You two really shouldn't be driving such a long distance this late at night. There will be crazy drunk people on the road. Stay. You know we have plenty of rooms and you two can stay on the complete opposite end of the house from your father and I with plenty of privacy."

I've had a few drinks and probably shouldn't be driving, and Livia looks like she might not make it under her own steam to the car.

"Thanks, mom," I say, even as I know she planned this. I get my calculating nature from her, though hers comes from a kinder place than mine.

She turns to Griffin and Dayne. "You guys should stay, too. I'll worry about you. We need to make sure the best man and groomsman stay safe. By the way, which of you is going to be the best man?"

They both shrug. "Hell if we know," Griff says. "Maybe we'll flip a coin for it." But Griffin knows he's the best man. We're going in order of meeting Livia. Groom, best man, and groomsman.

"So you'll stay?" my mom pushes. "Plenty of rooms."

Griffin and Dayne both get evil glints in their eyes which I hope my mother is too tired to notice.

"Sure," they both say.

My mother, of course, assumes Livia and I are sleeping together, so she puts us both in the largest guest suite with Dayne and Griffin in rooms a respectable distance down the hall.

As soon as she's gone back to the other end of the house, Dayne and Griffin come into our bedroom.

"No way," Griffin says. "You're not sleeping with her if we can't."

"I'm *not* sleeping with her," I say.

Livia is too tired to be distressed by this whole thing and has already flopped back on the bed.

"You don't get to share a bed with her, either," Dayne says.

I point to the large plush sofa against the far wall. "I'm sleeping there," I say.

"Fuck that. She's getting her own room and we'll share down the hall to make sure nobody decides they're sneaking in here. Livia, lock the door behind us," Griffin says.

But she's asleep.

"I'm not into necrophilia," I say. "Look at her. She's not waking up until morning."

"I let you be the public husband," Griffin says like he plans to hold this over my head for the rest of our lives.

"*Let* me? I saw her first. I was *dating* her first."

"You were a shit head to her. She was crying over you when I met her!"

I look up to find Dayne undressing Livia.

"What the fuck do you think you're doing?" I growl.

"Chill, Soren. She can't sleep in this. You assholes keep arguing while I put her to bed."

Livia groans in her sleep but doesn't protest as Dayne slips off her shoes and gets her out of the dress. He takes her jewelry off and puts it on the nightstand, then tucks her into the bed.

I turn back to Griffin. "I can't sleep down the hall in your room. What would my parents think of that?"

"Your parents aren't coming to this wing, period. They think you're fucking your bride-to-be silly morning, noon, and night. They won't risk it."

I take one more look at the sound asleep Livia and follow Griffin and Dayne down the hall to their room, grateful at least it's another suite with a very large bed.

CHAPTER THIRTEEN: LIVIA

THE FIRST DAY OF THE YEAR I'M GETTING MARRIED

A little less than six months ago. New Year's Day.

I WAKE in a giant bed in a strange room with sunlight pouring in through the huge windows. This isn't Soren's house. Are we still at his parents'? It must be close to ten a.m. by now. My head is pounding. I drank too much last night. I wasn't sloppy drunk or anything, but I had a few too many glasses of champagne, and my head is not happy with that choice this morning.

I glance to the nightstand looking for a clock, but instead I find two aspirin with a note that says "Eat Me", and a glass of water with a note that says "Drink Me". I roll my eyes at the Alice in Wonderland reference but take the aspirin anyway.

That's when I realize I'm in my underwear and I don't remember undressing myself. In fact, I don't remember much of anything at all past midnight. Did Soren and I sleep together? I'm horrified by the idea that we might have. But I'm sure I'd be sore if that were the case since it's been so long.

Lying across the foot of the bed is a pair of dark grey lounge pants and a pale pink sweatshirt and a pair of thick fuzzy white socks. I put the clothes on, grateful to have something reasonable to wear and even more grateful that me and Soren's mom are about the same size. Putting the dress back on for breakfast would have been embarrassing.

Where *is* Soren? I wander down the hallway. This house is far bigger than it looked even from the outside, and there's a never ending labrynth of hallways on this floor. I finally find the staircase and go down to the main level. I can hear voices and laughter coming from close by. I follow the sounds into a large, bright airy kitchen that's done in cream and a sunny pale yellow, with just a touch of spring green.

It's big but feels the most like a real home of any room I've been in so far. Everyone looks up from the table.

"Sleeping Beauty finally joins us," Soren's father says.

I blush at this and sit in the chair between Dayne and Soren.

"Did you take the aspirin I left for you?" Soren asks.

"Yes, thank you."

He nods.

"Don't worry, I was about to come up and get you," Lillian says. "The food is all on the island behind you, and it's still hot. Help yourself."

I have the feeling Soren's mom had planned from the beginning for us to stay overnight. I find it hard to believe there would be this much food prepared and this much variety otherwise. I doubt this is normal breakfast fare for a woman so fit.

There are cinnamon rolls and pancakes and fruit and biscuits and sausage gravy and eggs and bacon with coffee, orange juice, cranberry juice, and milk as beverage choices.

I get a bit of everything and some black coffee and sit back down at the table. Everyone else has almost finished breakfast. Soren's father is reading the morning paper—like an *actual* paper—and Lillian is talking wedding stuff with Soren and Griffin.

I jump when I feel a hand stroke over my knee. It's Dayne.

"Morning, Sunshine," he says, his voice so low they can't hear.

I give him a murderous look. He can't just touch my knee under the table while we're having breakfast with Soren and his parents. They'll think we're having an affair. What is wrong with him?

"Did you sleep well?" he asks, ignoring my near panic.

"Fine," I say.

Dayne leans down to whisper in my ear. "I liked that pink underwear I found under your dress last night."

I'm sure I'm blushing as I pull away and turn back to my breakfast.

"Don't worry," he whispers. "I didn't do anything inappropriate. Griffin and Soren wouldn't have allowed it."

Lillian catches the last moment of my discomfort and thankfully misreads it. "Is the food okay?"

I smile at her through a bite of pancakes. "Yes, Lillian, it's delicious." I almost called her Mrs. Kingston, but remembered from the party last night—before the alcohol started flowing—that she wants me to call her Lillian.

I didn't even realize Griffin and Dayne stayed overnight, but Soren's parents don't seem to be weirded out by this breakfast set-up.

As if in answer to my silent question, Lillian says, "Griffin and Dayne have had New Year's Day breakfast with us for . . . gosh, close to twenty years now. It's hard to believe it's been that long."

"Since college," Soren says.

His mother sits on his other side. "I'm so glad you're settling down and with such a nice girl," she says. patting him on the arm.

I don't know how Lillian knows I'm a nice girl, but Soren doesn't contradict her. I'm pretty sure she wouldn't think I was such a nice girl if she knew the real relationship with Soren and his best friends.

It occurs to me suddenly that if this has turned into such a big tradition, that probably means we're all going to continue to have New Year's Day breakfast together even after the wedding. I'm not sure if I'm that good of an actress. Once we've all been intimate together will I be able to act as though Dayne and Griffin are just Soren's friends and nothing more?

I realize suddenly that Dayne's hand is still on my knee. I reach under the table and pinch him. Hard. He pulls back, giving me a wounded puppy look. Given my experience with actual wounded puppies, this doesn't faze me.

After breakfast I learn that actually the New Year's tradition is for Soren, Griffin, Dayne, and now me, to stay the entire day. There's traditional New Year's Day fare including black-eyed peas and ham planned for later this evening. It seems that Soren tried to get out of it this year —maybe for fear his parents might detect a vibe with me and the other guys.

But Lillian basically just kept giving us all alcohol last night until we were too tired and sloshed to drive, and now we're in it for the duration. Soren has surrendered.

The men watch football for most of the day, and Lillian brings me a giant armload of bridal magazines and wedding planning books she must have bought the second Soren told her he was getting married. I feel kind of bad. She doesn't have a daughter to do all this with.

I can't believe I was so worried about meeting Soren's parents. They seem so... normal. Despite the very fancy house, they don't act like snobs. They haven't treated me like I'm not good enough for their son—quite the opposite, in fact. And Lillian doesn't seem even remotely like the mother-in-law horror stories I've heard.

"I hope you don't mind," she says as she lays all the books and magazines down on the coffee table, "I'm just excited. I thought I'd never get to go to Soren's wedding. I was sure he'd stay a bachelor forever. He seemed so stubbornly anti-commitment. I don't know what you did to him, but I'm glad you did it."

"Of course I don't mind," I say smiling at her.

We're sitting together on a sofa in front of a fireplace in a large but somehow still cozy living room. It's several doors down from the game room with the big screen TV, but we can still hear the men shouting at the players.

The snow continues to fall lightly outside, and we drink cocoa as we look through the bridal magazines and wedding books. It's really only just now fully processing through my brain that there's going to be an actual wedding. Like a nice wedding—the kind of wedding every little girl dreams of.

This is the first real opportunity I've had to sit and look at wedding books and bridal magazines. I've been afraid to. I'm afraid to get sucked into this fantasy, to start believing in it. How can I believe in it? How can this possibly work? No princess in fairy tale history ever ended up with three princes. I'm pretty sure the happily-ever-after universe won't allow it.

For the rest of the day until dinner we circle cakes with sharpie markers and dog ear wedding dresses. We discuss colors and flowers and venues and music. And day or nighttime wedding? Lillian thinks nighttime weddings are so elegant, and I agree. It's all theoretical, all just fantasizing and imagining. Nothing is planned or set in stone yet. But can't I just let myself have the dream wedding at least? I know Soren will let me have it. Money is no object to him and after the ring he bought, there's no question he intends to let me have a beautiful fairy tale wedding to go with it.

Yet despite all his charm and all he's giving me, I've seen the dark edges, the shadow underneath the surface. And with his threat... I know I'm marrying the villain, not the prince.

CHAPTER FOURTEEN: LIVIA

THE REHEARSAL DINNER

resent-ish.

"Oh my God, Livia. Griffin is so freaking hot. Do you know if he's dating anyone?"

I resist the overwhelming urge to say "Me." That wouldn't go over very well. Macy, as the maid of honor, will be escorted down the aisle by Griffin, the best man. My cousin Cheryl is walking down with Dayne. Despite having such a large, elaborate wedding we're only having two adult attendants each.

The wedding planner, Patrice, nearly lost her mind over this issue. Apparently this just isn't done. She thinks it looks weird. With such a big historic church and such a nice reception and two hundred and fifty guests it's just odd, she says. She thinks we should have five attendants each. She's said about fifty times now that having only two each makes it look as though we are homeless vagrants without friends.

In fact, she's sure vagrants have more friends than that and could probably come up with more than two people each to stand up with them. She's offered to hire people to be part of the wedding party if we really are this hard-up for friendship.

But Soren was firm on this. He doesn't want anyone but Griffin and Dayne standing up there with him. And to be honest, I couldn't think of anyone I really wanted in the wedding except Macy. My cousin Cheryl was to just have someone to walk with Dayne so it wouldn't look even weirder.

Patrice's head might explode if Macy were to be escorted down the aisle by both Griffin and Dayne.

Vivie, who has just turned three, is the flower girl. She looks enough like me that someone on the groom's side thought she was my daughter. During the rehearsal, she tried to carefully place each rose petal on the aisle as she walked down instead of just tossing them. I thought it was cute, but Patrice decided she needed to show my niece how to do this right. The wedding planner and I almost came to blows when Vivie nearly broke into tears thinking she was messing up my wedding. I'm so glad I'll be rid of this she-beast after tomorrow.

From the looks of things, Soren is pretty much over Patrice too, if the death glare he shot in her direction after she upset my niece is any indication. I find a small bit of comfort in this protective gesture toward Vivie. It gives me hope that I'm not giving myself to a complete monster.

"Well?" Macy says.

"Well, what?" I ask. We just finished the rehearsal and

we're at a steakhouse Soren booked for the dinner. It's just the wedding party and our families in the whole place.

"Is Griffin seeing anybody?"

Before I can answer, the devil appears.

"Soren asked me to come get you," Griffin says, taking my hand and pulling me out of my chair before I can protest.

Macy looks up at him dreamily, and he winks at her. Those electric blue eyes of his should be illegal. I feel the slightest tinge of jealousy at his minor flirting. I mean, I get it, he can't make it look like he's into me. And it's practically tradition for the best man and the maid of honor to hook up at some point during the festivities. But he wouldn't... would he?

I follow Griffin outside. He grips my hand tightly and takes me a couple of blocks down, slipping into an empty alley. As soon as we're out of sight, he pushes me against the brick wall and starts kissing me, his hands crawling all over me, trying to find secret entrances under my clothing.

His hot tongue entwining with mine sends an electric current shooting through my body as I press myself harder against him and his questing hands.

I pull away from his mouth, breathless. "What about Soren? I thought you said..." but of course it was a ruse. He's not taking me to Soren. He's having a stolen moment. There's a battle between Griffin and Soren. I can sense it. Soren may be the one in charge, but Griffin pushes at the boundaries every chance he gets.

"Fuck Soren," he growls into my mouth, hiking my skirt up, his hand slipping between my thighs. I groan as my wetness coats his fingers.

A throat clears, and we look over. I'm terrified we've

been caught by a family member, but it's only Soren. He stands a few feet away, his arms crossed over his chest.

"Fuck Soren," Soren says calmly. "I'm fairly certain I need to be present for that to happen. And lucky for you, here I am."

Dayne steps out from behind him, and it appears the gang's all here. Dayne and Soren stride into the alley, and then the three of them are taking turns ravishing my mouth, grabbing at me through and under my clothes, pinning my wrists over my head. A part of me is afraid they're going to take me right here and now against the brick wall.

Before it can go that far Soren—with the self-control of a saint—releases my wrists, steps away, and says, "Stop."

"Goddammit," Griffin says. "We could make her come. Or she could make us come. A hand job or blow jobs..." He's actually trying to negotiate orgasms right now.

Soren grabs Griffin by his shirt collar and pulls him off me.

"I said... wedding night," he growls.

He has gotten so intense about this issue. When I'd originally said I didn't plan on having sex again until I was engaged, he'd been upset, now it's like he's trying to outdo me in traditional fuck-etiquette.

Part of me wants to do this right now—the anticipation is killing me—but another part of me is grateful for the 24-hour reprieve—one more day I can maintain my ménage innocence.

I'm still terrified of how this will go down with three men. And I know Soren is doing this to punish me... for what? Dating all three of them? I don't even know anymore what I'm being punished for, but it does feel as though I'm being punished. He doesn't want to slowly build my comfort. In fact, this is the most heated things have gotten with the three of us so far. And we've definitely never all been together even like this.

"Fine, but you're not pulling this shit after tomorrow," Griffin says. He is fuming, and I worry how it will look if he goes back to the restaurant so pissed off.

I put my hand on his arm, and his face softens when he looks down at me. Dayne just watches this whole exchange, taking it in, no doubt making notes in his head—for what purpose I'm not sure.

Dayne is the most nonchalant about the whole thing. It's not that he doesn't want me, the passion of his kisses tells me he does. In fact, a part of me is wildly curious about Dayne. That night in the penthouse I got the tiniest hint of how much restraint he holds behind his usually calm exterior.

Dayne is the kind of man who calmly thinks things through. Griffin is the impulsive one who goes with whatever he feels. Soren... ruthlessly calculates.

Soren approaches me, and I flinch. He's never physically harmed me, but sometimes I act like a battered woman around him. I can't help it. There's darkness in him, and I'm not sure if I can ever be safe from it. I'm not sure if the beast that lives inside him will be turned on me—and in some ways it already has been. I can't forgive him for the threat, for taking away my choices. We haven't talked about it since that night. It's like the words were never spoken, but we both know they were.

I tried to tell myself that threat was decided on by the three of them together, that it was a shared sin, but it isn't. I can't lie to myself anymore to spread out the blame and soften it. I know Soren made the decision. Soren chose to take my choices away, to turn me into his slave, his captive, instead of his willing wife.

It doesn't matter how much my body begs to be filled with his. It doesn't matter how attracted I am to him. He's still the man who decided he would own me and I would comply, and that combined with the way he looks at me right now, yes, I flinch, yes I shrink away, because this man scares me even while he lights me up inside.

But he only smooths my hair down and runs his thumb under my lower lip where my pale pink lip gloss has smudged against my skin. He straightens my dress and my bra straps which have managed to slide down my shoulders in this exchange.

"We'll go in to the restaurant together. You two will follow after five minutes," he says, his eyes never leaving mine.

He moves another step back and extends his hand to me. I take it without looking at either Griffin or Dayne.

When we get back to the restaurant the food is being served. It's Salisbury steak covered in brown gravy with mashed potatoes, green beans, and some of the best dinner rolls I've ever had. It's just about the most non-pretentious meal I could think of, and the steakhouse was happy to provide it for us. Plus it reminds me of my first date on the riverboat with Griffin. There's a chicken finger option for some of the kids who didn't like Salisbury steak. And everyone gets a slice of a fluffy chocolate silk pie.

I sit with Macy on one side of me and Soren on the other. Well actually, Macy is seated two seats from me on my left. There's an empty seat between us for Griffin.

I think this looks weird. Macy should be sitting next to me with Griffin on the other side of her, but Patrice did the seating chart. Does she know all four of us are together? I hate the idea of that woman knowing what's really going on here.

A mutual friend of mine and Macy's is seated on her other side, so maybe it doesn't look too weird. Maybe Patrice doesn't know and it just seemed like a logical seating choice to her. Maybe I'm being paranoid.

Macy takes one look at me and her freckled cheeks turn a bright shade of pink. She quickly glances away from Soren when he greets her and lets out a mumbled, "Hi".

Once Soren is seated and talking to someone else, she turns to me and whispers. "Oh my God, did you two just have sex?"

Great. Is it that obvious something just happened? Before I can come up with some sort of answer, Dayne and Griffin appear in the doorway. Dayne sits next to Soren, with Cheryl on his other side and Griffin comes to sit beside Macy... and me. His fingertips trail lightly across my shoulders as he passes me, and I shiver.

CHAPTER FIFTEEN: GRIFFIN

THE REHEARSAL DINNER

resent-ish.

My fingertips skim over Livia's back as I pass her. I swear I can feel the goosebumps that pop up in response to my touch. I want to fuck her so badly I can barely breathe, but instead, I sit down between her and the maid of honor.

I insisted to Patrice that she needed to do the seating this way. I told her that the girl now sitting on Macy's other side doesn't know anybody at the wedding but her and Livia and that it would be nice if she could sit next to someone she knows at the rehearsal dinner. I'm not sure if that girl knows anyone else here or not. I do know she's not family so she must be pretty good friends with Livia and Macy to be at the rehearsal.

I smile at the Salisbury steak placed in front of me. Food from our first date. I wonder if Livia thought of me when she chose this.

I glance down at my watch. By my estimation of how long the wedding and reception will take, it's almost twenty-four hours exactly until my mouth can be buried in Livia's cunt. Until my cock can take a ride. Until her mouth can be on my dick. Until I can watch Soren and Dayne fuck the shit out of her. Until we can pass her back and forth like our own private whore.

Twenty-four hours and she is ours.

I turn to find Macy smiling at me and then looking shyly away. She's a cute little thing. Dark auburn red hair against fair skin and freckles, green eyes so light and pale they rival rare gemstones, and dark-rimmed glasses that make her look like a hot librarian. In another lifetime I most certainly would fuck her, and I know from the way she looks away that she's hoping we hook up tonight or tomorrow night after the reception.

I wonder if Livia knows her best friend wants to fuck me, not that it matters. It isn't as if her friend is trying to steal her man. How could she know that everyone who'll be standing at the front of the church tomorrow in a tuxedo are *all* Livia's men? We even have this bizarre ritual worked out with the ring. Dayne will be holding it. He'll pass it to me, I'll pass it to Soren, and Soren will put it on her finger.

"Is your girlfriend coming to the wedding?" Macy asks.

It's obvious she's fishing, but she's so sweet about it that I almost don't mind.

I hesitate a moment before answering. After all Livia will be at the wedding, but she's not exactly my girlfriend. "She's out of town," I say.

Her face falls, but what could I do? Give her hope that something could happen? Do I want her trying to dance with me while I'm trying to dance with Livia at the reception?

I'm relieved when Macy turns and starts a conversation with her other friend. I turn my attention to Livia. She's strung tight like a bow string. I slip my hand underneath the table between her legs, but Soren is already touching her. My eyes meet his over the top of her head.

Livia is doing her very best to seem unfazed, slowly chewing and swallowing each bite of her dinner. She jerks in her chair, her eyes going wide when she realizes both Soren and I are fingering her together under the table.

I lean in close and whisper in her ear. "Maybe you should have worn jeans."

I plan to keep an eye on Soren until tomorrow night. Isn't this violating his "not until the wedding night" edict? This is the first time our fingers have been inside her pussy, finger fucking her. Ever.

"Please, Griffin," she whispers. She knows it's useless to appeal to Soren.

I don't have to ask what she's begging for. She wants me to stop. She's afraid someone will see and figure out what's happening underneath this table. The tables are covered in long table cloths and our table is set up so that our backs are against the wall, but it isn't as though our family and close friends can't see her face, and anyway the toasts are about to begin.

I reluctantly remove my hand from between her legs.

"Soren," I say.

He gives me an annoyed look but he does the same, and Livia lets out a relieved sigh.

"Thank you," she whispers. I'm not sure if she's speaking to just me or to both of us. Dayne is deep in a conversation with Cheryl about some mundane topic or other, completely oblivious to what he just missed out on.

CHAPTER SIXTEEN: LIVIA

WEDDING PLANS

Five months ago. January.

When I surrendered to Soren's plans, a part of me had thought I had a year of freedom left. I mean, isn't that how long it takes to plan a fancy wedding? Somehow I had rested safe in the idea that I wouldn't have to figure out how to exist with the three of them together for another whole year. Maybe in that time I could shake my dangerous attraction. Maybe I could figure out a way to get out of it.

But as it turns out, Soren knows a guy—because of course he does—and we were able to book The Fremont for the reception along with the presidential suite for the wedding night with only a six month lead time. And the church for the ceremony? It's the biggest and most historic Catholic church in the city. Soren attended as a child but he's not so big on church these days—still, he gets nostalgic about tradition.

They were booked two years in advance but Soren made an impressive donation, and so now the Franco/Kit wedding will be happening somewhere else. Don't feel too bad for them, they're getting an all expenses paid first class honeymoon in Greece, courtesy of Soren.

I've been armed with a black card and my very own wedding planner: Patrice Beauchamp. I'm fairly certain this woman could get a rabid pit bull to wear a tuxedo and walk down the aisle in perfect timing to The Wedding March. She is the most persuasive one human I think I've ever encountered.

I know this is starting to sound like poor little soon-to-be rich girl with the sky's-the-limit dream wedding. I get it. But you can't understand how the world shifted under my feet the night of the proposal. You didn't feel the ice that flowed out of Soren and covered me like my own personal never ending winter. I'm not much more certain about Griffin. Even Dayne isn't as non-threatening as he appeared when we first met.

I'm no longer sure if I would have said yes if only one of them had proposed and if they'd never known each other. Maybe I've always known I was playing in a fantasy world that could never be real. I didn't want men wasting my time, sure. And I did want marriage and a family—I *do* want that—but I also want love, and I'm no longer convinced that's what I'm getting—from any of them. It feels like what I'm getting instead is a gilded cage and no safeword.

"Earth to Livia," my mother says.

I look up and blush, embarrassed that I've been lost for the past fifteen minutes inside my head. Today has been an intense day of wedding planning. So far I've tried on about fifty dresses and can't make up my mind, so we've tabled that issue for today.

My mother, Macy, and Patrice are about to taste wedding cake with me to see if I can make my mind up about that. I feel like Patrice is judging me for not being a more excited or decisive bride. I haven't been oohing and aahing over all the things her brides normally get excited about.

Soren should be here for this, but he said whatever I wanted would be fine with him. He apparently has no opinions on anything about this wedding except that I get whatever I want. I feel like I'm marrying myself, and if I'm being honest none of this even seems real at all. It feels like a show.

It's so tempting to believe in these kind gestures, "the sky's the limit", "you can get whatever you want", but my mind continues to flash back to that night in Griffin's penthouse when Soren exposed my breasts to all three of them and set upon me like a devouring animal before Griffin stopped him. What would my family think if they knew it wasn't just Soren? They'd be mortified by this sordid arrangement.

My mother hasn't been able to stop talking about the *gorgeous Tiffany engagement ring* and what a catch Soren is. She has bragged to every woman she's ever met about that ring and this guy. I'm pretty sure half the women in this city could pick Soren out of a line-up now after the way she's flashed his photo around.

"Livia!" my mother says because yes, I have just drifted off again!

"What?" I say, sounding just as irritated.

But I don't need her to answer because all the little

cakes are here sitting delicately on the table in front of me, their warm fresh-baked scents perfuming the air with sweetness. Soren should be here for this. That thought won't stop flowing through my mind. It's one of the few wedding planning activities the groom is usually present for. Maybe he can't keep up the charade that all of this is just another normal dream wedding in front of my mother, best friend, and the wedding planner. Though truthfully Patrice is the only one I worry about. Both my mom and Macy are completely smitten and have fallen into this whole thing as though it's an internationally televised royal wedding.

"Soren should be here," my mother says, like she's become a mind reader. She says it with almost accusation in her tone like suddenly Mr. hot, wealthy, Tiffany ring guy just isn't good enough for her daughter.

"He's out of town on business," I say. He's not really out of town, but it seems like the only reasonable excuse for why I've been left alone to make this momentous confection decision.

My mother sighs but seems to accept this explanation.

Lillian was with us earlier in the day for dress shopping and lunch, but she had an appointment and had to miss the tasting. So she can't contradict my story about why Soren didn't meet us here.

I'm given German chocolate, hazelnut, lemon, vanilla, marble cake, red velvet cake, strawberry cake, and cinnamon spice cake. The owner of the shop tells me there's a menu of several other options if one of these doesn't meet my needs, but these are their most popular.

Because the wedding is coming up so fast they decided not to overwhelm me with their entire menu all at once, something for which I am deeply grateful.

Each piece of cake is on a beautiful bone china plate. These plates will be available for the wedding, or she has five other patterns I can choose from. The multiplicity of choices in this entire process is exhausting. I suddenly realize why this normally takes at least a year.

Each of us has a beverage in front of us. My mother has unsweetened iced tea, Macy has water, and I have black coffee. Patrice has chosen to simply observe this ritual, which is probably wise. She'd never fit into that tailored Chanel suit if she participated in every wedding cake tasting. I'm already afraid I won't fit into the dress I haven't even bought yet just from looking at all this cake.

Macy has her head buried in a glossy color photo book all about wedding traditions. Almost every place we have visited for every aspect of this wedding so far, Macy has been confused for the bride because she's just so into it. Her freckled cheeks are flushed, her pale green eyes are glittering behind her cute librarian glasses, and I swear she's living vicariously through me, but she's too wrapped up in the fantasy herself to notice that I'm not as excited about all this as she is.

I think my mother *has* noticed that I'm pre-occupied, but she probably thinks it's just normal wedding planning stress.

Macy looks up suddenly, pushing her glasses back up the bridge of her nose. "Livia, did you know that the first wedding cakes were meant to encourage the bride's fertility? And originally the top of the cake was saved not for the first anniversary but for the birth of the first child? How soon are you two having kids, because you could follow the original tradition and have the cake on the day the first baby is born. That would be soooo romantic," she gushes tucking a strand of curly red hair behind her ear.

All eyes are on me now, and I realize there was a question in there. My mother chimes in with, "Yes, Livia, when will I get to be a grandmother? I hope you're going to try for babies soon. Babies are so wonderful! I've wanted to hold another fat chubby-cheeked cherub in my arms for just ages!"

I swear the longer my mother is involved in this process the more she sounds like the affluent older women at the country club. It's like it's contagious.

"We haven't really talked about it yet." I'm not even sure if Soren *wants* children. It's probably something we should have already discussed but I was expecting someone to make a normal proposal after which obviously we would have started discussing things like kids, but the subject hasn't come up so I don't even know if he wants them.

But if he doesn't, maybe Griffin or Dayne? What happens if I get pregnant? Will there be jealousy or anger? Will it all fall apart?

"Livia, you need to talk about it!" my mother chides. "What if you don't want the same number in the same time frame?"

What if the father could be any of three different men? I ask silently in my head as if I would ever say these words out loud. And then I have a new fear. What if I have a kid and it looks like the father—not me—but the father isn't Soren? Will they notice? Or will they imagine they see one of our family member's features in the baby's face, making everything okay again?

My mother pushes the strawberry cake toward me. It's far more delicious than I expected. I have to stop the moan from slipping past my lips. It's moist and fluffy and perfect. And it's the most beautiful shade of pink, prettier than any strawberry cake I've ever seen. Suddenly I'm imagining myself in the blush-pink wedding gown I tried on at the third wedding dress shop and thinking maybe the cake is the secret to making everything come together.

Macy and my mother each take a bite of the cake as well.

"What do you think?" Claudia, our award-winning baker, asks.

"It's incredible," I say, feeling pretty certain I'm never going to narrow this down.

She already has all the important information, the wedding date, the venue, the number of guests. Patrice sent her a three page missive which I was email cc'd on last week to organize this tasting.

Claudia is in high demand, and Patrice told me I was lucky she was willing to squeeze me in and do my cake. And I am now a true believer.

I'm less enthralled with the hazelnut, marble, red velvet, or vanilla. They're all very good, don't get me wrong, but they don't have the same magic as the strawberry.

Patrice is furiously texting in her phone all of a sudden. She looks up after a frantic back and forth. "Sorry, strawberry is out," she says.

"Soren doesn't like it?" I ask, feeling somehow betrayed.

"His uncle is allergic to strawberries."

I sigh. "No strawberry." But I finish that slice of cake, knowing it's probably the last time I'll taste such a perfect strawberry cake.

The cinnamon spice is really promising, but it's a summer wedding and cinnamon spice feels more like a winter wedding cake. The last two remaining choices, German chocolate, and lemon stare back at us—the last two kids picked for dodge ball. All of us have already had a bit too much cake, but we soldier on for these last two options.

"Holy shit, that's amazing," Macy says when she tries the lemon. "Oh my god, Livia, you have to try this."

"Oh. My. God," my mother says when she takes a bite of the German chocolate. "This is the one, Livia, I'm sure of it."

"You haven't tried the lemon," Macy tells my mother.

I haven't tried either of them. I grab the plates before the two of them can devour these last two choices, and I take a bite of each.

"I can't decide. I love them both," I say, much to Patrice's annoyance.

She sends another text, and I'm sure she's asking Soren for more money for babysitting me.

"Great news, nobody is allergic to lemon or German chocolate," she says cheerily a couple of minutes later.

But I still can't decide.

"We could do the lemon for the wedding cake and chocolate for the groom's cake if you like," Claudia says.

"Yes! That would be perfect." And I think I might be developing just the tiniest bit of excitement about this whole wedding thing after all.

Assistants come in and clear the table of all the cake plates, careful to wipe up the crumbs before Claudia places a large book on the center of the table. The book is filled with huge glossy color photos of cakes.

"These are all my designs. I can do any of these or we can discuss something else if you don't find anything you like in here."

If I had to guess there are about five hundred photos in this enormous book.

Sensing my overwhelm, she says "Would you like fondant or buttercream for your frosting? I've got the book divided into two categories by frosting type so it'll narrow the choice down quite a bit either way."

"Well, I like the sleek look of fondant but I like the taste of buttercream," I say.

I'm sure this is going to earn me another sigh from Patrice, but Claudia speaks before that can happen.

"Oh, I have just the thing!"

She leafs through several pages in the book and opens to one of the most elegant cakes I've ever seen. It's a large three tiered cake with greenery and delicate white flowers on the top of each layer. The top of each layer is flat, with the most perfectly even spread of frosting.

"It's not fondant?" I ask.

"Nope. This is the looks-like-fondant-but-really-is-buttercream compromise. It's a very popular choice. The frosting is just a tiny bit thinner than usual but it doesn't affect the flavor. If you look at the side of the cake, you can see where the frosting is spread."

I can see it now. At first glance it does look a lot like fondant, but now that I'm looking more closely, I realize it's not.

"It's perfect. Lemon cake with buttercream frosting and this design," I say decisively.

"I can change the flowers on it to something else if you like," Claudia says.

"No, I want it exactly like the picture."

"Fantastic. What we'll do is have a few sheet cakes which will be cut in the kitchen for guests so you don't run out of the pretty cake. You'll want to save and freeze the top layer for your anniversary, and you'll be cutting into the second layer at the reception when you feed each other. For this particular cake there won't be enough for two hundred and fifty guests but with the sheet cakes there should be more than enough."

Patrice is practically beaming. I haven't seen this woman this happy since I met her. I can practically read her mind. *Finally an easy decision.*

"Do you want the same kind of frosting look for the groom's cake or something different?" Claudia asks.

"We can do more traditional-looking buttercream for that," I say.

"Chocolate frosting on the German chocolate cake? Or I could do a cream cheese frosting."

"Chocolate," I say, earning further brownie points with Patrice for my rapid-fire decision making in the face of infinite sugary possibility.

"Great," Claudia says, jotting down notes. "Now, what I would suggest for this is having a groom's cake for the guests who might want it at the reception, but since a lot of people won't eat two different cakes at the same time, you could additionally do these as cupcakes and send them home with the guests. I've got these fantastic little boxes for them." She shows me a picture.

"Yes!" I say, and suddenly it looks like Macy isn't going to be confused for the bride anymore. Who knew all it was going to take was sugar?

Claudia shows me a few photos of groom's cakes. "I can do any of these but I can also do something completely custom. Most groom's cakes are unique to match the groom's hobbies or something he likes. Do you have any ideas of what he might like? You can take a day or two to think about it and ask him. I know this is all overwhelming."

I take just a moment to think about it, not wanting to

have a goofy groom's cake marring such an otherwise elegant event.

"Well, we met at the art museum on third and main," I say. "This may be too difficult but what about a cake to look like the museum building?" The museum is a sleek and interesting design that, if possible, would make an amazing cake. And though it seems a bit insane and extravagant, I have full confidence Claudia can make this happen.

"Yes!" she squeals, having caught the excitement bug I've come down with. "I can absolutely do a groom's cake of the art museum!"

The meeting ends and I part ways with my mother and Macy who came together in a separate car to meet me.

Patrice walks with me out to my car and shoves a black binder into my hands. "This is a list of all the things we still have to do and decide and the dates by which everything must be done to stay on schedule. I'm afraid we don't have a lot of time to lock everything down." I can feel the judgment in her voice.

She goes to her own car and I'm sure she's going to leave, but she comes back with three books full of wedding invitations to choose from. There's a trendy high-end local designer option, Vera Wang, as well as Crane and Co.

"I need a decision on your invitation design by the end of the week. I would go with Crane," she says, piling them onto my passenger seat and closing the door. I'm sure the weight will make the electronic sensor in the seat think there's a passenger, and I'll have to click the seatbelt around them to keep the beeping light off my dashboard.

"Why Crane?" I ask.

"Tradition. Soren loves tradition."

This confirms my suspicion that she and Soren know

each other somehow and he didn't just randomly pick her out of a list of wedding planners.

She tells me this about Soren and tradition like it's some new revelation. I fight not to roll my eyes at her. I know it sounds stupid and paranoid, but there's this small part of me that thinks Patrice is some kind of spy and that she'll report back anything I say to him.

She continues on, starting to sound a little like Macy. "Do you not understand the history of Crane? This paper is used for our currency. It's 100% cotton. Paul Revere used it. Franklin and Eleanor Roosevelt used it. Even the Queen of England has favored this brand."

"Why even give me the other books then, if everybody's so sold on Crane?"

She shrugs and sighs. "It's your day." She says this almost half-heartedly, and I wonder if she's got stock in Crane.

"Oh and do be sure to go with the engraved stationery. This is very important. Under no circumstances should you go with thermography. I don't care if there are more color options. This isn't a high school bake sale; it's your wedding."

I sigh. Apparently this woman thinks I'm some country bumpkin who needs to be schooled in these things.

"I need you up bright and early tomorrow to meet with the florist. And dear, do try to get a handle on what kind of dress you'd like. It's the most important part after all. All eyes will be on you. And to be honest I'm not even sure if it's safe to decide on the flowers if the dress isn't in place. We only have five months," she reminds me.

Yes, the countdown clock has been running through my head since the date was set, but thanks for that update, Patrice.

CHAPTER SEVENTEEN: LIVIA

THE PRE-NUP

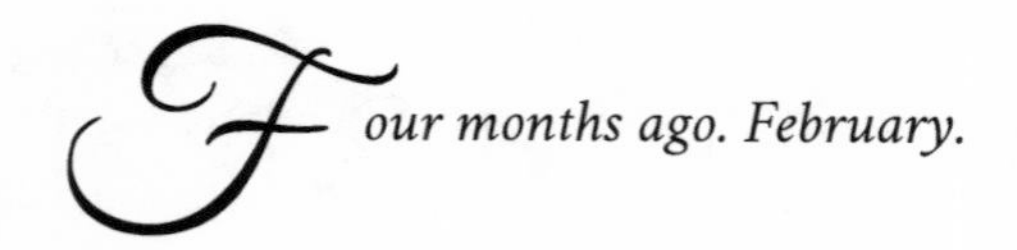

Four months ago. February.

When I walk into the conference room of Blake, Darcy, Henley, and Associates, seven men—mine, plus attorneys—turn their gazes to me in one sharp predatory swivel of heads. All eyes lock on mine as though honing in on a target to destroy. They stand as a collective when I step into the room, and it's as though the room itself takes a deep, cleansing breath. Soren pulls out the burgundy leather chair at the head of the table. I murmur a thank you and sit in it.

It's strange because this seat should be the position of power in a room, but in this case it isn't because the person with the least power is sitting in it. Soren, Griffin, and Dayne each have their own attorney to handle their own legal contracts with me. Today we are finalizing a complicated web of private contracts and trusts that ostensibly protect all parties.

Their attorneys are the three gentlemen whose names are on the sign out front. My attorney sits to my left. He isn't with this firm, but was hired by Soren. And I get the distinct impression that he takes his real marching orders from Soren—not me—though we've all decided to engage in this fiction that I'm being represented in a true and legal way.

I know this is not normal. When signing a pre-nup, my own interests should be defended. I should have a real attorney who only answers to me. But I know I have no negotiating or bargaining power here. I know these men would make good on their threats. I can never break these contracts, so any argument over the sordid details is the equivalent of crying and flailing about while being walked down death row. All it will get me is embarrassment.

This is only a formality to protect them if they ever decide they're finished with me. In private last night, Soren actually made reference to the crazy attic wife in Jane Eyre—intimating that if I tried to leave them, he'd literally lock me in a tower to prevent my escape. Charming. He actually has a tower on his estate. Two, in fact. Soren is every little girl's fairy tale gone wrong.

I take a steadying breath, willing myself to not start crying at this table. Soren is sitting to my right. His hand covers mine, and then his thumb begins to move almost imperceptibly in soothing strokes over the back of my hand. I look up to find those deep dark fathomless pools of green. No one but this man has eyes this color and they suck me into their depths each time I fall helplessly into his gaze.

I had been so sure about all three of these men when they were just some guys I was dating. I'd eliminated so many others before them. I'd dropped every man who didn't treat me with respect, wanted to split the bill, or had some obvious deep-seated and barely disguised misogyny or weird mommy issues.

Griffin, Dayne, and Soren all got past every test I set up. They each slipped beneath my radar, and charmed their way into my heart. They were such gentlemen, so patient, so respectful, so generous and kind. Well, Griffin and Dayne were. It was touch-and-go with Soren for a bit.

And now here we are.

I want to run and never stop running. At the same time, my body longs to be claimed by theirs in such an all-encompassing way that I can't do anything but sit frozen in place, waiting for my fate to unfold according to their designs, waiting to read their terms in stark black and white.

I don't even know why they're putting me through this meeting except for the sheer pleasure of humiliating me. I fucking hate all three of them right now. I can't believe I thought I loved them little more than two months ago.

I can't believe I *still* thought I loved Soren when we made the fake video proposal. I glance down at the Tiffany diamond on my finger. The proposal may have been a fake, but this ring most certainly isn't. I want to believe in this fairy tale so badly. I think back to all the losers who wasted my time playing boyfriend while trying to gain wifey privileges from me. And I wonder if they were really so bad after all. Because this feels so much worse—this lie they've sucked me into. And I can't understand why they're doing it. Are they just that bored with the luxury and ease of their lives?

Maybe they do all three in fact want me. Maybe their declarations of love were once sincere. But they didn't give me a choice in any of this, and somehow ever since that night in Capri Bella it feels as though our relationship is some sort of twisted revenge against me.

"Ms. Fairchild all the contracts have been finalized. We just need you to read over them with your attorney, initial in all the marked places, sign, and date. Then we can all get out of here," one of the attorneys says.

Finalized. The contracts have been finalized. Yes, I know this is not in any way normal. That's not how these things work. It's supposed to be a negotiation. I'm supposed to receive an opening offer where I mark out the changes I'd like to see, and we discuss things until we come to an agreement that works for everyone. But no, this is only a formality. It's a boilerplate contract—the kind you sign as is or walk away, except I only have that first option.

My hands shake as I read the contracts. There are ways in which they're all the same, and ways in which each is unique, but all of them cover the basics of property and how it will be divided should these unions break.

Even though I can't leave, the attorneys don't know that.

So according to the contracts, if I leave, I get nothing. If I cheat, I get nothing—though I can't imagine the ravenous sexuality of a woman who would need *more* than three dicks to service her. It's all quite comical. Weirdly, there has been a notation inside each of these contracts that explicitly states sex with any of these three men isn't considered cheating on the others. I wonder how that would hold up in court for the pre-nup?

Probably it wouldn't, but since it is an agreement we've made beforehand and the pre-nup itself isn't the marriage, maybe? Who knows? I'm sure they've come up with just the right legal language to make all of this work somehow. And I'm equally certain that should any of this ever reach a courtroom, there would be a bought and paid for judge who would go along with whatever they want even if their cleverness in legalese should fail them.

If *they* leave, however, I do get things. They are at least ensuring that if they discard me and destroy and ruin me that I won't starve. I'll have a nice life, at least on the outside. I take another deep breath, forcing the gathering tears not to spill out. I will not cry in front of these men and all of our attorneys. It would look far too weak.

If I were the person I've been pretending to be and convincing myself that I was, I'd view today with triumphant glee, seeing myself as somehow locking down, not one, but three eligible wealthy bachelors and having lifetime access to a lifestyle I only could have dreamed of before. But I'm too worried about what will happen to my body, mind, and soul once I am fully and finally inside their bonds.

The legal contracts are only the first layer of the rough tight rope looping around me and squeezing like a vice even in this moment.

What must these attorneys think of me? Binding myself romantically, sexually, and legally to three different men concurrently? I wonder if they jerked off thinking about it while putting the contracts together—or if they fantasized about somehow getting in on the action. I can only hope that Griffin, Dayne, and Soren have no plans or desires to allow any other man to touch me.

My mouth falls open when I find in each contract the topic of heirs. Heirs. Are they fucking kidding me? It's not that I don't want babies—of course I do—it's just this archaic caveman language. They are actually *demanding* heirs, like it's some God given right. In fact, it's another stipulation. Failure to produce an heir forfeits the right to resources should the male with no paternal interest leave the arrangement. What in the fuck?

I look up from the contracts. "Heirs?" I say, to no one in particular.

It's no surprise to me when Soren takes the lead here. "Yes, Livia, heirs. We each need an heir. We have generational wealth. Do you know what generational wealth requires?"

When I just stare at him blankly, he says, "Generations."

I roll my eyes at this—the first moderately brave thing I've done in weeks with these men. "Must these heirs be male? If they aren't, are you going to lock me in the tower and chop off my head?"

"Don't be ridiculous," Soren says. "Of course they don't have to be male. They just need to be ours."

"And how exactly would that work? How would we..." I can't even think of how to phrase this question. How does one juggle the logistics of paternity in this situation?

Soren arches a brow at me, but it's Griffin who answers from farther down the table.

"How it would work is... we all fuck you raw—no protection—until you have the first child. Then we do a paternity test, and the father doesn't get further access to your pussy with his dick until you're pregnant again and it's safe. But he can still claim your mouth and ass—so, he'll live. After we each have an heir you can get your tubes tied if you so choose. It's always nice to have backup heirs, but even we thought six pregnancies was cruel. Though twins run in Dayne's family, so there's that."

My face flames at these crude words, though the attorneys remain stoic as if nothing happened. I can't believe Griffin just said these things to me in front of these strangers. And yet. There's the part of me that is excited by all the things I should be shocked and horrified by. My libido is the biggest chain that binds me to these men because I'm pretty sure they're offering me every dark fantasy my mind has ever concocted.

I glance back down at the contracts to find that, in fact, a statement about the right to a tubal ligation has been mentioned *after* I've done my breeding duty. Though it is stated in the classier "heir" language.

I don't know what the hell is wrong with me, but my body practically sings and begs for each of them to take their turn impregnating me. It's so sick and twisted, this demand that I be their broodmare—livestock so they can pass their money along using me as a mere container for this wealth transfer. But it makes me so fucking wet I can barely stand to have the eyes of so many strangers on me while I process all of this.

"And what if I can't have children?" I ask.

"That's the next clause," Soren says.

He's right. I look down to find a place I have to initial regarding submitting to fertility tests with a doctor of their choosing as well as steps which will be taken to ensure heirs.

"This is insanity," I say. "You do realize that infertility isn't just a woman problem, right? Men can be infertile as well."

"We've already had all the appropriate tests. All of our swimmers are in top competition shape, I assure you," Soren says.

I look over to Dayne who hasn't said a word about all

this, but I swear he's imagining my belly swollen with his child—or children, if Griffin's comment about twins is correct.

I continue reading. Should these unions break by their choice, I will be allowed to keep the children with me, but Griffin, Dayne, and Soren will have access to their children whenever they choose. All needs for the children and for me will be taken care of and amounts and percentages are stipulated. If I leave, they get full custody and I get visitation.

I wonder if they're worried their past threats aren't strong enough to hold me. Maybe they need the future threat of surrendered custody of my own children to superglue my life to theirs. Or maybe even Soren isn't cruel enough to put the mother of his child in prison.

"You won't have to do all the childcare duties. And of course we'll want to have access to you whenever we please, so there will be help at the estate to take some of the burden of motherhood off you," Soren says.

Of course. After all, three little *heirs* could get in the way of the men getting all their depraved needs met inside my body. I cross and recross my legs, trying to stop the throbbing ache that's been going since this meeting started.

I don't say anything more. I just finish reading the contracts, then I hand them to my placeholder attorney because I'm supposed to. I'm mortified for him to also be consuming these words. He takes out a pair of reading glasses and takes his sweet time poring over each word—probably getting off on it. The room is pin-drop silent while he engages in this show trial.

Soren is back to stroking the back of my hand. I wish he would stop. It does things to me. It makes me want to be his little spoon for the rest of time. And I can't feel that for this man. I don't understand why these small acts of kindness—if they are kindness—ignites an urge in me to please him, to be close to him.

I'm confused by how things have shifted or what any of it means. Both Dayne and Griffin still inspire the same feelings in me as before. And we still have our time together, time that is just ours. But increasingly Soren is taking up more and more space in my mind.

Maybe it's because he's the one who will be my husband and the other two are... what? Illicit lovers? Extras on our porn set? I don't understand how any of this can work. But I just sit quietly like the good girl I apparently am, while my attorney finishes reading the contracts.

Finally he slides them back over to me and nods as if this means anything—as if my interests have really been taken into account in this joke of a meeting. But in truth, the contracts are better than I expected. They do protect me if these men abandon me, and while they want heirs, these would be my children as well. And they'd be going into a life far better than I did. I always wanted children—three, coincidentally—and now those children have a future. I have a future. If I can survive it.

I dutifully initial on all the pages marked by a thin neon sticky note, then I sign and date the last page of each contract. I stack them together and place them in front of me on the conference table. I stare at the papers. A strange visual pops into my head of me transforming into a dragon and burning the contracts to ash with my flaming breath.

"Livia," Soren says, interrupting this brief fantasy interlude.

I look up. "Yes?"

"I'd like you to wait out in the hallway for us. We have some business to discuss that doesn't concern you."

Yeah, right. But I only nod, too dazed to argue or fight after legally binding myself to these men, after the words that just passed across this table and the strangers who heard it all. My face flames again, but I stand. Everyone else in the room stands as well, and I walk out, shutting the door softly behind me.

After the meeting with the attorneys, I'm taken directly to *a doctor of their choosing* to get those fertility tests. I expected it to be some creepy frail man—part of their old boys network. But it isn't. It's a kind, middle-aged woman with curly brown hair and delicate gold-framed glasses. She explains all the tests she's running before doing the exam and taking samples for testing. She reassures me and tells me about the new developments in fertility treatments should they become necessary, including options like surrogates, even donor eggs if I really and truly were infertile. Depending on the circumstances I could carry the baby or someone else could. My egg or someone else's.

Soren briefly outlined some of these options on the ride over. They want the babies to be ours together biologically, but they need heirs. My biological material isn't strictly required.

The sky really is the limit here. At this point fertility tests seem like just another humiliating exercise, reminding me of the totality of their ownership over my body.

All three men have chosen to be with me in the room. The doctor makes zero comment about this—even though, just like the pre-nup meeting, this is highly irregular. Every time some weird thing like this happens, I'm reminded of just how much power these men have and how little they care for any laws or rules of society, how easy it is for them to bend all of those laws and rules. Money talks, and all they need is the right people to listen.

I'm not in a paper gown like I might be in a normal gynecological setting. This is what I can only describe as a luxury medical spa and fertility clinic. I had no idea such things existed, but here I am, so clearly they do.

So no, it's not a paper gown.

When everything is finished, I'm directed to get dressed and meet the doctor back in her office. The men and doctor leave me, and I put my clothes back on. When I get to the doctor's private office, a cup of hot tea in a delicate porcelain cup along with a couple of what appear to be bakery-fresh shortbread cookies are waiting for me.

The teacup has three delicate light blue robin eggs nestled inside a small nest hand-painted on the side. I wonder briefly if this was a thematic choice on the part of the fertility clinic or if they just liked the design. It does, after all match the office's décor. At the same time... eggs are a little on the nose.

"Do you have any questions Ms. Fairchild?" the doctor asks turning her attention finally from her conversation with Griffin, Dayne, and Soren over to me. Finally, I exist again. It's only *my* body which will be bearing the burden of these heirs after all.

I shake my head. After all, what could I possibly ask in this situation? I've just finished my tea and cookies when Soren thanks the doctor for her time and discretion and offers me a hand to help me out of my chair and to the door, Griffin and Dayne following close behind us.

When we get out to the car, Soren says, "That will be your doctor when the babies come."

"You mean the *heirs*?" I ask a bit acidly.

"Careful, Livia." But as he opens the car door for me, I feel somewhat relieved and comforted to know that sweet woman will be the one who is there for me while I'm delivering my part of the contracts.

CHAPTER EIGHTEEN: LIVIA

WEDDING PREPARATIONS

Four months ago. February.

AFTER THE DOCTOR'S appointment this afternoon, Soren put me in a separate car with a driver to escort me home. The phone rings at nine p.m. Like clockwork. Every night when I don't go out with one of them, I get this phone call at nine. When I do go out with one of them, I get the call at midnight. They've decided to go back to this dating situation we had where they each get alone time with me. On these dates, the others aren't discussed, and it's sometimes easy to forget they all know each other and everything has changed forever.

I pick up on the third ring.

"Are you home alone?" Soren asks. As if he needs to ask. He knows I am.

"Yes," I whisper. I don't know why I whisper, but I can't help it when Soren calls. He's the only one of the three who calls like this. But his dominance in the pecking order has been established.

Soren doesn't bring up the phone calls when I see him. In person, he acts as if they aren't even happening. And I don't bring it up either. The phone sex is a separate thing, a separate world and as long as I keep it separate I can look him in the eyes.

I don't even know if Griffin and Dayne know about these nightly phone calls. Then my entire body flushes as I realize Griffin and Dayne may be listening at this very moment. After all, Soren calls from his land line at the estate. Someone else listening in is a distinct possibility because there's more than one phone in his house—all connected to the same phone line. It feels oddly old-fashioned, and yet, he refuses to give up his land line even as he handles most business with his cell phone. He is the oldest thirty-seven-year-old man I know.

"Was your pussy wet at the pre-nup meeting today?" he asks without any warm up. And now that it's occurred to me that Griffin and Dayne may not be making calls like this only because they're enjoying the pleasure of listening to them, everything takes on an even more illicit tone.

"W-what?" I stammer.

He laughs. "You looked really turned on. I know that look." And he does. They all know that look. Even though they've behaved like monks when we're together, it's only because they don't want me to get too comfortable with them before they've stolen all my freedom away. This act of waiting for the wedding night has become its own brand of kink. We don't talk about it out loud, but I know we all feel it.

They've gotten used to this fantasy idea of me, the untouched virgin on her wedding night. And even though it isn't true—I'm not in any way untouched—my long bout of celibacy means in some ways it'll be like my first time. And it will definitely be my first time with three different people all touching me together. So there's a strange truth to this extended role-play.

"I wasn't turned on," I say, "I was upset. I was mortified and humiliated, especially by what Griffin said." I still can't believe he said that. I've been romanticizing him somehow as my protector for months on the basis of a single interaction where he stepped in against Soren.

"Sure, Livia. You know, these lies won't be tolerated when we're married. You may get away with it now, but if you try this after you've pledged to honor and obey me, you will be punished. By all three of us."

I swallow hard at this, trying to tamp down the stupid fucking excited arousal flooding my panties again. My body is in an all-out mutiny against my mind these days.

"You're wet right now, aren't you?"

"Y-yes," I confess, clutching the phone more tightly.

We're reciting traditional vows at the wedding. *Very* traditional vows—the ones where I will promise to honor and obey him in front of hundreds of people. Royal weddings don't even include the word *obey* for the bride anymore. But the idea of saying those words in front of all those people sends an erotic thrill down my spine. There is something deeply wrong with me.

"Are you ready for wedding preparations?" he asks.

The first time he called me and asked this question I thought he meant things like flavor of cake, or the dress, music, flowers, invitations, or the thousand tiny details of a wedding this large and lavish.

But that wasn't what he meant. He was talking about me preparing my body so that I could *receive them* on the wedding night. He actually used those exact words, and my knees almost buckled beneath me as my breathing became more erratic. He'd only chuckled at my reaction.

"Yes, I'm ready for wedding preparations," I say quietly. Demurely. Who is this person I become under the spell of his low rumbling voice?

"Good girl," he growls. "And let me remind you, sweet Livia, these wedding preparations are for your benefit and protection. If you're lying to me and not doing what I ask, it's going to be a very painful and difficult wedding night for you which would be a fitting punishment for your deception. We're all very large—me especially—so you have to prepare yourself every night so you'll be able to take us."

My breath hitches in my throat. It doesn't matter how many times he speaks to me in this way, it always has the same effect on my frazzled nerve endings.

Eight and a half inches. He could be lying, but somehow I don't think he is. Even so, the concerning part isn't the length, but the girth. And honestly I'm a bit scared to have his monster dick inside me.

He interrupts my near panic attack over the size of his cock with, "Now go get your gift."

Every few days a gift is delivered to my house. It's always in a black box, wrapped with elegant embossed silver paper and a black satin bow.

I'm both excited and afraid of what may be inside the box because I know I'll have to obey him and use it while he listens and jerks off on the other side of the call.

"What are you wearing?" he asks.

"I... um..." He'll know if I lie. I can't do that thing women usually do where they pretend they're wearing something sexy when they aren't. It comes out in my voice. And I know he wants me wearing something sexy when he calls. "Jeans and a T-shirt."

There's a long pause. "I think you *want* to be punished. Perhaps I should keep a list of your offenses against me so I can be sure all penalties get paid. Go to your bedroom and put on that see-through red thing."

Soren has seen all the lingerie I own. Ninety percent of it he's purchased for me the past few weeks. Often it comes in the silver and black wrapped boxes along with various toys. Sometimes it comes separate. Sometimes he takes me into the store, and makes me try it on first.

But he's never seen me in any of it. He doesn't even ask for photos. He's said he wants to take it in all at once on our wedding night and honeymoon at the same time that Griffin and Dayne get to take it all in. What he really wants is my discomfort. Rather than slowly easing me in to intimacy and the vulnerability that comes with clothes coming off or lingerie going on, he wants it to all flood my system in one moment of pure adrenaline.

He feeds off this anxiety. He gets off on it so much that he's more than willing to wait just so he can keep me on this razor edge of fear and anticipation.

I take the red lingerie he requested out of the closet, remove my jeans, T-shirt, and undergarments, and put it on. I know I could work on being a better liar. I could rebel and put different lingerie on or just be naked, and he'd never know. But a part of me wants to obey these commands.

"Is it on?" he asks. I'm pretty sure he's begun to slowly stroke his cock by now. His tone and breathing have changed.

"Yes."

I want to say *Sir* after that so badly. And I know with

the way he orders me and the threats of punishment, and the many times he's explicitly described to me the way his cane will feel across my flesh as I've been made to finger myself to his filthy descriptions. This part started only a few weeks ago, the explicit overt hint of kink. I'm not innocent. I know there should be a title.

It feels wrong without one. But he hasn't requested one. And he makes me so ridiculously shy that I can't initiate it. And what if I did, and he didn't want it? What if he doesn't like it or doesn't get off on it? So every time I answer him, I bite back the increasingly strong urge to offer this verbal submission.

"Good," he says. "You may buy yourself back into my good graces tonight after all. Open the gift."

I take a deep breath and untie the bow. He's always patient as I carefully unwrap the box. I don't like to rip this beautiful paper. And I save it. I don't know why I'm saving it. It's so absurd. It's not like more isn't coming. It's not like I won't be able to afford wrapping paper. Heat races up my neck and into my face as I imagine giving gifts to others using this paper. It would be like inviting guests to sit on a couch you know people have recently fucked on—a couch *you've* recently fucked on.

When I finally open the box and pull back the black tissue paper, I let out a small whimper. The toys vary, but today it's a dildo. Not glass, which is often his preference. I have a growing and impressive collection of glass dildos in all colors with all manner of bumps, ridges and swirling curves. They are each beautiful in their way, each a new piece of erotic art, each creating different sensations as they slide back and forth against my wet swollen flesh.

"Run your fingers over it and tell me how it feels," Soren says, interrupting my thoughts.

I reach out and stroke the length of the sex toy. "I-it feels like real skin."

It's been so long since I've touched a real dick that I'm surprised I remember what it feels like, but it does seem remarkably real against my fingers. It's also bigger than the other toys he's sent in the past.

"Soren, I don't know if I can..."

He chuckles, and I know he knows exactly what I'm thinking. "You better find a way, princess. My dick is bigger. The toy is only seven inches, and it's nowhere near my girth."

I stifle another whimper. I am terrified of his dick. It's too fucking big. There's no way I'll be able to take it. And then I torture myself with the reality that the three of them won't just want my pussy, but my mouth and ass as well. And what if they all want to take me together? He hasn't done any kind of anal preparation with me so what does that mean? Does it mean I'll be spared that on the wedding night?

I hope that's what it means.

It doesn't matter how much it scares me, it excites me more. I want to be impaled on his terrifyingly large dick. I want to gasp with shock and a little bit of pain as he drives into me. As Griffin and Dayne watch. As they take turns using my wrung out body for their own pleasure.

There's something else in the box—a new bottle of lube. Soren buys me what I can only describe as luxury lube. It doesn't irritate my skin and feels like silk inside me. I've developed a Pavlovian arousal response every time I see the elegant bottle because I know the magic it contains—the ability to at least double the pleasure I would have without it.

It's safe for use with all toys and condoms, which is just

a bonus. Though it's my understanding there won't be any condoms, at least not until the three *heirs* get here.

"Take the dildo and the lube and go lie down on your bed. Spread your legs wide when you get there."

I do as he says and position myself on the bed. I turn out the main lights, leaving only the light spilling in from the bathroom. Even alone I can't stand to obey his orders in full light. It feels too exposed even when there's no one here to watch.

I wonder if *lights on* should be part of the *wedding preparations* since three sets of eyes will be on me that night and every night after. I'm pretty sure they won't let me shroud myself in darkness.

"Okay," I say, my voice going even softer.

"You know what I like," he says. "Do it."

I do know what he likes. We've been doing this since three days after Griffin drove me home from the penthouse when everything was decided. It was the first black box with silver wrapping, and my first orgasm under the power of his voice.

I put some of the lube on my fingers and begin to stroke myself. Soren hears it the moment my breathing starts to change. I'm so wet naturally that I don't really need the lube for this part, but Soren still demands it. He wants the lube. There's something more dirty and deliberate about adding lube to an already wet pussy.

His deep seductive voice pours into me. "Don't touch your clit. I don't want you getting there until I'm ready for you to get there."

"Okay," I whisper. God, I want to say *Yes, Sir*. Why hasn't he asked for that? Of everything else he's said to me, every dark and dirty promise... I know he's a freak. Fuck, he's sharing me with two other men. So why am I not allowed to call him Sir? Why doesn't he demand it?

"Lube the toy. I want you to use a lot so it slides right in."

I take a deep breath as I do what he says. Even with lube, it's been a long time since I've had something this large inside me and I know we've been gradually easing to larger toys, but I get nervous and close up.

"Now, Livia. Fuck yourself. Penetrate that tight little pussy and imagine it's me."

I let out a yelp as I push the toy inside. I spread my legs and arch my hips up to relax my muscles. My body finally lets the toy in. It's just a couple of inches at first, but finally after some patience I'm taking the entire thing.

Soren knows I've obeyed him because he chuckles and says, "Good girl."

CHAPTER NINETEEN: GRIFFIN

THE PHONE CALL

Four months ago. February.

I'M on my hands and knees in the middle of Soren's bedroom while he fucks my ass. He's still moving slowly inside me—almost gently—which only makes me impatient for more, but I can't make demands right now. He's on the phone with Livia, walking her through the next escalation in penetrative sex toys. He's using the same lube with me that he buys for her gifts. And I don't know how it feels for her, but it's the best fucking lube I've ever had inside my ass.

Today, I selected the gift, and I wish it was me on the phone with her. But we've all agreed Soren will be the only contact point for overtly sexual behavior until the wedding, because there needs to be one overwhelmingly dominant point of power to organize this shit. And if that's not Soren, it's nobody.

I bite back a moan at her loud begging and whining which drifts out through the phone as he voice fucks her and forces her to impale herself repeatedly on a dildo that isn't even as big as him. But it's very big for her.

It excites me that she's so tight, that she has to work so hard to accommodate even the toys we've used with her. Her obedience and surrender to each new demand only makes me harder. I want to bury myself inside her and feel her sweet cunt grip onto my dick.

We'll have to keep her at this size for the next week before giving her more. That very thought is about to send me over the edge, and Soren isn't even fucking me like he's serious yet. I have no idea how the fuck we're ever getting inside her ass, but we're all used to accomplishing big goals, so I'm sure we'll figure it out.

I'm jealous I only hear bits and pieces of the conversation, not the whole thing like Dayne and Soren are getting. Dayne sits at the other end of the room in a large overstuffed chair, his dick out, languidly stroking his length. A cordless phone is pressed to his ear as he listens to Soren and Livia having phone sex.

I know I'll get to listen next time. And then it will be Dayne either sucking Soren's cock or taking it up the ass.

I never expected this to be my life. When I met Dayne and Soren, none of us would have considered ourselves gay, and on a certain level I don't think we really consider ourselves that now. We aren't really into labeling things, and we're definitely also into women. We love women. But there's something carnal and animal and purely physical about what we share between us.

It's lust without parameters, without softness. It's hard fucking without the promise to call. It's pleasure without the risk of unplanned offspring.

Livia is the luminescent full moon that shines down on all of us, offering her soft glow to light up the night. But we are the men who shift to animals under that same moon.

I don't love Soren or Dayne. Not like that. I love how I feel when we fuck. I love the pure physical release. We don't cuddle after or say sweet things to each other. Nobody gently caresses anybody or buys anyone presents. We save all that tender shit for Livia—even though she doesn't understand just how careful we are with her.

Although none of us have fucked her yet, we've kissed. We've touched over clothes. I feel like a teenager acting like this. Suddenly second base is some new big deal again. It was Soren—of course—who decided we'd all just fuck each other until the wedding night, that we should all take her for the first time together after everything was finally and fully legally sealed.

I agreed, because why not? Increasingly she's the one left hungry, and we're the ones satiated. Watching her squirm while our needs are quietly fulfilled in the background is a just punishment for the way she played us. She doesn't think she played us, but what else could you call it?

I let out a groan as Soren's dick hits me just right. He's picking up speed, Livia's soft moans and whimpers and begging driving him toward violent release. Mother fuck he knows exactly how to thrust for maximum impact, but he isn't thinking about me or my pleasure. He's thinking about her. I'm just riding this roller coaster.

"Harder," Soren says into the phone. "Fuck yourself on it like you mean it. Hold the phone down next to your cunt so I can hear those beautiful sloppy wet sounds."

She must have done it because in the next moment Dayne says "Oh, fuck, yes." Thankfully his phone is on mute, and the room is big enough that his words don't make it through the speaker of Soren's phone. Though I'm not sure Livia would even hear him if they could. From the small bit I'm getting, she's too lost in lust and mounting pleasure which has finally squeezed past her discomfort to hear anything but Soren's demands.

I wonder what she'd think if she knew she isn't truly alone with him. Maybe she suspects. After all, in what reality would two of your three future lovers agree to stay completely away while the third one gets nightly phone sex? She can't be that naïve. She may not realize we fuck each other, but she has to know we listen to her.

The phone is back to her ear again because he tells her what a good girl she is. And he's fucking me harder. Dayne strokes his own dick with more intensity, fisting it in his hand as though he's punishing it for a serious crime.

"Tell me how good it feels. That's going to be my cock very soon. You will take every inch of me and you will thank me for it," Soren growls against her increasingly loud whimpers.

A moment later, he orders her, "Come."

She screams, and I know it isn't an act. Soren fucks me with a harsh intensity that steals my breath and we both come almost simultaneously to the sweet sounds blaring over the phone. When I look up again, Dayne has come on the hardwood floor and is back to languidly stroking his dick as if nothing has happened. I think Dayne shouted when he came, and I wonder if Livia heard it, if she realized that wasn't Soren's growl of pleasure. I wonder if Soren muffled Dayne's voice with his own release.

Soren pulls out of me, and I collapse onto the floor, my breath still coming in hard pants as he soothes her and tells her what a good girl she is and what a good girl she will be for all of us.

He hasn't made her call him Master yet. It both surprises me and doesn't. After all, it's just another thing he can add to his wedding night plans, just another chain he can lock around her that we'll all get to witness.

"Don't touch yourself again until I call you tomorrow night. Do you understand, Livia?"

I don't hear her response, but it must have been yes because he disconnects the call.

"That was hot," Dayne says. "I'm not sure I can wait four more months to fuck her."

"You'll wait if I have to put your dick in a chastity cage," Soren says. And he is dead fucking serious.

Dayne doesn't take his bait. He just calmly holds Soren's challenging glare.

"No oral either," Soren says. "You too, Griffin. I need to know I can trust you two. I want our little bitch on edge until we all consummate this thing together. I want us to own her so completely she can't remember her own name. And that requires patience."

"I already said I was in," I say. And I am. Dayne and I are both getting fucked by Soren, and fucking and sucking each other. There's no immediate need to release inside Livia. For now, our physical needs are met, fortifying our patience to wait to fully and completely possess our shared toy.

CHAPTER TWENTY: LIVIA

THE WEDDING NIGHT

he Present.

SOREN HOLDS my hand tightly in his as he leads me to the presidential suite as though I'm a prisoner who might get away or scream for help. I admit these aren't the craziest of ideas right now. A moment later, we're standing in front of the door.

He doesn't go for his key card immediately. He just stands there, taking me in, a small smile curving his features. It's not a kind smile, but it isn't an evil demented one either. I'm not sure quite how to class it. It does denote triumph, though. Like he won.

His eyes are every dark forest any fairy tale child has ever gotten lost in. They're deep green and completely impenetrable. Wild animals lurk inside them, watching me like prey. My heart flutters erratically in my chest as his hand raises to my cheek. I flinch like he's going to hit me.

But that's not Soren's style. I know it's not. He would never strike me in this way. If he's going to do it, it will be with a belt or a flogger or a cane, and I will come undone helplessly beneath him directly afterward, screaming out my pleasure. I know this because he's told me during our nightly calls many times. He's told me exactly what I'm in for with him and with Griffin and Dayne. And yet, I didn't put up much of a fight—at least not much beyond the good-girl protests of them sharing me.

He strokes my cheek. "You're trembling." But he doesn't say it with concern, more like pride. Satisfaction. As though my terror of what may be about to unfold in this room is the absolute best thing about this day for him. He leans forward and presses a chaste kiss to my forehead, and somehow I know it's the last chaste moment we'll ever share between us.

"Welcome to your future, Mrs. Kingston."

With this pronouncement, he swipes the key card he's smoothly produced from his jacket pocket, scoops me up, and carries me over the threshold. The tradition of carrying the bride over the threshold started because it used to be believed that evil spirits attached easily to the feet of brides and so to keep them from coming inside with the happy couple, it was just safest for the groom to pick her up and carry her.

I know this fun fact courtesy of Macy—the new and reigning queen of wedding history.

This avoid-the-evil-spirits trick is a wasted effort though because Griffin and Dayne are already waiting in our suite, removing their tuxedo jackets and ties, raw hunger in their gazes.

"Boys, I have our new toy," Soren announces, before the door has even shut completely. Griffin's normally lighter blue eyes seem nearly as dark and fathomless as Soren's. And Dayne's warm brown are now dark pits. They are each a forest for me to lose my way in, and I don't know which one of them is hiding the bread crumbs that will get me back home safe.

Soren sets me down on my feet but pulls me immediately back to him. His lips are at my ear as he speaks low to me, so softly I'm not sure if the other two can hear. "Go stand over there, face the wall, and put your hands on it, palms flat against it on either side of your face."

"O-okay," I say shakily. I'm used to orders over the phone, but it's an entirely different thing in person.

He shakes his head at me. "No. When we're together in private about to do something sexual, you will call me *Master* and Griffin and Dayne you will call *Sir.*"

My face heats at this, but my mind can only scream *finally*. I let out a long, shuddering breath, and in some ways it feels like the first moment of peace and relief I've had since Capri Bella. I have longed to offer him a title. Maybe deep down I always knew it would be Master and not Sir. Soren is too big, too all-encompassing to be Sir.

It's been so long since I've had sex I'm not sure I remember how to even do it the regular way. But while my body has been chaste, outside of toys my mind has been a nightly kinky whorehouse—and not all of it due to Soren's calls.

"O-okay, Master." A flood of wet heat blooms between my legs when this word comes out of my mouth. A tear slips down my cheek but there's no pity in his eyes. He takes a step toward me and pulls me close, his hand gripping the back of my neck. I hold my breath, thinking he'll kiss me in that aggressively passionate way he did at the altar in front of all those people, the way that made me blush as though I really were a virgin—worrying what our scandalized guests thought of that display, what they thought it might mean about what would happen between us tonight and every night going forward.

But Soren doesn't kiss me. Instead he leans in and licks the tear off my cheek. "Go," he whispers against my face as he releases me. I stumble back, but turn and go to the wall as he told me, avoiding Griffin and Dayne's gazes. I'm still having a hard time processing the fact that this night is finally here, no more excuses. No more delays. We are doing this thing.

It's my wedding night, and I'm not even wearing makeup. Macy brought an entire kit of professional quality makeup, naturally assuming she'd be painting my face today, but I'd told her no. Soren doesn't like it.

She'd been aghast, saying surely he wouldn't mind for just one day, it's my *wedding* day. But I refused. I told her only lip gloss which I let her swipe across my lips. It was a bit like giving an addict just a tiny bump of cocaine. It was just enough to light the fire and cause a thirty minute tirade about how this was crazy and I should wear makeup on my wedding day... after all what about the photos? But I held strong and eventually she gave up the fight.

I'm grateful I don't really need makeup and wasn't in the habit of wearing it anyway. So I didn't feel self conscious without it, particularly going down the aisle with the veil covering my face. And the photos can be retouched if necessary.

As I move to the wall to obey his orders, I realize his dislike of makeup is because of moments like what just happened. He doesn't want there to be any barriers between my skin and his tongue, nothing that tastes of foundation and mascara. Just me, clean and ready for him at all times. A shiver runs through me at this thought.

Griffin strokes my breasts through my wedding gown as Soren painstakingly releases each tiny button from its looped cage.

At the same time I hear a zipper and pants hit the floor, and then Soren is groaning, "Fuck yes, just like that."

My eyes go wide as they meet Griffin's, as I understand exactly what's happening. I can't look behind me to see, but I know Dayne is stroking Soren's cock. And now all at once everything clicks into place.

It never occurred to me that they had something going on with each other. I'd wondered all this time how they could possibly be keeping their lust in check. I'd worried, what if they were fucking some other girl—or more than one? It never occurred to me they were fucking each other, biding their time, waiting for me to join them.

Soren isn't making sacrifices to share me with two other men. No, he's getting three mouths on his cock, three bodies to penetrate and mark and claim with his release. And yet, even so, he doesn't own them. They all own me. Like a pet.

They may be his lovers, and he may be in charge, but in some way, they are equals. They are brothers with secrets and history. I'm dessert. I'm their shared toy.

Soren finally reaches the last button on my gown, and he and Griffin together help me out of it. Then I'm standing face-to-face with Dayne.

"I drew the winning straw," he says. His gaze is intense on mine, with promise, with intent. With triumph.

At first I don't understand what he means but then it hits me. He's the one who gets to fuck me first. I look to Soren, but he doesn't react to this. He doesn't seem jealous or like he'll fight Dayne on it. A part of me is relieved Dayne is first, I'm not sure if I could take Soren first. Soren is so large, and even with all the toys to prepare me, I'm afraid he'll hurt me with his size.

Another tear slides down my cheek, and Dayne wipes it away. "Shhhh, sweet. I've got you. It's going to be okay." He exchanges a look with Soren; I turn in time to see Soren nod. Dayne takes my hand and leads me into the bedroom, shutting the doors behind him.

"Dayne?" I question.

A stern look falls over his face, and that power he has that is so quiet suddenly becomes very loud. "I believe Soren told you how to address us."

"S-sir," I say, hurriedly.

He nods. "Come here."

I'm shaking and afraid I'll fall into trembling sobbing fits. I'm so overwhelmed, and I don't know what's about to happen. It's been so long, and now being faced with three men who all have expectations, being bound to all of these men, I don't know what I'm doing or how I even got here. But I go to him because what else can I do?

When I reach him, he pulls me into his arms and holds me, stroking the back of my head, his fingers moving gently through my hair. "Shhh. We're going to take good care of you."

He just holds me like this for several minutes, then guides me quietly over to the bed. He turns me facing the tall ornate Mahogany bed post.

"Hold onto it."

I grip the post, while he stands behind me unfastening the hooks on my corset. He helps me out of the last scraps of fabric that covered me then directs me to lie down on the bed. He's still fully dressed. Instead of joining, he sits in a plush dark blue armchair across the room, watching me.

It unnerves me to feel his gaze on me like this. It makes me feel more exposed even than my nudity. And while the room may be cast in soft light, it's plenty light enough for him to see every line and curve of my body, every imperfection. And still, he just takes me in, as if he has all night to make this assessment.

Finally he speaks. "Livia, do you understand what will be expected of you going forward?"

I shake my head, "No, Sir." Because despite Soren's dirty talk on the phone, I really don't. I don't know how much of that was talk, and how much will actually happen or what other things may happen. I don't even know how tonight is supposed to go. I don't know how to be with all of them. And I'm afraid of having to take them all at once.

He sighs, but his eyes never leave mine. "You will obey our every command. You will cry for us, beg for us, come for us. You will be sweet and pliant and take all of us into every orifice on demand. You will deny us nothing. Any kink, any request, you will happily comply."

My body screams yes to all of this, even as my mind is still unsure and anxious.

"And if I don't?"

"Soren has been very clear about this in his nightly calls. You'll be punished. And Soren really enjoys punishment."

I'm crying softly again because his words are terrifying, especially with the solemn way he delivers them. He isn't kidding. None of them are kidding. When Soren first said I belonged to them, I didn't realize he meant it so literally, or that everyone was equally on board with these terms.

These men are every fantasy I've ever had, offering to

act out every fantasy I've ever had. But it's one thing to touch yourself privately to your own dark thoughts; it's another to actually do those things. And it's still something else to be in the situation I find myself in.

He doesn't acknowledge my tears. Instead he says, "I've heard you over the phone, Livia. I know this is inside you. If I didn't think it was inside you, if I didn't think you needed this, I wouldn't be here."

"What about Soren and Griffin?"

"I don't know about Griffin, but I know Soren would have taken you on any terms. And he will keep you under any conditions and at any cost. There's no negotiating with Soren so don't even bother."

I allow this to sink in, even though I've never doubted for one moment Soren's ruthless nature. But Dayne isn't finished yet.

"And it isn't just the phone calls. The night of the proposal I tested you. When I shoved you against the wall and called you a cock tease you didn't cry or panic. I felt how wet you were, the way you pressed against me, your body begging for more. The others tested you, too. Even though he wasn't bluffing, Soren's threat was its own test. You were afraid but you didn't try to run. You were more aroused than you were scared. You just needed permission to do this forbidden thing with us. You needed permission to be selfish, wanton, slutty, obedient, and submissive. Livia, let me be clear, you have all of our full permission to be all of those things. And you will be all of those things, or there will be consequences."

My breath hitches as he rises slowly from the chair and begins to unbutton his shirt.

"We're going to go very easy on you your first time with us. Nothing crazy or extreme. But don't get used to it.

Things will change—especially on the honeymoon. You need to be prepared for that."

Dayne is absolute pure masculine beauty. He is a god—the kind of man all women fantasize about but few dare to dream they can truly have in real life. And here he is, prowling toward me like a jungle cat.

He finishes undressing. "I want you on your hands and knees. I'm going to take you from behind."

My womb clenches at this statement.

I obey his quiet command, and I somehow know he wants me from behind because he doesn't want to see the tears on my face and feel like a monster, even though I *do* want him. I want all of them.

I'm just scared because all of this is far too big for me.

I feel the bed dip behind me, and then he's gently stroking my back and my ass. He continues these soothing caresses until my body relaxes. I gasp when his hands move around to fondle my breasts, and then fingers are inside me.

"God, you are so tight," he says.

He flips me over onto my back and before I know what's happened, his head is between my legs, his tongue flicking over my clit as his fingers move in and out of me, stretching me, easing me farther open so I can take them. I move with him, chasing the pleasure his mouth and hands are building within me.

Ragged animal sounds begin to flow out of me, sounds I know Soren and Griffin can hear in the next room. I wonder if the two of them are fucking in there, or if they're jerking off or simply waiting for their turn to take me.

When I'm close, he flips me back onto my hands and knees, and a moment later he's inside me. I let out a moan at the intense pleasure-pain feel of his first hard thrust.

He grips my hips as he drives relentlessly into my body, my climax racing headlong into me until I come apart beneath him as he rides me harder still. A moment later his orgasm joins mine, and then he pushes me down until I'm flat on my belly and he's lying on top of me, still inside me.

"You are *such* a good girl," he whispers in my ear, and that praise creates another flutter of pleasure low in my gut.

He pulls out of me, and a moment later, Griffin and Soren are in the room with us. Griffin helps me stand. I'm so wiped out from the pleasure with Dayne that I don't have the presence of mind to feel self-conscious about my nudity. Soren offers me a bottle of water and I sit on the edge of the bed and drink, trying to collect myself.

I glance over to find that Dayne has put on a pair of lounge pants and is back to sitting in that blue chair, watching with the same intensity he watched me the first time. Soren takes the bottle from me and helps me to my feet.

"Hold her for me," Soren says.

Griffin stands behind me and holds me in his arms facing Soren. He cups and squeezes my breasts and nips and kisses my neck while Soren slowly undresses, his eyes never leaving mine.

"Did you warm her up for me?" Soren asks, the question aimed at Dayne.

"See for yourself," Dayne says.

I glance over to find Dayne's eyes trained on mine. He's poured a glass of scotch from a side cart a few feet away. He sips it as he watches the rest of this show. There's a minor power play going on between Soren and Dayne. Soren may not be jealous exactly, but he doesn't like not being the first to fuck me. He doesn't like a single moment passing without him in control of it.

"Spread her open," Soren says, this time directed to Griffin.

Griffin's hands are suddenly between my legs, spreading me lewdly open, angling my hips up so that Soren can get a full unobstructed view of my recently waxed pussy. I feel my entire body flush at the heat in his gaze.

"She's so fucking wet," Griffin says.

"You're welcome," Dayne says.

Soren only chuckles. And then his terrifyingly large dick is inside me. It's an even more intense fullness along with that pleasure-pain again as I adjust to his size, so grateful that Dayne warmed me up for him.

I'm overwhelmed by the intensity of being pressed between Griffin and Soren's hard bodies while Griffin holds me and offers me up like a sacrifice to Soren's primal hungers, all while Dayne sips his drink and watches. After a few minutes, Dayne pulls his dick out and begins to stroke it, already ready to go again.

"Come, now," Soren orders.

My pleasure shouldn't be voice-activated, but with Soren it is. I'm too used to his orders to come, his voice low and growling in my ear over the phone, that my response is immediate and well-trained. I come again as he releases inside me, fucking me even harder until he's emptied himself completely. His mouth claims mine again in another of those searing possessive kisses as he pulls out of me. Part of his release slides down my thigh.

Before I can catch my breath, Griffin pushes me onto the bed. "On your hands and knees," he orders. Just like Dayne, he wants to take me from behind.

"Wait," Dayne says.

Griffin stops. Dayne rises from the chair in that slow graceful way he does and hands his scotch to Soren. Then he joins us on the bed, sitting in such a way so that my head rests in his lap. I glance over to find Soren taking Dayne's chair, and finishing his drink while he watches the rest of what genuinely somehow feels like my deflowering.

Griffin strokes my back while Dayne pets my hair, and all at once I feel very safe and cared for. But a moment later, Griffin is inside me, and once again I'm not prepared for the harsh intensity, and the way that initial thrust steals my breath away.

While Griffin is fucking me, Dayne strokes my cheek. I whimper in response.

"Let me inside your mouth," he says.

The way Dayne gives commands is primal ferocity cloaked in gentle civilized language. I take him into my mouth, trying to focus on sucking him and at the same time relaxing my body so that Griffin can take his turn inside me. I'm so hot right now at the idea of both of them taking from me like this.

The two of them are still soothing me and stroking me as their dicks thrust without apology, seeking release. And all the while Soren sips on Dayne's abandoned drink and watches them take their pleasure. By this point I'm floating on waves of sensation. I am their vessel to fill, to pour into. I am their plaything, their toy to use.

I don't think I can come again, but then Griffin shifts the angle of his hips and hits my g-spot. I whimper and moan around Dayne's cock as I come for Griffin, giving him my pleasure just as I gave it to the other two men. Dayne no longer requires my effort, he's holding my head in place, fucking my mouth. I allow him to use me in this filthy carnal way. Both he and Griffin come inside me at the same time.

"Be good and swallow for me," Dayne says, gently stroking my throat.

I obey him and then glance over to find Soren's gaze is full of fire, the grip on his glass so tight I'm afraid it will break. His dick is hard and ready to fuck me again.

CHAPTER TWENTY-ONE: LIVIA

AFTERGLOW

he Present.

THE HOTEL HAS A HONEYMOON SUITE, but we didn't take it. The bed in the presidential was larger. We still got all the romantic honeymoon perks, except for a heart-shaped jacuzzi. Ours is regular shaped.

I lie in bed between Griffin and Dayne who both absently stroke my bare breasts. The touch somehow isn't sexual right now. I'm not even sure they realize they're doing it.

But I don't say anything. I'm so wrung out all I can do is lie here trying to put together the shards of who I was before tonight. There is an absolute and complete rift in me. There is Livia before and Livia after consummation. And these two Livia's exist worlds apart.

There was an agitated tension with the men that has finally faded away which I'm not sure I was fully aware of until the moment it was gone. But now that I think about it, I realize the tension started the day of the pre-nup because in a very real way I was married to both Dayne and Griffin on that day, but still not yet married to Soren.

People often don't think of marriage as a contract, but it is. They usually try to blend the legal event—which happens behind the scenes as if by magic—with the social/spiritual event that happens in front of friends and family in whatever sacred space they've chosen for the ceremony.

The typical marriage is a boilerplate contract with the state. A pre-nup is a way to legally alter the non-negotiable rules you'd otherwise be forced to follow in the event of breech of contract... better known as divorce. Marriage is the only contract that extends for a lifetime but which you can't actually negotiate the terms of.

I'm not sure why Soren decided not to just make his own private contract with me and leave official legal marriage out of it. We still could have had a wedding. Nobody would have known the reality behind the scenes, but Soren is too traditional—from his engraved stationery to the way he legally bound himself to me—that's why he's the legal husband, not because he's the scariest or has the biggest estate—even though both things are true—but because he's the most traditional even if he tries to hide it.

I watch Soren as he speaks low over the phone from across the room.

"Food will be here in about thirty minutes," he says when he disconnects the call.

"Huh? It's after midnight," I say.

"The room service here is 24 hours. I'm not finished with you yet, but you need to eat."

He's right. Now that I think about it, I'm starving. So

much was happening, and I was so scared that I didn't eat very much at the reception. It makes me sad because I pored over about thirty different menu options, and chose food that would have been really delicious if I'd had the appetite for it. As it was, I'd just managed a few bites.

"I wish we had leftover wedding cake," I say to no one in particular. I literally got the one bite Soren fed me, and that one bite was incredible. It might be the best cake that was ever created, and I got a single bite of it.

"We *do* have leftover wedding cake," Soren says. "I can call down and have some brought up with the food if you'd like."

"Thank you." I feel so shy right now after what we all did together.

He nods and crosses back to the phone and makes another brief call, then he sits in front of the television in the adjoining room. Everything feels so strange. After what the three of us did together one would think I'd be more comfortable with them, but I'm less. I know they aren't going to just disappear on me now that we've slept together—there are legal documents after all—but I feel more unbalanced than I did when this day began because the reality of being permanently in the bed of three men is finally truly settling into my brain.

I'm on edge because I know so much more is coming on the honeymoon. I would berate myself for agreeing to this except that there's no blame to be assigned to me. Soren took the illusion of free will away, and in this moment I'm grateful for that small kindness.

Griffin and Dayne have moved from stroking my breasts to alternating between kissing them and the side of my neck. I arch first into the touch and mouth of one of them, then the other.

Dayne's hand slides between my legs, and I am suddenly awake and hungry again for something more than food.

I wonder if they'll keep me up all night feeding their insatiable lusts, and I'm grateful we don't have a flight to catch in the morning. The jet leaves when we're on it.

By the time room service arrives Dayne and Griffin have shifted back to innocent cuddling. Soren answers the door and steps aside to allow the food to be rolled in. Shock and embarrassment cover the young attendant's face as he quickly looks away from the sight of me in bed with two men who aren't my husband.

And he knows we're from the wedding. Everyone working at the hotel today knows who is in the presidential suite. And even if that weren't true, it shows in his discomfort at what he's walked in on as well as the fact that my wedding dress is discarded on the ground in clear view of the door. It doesn't take a genius to put the pieces together, unconventional though they may be.

The bedroom is a separate room from the main part of the suite, but the doors are sliding doors that at this moment are pulled wide open, disappearing into the walls on either side. So from the bed, the three of us have a clear view of the door that leads into the hallway, and the attendant has a clear view of us.

Soren slips him a few hundred dollar bills and whispers something in his ear. The man nods quickly and flees the room as if he just witnessed a mob hit.

Soren rolls the cart the rest of the way to us and parks it next to the side of the bed Griffin is on. No one makes any comment about the fact that the attendant saw this or that the groom just paid him off to keep what he saw to himself.

In fact, I'm sure that besides the attendant, I'm the only one uncomfortable about it.

Lids are removed from the food to reveal club sandwiches and fries, and a platter with several pieces of our wedding cake on it. Soren passes me a soft drink and a plate with a sandwich and fries, and lets Dayne and Griffin get their own.

I barrel through the food like a twelve year old who has yet to learn table manners. It may not be the food I picked for the wedding, but after not having a full meal since lunch, it seems like the best thing I've ever eaten.

"All right, Eliza," Soren says. "Will I need to pay for etiquette lessons as well?"

I roll my eyes at the reference. "The rain in Spain stays mainly in the plain," I recite.

"Smart ass."

I pass my empty plate to him, and he trades with a piece of the lemon cake and a fork. I let out a moan of pleasure as the moist tangy sweet cake slips past my lips.

"My God this is incredible," I say. Without even thinking I offer a bite of my cake to Griffin. He has a piece of his own, I'm just so thrilled with this cake I want to share it. His intense blue gaze is locked on mine as he slowly chews and swallows.

Then he feeds me a bite of the cake from his plate. And now that we've accidentally done this feeding-each-other-cake wedding ritual, I feel compelled to turn and offer a bite of my cake to Dayne. Everyone has gotten strangely solemn in this moment as if this is the most serious wedding ritual any human being has ever participated in. Dayne takes the offered cake from my fork, then feeds me a bite from his own plate.

Then the four of us sit and stare at each other. I don't feed Soren. I did that at the reception.

All of us have shared cake. All of us have consummated whatever this is together. And there was a witness to this union who scampered off two or three hundred dollars richer for a two minute delivery.

No one speaks another word as we finish our cake, then Soren takes plates and glasses, and rolls the cart out into the hallway to be collected later.

"Put on your bikini, we're going to the pool," he says when he returns as if the moment we all just shared never happened.

I should complain of fatigue and beg for sleep but I am way too amped up to sleep. Besides, Soren isn't done with me yet.

CHAPTER TWENTY-TWO: GRIFFIN

AFTER HOURS SWIM

he Present.

IT'S a little after one in the morning when the three of us escort Livia to the pool. Despite the things we just did with her and to her, she's still such an innocent lamb, having no true idea of the wolves who surround her, or our intentions. She is far too easily led through the forest.

Soren plans everything to the tiniest detail, and we've known for weeks exactly how this day and night would go. What seems like a spontaneous after hours swim is anything but. She's wearing a black bikini and cover up as we guide her down the hallway having just gotten off the elevator.

How quickly she's moved from the innocence of the white dress to the sin of the black bikini. I can't say I'm complaining.

The three of us wear swim trunks, but mine and

Dayne's are mostly for show so she doesn't become alarmed and spook like a frightened young colt before we reach our destination.

"It's closed," she says when we reach the door and the sign with the hours on it. She seems disappointed, and I almost want to hug her. And I know Dayne does. Dayne has always been the softest with our women. And he's become even more taken with Livia than usual.

Soren says nothing but simply slides his key card into the slot beside the door. The light flicks from red to green, and the door lock clicks open to allow us entrance. Soren arranged to have things set up for us, to disable the security codes that lock down the pool even with a key card after midnight.

Livia looks uncertain. "Won't we get in trouble?"

Soren just laughs and guides her inside. It's sort of hilarious that anyone would come scold us for swimming past midnight with the rate we're paying.

Dayne and I stand outside the door as bodyguards, lest another rule-breaking guest attempt to walk in and interrupt. He and I exchange a glance and look in through the window.

I know what Soren is telling her. He's telling her to take the bikini off. He's telling her it's okay because Dayne and Griffin are guarding the door. No one can get in, and no one will be allowed to peer in through the window. But she sees right through the faux concern for her public modesty.

She points now, having seen the black shiny globes overhead. They're meant to look like part of the décor, and probably most people don't even think about it, but she knows they're cameras. Livia is both one of the smartest women I've ever met, and somehow also one of the most naïve. She is both light and darkness, innocence and sin. And as it all unfolds before us in the most beautifully fucked-up story, I'm glad Soren insisted that we all initiate her tonight, on her wedding night.

I feel bound to her now in a way I didn't feel with just the contracts we signed, even though it was those legal documents that truly tied us together.

First-time sex between a couple on the wedding night is one of many traditions that still contains an unexpected thrill. And it's every too-greedy man's loss not to get this experience. Consummation means so little when you've already been consummating for months or even years. The specialness is gone. People talk about the importance of sexual compatibility—and I agree—but there are a lot of sexually dissatisfied married people who took each other for plenty of test drives before vows were ever exchanged.

The cameras in the natatorium are all in working condition, filming everything that happens with both sound and image. At this very moment there are a couple of men in a room on the basement level who can see the video and hear every word of what happens between Soren and Livia.

I adjust my dick, the uncomfortable tightness causing my mind to scream to be inside her again. I don't technically have to stand here. Dayne is enough of a deterrent. There's no need for this Secret Service level of security on one door. For fuck's sake. Soren and Livia aren't royalty or celebrities, though I'm sure despite the bribe, the late night kitchen staff is abuzz with what's really going on on the wedding night of the Fairchild/Kingston wedding.

I could watch and listen from the security room. After this is over Soren will have the footage. It'll end up in a safe at the estate, and when we're feeling nostalgic one of us will no doubt take it out and watch and jerk off. Maybe all three of us will. Maybe we'll make Livia watch it and touch herself while we watch her.

We could have arranged this late night pool access with money and had the cameras turned off. I could go to the basement right now and shut it down—though not without a serious confrontation with Soren later, and I want that video footage as much as he does. I want this wedding night souvenir.

The price that was agreed to for having the security code disabled was that they'd be allowed to watch. Soren wants them to watch. He gets off on it. I do, too. And the erection Dayne is sporting speaks for itself.

As soon as this is over, I'll go get a copy of the video and the original will be deleted from their system. I should go down there now to make sure they don't secretly make their own private copy, but I can't bring myself to move from this spot where she exists in full color only a few yards away from me.

Livia isn't playing along, though. She's still wearing her cover up. She moves swiftly back toward the door, practically in a full run, reaching for the knob. Her face says she's sure that Dayne and I will save her, that we'll protect her from Soren. I put one hand up against the door to block her escape. Dayne and I exchange a glance, and I'm surprised to see he doesn't waver. I always thought he'd be the weak link.

Soren reaches her and drags her kicking and screaming back to the pool's edge, back to the spot in the best view of the cameras.

"I'm going in. Guard the door," I say to Dayne.

"You know what Soren said."

"I don't care. I want to be in there."

"*I* want to be in there," he says. It's clear the only reason he agreed to play bodyguard is that this was Soren's thing. He's not going to go along with me joining in while he's left out in the cold.

"I'll go in for a bit then I'll trade places with you," I offer.

Dayne seems to consider this. "Soren won't like it."

"Fuck Soren. I know he thinks he's the big bad alpha male but we've got to stand up for ourselves or he'll run right over us. Is that really the way you want to spend the rest of your life? Playing his butt monkey and needing to be *allowed* to fuck your own girl? We have contracts with her, too. We're just as *in this* as his royal highness in there."

We all agreed we'd share her equally, but I know Soren has been establishing the pecking order, and if he thinks I'm going to just quietly go along with that, he's wrong.

Dayne lets out a sigh because he knows I'm right. "Go. I'll cover you."

I slip my key card into the slot and go inside.

"I thought I told you to guard the door," Soren says, his voice far colder than I expected this early in the game. But he doesn't like being told no. And our Livia is turning out not to be as obedient as Soren might have preferred. But I'm good with it. I like a little fire. I like the struggle.

"And I thought I told you I wasn't taking orders from you," I say.

We stare each other down. If he thinks I'm looking away just because he's got a good solid thirty pounds of pure muscle on me, he doesn't know me as well as he thinks he does. I'll take this motherfucker to the mat for the next five decades if need be.

Livia practically flings herself on my mercy. I wrap my arms around her, feeling her warm soft skin pressed desperately against me. I place a gentle kiss to her forehead and stroke her hair. I'm not about to save her, but I'll let her believe it—for a moment at least. I enjoy this role as the hero, her savior from the evil villain, Soren.

He can play the big bad wolf all he wants to, as long as she runs to me for protection. I was the one who held him back the night of the proposal after all. In that moment when I'd put my hand on his shoulder to stop him, the gratitude in her eyes was so intoxicating that it was all I could do to keep my hands to myself when I drove her home. But I was a good boy. I didn't want to destroy the role she'd given me in her life. A part of me still doesn't.

For months I've fed on this hero worship from that single moment.

She thinks something similar is about to happen now, and a part of me hates that I'm not about to receive that same gratitude, that I may erase everything I've built. But the problem is, I'm just too greedy. I've had a taste of her. She's in my system. There are no brakes on this train anymore.

She begins to understand the true state of things as my hand slips underneath her coverup to slide inside her bikini bottoms, stroking her ass. She tries to struggle, but within a few moments she's grinding her tight little body against me, whimpering.

"Please, Sir," she says to me, and I groan at that. I hadn't expected her to remember these rules, not when she's scared and it's all so new. From the way she's grinding on me it's impossible to tell if she's begging me to keep touching her or if she still wants me to rescue her from this situation.

I know I can't take Soren in a fair fight, but if I wanted to save her, Dayne would burst in here and back me up. I look back to the door to find his shrewd gaze observing this entire scene. Oh yeah, he's up for playing hero if need be. That's the beauty of this little power triangle. Soren may be the strongest, but Dayne and I tend to form alliances when he goes too far.

I bend to whisper in Livia's ear, "I'll make sure the footage gets deleted." I hope this small protective gesture keeps her looking at me the way she's been looking at me since that night. I thought I'd lost her after my lewd outburst at the attorneys' offices the day the contracts were signed. But lust had too quickly overpowered her distress, and by the next day it was forgotten and I went back to pretending I wasn't the type of man who'd say something like that in front of strangers just to humiliate her—that I wasn't the type of man who deliberately did things like that because I got off on it.

She looks up at me, unshed tears in her eyes. "How will you make sure?"

I arch a brow as if to ask *how do you think?* But I answer the question anyway. "Money, of course. People will do anything for the right price."

I immediately regret these words because I know she thinks I'm putting her in that category as someone we bought, but I've known for months now that she wasn't quite what we first assumed. Even so, it was threats, not promises, that sealed her to us. With the way this was handled, she shouldn't care what we think of her at all. But I know she does.

I continue to stroke her hair as she leans against me.

"Please," she whispers. And I know she does want a rescue. I can't pretend I don't know what she's asking for. She doesn't want to perform for the cameras.

I want to lie to her and say there's nobody in the security room—no one will see this at all—but the one thing I won't do is lie to her. I tilt her chin up to mine and capture her mouth in a kiss that steals her breath.

"That's it," I growl into her mouth. "Be a good girl for us."

She gives up the fight and melts into me. She doesn't resist when I pull her cover up off. Then Soren is behind her, unhooking her bikini top.

She pulls away and looks in my eyes again, a silent plea.

"You're safe. I promise," I say. I don't know what she needs to feel safe from. Is it safety from exposure to other leering gazes? Does she worry that we'll judge her? For something we set up?

I'm not fully sure what I'm promising her, and I'm not sure she does either, but she lets Soren take her top off. Then he pushes the bikini bottoms down over her hips.

She jumps when he smacks her ass.

"Get in the pool," he says.

She's still clinging to me. She only lets go so I can pull the T-shirt over my head.

"You're loving this shit, aren't you?" Soren asks, giving me a derisive glare.

"What shit?"

"The way she clings to you like you're the good guy."

"Maybe I am the good guy."

He laughs at this. "Sure, Griff. You're on the short list for new saints."

I ignore his barb. He's jealous that Livia responds to a bit of softness, something he isn't as equipped to give. He knows it puts him at a disadvantage, and so he plays raw power instead.

I take her hand and guide her into the pool with me. Soren raises a brow at this.

"Okay, fine. You can help." He doesn't have to tell me

what to do. I've been jerking off thinking about this for weeks. Except in the original plan he'd simply order her to do it. Somehow it's hotter if I hold her in place.

I move her to the wall near Soren, positioning her right in front of the jets. You can't tell me pool manufacturers don't know what they're doing when they place these jets where they do. They're at the perfect height for the average woman to press her pussy against it, letting the water pulsate and massage her to orgasm.

Livia grips the edge of the pool and lets out a gasp as the powerful jets force water against her clit. I hold her hips in place so she can't pull away from the relentless pulses.

I grab her breast roughly with my free hand and bite at the side of her throat like some out of control animal. She's moving, but not pulling away. She's moving with the water, rotating her hips to enhance the experience, moaning as she gives herself over to the water, to us.

I look up to find Soren moving closer. He's discarded his swim trunks. He sits on the edge of the pool, fully erect, his legs on either side of Livia. Without being told, she bends closer and takes him into her mouth, but he pushes her off him.

"I didn't say you could touch my cock," he says, clearly displeased by her show of initiative.

"I-I'm sorry, Master."

This just makes my dick harder. I know she isn't ready, I know she can't take it yet, but I desperately want to fuck her ass right now while the jets continue to ravage her cunt. I tease her back entrance with the tip, and she whimpers.

"Please, Sir," she whispers, panicked, trying to turn to

look at me, trying to protect her vulnerable ass from my probing dick.

"Don't you dare. I will fucking drown you if you take her ass," Soren says. And a part of me isn't sure if he's saying this for effect to try to steal the hero title from me or if he's serious. "You know I get to take her ass first."

Another whimper from her.

Last night when we drew straws for who gets to do what when, Dayne got first fuck, Soren got second, which meant he got her ass first. I got the leftover first—first punishment, something I know Soren wants, so maybe I can negotiate a trade on the honeymoon.

But for now I just say, "Oh be serious, Soren. You know she'll never be able to take you first. You're too fucking big and you know it. It needs to be me or Dayne first."

"Never," Soren says. He looks from Livia to me, back to Livia again, and then finally to me.

"Jerk me off, Griffin."

I swear there's some kind of psychic link between the two of us or maybe we've just been sharing women too long because I know exactly what he wants. I can read his unspoken demand as if it came engraved on his pretentious-as-fuck formal stationery. And all at once, he and I are back on the same team.

I grip his cock and jerk him off as requested. He leans back, bracing himself with his hands pressed against the concrete behind him. I can't help admiring the way his abs flex when he moves. We all work out, and we're all fit, but he has that natural extra bulk that helps him command every room he enters.

"Harder, don't be a little girl about it," he says.

I squeeze harder, trying to actually cause him pain now for that remark, but he doesn't give in. instead he bucks his hips with my movements, and I relax my strangle hold on him just enough to give him actual pleasure.

I can see when he's close. Just before he comes, I lean down to Livia's ear. "Open your mouth."

She does, and I grip the back of her neck with my free hand, and then aim his cock into her mouth. He releases into her as I'm careful not to let her lips close fully over his flesh. I move a hand to her throat, urging her to swallow.

"Such a good girl," I growl in her ear. She's moving again, bucking hard against the jets as they finally take her over the edge. Soren finishes and slips from her mouth as she screams out her release.

I press her harder against the pulsing water not letting her go until she's fighting and struggling to escape the overstimulation.

"Kiss it and thank me," Soren says.

I finally let her move away from the flow of water. She obediently kisses the tip of his cock and says, "Thank you, Master."

In this moment she is so soft, so demure. So inviting.

I spin her around so her back is to the pool's wall and hike one of her legs up over my hip. She lets out a whimper of surprise as I surge into her. A moment later I'm fucking her and she's gripping onto my shoulders trying to hang on for the ride.

Soren has recovered by this point and sits up and moves closer to us, he strokes and squeezes her breasts from behind, then drags one hand up her throat until he's pressing his thumb into her mouth. She sucks on it and moans while I fuck her even harder.

I roar out my release as she comes again, her cunt quivering and gripping and milking my cock as if her life depended on my pleasure.

And I am very pleased.

I pull out, get out of the pool, and put my T-shirt back on. I leave Livia with Soren and go into the hallway to tag out with Dayne.

"Use one of the metal chairs inside to block the door," I say when I get outside.

"What? Why?" Dayne asks.

"Because I'm going to the security room to make sure those fuckers don't think they're going to make their own private porn backup before I get down there."

"Why didn't we just do that to begin with?" he asks.

"In case she ran, I guess. You know Soren. She's too far gone to run now so a chair will do."

Dayne is beyond annoyed, and it takes a lot to annoy him. Usually he's pretty laid back, the least likely to fight about anything because half the time he just doesn't care. But with Livia it seems all bets are off.

I wait and guard the door while Dayne shoves the metal chair up under the metal handle, glaring at me as he does it. We're lucky the door pushes inward instead of opening out, so we even have this option. Fate apparently smiles down on us.

When everything is secured, I take the elevator to the basement level. I go down a long depressing slate gray hallway, past the laundry and maid's areas filled with giant metal racks of cleaning supplies. Finally I get to a small room at the end right next to the emergency exit.

I open the door without knocking, mostly because I want to see how badly these guys spook. And it's a sight to behold. You'd think being the security team, they'd lock this door—at least when they've got their dicks out, jerking off to X-rated security footage.

They both jump nearly a foot out of their chairs when I let the door bang against the wall and step inside.

"Mr. Macdonald," they say in unison like I'm a visiting dignitary and they've spent hours practicing this greeting. It doesn't have quite the right tone with their dicks hanging out, though. Realizing the problem, they both zip up quickly.

"What are you doing down here?" one of them asks. His name tag says Drake, and I'm pretty sure that's not his real name.

I cross my arms over my chest. "I came to make sure that when this is done one copy and *only* one copy gets made, that it is given to me, and that the main files are deleted. I've got extensive computer security knowledge so don't think you'll slip something past me. I'll be checking to make sure everything's properly wiped, and there isn't a hidden backup somewhere."

I can tell from their faces my suspicions were right. They *did* think they were each getting a video to take home with them.

"Oh, come on!" the other one says. "Help a guy out."

"That's my wife on that screen," I say. It's the first time I've said this word out loud or even thought this word. And while I know my name isn't on the marriage license, My contract with her is just as binding as any marriage, covering all the same things and more.

"I thought she was married to that other dude."

I'm saved from having to entertain this asinine comment as I watch Livia, Soren, and Dayne on the screen leaving the pool area.

"Just make me a copy of the footage," I say. I'm impatient with this and want to go back to the room.

CHAPTER TWENTY-THREE: SOREN

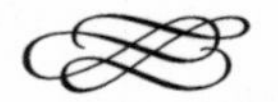

THE MILE-HIGH CLUB

*he Present.*

WE SLEPT in and had a very late lunch, so we didn't get on the jet until three pm. We should arrive in Costa Rica by eight or eight-thirty at the latest. Because the flight is short, no one will be sleeping, but that doesn't mean the bed won't get used. It's the pilot, co-pilot, Dayne, Griffin, Livia, and me today.

Dayne and Griffin are on their laptops trying to catch up on some work before they get side-tracked and distracted by the honeymoon. Livia is reading a book. Or she's attempting to. She hasn't turned the page in over five minutes, so either she's pretending to read or she's reread the same paragraph twenty times. If ink could show wear on a book from being looked at too much, Livia's intense gaze would have melted several lines right off the page, leaving only blank space and a mystery behind.

She glances up, and I capture and hold her gaze in mine.

"Nervous?" I ask.

"A-about what?"

For months she's been distracted by the wedding planning and the wedding, too distracted to properly internalize the fact that three men are taking her on a jet out of the country to a honeymoon and a location she doesn't know any details about. Beyond the country, she has no idea where we're going or why we're going there. Dayne was responsible for those details since it's his resort we're going to. He's got someone else managing it for him and doing all the work, but he owns it and gets monthly reports on operations.

"Come with me," I say.

"Where?"

Dayne and Griffin look up from their laptops. They watch her like I am watching her. I don't know how long this nervous uncertainty will last, but I want to drink up every last drop of it for as long as it does.

I glance to the back of the plane where the bedroom is, then to her. "You know where." My cock pushes tight against my pants. She bites her lower lip when she notices my erection. She knows we're about to finish what I tried to start almost a year ago—that I will finally win this battle. Only this time it's better than the first because it won't just be the pilot and co-pilot who hear her come; it'll be Dayne and Griffin as well.

She turns to the guys as if hoping one of them will save her, but neither of them steps in to answer her silent pleas. They go back to their laptops, but they aren't working anymore. They're listening and waiting to see what will happen next.

I stand and move into her space just like I did almost a year ago. I tower over her, and her gaze drifts back to the guys on the other side of the plane.

"No," I say. "Look at me. They won't help you."

Her gaze drifts back to mine. I stroke her cheek. "I could just *take* it," I say.

The look in her eyes is equal parts fear and arousal. She wants me to just take it. She wants me to throw her down on the bed and just take it. She's not brave enough yet to be that honest, but I got a taste of her last night. I know where she lives. I know she's not the vanilla suburban hell trying to trap me that I feared. She is my equal, my perfect match, my opposite polarity. She is the fire to my ice, the surrender to my conquest. She is perfect.

I lean down closer, my voice going lower. "Do you not remember the vows you spoke to me not twenty-four hours ago? How you promised to honor and obey me for the rest of your life?"

"Yes," she whispers.

"Yes, what?"

A long tremulous breath flows out of her, and then she says in that same soft whisper, "Yes, Master."

"Good girl, now come with me."

I step back to give her space to obey me and extend my hand out to her. She takes it, color flooding her cheeks as she allows me to lead her back to the bedroom.

I lock the door when we get back there, not because I really need to, but because it pushes the final nail into the coffin, it puts hard punctuation on the end of the sentence.

"Now, where were we?" I say as if I'm picking things right back up where we left them now that I've fulfilled her requirements for letting me inside her, now that I've put a ring on her finger. And though I've already been inside her

—and it was exquisite—this is the first time I've had the pleasure of taking her alone.

She's wearing a dress today—not the same dress she wore the night of the underwater restaurant date. This one is more of a casual flirty sundress, white with yellow flowers sweeping up along the flared base. Her shoes were left behind next to her seat so her feet are bare. She has light pink polish on her toes and a yellow flower painted on the largest nails. I realize she got a pedicure to match this dress.

She looks so innocent, and she feels equally innocent on the inside. Even with all of our toys and preparation, she is tight.

I look her slowly up and down. "Turn around."

"S-Soren," she whispers.

"Master," I correct.

But she doesn't say anything else, she just turns away from me. The dress has a zipper, and I take my time dragging it slowly down her back as goosebumps chase the path of the zipper. I slip the straps off her shoulders and push the dress to the floor. She's wearing the most innocent sweet white cotton panties and no bra. I let her keep the panties for now because I like looking at them. I like the way she makes me feel when she looks so vulnerable.

"Go lie down on the bed on your back," I say. I can barely keep my voice under control.

While she does this, I go back to the door, unlock, and open it.

"W-what are you doing?"

"I changed my mind about the door. I want everyone on this plane to hear you."

Dayne and Griffin are only a few feet away. Griffin's seat allows him a glimpse with the door open, but not enough to consider it a front row seat. He and Dayne would both have to get up and come in here for that. But they know I don't want them to, and they'll stay in their seats and let me have her the way I want her.

"Master, please," she whispers.

I strip off my own clothes and watch her. "Spread your legs and slip your fingers underneath your panties. Play with yourself."

She only hesitates a moment before doing what I ask. I can tell from where I'm standing that her panties are already soaked. She can protest all she wants. She can display her fear like a badge, but every part of her body is excited by this, by the power I wield over her, by the idea of her other two lovers only a few feet away, by the idea of the pilot and the co-pilot behind only a divider wall. There isn't a proper door to separate them from the rest of the plane.

I crawl onto the bed with her and pull her hand away from her pussy as if catching her misbehaving instead of doing exactly as I asked. I cup her over her panties, my grip hard.

"Whose cunt is this?"

"Y-yours, Master."

"And?"

"A-and Griffin's and Dayne's."

"Good girl. And you will honor and obey all of us. That vow applies to all of us. Do you understand?"

She nods.

Her hips arch up into my hand as I begin to rub her hard through her panties. I don't warm her up with gentle caresses, and she doesn't need it. The rougher I handle her, the more her body responds to me.

I grip her throat, holding her down as I continue to

stroke her with my other hand. She struggles and fights between the panic of my hand around her throat and the close cresting of her orgasm.

"You want to breathe, princess?"

She nods to the extent that I allow her movement.

"Then you must promise when I remove my hand from your throat, you will come and you will scream your pleasure loud enough for everyone on this plane to hear."

She nods again.

"Good girl."

I release her throat while the fingers of my other hand stroke feverishly over her clit. She bucks and moans and screams. When her body finally settles and she goes quiet and still again, I rip off her panties. She lets out another loud gasping moan when I shove my cock inside her.

She's so fucking tight. There are tears in her eyes when I look at her face again, and I'm not sure if it's the force of her orgasm or my giant dick slamming into her that put them there. But her hips begin to move, urging me on.

Her small hands claw at my shoulders trying to pull me deeper into her even though I'm buried to the hilt. She makes the most gorgeous panting moans in rhythm to my thrusts. She comes again right as I do, as I'm spilling inside her, hoping she'll be carrying my child soon.

It isn't until I pull out of her and spoon her against me that I realize... even though she struggled and bucked, she never clawed at my hand when it was around her throat. Some small part of Livia trusts me, and while her fear may excite me, her trust fills me with warmth.

CHAPTER TWENTY-FOUR: DAYNE

THE HONEYMOON

he Present.

THE JET LANDED in Costa Rica a few minutes after eight. Livia can't hide her surprise at all the people greeting me with "Hello, Mr. Montgomery," "How was your flight, Mr. Montgomery?", "Everything is prepared for you, Mr. Montgomery," as we're led through the resort by an entourage of eager help.

They take us to a large two-story house done in the same style as the rest of the resort. It's a separate private building, and it's never rented out to guests. It's always kept on reserve for me and my private guests. Both Griffin and Soren have been here on many occasions. We've kept toys here for weeks at a time in the past—women who begged to be ours forever by the time it was over.

Unfortunately we all have work to get back to and don't have as much free time in our schedule right now, but we'll be back. Maybe a shorter stay is better this time to avoid overwhelming Livia. Soren has a respectable dungeon set-up at his estate, but the public stuff is fun, and we only get that here. It's the only time and place we can be truly out and open about our arrangements without judgment or risk of scandal. After all, every member has their own secrets to keep and everyone signs about half a dozen contracts, including NDAs.

It's an underground—as in secret—resort where those with money and power and the password—which changes frequently to control security leaks—can come and engage in open public kinky debauchery with those they bring as guests. Guests are carefully screened and have to be open to being shared, passed around to the other members, and anything and everything we choose to do with them while they're here.

But Livia, because she's mine, won't be shared with anyone but Griffin and Soren. She gets this one mercy which only exists because the three of us don't want anyone else getting close to our dynamic or fucking with it. We've made that mistake in the past. We won't make it again.

Livia is slowly awakening to my power in this arrangement. I think she believed at first that I was just an extra, or somehow submissive to Griffin and Soren. But I'm not. There isn't a submissive bone in my body. It takes a woman in our grouping to keep things stable which is why we almost never fuck each other unless there's a woman in the mix. We're all far too aggressive and dominant to make it work with just us.

The fucking we do happen to do—just the three of us—is for pleasure. But we don't get the same psychological rush we get when we have someone to share, a girl completely under our power. We've all been on the receiving end of anal—even Soren, though he would go to his grave before admitting it. There's something vulnerable in that act which requires a high level of trust.

We couldn't do it with anyone else but each other. It's because of the things we went through at Dartmouth during rush that allows us to trust each other enough for that. Otherwise, despite the intensity of the pleasure afforded, we could never bring ourselves to do it, to surrender in that way to someone else.

When it's more than just fucking, when there are feelings beyond brotherhood, when there's a relationship, there has to be someone at the center of it all to bend to our will. That's where Livia comes in. It's a delicate dance and trade of power across the board. Even so, there has to be a power that can hold everything together.

Griffin's power is too impulsive and uncontrolled—wild like an unexpected rainstorm. Soren's is too ruthless. He knows what's right, but he'll do whatever he wants anyway. And even though I came to this party late, I know why Soren invited me rather than just keep her between him and Griffin—even if he himself doesn't know. And it isn't just access to the resort and all its pleasures.

It's because I'm the stable power, the safe power, the one who subtly manages things behind the scenes. Livia is the soft power, but she doesn't know that yet. It may take years for her to realize and step into her own power. It may take her years to understand just how much all of us would sacrifice for her, how much wealth and luxury and pleasure and safety and protection we will gladly lay at her feet because she makes everything possible. She's the first one we've all seen a real future with, the key to all our locks.

I don't think any of us believed we could ever have this in a real and permanent relationship. It was always just supposed to be fucking around. And it always was. Before her.

I've had my hand on the small of Livia's back since we got onto the property, and I keep it there the entire walk through the resort until we're safely inside our home away from home. The staff and members need to see her; they need to see this. They need to know she's with me and under my protection. I will remove any member who tries to violate this boundary and revoke all their future privileges, as well as those of their families, friends, and even descendants because the blacklist here can stretch through generations. There are people who will never gain entrance because their grandfather fucked up and pissed off the wrong person fifty years ago.

We're finally alone, the four of us. Our bags have been brought in and all resort employees have taken their leave. Livia looks shaken by what she saw in the lobby and on the grounds. People half dressed. People naked. People in leather. People in collars being led crawling through the resort like it was nothing.

It *is* nothing.

I call and order room service to the house, then I do a walk-through to make sure everything is as I requested. When I'm finished, I go into the master bathroom and run a bath for Livia.

I turn a few minutes later to find her standing in the bathroom with me, looking almost as timid as she did last night coming into our suite. "Griffin sent me up here," she says. She can't meet my eyes, instead looking to the large jacuzzi tub as it fills.

I pop the cork on a bottle of champagne and pour her

some in the single flute that was left on the counter. She gasps as I pour the rest of the champagne into the tub with the water and sprinkle in the still fresh fragrant cream-colored rose petals the staff left before we arrived. I light the candles around the tub and hand the champagne to her.

"Drink this. I need you relaxed. The champagne bath will help, too." If possible, this pronouncement makes her more nervous.

She takes the flute and chugs it back like it's beer. Well, that's one way to do it.

"Dayne? What's going to happen to me here?"

It's moments like this when I wonder if I'm wrong about her. Can she handle us? She sends such mixed signals. I choose not to answer because I'm not sure there's an answer that will put her at ease. She was already warned last night that things would escalate, but I know she didn't expect this. She expected a normal honeymoon—at least on paper. And she hasn't even seen the half of it yet.

I take the empty flute from her and place it on the counter behind me. "Turn around."

She does, and I carefully unzip her sundress and push it to the floor. Oh I like this. No bra and virginal white panties. I bet Soren liked it when he had her on the plane, too. I push the panties down over her hips, and help her step out of them when they hit the floor to join the dress.

Then I guide her into the tub. I lean over and press a kiss against her forehead when she's settled. "Just relax. I'll come get you when dinner arrives."

The guys are stretched out on sofas in the main room when I get downstairs. "New plan," I say. Most of the planning has shifted to me now that we're at my resort, but Soren will be happy to take the reigns again when we return home, on his turf—the estate. But this is my castle. My rules.

"Oh?" Soren says. "I thought we were taking her to the dungeon to show her off and play."

I shake my head. I remain convinced that this is inside Livia, but if we push her too far too fast, we could lose her. We could break her, and then we're left with the mess we made.

"It's too soon. She needs a night to relax and acclimate. She needs a night that feels normal and safe."

"Bullshit," Soren says. He practically spits the word.

"Hey," I say, my tone hardening. "Settle your ass down. I can ban you from the resort just like anyone else. Fuck around with her, and we won't be able to undo the damage. I want her tonight when we go to bed. Alone. For the whole night."

"Fuck that noise," Griffin says.

"No," Soren says, flatly.

"We're here for a week. You can each get her alone for one of the nights, too. And Soren, you already had her alone on the jet."

"Why should you get her alone all night first? You had her first last night," Soren says.

I know what he thinks. He thinks I'm trying to usurp his territory. He thinks I'm trying to unseat him and run this quad. I've never attempted a direct power takeover, and I'm not attempting it now. But they've both noticed I'm more possessive of Livia than I've been of the others and just how fast that possession took hold.

"Because I'm the one who can be the most gentle with her, and that's what she needs right now. She needs eased into our world. She's not like the other girls who voluntarily came to us and knew what they were getting themselves into."

A lot of those girls were guests of other members here at the club. They'd already been passed around to at least a dozen men and some couples before ending up in our bed and under our control. Livia is different. In so many ways.

Griffin nods. "Yes. Okay. I agree with Dayne. Just for tonight. Come on Soren, you know he's right. He's not trying to take over."

"When we get back home..." Soren says, warning.

"Your castle, your rules," I say, holding up my hands in mock surrender.

He nods his agreement. "Fine."

Half an hour later our food is here. I ordered normal casual American fare. Nothing fancy. Nothing foreign. Nothing unpronounceable. Livia doesn't need to navigate bizarre spices and mystery sauces right now. She needs normality. So it's burgers and fries. We're all going to have to hit the gym hard as soon as we get home.

When I go back upstairs to retrieve Livia, I find her sobbing and shaking in the tub. If even a champagne bath can't calm her nerves... I was right about this. I blow out the candles and pull the plug on the tub and lift her out. She clings to me even as she's clearly afraid of what I—what we—will do to her here.

I've seen girls break down like this in the dungeon, and I haven't intervened. But those girls weren't mine, and it wasn't my business to know what they could and couldn't take. They signed contracts. They knew what they were getting into, but Livia doesn't.

I carefully dry her off then get her into a soft terrycloth robe and pull her into my arms.

"Please, Sir," she whimpers. And that broken sob breaks my heart.

"Shhh," I say. "We aren't going to hurt you. We're going to have dinner and cuddle on the sofa and watch a movie. Then you're coming to bed with me—just me. We aren't leaving this house tonight."

"But you said..."

"I know what I said, and you aren't ready. We have our entire lifetimes. We'll go slow with you. I'll protect you."

"But Soren..."

"... isn't in charge here. This is my resort. I'm running the honeymoon. Relax."

Inexplicably these words have a stronger effect on her than the champagne she drank or just soaked in, and I feel her sigh as the tension finally rolls off her body and she melts into my arms.

It was worth it waiting for the wedding night to initiate her, but the side effect of that is that we've lost time we could have used seducing her into our world. Soren may like her fear—fuck I like her fear—but it's too much too soon.

I wipe the tears off her face and kiss her. I shouldn't have left her up here without any explanation, but I needed to manage Soren and Griffin.

She's much calmer by the time we get downstairs. We all sit together at the big kitchen table with our ginger ale and burgers and fries. Livia picks over her food at first, but then her appetite shows up and she digs in.

"There's our healthy eater," Soren teases. And I see the corner of her mouth twist up in a smirk.

"Soon you'll be eating for two," Griffin says.

"Or three," I say because I can't help myself.

Livia's gaze goes solemnly to mine and then back to her

food. I wonder if she's already pregnant. The timing of the wedding couldn't have been more perfect. Last night she could have conceived. There could be the tiniest proto-person growing inside her at this very moment.

After dinner I let Griffin and Soren cuddle with her on the couch for the movie. I don't need to be in the mix because I get her all to myself tonight. Griffin chose a romantic comedy with a fake wedding of all things, but she's smiling and laughing at least, and that's a vast improvement from the state I found her in an hour ago.

She falls asleep about halfway through the movie in Griffin's arms. I allow it because she needs this nap. All that champagne both drinking and soaking was bound to fully hit her once the adrenaline subsided. And even a healthy meal wasn't going to stop it from claiming her.

"Enjoy your night with her." Soren smirks.

I laugh. "Oh, I'll wake her up after the movie. Don't you worry."

The house has three bedrooms, and all of them have a bed large enough for the three of us and a girl. Officially we each have a room, and the girl gets passed between rooms, though many nights we've ended up all in one bed. Each room has an attached bathroom, but the room with the master bathroom with the jacuzzi is mine. As the movie finishes, I take my bags to my room and make sure I have everything I need.

I'm not kind enough to let her sleep until morning, but I will let her sleep a little while longer.

Soren has already gone up to his room for the night by the time the credits roll.

"I'm afraid I'll wake the octopus if I move," Griffin whispers, his arms outstretched to show the problem he has on his hands. Livia is pretty aggressively snuggled into him, her limbs wrapped snug around his body. I help him untangle her, and he carries her up to my room.

"Don't wake her," I whisper.

"You're letting her sleep?" he whispers back, surprised.

"Fuck no, but I want her to wake on my terms when I'm ready."

Griffin nods and deposits her gently on the bed then retreats, leaving me alone with my prize.

CHAPTER TWENTY-FIVE: LIVIA

THE HONEYMOON

he Present.

I WAKE IN TOTAL DARKNESS, fabric covering my eyes while soft lips devour my mouth. I moan into the mouth on mine as I try to remember where I am and who I'm with. He must feel me stir because he pulls back.

"D-Dayne?" I ask. He said it would be him tonight. Just him. Though I feel almost equally safe with Griffin. I wonder if I'll ever feel as safe with Soren.

"You know that's not what you're supposed to call me," Dayne says.

I let out a slow breath. "Sir," I say.

"Good girl."

I'm naked under the covers, I assume in his bed, in his room. I move my hand up to remove the fabric covering my eyes.

"No. Leave the blindfold on."

He pulls the covers back and I shiver as the cool air touches my bare skin. I turn my head as if by doing so I can somehow see through the blindfold.

"It's just us. Like I promised," he says, knowing my question without me asking it.

He strokes my cheek, and I lean into him. Then he goes back to kissing me. I should have known when I woke that it was Dayne. They all kiss so differently—each a unique signature none of the others can forge.

Soren's kisses are like a tornado spinning through me and breaking me apart, rough and ravaging and demanding I submit. No matter how much I already think I have, Soren's mouth always disagrees and demands more. Griffin's kisses are passionate and frenzied but they don't have the fear I might disappear behind them. They don't have the need to lock me in a tower and throw the key away.

Dayne's kisses are all calm command. They are strong and silent but soft and gentle at the same time. His tongue doesn't dominate me or conquer me when it slips into my mouth. It coaxes my tongue to join his dance. Maybe he's the one with the bread crumbs that leads me safely out of the forest.

When he touches me he makes me want to swear ancient blood oaths to him—not due to any overwhelming fear or excitement, but because of how calm and peaceful he makes me feel inside. How safe and protected.

His mouth moves from mine to trail over my throat, across my collarbone, then briefly nipping each breast. He places soft kisses on my belly and holds his hand there for a long time as if he's willing his child to grow in there—or sensing its essence.

But even if I were already pregnant with someone's child, it would be too soon to know.

Then he moves lower still, his mouth between my legs. I gasp and arch up into him, but he's only teasing me.

"You're already quite spoiled," he says, pulling back. "Roll over onto your stomach."

"Sir?" I'm sure he can taste my fear on the air in the stillness of the room.

"Don't worry. I'm not going to fuck your ass tonight."

I roll onto my stomach.

"Good girl."

I feel the blankets that were pulled back partially only a moment ago, now removed completely.

"Stretch your arms and legs out like an X," he orders.

"A-are you going to tie me?"

"Yes. I want your complete surrender. Do you trust me?"

I don't answer him in words. Instead, I spread my arms and legs out in an X like he requested.

He presses a kiss to my back and murmurs, "Good girl" against my skin.

I gasp as ropes are tied around my wrists and ankles, then tied to what I assume must be the bed posts. I don't know, I haven't actually seen his room. From the roughness of the ropes, I know he wants to leave marks on me. After all he could have used silk, or soft cords, or ties. Does he want Soren and Griffin to see them? Does he want to watch as I sit uncomfortably through breakfast, rope burns on display in the morning light?

I wonder if there's a bigger power struggle than I thought and what that ultimately might mean for me. Whatever's going on with them, it doesn't feel like jealousy. It isn't as though they're each fighting to be the one to win my heart. It's nothing so quaint and prosaic as that. It's about power. Control. It's about who gets to move the pieces across the chess board.

The queen is supposed to be the most powerful piece, but I don't feel it. Maybe I'm only a pawn after all.

Dayne's voice interrupts my thoughts. "I need you to relax for me. Take a deep breath in and then slowly let it out."

I obey him, and when I exhale, I gasp as he pushes something hard and cold and wet inside my ass. Metal? Glass? I don't know what it's made of. But it's only about the thickness of a man's finger.

He presses a hand against my back. "Shhh, Livia. Relax. Everything is okay."

I'm pretty sure Dayne could make me believe this even if the world was literally burning down around me. Just his skin against my skin and his soothing words can make me believe anything. It's a dangerous power to have.

He eases the toy in deeper. At first my muscles tighten against the invasion, but under his calming caresses and his steady voice, I relax, and I feel the tiniest tendril of something that's surprisingly more pleasure than pain. It shouldn't feel good. It's dark and dirty and makes me feel vulnerable and self-conscious in a thousand different ways.

And I wonder if he's in the dark like I am, or if it's merely the illusion of the blindfold and he has full light.

"Stop thinking. Just feel. Surrender. You have no control over this situation."

Even as he says these words, I know if I cried or begged he'd stop. I know this because Dayne's darkness is cloaked in honor, unlike Soren's ruthless storm.

"Give me another slow breath. In. And out."

Dayne could have been a yoga instructor in another life. I follow his direction as he begins to slowly ease the lubed toy in and out of me. My pussy responds with arousal and jealousy that another part of me is being penetrated, and suddenly I want to be fucked. Suddenly I want to feel fullness from both sides. In my cunt and in my ass at the same time.

I'm shocked and unnerved by this thought. It's not possible. I'm not anatomically set up to be able to handle it. I know I'm not. This silent struggle goes on in my mind while Dayne continues to send my nerve endings into overdrive.

The ropes dig into my wrists as I struggle, but I'm not struggling to get away, I'm struggling for more without having to ask for it.

Dayne stops and removes the toy.

"Please," I whisper.

He chuckles. "You want more?"

"Yes, Sir."

He raises my hips and places something underneath me, then he presses me back down on it. It feels like a spongy rubber ball, except it must be flat on the bottom. It's pressed between my legs. And then it starts vibrating.

Without meaning to, I begin to grind on this new toy. Then I feel more lube being pressed into my ass, followed by a toy a bit larger than the last.

"Breathe," he reminds me.

I do, and he slowly eases it inside me.

"Good girl."

I move with both the rubber ball stimulating my clit and the other phallic toy awakening me to surprising new sensations I never knew I could access. I didn't know this could feel good for women. I thought it was only men who could access pleasure this way—as the receptive party.

That's when I notice Dayne's breathing has gone

ragged, and his hand is no longer on my back. He's jerking himself off while he slowly fucks my ass with the toy and the vibrator drives me insane from beneath.

My orgasm crests over me in a sudden wave too powerful to stop. He doesn't turn off the vibrating toy, nor does he stop moving the other one inside my ass. A few moments later he lets out a growl, and I hitch in a breath when I feel warm wetness hit my back.

Dayne removes the toy from my ass, and turns off the vibrations that were pulsing against my clit. But he doesn't untie me immediately.

I'm silent. I can feel his eyes on me. He doesn't go get a towel or wash cloth to clean me up. Instead, he uses his strong steady hands to massage his release into my skin. It's one of the most filthy and erotic things I've ever experienced. And I can't help the moan the slips out of my throat in response.

CHAPTER TWENTY-SIX: LIVIA

THE HONEYMOON

he Present.

IT'S the last day of the honeymoon. Most of the trip has been surprisingly normal after what I witnessed when we first arrived at the resort, and I'm feeling silly for my emotional meltdown that first night. I was just... overwhelmed. And shy. And unsure of who and what I was bound to. For the most part we've spent our resort time at the house, using the attached private pool. They've taken me to several nice restaurants but nothing on the property. When we haven't gone out to eat, we've ordered room service.

On the first full day, the guys took me to Manuel Antonio which has a huge national park with the cutest capuchin monkeys. It was kind of crowded and touristy but nice. We spent time on the beach as well as exploring the varied wildlife that lives in Costa Rica, including the sloth sanctuary. Dayne booked us a behind-the-scenes tour so we got to see baby sloths up close in the nursery and even feed them. Watching Soren feeding a tiny baby sloth while it just stared up at him was surreal and caused me to drift off into a fantasy about him holding our baby.

Over the past few days, we've zip-lined over the rainforest, soaked in natural hot springs, painting each other with warm mud only to get back in the springs to rinse off. And we walked across a huge swinging bridge that I had to be reassured about twenty times wasn't going to snap and kill us all.

With each passing day I feel more comfortable with all of them, not just sexually attracted, but safe—more like the way things felt before I knew they all knew each other. And I'm starting to think somehow this actually could work.

After the first night alone with Dayne, it was a night alone with Griffin, then Soren. It was nice to be able to spoon with each of them in something mirroring traditional intimacy. Then there was a few nights with all of them. Those nights went kind of like the wedding night.

Each night they've prepared me with a range of ever widening anal toys. And aside from that one aspect, this thing with us is starting to feel somehow normal. Domestic almost. Well, and the titles. Even though nothing especially kinky has happened in Costa Rica, they've demanded the titles when we've gone to bed. It's still *Sir* for Dayne and Griffin, and *Master* for Soren—something Soren wants to make sure I don't forget during the power shift of this vacation interlude.

Soren is the roughest when he fucks me. He fucks me like he's trying to use his cock to brand me, to remind me that he will always be inside me and I can never leave him.

I can never go anywhere. But increasingly it's hard for me to think of anywhere else I'd want to be but with them. Even Soren's terrifying nature has started to feel comforting.

The idea of going back to my small lonely apartment and sleeping by myself seems suddenly far more horrifying than the way Soren holds me down, chokes me, and fucks my mouth. The way they pass me back and forth between them, the way they grab and paw at me and make me feel both completely used and completely desired by the time they're finished each night.

It has all started to feel less threatening because they've kept everything private as they've slowly gotten me used to the myriad ways they might take me together.

When I step out of the shower and into Soren's bedroom, there's a black evening gown on the bed, strappy black heels, long black opera gloves, a masquerade-type mask—yes, also in black, and a note:

Put this on, and come downstairs. We're going out. -D

I know Soren hates the way Dayne has taken charge of things on the honeymoon. And I know it won't always be this way, but I've felt safe with Dayne in control. But this... the dress, the sexy shoes, the mask... *we're going out.*

I know what this means. It means he's ready to stop shielding me from the rest of the resort. I take a slow, calming breath and remind myself we're going home tomorrow. Whatever happens tonight, it's just for tonight, then we're going home, and I'll never see any of these people again. And I'll be partly shielded behind a mask. That's something, isn't it?

In these last few days, I've started to trust they'll keep me safe. I jump when I see a reflection in the full length mirror besides my own. I turn to find Soren leaning in the doorway, his arms crossed over his chest. He's dressed sharply in a black suit with a black shirt and tie.

"Drop the towel and dress for me."

My gaze goes to the ground. He always makes me feel so shy. I don't know who this demure girl is that blossoms out in his stern presence.

"Yes, Master." I glance up to find the satisfaction and pleasure on his face at that title.

I drop the towel and obey him. Sometimes putting clothes *on* for Soren is as erotic as taking them off. The dress is form fitting but not too snug and has a high slit up the side that goes so high it reveals the strappy band of the black thong panties I just slipped on. The zipper for this dress is in the front, instead of the back, the little pull dangling right between my breasts. One tiny tug on it and I'd be exposed.

My breasts practically spill out of the dress under Soren's watchful gaze as I sit on the bed and bend to put the shoes on. They have snaps where buckles might otherwise be, making them quick and easy to get on or off.

Next I put on the elegant masquerade mask then the opera gloves.

Soren nods, satisfied with this performance. "Come downstairs."

I follow him down to the main level where Dayne and Griffin stand waiting, both wearing black suits with black shirts and black ties just like Soren's. There are three additional masquerade masks on the table for them. We look like we're attending a secret society funeral.

"Kneel," Soren says, snapping his fingers and pointing to the floor in front of him. And I suddenly understand why this slit is so high. Without the slit, kneeling in this dress would be impossible.

I get on my knees in front of him.

"Take the shoes off and sit back on your heels," he says.

I let out a sigh of relief as I remove the shoes I just put on for him and settle into this more comfortable position. Soren produces a black velvet box from his jacket pocket. He always seems to be the one giving me jewelry. It's somewhat thin and square. He holds the box out to me.

"Open it."

I open it to find a solid gold band. A collar? It's not like the other collars I saw the first night in the lobby. Those collars were all leather dog collars with metal loops and leashes. This is actual jewelry.

Soren takes it out of the box, unlatches it, and locks it around my throat while my head is still bowed.

"It protects you," Dayne says. "No one is allowed to wear jewelry collars at the resort—only the leather ones. A girl in a gold collar is marked as mine and protected. No one else is allowed to touch you but us. Do you understand, Livia?"

I nod. "Yes, Sir."

"Good, let's go." Dayne and Soren walk out the door while Griffin offers a hand to help me up. He steadies me while I put my shoes back on.

I felt a shift in Dayne just now. It's that darker more commanding side—the side that scares me a little and reminds me of Soren.

When we get outside, Dayne holds an arm out to me, and I loop my arm through his as though he's escorting me to Homecoming or something. Griffin and Soren walk directly behind us like they're our bodyguards. The guys are wearing their masquerade masks as well now.

Dayne leads me across the resort grounds into the enormous main building I only caught a glimpse of that first night. I keep my gaze straight forward, avoiding eye contact with the guests we pass. My heartbeat thunders in my chest.

They take me to an elegant ballroom which seems to be dripping in gold, which I'm pretty sure isn't fake. Gold accents on the walls, gold chandeliers, gold accents on furniture. The ceiling is white with complex swirling designs carved into it.

The lighting is low. There's enough light to see everything, but it's an understated illumination. A string quartet plays on a stage at one end of the ballroom. They aren't playing classical music. They're instead playing a darker rock piece re-imagined and arranged for strings.

Champagne and hors d'oeuvres are passed around on trays around us. Dayne grabs a champagne flute from a passing tray and hands it to me. This time I sip. There are no tables in the ballroom, just a wide open space with different types of sex dungeon furniture, as well as leather couches scattered about, mostly along walls. There are large leather tables which double as beds—at the very least they're surfaces to fuck on, judging by the presence of people fucking on several of them.

A couple of the walls are covered in padded leather in what appears to be a supple rich brown with restraints bolted into the walls. All the leather is this color, complementing the white and gold.

Hooks along the walls hold various implements like paddles and crops and floggers and whips. A shelf with a small recessed light shining down on it showcases an assortment of canes. There's already an orgy going on around us, and nobody seems to be shocked by any of the fucking and sucking and whipping occurring in this space.

I take a deep breath as I take it all in and take another gulp of champagne.

We pass several people, including many couples and threesomes. There are a lot of women in collars, some scantily clad, some nude. Everyone wearing clothing is dressed in black. I'm not sure if this goes on all the time or if this is a special event.

Several people say things like: "It's good to see you, Mr. Montgomery," "We haven't seen you in months, Mr. Montgomery," "Is this your new toy, Mr. Montgomery? She's lovely." Absolutely nobody calls him Dayne. They all know him, but it's like they aren't allowed to be familiar with him —at least not in public.

Near the stage with the string quartet is a second raised platform with a very nice very large leather chair adorned with tasteful gold accents. Dayne leads me up the stairs and my heart rate escalates higher. Griffin and Soren are right behind us. They stand on either side behind the chair, looking even more like bodyguards than they did on the walk down here.

The music stops playing, and a spotlight shines down on us. Everyone in the ballroom stops what they were doing to turn and look at us. I think Dayne is going to say something to the assembled guests—like maybe some sort of welcome speech—but all he does is nod toward the string quartet.

Slow dark strains of cello music fill the otherwise now quiet ballroom. The cello is soon joined by one of the violins. Dayne turns me to face the assembled guests, his large hands wrapped possessively around my shoulders.

He leans next to my ear. "Are you going to be a good girl and do everything you're told?"

"Yes, Sir," I whisper.

"Good. Take off the shoes." He relieves me of my champagne flute, the alcohol starting to give me just enough buzz to bolster my courage. I remove the shoes, grateful for the easy snaps at my ankles.

When I'm finished, he turns me to face him, Griffin, and Soren. He pulls the front part of my dress back to reveal my thong—but only to the guys. My back is to our guests and the rest of the dress still shields me so no one else can see. He slides the panties down over my hips and orders me to step out when they reach the ground. Then he picks the thong up and tosses it out into the crowd.

I'm turned back around in time to see a man snatch it out of the air and put it into his pocket. He smiles, raises his glass, and nods at Dayne. I shiver at this, growing wetter between my legs thinking about my panties in that stranger's pocket, my panties that were already soaked with evidence of my arousal.

Dayne doesn't have to tell me what's about to happen. I know. At least I have some idea. He gently tugs the zipper down until the gown is fully unzipped, then he pushes the straps off my shoulders, and the dress falls to unveil me. I feel like a statue being revealed at an art opening.

I'm not sure how to feel about the fact that I had a spa day and got waxed a couple of days before the wedding. On the one hand I'm well-groomed, but on the other, there's nothing to hide behind. It's a far more intimate level of exposure than if I'd skipped that task.

Soren moves the dress out of our way as Dayne helps me step out of the gathered silk. Then he sits in the chair and points to a spot at his side in front of Soren.

"Kneel," he says, "Facing that way." He gestures out toward the assembled onlookers. I'm still wearing the opera gloves.

I take a deep breath but do as he says.

"Spread your legs. Let them see," he says. He says it loud enough that many of the guests at the party can hear, judging by the anticipatory smirks that grace their faces.

But I comply. His order sends a flutter of excitement into my belly. After I'm positioned the way he wants me, the spell that seemed to fall over the room slowly lifts. Voices begin speaking again in murmured tones that gradually crescendo louder into a din. After another few minutes the sounds of fucking and whipping start to compete with the quartet for dominance and the elegant strings fade into the background.

I feel Soren's hand suddenly move around to grip the front of my throat. He leans close to my ear and whispers, "I need to fuck your mouth. Turn around."

I look up to Dayne as if I need permission for this, but he's talking to Griffin about something. So I turn around, still on my knees. My hands shake as I unzip Soren and free his huge cock from his pants. I'm still not used to his size. Griffin and Dayne are big, but Soren is... frightening. And I'm not sure the impact will ever truly lessen.

He doesn't let me take him at my own pace, instead, he pushes his hardened cock between my lips and begins to fuck my mouth just as he promised. I start to panic, but when I do he backs off and lets me control the pace so I can lick and suck him the way I know he likes.

Then he speaks. But not to me.

"Colin," Soren says, "I didn't expect to see you here this week."

"Your secretary is a bulldog. The only way I could get to you was to fucking fly to Costa Rica and intercept your honeymoon."

I flinch at the unfamiliar man's voice. I didn't hear him

step onto the platform, and my field of vision has been narrowed to Soren's cock for the last several minutes.

"I'm sorry, we've been busy with the wedding," Soren says. "What was it you needed?"

"I had to find a new CPA because of you, and I had to get ahead of a scandal from rumors which I *believe* originated with you."

Soren continues to stroke my hair. "It wouldn't have happened if you'd kept your mouth shut about my private activities. I'm fairly certain that story you told Harold happened here at the resort. I could get you blacklisted for breaking the NDA."

I freeze at the sound of my father's name. It could be another Harold, but Colin *did* say CPA and while there are fewer names that sound more like they could belong to an accountant than Harold, I'm pretty sure they *are* talking about my father.

"Oh fuck you," Colin says. "You owe me."

Soren laughs. "Oh really? And what do I owe you?" his grip around the back of my neck tightens as he realizes I'm doing more listening than pleasuring. "That's it," he coos softly to me when I return my focus to him. "Good girl."

I feel my entire body blush because this stranger is standing far too close to us and is no doubt leering down at me, no doubt appraising my technique.

"Well," Colin says, "You could loan me your girl for a night. That might make up for it."

I tense, and for a moment I'm actually afraid Soren might agree to this. Even though I'm sure Dayne and Griffin would put a stop to it. Even though I'm wearing the gold collar that's supposed to protect me. Even though I know how possessive Soren is.

Soren laughs. "If that little business of yours doesn't work out, you could go into comedy."

"The little business that sits higher on the Forbes list than yours? Okay, Soren. I'm sure your stockholders would love to know about this arrangement you have. Can you afford the scandal? Can she?"

There's silence for what feels like forever where I assume there's some hostile manly stare down going on. Finally Soren says... "I could get you something. Something soft and sweet, and you can keep her forever. With conditions of course."

"I'm intrigued."

"Give me a few weeks to arrange it. I'll have my bulldog secretary set up a meeting."

While I didn't hear Colin come up on the platform, I do hear him leave. My mind is spinning trying to figure out what Soren plans to give this dirtbag to keep him quiet.

When he comes, I'm so distracted I don't swallow. In truth I can't believe he managed to keep a hard-on during that tense discussion, but maybe it was the thrill of his frenemy watching him getting his cock sucked by a woman he wanted to *borrow*.

Soren puts his fingers under my chin and raises my gaze to his. "Stand up. Now." His order is harsh, even harsh for him. It calls both Griffin and Dayne's attention when I stand.

"What's going on?" Griffin says. Dayne is standing too, now.

"I'm going to punish her."

"What the fuck for?"

He raises my face to show Griffin and Dayne the evidence of my crime.

"No. I don't know what the fuck is wrong with you, but

you're not taking whatever shit you've got going on out on Livia," Griffin says.

"You were the one who wanted a trade," Soren says. "This is *mine*. Do you want to trade back?"

Trade what for what? I have no idea what deal is going on behind-the-scenes with these two, or what they've been bartering that has to do with me. And then I can't take it anymore. I just crumple to the ground and start sobbing, just like the first night in the tub. Then one of them is on the ground with me, holding and rocking me.

I think it must be Dayne or Griffin, but it's Soren's voice in my ear. "I'm sorry. Griffin's right. I can't punish you when I'm angry. I'm not even angry at you. It's that dipshit, Colin."

He presses a kiss to the top of my head.

Griffin shows up a few minutes later with a warm wet washcloth and cleans me up. The mood, my arousal, everything is ruined. And this is the last night of the trip. I know they wanted to do things with me here at the party. And there's a part of me that wanted to do those things too. I was just getting to the point where I felt like I could trust them to start exploring these fantasies. These are *my* fantasies. It's not just theirs. I'm not just their puppet being forced along to obey whatever. I get off on this too. I don't like to admit that to myself but I do.

"Come on, let's go back to the house," Soren says.

I shake my head. "No, we were going to... do things, and it's our last night here."

"It's not the end of the world," Dayne says. "We've each got some work we have to get caught up on, but we were planning on coming back in a couple of months. We could stay longer then. There's plenty of time for this."

I take a long look around. Despite what felt like the

hugest drama in the world to me five seconds ago, I realize everyone at the party is too busy with the party. They aren't watching us right now. They've got their own stuff going on. Nobody saw what just happened so there's no reason for me to be embarrassed about it. They didn't see Soren lose his temper, and they didn't see me crying. And they can't see anything now with me shielded by Soren's broad body.

"What was going to happen here tonight?" I ask.

Soren sighs. "We drew straws and Dayne got first sex. I got first anal. And Griffin got first punishment. Griff decided he wanted to be a hero and save you from first anal with me and he knows how much I like punishment. So we traded. I was going to punish you tonight anyway. Not because of anger, but because I wanted to do it."

I let all that settle in. Half of me thought Dayne was kidding about drawing straws for me. It's at once both juvenile and barbaric. And I am grateful that Griffin made that trade, though I'm not sure a punishment from Soren is much more comforting.

"And I was going to fuck your ass," Griffin says.

I take in a deep breath. And what? Now we're going to go back to the house because Princess Livia cried? Seriously fuck that. We're doing this.

"Let's do it then," I say.

"Excuse me?" Soren says. It comes out a half laugh.

"Let's do the stuff. It's our last night. I want to do the stuff." I turn to Dayne, "But can you make that Colin guy leave, please?" The idea of him watching this after the conversation I overheard feels wrong.

Dayne arches a brow. "You're asking me to ban Colin?"

"Not like forever. Just... until we leave."

The guys exchange looks. Finally Dayne shrugs. "Sure,

why not? It would amuse me to put Colin in the time-out corner for a while."

Dayne hops off the platform and goes to talk to some guys who look like bouncers. They nod and then go off in search of Colin.

CHAPTER TWENTY-SEVEN: SOREN

THE PUNISHMENT

he Present.

WHAT IN THE fuck is happening right now? So much for thinking Livia couldn't handle my darkness. Though the night's not over yet. I look at her to find she's got this sort of defiant look on her face, and fine. She doesn't want to be spared? I won't spare her.

Before she can catch her breath, I grab her arm and jerk her to her feet. Griffin has showed up again with a black robe to cover her, but I wave him off. No, she's in this. If she's in it, she's in it. There's no sense or point in covering or protecting her modesty now. They've seen everything.

She yelps as I half drag her down the stairs.

"Soren," Griffin warns, ever the hero.

"What?" I snarl. "You heard her. She wants to do the stuff. So I'm going to do the stuff. You're welcome to come watch. And then you can do your stuff. Deal?"

Dayne doesn't try to interfere at least. This whole honeymoon setup is grating on my nerves. I know I agreed to this. I'm the king at home. He's the king at the resort. Griffin is... second at home? Third at the resort? Fuck I don't know. We've always just shared girls with no drama. We've rarely felt the need to create this hierarchy of possession or keep score. Because with every other girl we knew it was only temporary. And then there would be someone else to amuse us.

So if we didn't like how the power structure played out, we could just reset with the next one. But Livia is the last one. We all know this on a deep level so we have to get it right. And Dayne has enough sense to back the fuck off right now and not try to play his king of the resort and secret underground kink club card.

Though part of it I think is reputation. If he steps in and rescues her too much in public it makes him look weak. Welcome to my world, motherfucker.

By this point the music has stopped, and we're drawing attention. Guests are becoming interested again in our activities. Fantastic, I love giving a good show. It's been a long damn time since I've been able to do this.

I can feel the tendrils of fear and adrenaline coming off Livia. It's like it seeps out of her skin, into mine, into my bloodstream making my own blood pump harder and my own heart match the erratic rhythm of hers. I don't reassure her because I don't want to reassure her. She needs to know what she said yes to and that she doesn't get to fuck around with these things. So she'd better be sure.

I'm not angry now at least. Not at her. Not even at Colin. I know something that will get Colin off my ass and appease him, but all I care about in this moment is the gift I've just been given. Finally, I get to punish her.

I take her to the center of the room and space is made. People break their scenes and move out of the way, forming a circle around us. Every eye in this place is riveted to us. I turn to the string quartet and they rush to fill the empty space with music again.

I don't know the name of the piece they've selected, but it's dark, intense, and seductive.

I point imperially at the ground in front of me. "Kneel," I say. My voice is hard, short, and clipped. And it makes her flinch.

She gets down on her knees and looks up at me. Real fear is back, and I'm a sick son of a bitch for being turned on by it. A tear slides down her cheek and I grip her chin, lean down, and lick it off her face. She shudders under the caress of my tongue.

"Tell me, slut, what is it you did to earn punishment tonight?" I ask the question loud enough that our assembled audience can hear. They are hanging on every word now.

They've no doubt spent the entire week trying to catch a glimpse of our new toy, wondering when we'd make an appearance with her and if we might share her. They know the gold collar means no. But they can still watch. We'll allow them that privilege at least.

Well not Colin, poor guy. He's been escorted off the property. I have no idea how long Dayne banned him for, but I do sort of love it. He earned that for even asking to touch her. He's not new. He knows the rules here.

"F-for not swallowing, Master," she says. Her voice is so quiet.

"Louder. They need to know your transgression."

"For not swallowing, Master," she says louder, and when she looks up at me her eyes are those twin blue flames again. They say *I can take whatever you have to give.* Oh yeah? Show me.

"And what else are you being punished for?"

She looks confused. "I-I don't know, Master."

"Don't you? Don't think I didn't catch you looking to Dayne for permission to suck me off earlier. Let's be clear... I saw you first. If you need anyone's permission for anything, it's mine. Is that clear, Mrs. Kingston?"

It's the first time I've called her by her new last name in public. And I can tell our guests didn't realize things were so much more permanent with Livia. They thought she was just another diversion. I'm sure there will be gossip wondering why she isn't Mrs. Montgomery.

"Y-yes, Master," she says.

I glance up to the platform to find Dayne lounging in his big leather chair, shaking his head and chuckling. Griffin has moved onto the main floor and stands just at the edges.

"Be useful and bring me a cane, Griff."

"Soren..."

"Bring. Me. A. Cane. As soon as I finish here, you get to deflower our little anal virgin."

Multiple gasps ripple throughout the circle. People here are so jaded. Dayne doesn't allow anyone underage anywhere near the resort, so it's been a long time since they've gotten to see a virgin anything.

There's a part of me that wishes it was me doing the honors, but Griff is right, it's really too much for her first time.

A few minutes later, Griffin returns and passes a bamboo cane to me.

"Livia, I want you to bow all the way to the floor, arms stretched out in front of you, palms flat, head resting on the floor. And you will count. You're getting ten."

"Soren..." Griffin says again.

I round on him. "I swear to fuck, Griff. If you say another goddamned word, I'm caning your ass next."

He glares at me but backs off. Livia is trembling on the ground. The music has stopped again, everyone, including the quartet watches inside this pin-drop silence.

I turn my attention back to Livia. "After you count each one, you will say Thank you, Master."

She can only nod. She's already crying, and I haven't even touched her yet. What is this weird feeling in my chest? Is that fucking guilt? This only makes me want to cane her harder. I don't want to be soft with her. I don't want to be soft at all.

The cane slices through the air as I lay the first welt across her ass. She gasps in shock and surprise. She probably hasn't even been seriously spanked before. And I'm starting her with this.

"Mrs. Kingston?" I say.

"O-one. Thank you, Master."

Shit, I should have gone for five. I am an absolute irredeemable monster right now. But this voice in my head doesn't stop me because it never has before. And even as the guilt curls around my heart for causing her pain—my body still responds the same way. My dick is rock hard.

I continue the punishment, and by five, she is wailing. I glance over to find Griffin glaring daggers at me. He wouldn't succeed, but he looks like he may at least try to pull me off her. And soon. I look to Dayne, and he doesn't look thrilled either. But he's not going to intervene.

I can't continue this. If I wanted this, I should have trained her for it. As much as I hate to admit it, Dayne is right. This is too much too soon. I take a few steps away from her.

"Beg me for forgiveness," I growl down at her.

She's sobbing. She doesn't raise her head from the floor because I didn't tell her to. She is such a good girl.

"M-Master, please, forgive me. Please..." That last please comes out in a broken sob as she tries to catch her breath.

"What will you do to earn this forgiveness?" I ask.

"A-anything. Please, please I'll do anything."

I let out a long sigh. This girl is going to break me. "I'll offer you a trade. It's a one time offer because you are mine. Suck me off right... in front of all these people, and I will forgive you and cancel out the other five you owe me. Do you accept this trade?"

"Yes, Master," she says quickly.

She pushes herself up and crawls to me. She's so eager to please me now, to make the pain end, to stop me from leaving more angry welts across her flesh that she doesn't need direction. She doesn't need to be told to crawl. She just does it. She fumbles with my zipper, and I help her because that's the kind of guy I am.

I'm pulsing and hard and desperate to get inside her mouth. But I don't skull fuck her, I let her take this at her own pace this time. Tears are flowing down her cheeks as she looks up at me. I let out a groan as she takes me into her warm, wet mouth. I gasp at the hard suction of her mouth that can barely take me to begin with.

She relaxes her throat and takes me deeper than she's taken me before. Fuck that's amazing.

This is the most eagerly enthusiastic blow job I've ever received from her or any other woman, and it'll take me less than a minute to come at this rate. I wipe the tears off her cheeks as she fellates me like she has a master's degree in oral sex.

This time when I come, she swallows every drop. "Good girl," I say, as I massage her throat. "Such a very good girl."

My dick slips out of her mouth, and she zips me back up. I take her hands in mine and help her to stand. I press a kiss to her forehead.

"You're forgiven. Now you're going to offer your ass to Griffin like the good whore you are, do you understand?"

There is something soft, pliant, and completely surrendered in her voice when she says, "Yes, Master."

CHAPTER TWENTY-EIGHT: LIVIA

THE DEFLOWERING

he Present.

THERE ARE SO many eyes on me right now. So many strangers just watched me naked, kneeling at Soren's feet, getting caned and then... sucking his dick. I feel humiliated along with other things which I don't have words for. But then I also feel safe—and I don't understand that one after what just happened—but it's swirling around in the soup of emotions anyway. I could deny it, but it's still there.

And then the loudest feeling... I feel so turned on right now, so hot I think I might spontaneously combust. My wetness drips down my thighs, and I know that if I bend over anything right now, at least a few people will be able to see just how aroused I am. Though I'm sure they know. My nipples are so hard they're painful. And the ambient temperature in this room is comfortable, so it isn't from cold.

My eyes lock with Griffin's and then Soren steps aside as he takes over.

"Bend over that table with your palms flat stretched out in front of you," Griffin says.

I can see his erection through his pants. The table he points to is soft leather and is just the right height for me to lean over and stretch my body across, giving him easy access to my ass. The welts still burn from Soren's cane and Griffin spends a few minutes gently stroking them once I've assumed the position he wants me in.

Dayne pushes through the crowd and lays a black leather case that looks a bit like a briefcase on the table beside us then takes a few steps back. It's me and Griffin now, the center of attention.

My cheek rests on the table as I watch Griffin open the box. Inside are about ten metal phallic objects. I recognize them from the times we've used them this week. They're for anal penetration and training. The guys have also used butt plugs, keeping them inside me for long periods to get me used to the fullness.

The toys in this box start at finger-size and they slowly move up until they are at least as big as Griffin's cock. If I can take that last toy, I know I can take him. We haven't yet made it through all the toys but we've come close.

Also inside the box is a large tube of lubricant. I gasp as he massages a healthy amount around my entrance, pushing a heavily lubed finger inside me. I can't help moving against him. Over the past week I've started to really like this—much more than I'm comfortable admitting.

Though it still feels intensely vulnerable and a little scary and a lot dirty. And though I'm still self-conscious, I can't deny the pleasure that comes with it. The fear, the tiny bit of pain that melts into surrender and sensations I've never felt before these men came into my life.

I feel an intense gaze on me, and I glance over to find Soren standing at the edge of the crowd. He holds my gaze in his as Griffin slowly works me up through the toys. At each addition in size, I have to remember to breathe and relax, and open to him.

He strokes my back. "You're doing great," he whispers. "Just open, accept it inside you."

These words make me wetter. I continue to watch Soren as Griffin prepares me for his cock. My body responds easier now, more quickly. I've learned how to relax, how to surrender this part of myself to them even though it's only been toys before tonight.

The string quartet is suddenly playing again, and I wonder if Dayne told them to play something. It's slow and soothing, and it helps me breathe. The music itself is a breath moving slowly in and out like the tide.

Griffin leans his body over mine, and I feel the fabric of his suit against my bare back. He's still fully clothed, I realize. He kisses my back, and then my shoulder and neck and the shell of my ear.

"Take a deep breath, Livia. The next thing going inside you is my cock."

He barely gives me time to take the breath before his lubed cock is pushing inside my ass. I let out a strangled cry but it's all pleasure, no pain. It's so different than the toys because it's the softness of naked skin gliding against naked skin. I grip and claw at the table seeking anything to hold onto as he drives into me stealing my breath with each thrust.

"You love anal, don't you, you dirty little slut," he growls close to my ear.

"Yes, Sir." It comes out on a desperate mewling whimper.

By the time he comes I'm about to lose my mind with need. I'm so close, it would take so little for me to go over the edge. But before I can, Griffin does. He pulls out and releases on my back with a groan.

My eyes find Soren's again. Something inside me wants to know how he feels about what he just saw. His gaze is filled with lust, and he's hard again, his erection straining against his pants. He breaks away from the crowd and comes toward me with purpose.

Griffin helps me up, but he doesn't clean off my back. Nor does he rub it into my skin like Dayne did the first night in his bedroom. Instead, it just slides down my back, making me feel so dirty, but in the best possible way.

One of the leather sofas is pushed out into this wide open space we've claimed and Soren sits on it. He undoes his pants for the third time tonight and motions me forward.

I don't walk to him. I crawl. And I know from his amused smirk that he's pleased with this.

When I reach him, he says, "Ride my cock."

I, rise from the ground, straddle, and sink down on him, trying once again to get used to his size. He's still fully dressed, just like Griffin was when he fucked my ass. I don't think they're shy about public nudity. It's about power. The power of their suits pressed up against my nakedness. Their command tangling with my vulnerability.

I ride him, my breasts pressing against his suit as he grips my ass, re-igniting the flaming pain from the cane marks. Then he soothes and strokes them, all the while urging me to ride him harder.

Then another set of hands is on me, pulling me back

enough so he can stroke my breasts, pinching my nipples. I turn to find my mouth captured in Dayne's kiss.

"You can't leave this room until I fuck your ass in front of my guests," he growls into my mouth.

He pushes me back on top of Soren, who has stopped fucking and holds me still. More cold lube is pressed inside my ass as Soren holds me wide open for Dayne. I blush harder at the people standing at just the right angle to see this lewd display.

"Breathe," Dayne reminds me.

When I exhale, he eases his cock inside my ass.

"That's it," he says, "Everything is okay."

It's a tight and uncomfortable squeeze, and at first I feel panicked with Soren filling me from one side and Dayne from the other, but they are both very still as I adjust, Soren stroking my cheek while Dayne pets my hair.

After a moment they begin to move in tandem, and it is the most exquisite feeling. All I can do is grip Soren's shoulders and hang on for the ride as the two of them fuck me together, their bodies demanding I simply receive them. Soren grips the back of my neck and pulls me in for a devouring kiss just as my orgasm is cresting.

I moan and cry into his mouth, tears streaming down my cheeks while he and I come together. He holds me in his arms as Dayne pulls out and comes on my back, joining Griffin's earlier mark. And all of it is sliding down over Soren's cane welts.

I look around, seeking Griffin. I find him sitting in Dayne's leather chair on the platform. He smiles, his devastating dimple claiming me from a distance, and he just winks at me. Then I drop my head back onto Soren's shoulder.

CHAPTER TWENTY-NINE: LIVIA

THE HONEYMOON'S OVER

he Present.

It's Saturday. We've been back from our honeymoon for almost a week and have spent most of that time—when we haven't been working or fucking—moving my things to Soren's place a bit at a time. Griffin and Dayne have been fully moved in for two months now, so all efforts have been focused on moving my things from my crappy apartment to Soren's estate.

It's hard to think of this as my home, even though I understand it intellectually. While I'd been stressing over the wedding and worrying about what would happen once we were all together, I hadn't had much time to realize that I'd never again have to contemplate which bill wasn't getting paid that month. I would never again eat another package of Ramen noodles standing over the kitchen sink. My parents could have helped, but I didn't want to burden them. And now that life and all its uncertainty is over, traded in for the new uncertainty of these men.

The front door stands open. Soren is outside getting another one of the boxes from the moving truck we finally got around to renting. I think Dayne is in the kitchen. Griffin grabs me from behind and spins me around, pinning me against the wall, holding my wrists over my head.

He claims my mouth with his and presses his knee between my legs.

"Ride it," he growls.

I grind against him while he continues to ravage my mouth. Then I hear a gasp. And it isn't coming from either of us.

We both look up, startled to find my mother and Macy standing in the entryway gaping at us.

"I-I'm sorry, the door was open," my mother says.

Macy looks from me to Griffin, then back to me, then runs out of the house.

By this point, Griffin and I have put several feet of respectable distance between us. Dayne walks in then with a bowl of ice cream, looking curiously from my mother to Griffin and then to me.

Soren walks in with one of my boxes and sits it down on the coffee table. "What's wrong with Macy? She's locked herself in the car and is hysterical." Then he takes in the scene, his eyes narrowing. "What's going on in here?"

My mother looks like she's about to have some kind of fit because she thinks Soren almost caught me cheating. She's got a disappointed look on her face like she can't believe I would do this to him. I wonder how much more disappointed she'll be when she knows that the truth is so much worse than she thinks.

Griffin finally breaks the tense silence. "Macy and Livia's mother walked in on us kissing."

"I—the door was standing open," my mother says. She can't meet my eyes. I know it's about to get worse because there's no way we're about to play out some fake cheating drama like a soap opera.

Soren sighs. "I'm sorry you had to see that, Judith."

"I—wait, what?"

He turns to Griffin, "Griff, what the fuck?" Then realizing he just cursed in front of my mother, turns back to her and says, "I apologize, Judith. It slipped."

"It's *our* house!" Griffin says. "I can kiss Livia in our house!"

"I'm sorry," my mother says, and I feel just awful for her.

Soren shakes his head. "Nonsense, Judith. It's the middle of the day, and the door was standing open. You saw me outside. You couldn't have known."

"Wait, what exactly is going on?" my mother says.

Griffin takes my hand in his. My mom notices, and her eyes grow large. She looks quickly to Soren as if expecting him to get angry and fly into a jealous rage, but Soren doesn't react.

I finally find my own voice. "Mom, I think you should sit down. Why don't you come into the kitchen and let me make you some tea."

Griffin lets go of my hand as I guide my mother into the kitchen. There's already a hot kettle of water on, so I pour some into two tea cups.

I turn to the guys. "Does anyone else want tea?"

They shake their heads and come join us at the table. Once I've fixed tea for my mother and myself with milk and sugar and some pink and green thumbprint cookies I picked up from the bakery earlier in the week, I sit and take a long deep breath.

We all look at each other as my mother sips her tea. She's a smart woman, and I know she has to suspect at least some part of what's happening here no matter how high her denial may be.

"Look," Soren says, "There's no easy or nice way to put this. And I don't expect you to approve, but I hope, for Livia's sake you'll keep this a secret. There's no reason to cause conflict within our families and none of our businesses needs a scandal. It's your daughter's future we're talking about. It benefits no one, least of all Livia, for this to get out."

"Keep what a secret?" my mother's voice is going shrill and she's about ten seconds from *Olivia Elaine Fairchild, you'd better explain what's going on right now*!

Dayne chooses this moment to interject. He's still eating his ice cream. "Judith..."

"I'm sorry, who are you?" my mother says.

"I'm Dayne Montgomery. I was the groomsman at the wedding. I'm Soren's best friend. One of them at least."

She turns back to Griffin. "And you? You were the best man, right? Griffin?"

"Yes Ma'am," Griffin says.

Dayne looks a little hurt that she remembered Griffin but not him, but he continues. "We're all married to your daughter, the three of us."

I'm not sure I would have led with *that* statement, but okay. I guess we're going with a *rip the band-aid off* approach.

My mother turns pale. "What do you mean you're all married to Livia? You can't all be married to her. The state doesn't allow... it's illegal... and immoral and..." She turns her glare on me now. "Olivia Elaine Fairchild..."

Here we go.

"Explain yourself this instant!"

I knew it was in there.

"It's true. I'm legally married to Soren along with a prenup, and I have private legal contracts with Griffin and Dayne. They aren't called marriage, but they address the same legal issues."

"But... what about children?"

"We'll raise them together," Soren says. "We're a family."

"But..."

Griffin puts a hand over my mother's which inexplicably seems to calm her. To be honest, I think all women have a bit of a crush on Griffin. It's the dimple. It's so disarming.

"We never intended for you or anyone else to find out about this because we know most people wouldn't understand or approve. And the last thing we would ever want to do is cause Livia any pain or harm," Griffin says.

My gaze shifts to Soren, wondering if what Griffin says is true and if Soren agrees with it. Obviously he *does* enjoy causing me pain, but maybe not harm.

My mother shakes her head. "I just don't understand how this happened. Livia, I don't understand why you couldn't just have a nice traditional marriage like your father and I have."

Dayne speaks again. "Actually, polyandry is quite traditional. At least it was with my ancestors. The church had a hell of a time getting the Celtic tribes to stop doing it."

"Poly what?"

"It means one woman with multiple husbands," Soren says. "And while it may not provide very much comfort.

Dayne is right. There was a time and place when normal respectable ethical society was just fine with the kind of relationship we have. It's not some new modern weird alternative lifestyle. We don't expect you to like it. We just need you not to try to break it."

Except that we *are* in some new modern weird alternative lifestyle. But my mother doesn't need to know that.

"And are you in relationships with other women? If she gets three men... then..."

"No," Soren says. "It's only Livia. And it will only *be* Livia."

"I just don't understand..." she says, still at a loss. "Aren't you jealous of each other?"

"No," Dayne says. "We're a unit. It's not as though Livia is going to choose one of us and dump the others."

Yes, because I can't. But I definitely won't be sharing that informational nugget with my mother. And honestly after the honeymoon I'm not sure I would ever want to pick one or leave any. Somehow in the space of a week I no longer understand why I resisted this.

Soren speaks again. "Judith, we don't expect you to understand. It's very unconventional, and to you it might feel unstable and insecure, or even dangerous. We just want you to know that we love your daughter and we will take care of her. She is safe. She is loved. She is provided for. All the contracts protect her financially should one of us be crazy enough to abandon her." He's looking at me while he says this.

Is all of that really true? Is this the only way he can say these words to me?

"Mom, you can't tell anyone, okay?"

My mother laughs bitterly. "Are you kidding? Your father would have a heart attack, then he'd rise from the grave and kill the three of them in their sleep. No, I won't tell anyone. Soren is right, no good can come of it. But when children come, you know eventually it might slip out. Kids won't understand why they can't talk about this."

"We'll deal with that when the time comes," Soren says. "By that point we'll have all been together long enough that more people will be willing to give us a chance because they'll see how long it's already worked."

"I need to go talk to Macy," I say. "Will you be okay if I...?"

"Go," my mother says. "I want to hear from them how this all came about."

I'm sure they're going to give her a very edited version of the facts, but I'm grateful to get away from the table and out of Soren's giant house which suddenly feels stifling and small.

I find Macy locked in the passenger side of my mother's car, bawling her eyes out. I knock on the window.

"Go away!" Even with the glass between us muffling her voice, I can still hear her clearly.

"Please, Macy, we need to talk." Suddenly I wish at least one of the guys was with me, though probably not Griffin.

Finally she rolls her window down. "You knew I liked Griffin! I can't believe you would cheat on Soren! He loves you! What? One rich perfect gorgeous man wasn't enough for you?"

Oh. Yeah. Macy still thinks she walked in on cheating.

"I'm not cheating on Soren. I'm with all three of them."

"All *three*? Who's the third one?"

I forgot she didn't see Dayne.

"Dayne," I say.

"So you're basically fucking the entire wedding party? Fabulous. Don't save any good guys for anybody else, Livia, it's fine. It's not like the dating pool isn't totally fucked up for all of us as it is," she says sarcastically.

I go around to the driver's side and knock on the window. She grudgingly unlocks the door, and I slip inside. The keys are in the ignition, and the AC is running on full blast.

"Are you going to tell anyone?" I ask. "You know people won't understand. And it would kill my father."

She looks away out the window again. "Liv, we've been best friends since we were five, since the day in kindergarten when you yelled at the kids who were bullying me and invited me to sit at your table for lunch. You know I'm not going to say anything. You know I have your back."

I bite my bottom lip and look out my own window. I can't tell my mother the real truth, but maybe I can tell Macy? I wonder if the risk is too great to have a single confidant outside of my official arrangement.

I risk it because Macy could already destroy everything if she wanted. She's seen too much and knows too much and already has the power, but I know she won't because she's still that little girl I rescued when we were five.

"I didn't intend on being with three men. You know how things were after I broke up with Robbie? How depressed I was because guys could just string women along and keep them as girlfriends, even live-in girlfriends without really giving them a life or commitment or any protection or security?"

Macy nods, turning more fully toward me. She's stopped crying at least. It's as if she knows I'm about to drop something big on her.

"Well, I discovered a way to stop them from doing that. My plan was to date multiple men casually while getting to know them well and seeing who was the most compatible and who was willing to offer me marriage. That way I wouldn't get overly invested in the wrong man or waste a lot of time on someone who couldn't give me what I wanted and was just stringing me along and playing with my heart. It put the power back in my hands. The plan was to end up with one man. The right man."

Macy just stares at me like I'm a complete stranger, which makes me feel more than a little defensive.

"Men date like this all the time! You know how it is... the confirmed bachelor playboy who plays the field indefinitely until he randomly decides to settle down, taking his sweet time about it. I was doing the same thing. Except I wasn't sleeping with them. I was getting wined and dined. You know this is fair."

"But you ended up settling down with *three.*" She practically shrieks that last word at me.

"Not by my choice," I say.

Her eyes widen. "What do you mean by that? How is it not by your choice? Did someone make you get together this way with three men?"

"Soren did. I was dating all three of them, and they found out about each other. It turns out they already knew each other. Fraternity brothers, if you can believe it. I mean I knew it was a small world at the top but... wow it really is. They decided they were sharing me, and if I said no, Soren said he would... Macy he knows about spring break."

Macy's eyes grow huge, and I know she knows exactly which spring break I mean. It wasn't like we were disposing of bodies every year in our free time. "H-how could he know about that?"

"I don't know. He had an investigator look into me... and... I have no idea how he could have found out. I've tried and tried to piece it together, but I can't. Somehow he did.

He's smart. There must have been some tiny odd thing that sent him down a rabbit hole. I don't know. But he said if I didn't marry them, he'd destroy both of us."

I can see she's deeply conflicted. Her anger has shifted from me hogging all the men in the world to Soren. I know she wants to kill him, or report him to the police, or something.

"We have to find a way to get you away from him, away from them. There has to be a way..."

I shake my head. "Don't, Macy." I take a deep breath. "I think I want this now—the three of them." This may be the first time I've admitted this to myself. Hearing it out loud is strange and unsettling.

"How? He's such a... monster." Her face is horrified, filled with a new kind of judgment.

"Just don't, okay? He's meeting my needs. They all are."

I don't have to say anything else because Macy and I have had big long talks about deep dark twisted fantasies. Over boxes of wine. Over margaritas. During late night slumber parties through the years.

"Oh." It's all she can say. And I can tell she's struggling between the absolute evil of Soren's behavior and the fact that it's *meeting my needs*.

"I don't understand how this is going to work," she says.

"That's what my mother said."

"Your *mom* knows?"

"Not what you do, not that this arrangement wasn't my choice. I'd rather she think I'm a slutty nymphomaniac than a hostage."

"Do you think they'd ever let you go?"

I shake my head. "No." I glance up at the tower on one side of the house—the one Soren threatened to lock me in if I tried to escape him. I still think he'd do it, and I wish I could be more angry and indignant about it. I wish I could hate him, hate them. The truth is, I want to be in their cage. It feels oddly secure.

I can see how torn my friend is. I've felt all those same feelings. I know her well enough to know there's a part of her that wants to rescue me, a part of her that wants to be happy for me, and a part of her that might be a tiny bit jealous, then a giant part of her that feels crazy for everything but the rescue part. All these feelings play across her face in quick repeating succession until I'm afraid she'll short circuit or something.

Finally she sighs. "Even if you weren't a hostage, how could this work? How can it last? This isn't realistic."

"Well, Dayne appears to be a history buff who knows all about how his ancestors supposedly made it work, so maybe he's got the recipe to the secret sauce stashed away somewhere."

Macy leans her head back against the head rest, looking up at the interior roof of the car. "Fuck. Don't hate me Liv, but part of me doesn't care if you're a hostage. Look at them. They're gorgeous and successful. I'm not going to lie, I'm totally jealous. I'd take that cage, too."

Is she actually teasing me about this? We might survive after all. I'll just have to remember to lock the front door.

"I'm willing to teach my dating methods for the low low price of your silence," I say.

She laughs, and that's when I know we're going to be okay. She won't tell my secrets, and she won't judge me. Deep down I think I already knew this.

"How big was your crush on Griffin?" I ask, still feeling bad that she'd hoped to get together with him.

Macy sighs. "I really liked him, and it hurt me when I saw you kissing him, but I mean it's not like we dated or anything. I just thought he was hot. I thought I could have the fairy tale like you."

This admission crushes me. If anybody deserves the fairy tale it's Macy with her adorable auburn hair and freckles and all her historical wedding facts.

"It's the dimple isn't it?" I say.

"God, yes, the dimple kills me. But he did say he had a girlfriend at the reception, so it isn't like he led me on or anything. Wait... he doesn't have a girlfriend, right? Like, someone besides you?"

I shake my head. "He doesn't have a girlfriend."

We sit in almost comfortable silence for several minutes until I finally say, "Macy?"

"Yeah?"

"Thanks."

"For what?"

"For being someone I could share this with. You don't know how big of a relief it is to have someone else who knows the truth."

We spend the next hour or so talking in more detail about how all of this came about. She's heard all about Soren but she'd missed out on the stuff about Griffin and Dayne and how I met them. I jump when someone knocks on the driver's side window.

"You're in my seat."

I look up to find my mother standing there. I open the door and get out.

"We're going to head back," my mom says. "Is Macy okay, now?"

"Yeah. We talked it out. Are *we* okay?"

"Why wouldn't we be okay? You're a grown adult, and I already liked Soren. Griffin and Dayne are working on winning me over. No promises that I'm ever going to be even a little okay with this, but we'll see. I'm willing to keep an open mind."

"And a secret?" I ask.

"And a secret," she confirms.

She gives me a hug and gets back into the car. I'm glad to see that at least her color is back to normal.

"Oh wait, Mom, what were you coming over for?"

She laughs. "We were just going to the spa for mani-pedis and wanted to know if you wanted to come along, but we'll do it another time. I think we all have a lot to process, and you've still got unpacking to do."

I watch them pull out of the driveway filled with the same worries they are, wondering if this can possibly last long term or if it's just a dream that must someday end in tragedy.

CHAPTER THIRTY: SOREN

HEIRS

New Year's Day. Eight years in the future.

WE'RE ALL AT MY PARENTS' house for our annual New Year's Day tradition. Except there hasn't been much football today. My parents, along with Dayne, Griffin, and I are out helping Dayne's seven-year-old twin boys build a snow man. Griffin's little boy, age five, sits on a sled watching us work, gripping pieces of coal and a carrot in his gloved hands. He's waiting to do the fun easy part, letting us do all the work. He's figured this shit out.

Livia watches us from the glassed-in sun room where she's nursing my six-month-old little girl, Lily—named for my mother. At first Dayne and Griff gave me shit for thinking of myself as the leader but not having the strongest swimmers after all—until it looked like we wouldn't be able to conceive.

We didn't understand it. Livia was obviously able to

have kids, and all my tests had come back good. We ran all the tests again and everything was fine. The doctor had joked that maybe my sperm got stage fright. Maybe they suffered from performance anxiety. Or maybe Livia's body saw them as invaders and was killing them on sight. It does happen.

Though it seemed unlikely since it didn't happen with Dayne or Griff. Maybe her body was simply rejecting *me*. Because of what I'd done. After all, it was me who decided we were going to share her—her wishes and needs be damned. It was me who decided to bring Dayne in. It was me who decided I'd find a way to force her hand so she couldn't say no to our proposal—because I couldn't stand the thought that she might say no, or worse, choose Griffin over me. So it would only be right if it was me who couldn't have a child with her—some kind of cosmic punishment balancing the scale and ending my genetic line on this plane of existence forever.

But I guess karma decided a more fitting punishment would be to give me a daughter—someone vulnerable I have to find some way to protect from men like me. I agree with the universe, it is the more fitting punishment. I worry about her and the men she'll date all the time, and she's still many years away from dating. Hell, she's still many years from her first day of school.

I understand with a whole new clarity and respect why Harold was so cold that Christmas Eve when he found out his baby girl was getting married to someone like me.

If some man walks into my house and snidely announces he's marrying my daughter, I might have to bury him in the backyard.

The snowman is done. Little Cade is wobbling in his

layers of clothes to our creation with the coal and carrot to give the snowman a face.

One of the twins, Weston—we call him West, what seven-year-old is called Weston—puts a hat and a scarf on him. And the other twin, Eric, adds some coal buttons to his front. Cade claps delightedly at this frozen miracle we've created.

"Okay, now boys, it's time to bake and decorate Christmas cookies," my mother says in an excited tone, shooing them into the house.

My parents know the boys aren't mine. Early on they didn't, and so they didn't initially know about the struggle Livia and I had to have a child of our own—we'd had to keep that pain secret. But soon after the twins were born we realized the logistical nightmare we'd taken on. It wasn't fair for the boys not to know their other biological grandparents. And when Cade came, the same became true for him.

We waited until the last possible second to tell my parents the truth, but they took it better than anyone else. They love Griffin and Dayne. I think they always wanted more children, and a part of them adopted my friends the moment they met them.

The rest of Livia's family did end up finding out. Her mother was right, kids talk, and it was impossible for them to understand why they couldn't talk about their family. And it was unfair to them. Livia's father did *not* in fact have a heart attack. He's tougher than they all thought. But he hates us guys—me especially—and no doubt spends large portions of his time planning our grisly deaths.

So far no scandals have rocked our businesses.

We spend Thanksgiving each year with Griffin's family, Christmas Eve with Livia's, Christmas Day with Dayne's, and New Year's Eve and New Year's Day with mine. These kids basically get four different Christmases. And I know Lily will be the most spoiled because she's the only little girl. I can tell my mother is lying in wait to start the Disney Princess indoctrination as soon as Lily can focus long enough to absorb it.

Instead of going into the house through the kitchen with everyone else, I enter through the sun room. I bend down to kiss Livia. She looks tired, and even though I'd love to have more kids, I honored the contract and didn't argue with her about getting her tubes tied.

"You want to hold her, Daddy?" she says. "She's all full of milk and content and snoring."

I chuckle and gather up the bundle of fat baby in my arms and sit in the rocking chair across from Livia.

Lily sighs in her sleep and snuggles in against me, her tiny hand splayed on my shoulder.

"Livia, if you could go back in time, knowing everything you know now, would you have said yes to our proposal?"

She arches a brow. "I wasn't given much of a choice."

"I know, I know. You've been a pampered and spoiled hostage practically living in a castle, but seriously, knowing how things have turned out, would you have said yes, voluntarily?"

She stands, and stretches like a cat. She's still got the tiniest bit of post-baby bump which I secretly hope she never loses. I like that last small reminder of her finally carrying my child. In a way I'm glad I was the last to conceive with her because this final form she has taken... it's all mine.

She leans down and kisses me in an echo of my earlier action, then she whispers, "I guess you'll never know."

CHAPTER THIRTY-ONE: LIVIA

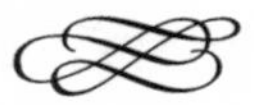

THE FIRST DANCE

Two weeks ago. The Wedding Reception.

THE FIRST DANCE of the bride and groom as a couple is announced, and Soren guides me out onto the dance floor. I glance over to the table where the wedding party sits to find Griffin and Dayne watching me and Macy watching Griffin. The men each watch me so intently I worry other guests will notice. But all eyes are on me and Soren as he expertly sweeps me around the dance floor. Spinning me and dipping me.

We hear "Woo hoos", from the guests and glasses clinking as they try to get us to kiss during our first dance. Soren finds a moment and does just that. He is so charming, and everyone in this ballroom is under his spell, even me—even knowing all that I know about him and fearing all that is to come. Even with this secret we carry with us—

this secret that weighs us all down and makes a happy ending feel so impossible.

I was surprised two months ago when Soren actually agreed to meet with a wedding dance choreographer to learn a dance to go with our song. He doesn't talk to me during the dance, but I don't think it's some Machiavellian strategy on his part, he's just trying to remember our choreography.

I miss a step because I'm so caught up in my head, but he rescues it, leading me so flawlessly through to the next part of the dance that I know no one noticed. They are all too taken with him to notice. Everyone on my side thinks he's the best thing that ever happened to me, and everyone on his side thinks he's a lucky son of a bitch.

And I know in this moment, they are forming opinions about the passion between us. With that kiss at the altar that brought shocked gasps from some of our guests, with this dance, I know they imagine we heat up the sheets with the ferocity of lightning splitting an ancient oak.

Everyone assumes we're already sleeping together. They have no idea just how traditional this wedding really is in that way. The song ends, and everyone claps. Three tables full of fraternity brothers offer loud wolf whistles. Patrice announces that everyone is invited now to join us out on the dance floor.

Soren smoothly passes me off to Griffin who has appeared out of nowhere to take his place. And I realize not only is this song another love song that could easily pass for a first wedding dance song, but it's one of the songs that played on my first date with Griffin on the riverboat.

I glance around to see if any of our guests find it odd that the best man is dancing with me right after Soren. Will

Dayne be next? How will that look? The dances with the parents haven't even happened yet.

I haven't been to that many weddings, but I'm sure this isn't normal. Still, everyone seems so caught up in the day and the party and drinking that no one seems to be paying much attention.

"What about the dances with the parents?" I ask Griffin as he pulls me in probably closer than he should in public, even for a slow dance.

He leans closer to my ear. "Patrice scheduled it this way. She set it up so you have the first dance with Soren, then all the guests can dance, and then the band will take a break. When they come back, the parents dances will be announced."

"Oh. Okay." I wonder who told Patrice to schedule it this way, and it makes me even more suspicious that the wedding planner from hell—someone who somehow knows Soren—is probably privy to far more details of our arrangement than I would like. Though maybe it's only my imagination. After all, Soren can be persuasive without offering any details or explanations.

"But what about the parents? Surely they think they've been skipped over?"

"Patrice told them about the schedule and how we're doing things. She made up an excuse that it allows the guests to get out on the dance floor sooner and get the party rolling and that right after the band break is the perfect time for the other formal dances."

Does the bride dance with the members of the groom's wedding party? I don't know. I feel like it's something I should know. Macy would know.

I wonder if Griffin got me next because of some hierarchy the men have fought out amongst themselves or if it's so Macy doesn't get to him first.

I glance over to find Macy dancing with Soren. So maybe it doesn't look too weird. He's dancing with the maid of honor. I'm dancing with the best man.

Griffin notices my nervousness about this and leans close to my ear to whisper, "It's perfectly normal for the bride to dance with the best man and the groom to dance with the maid of honor. Relax. And Dayne is next with you. Soren will dance with Cheryl while he's with you. No one will notice anything. No one will think anything we don't want them to think."

But *we* know why the dances are happening in this odd order, because all three of my men take precedence over any of the other dances, and it's been smoothly organized to make it so. All the guests are crowding the dance floor so no one can take too strong of a notice of the chemistry between me and Griffin or me and Dayne for that matter.

"Why wasn't I told about this?" I ask. At no point during the wedding planning was any of this mentioned.

"We didn't want you to be more stressed out than you were," Griffin said. "Anyway, you knew you'd be dancing with us at the reception."

That's true, but it didn't occur to me that they would get me first right after Soren. But I agree it's best I wasn't told. I would have been a nervous wreck worrying someone would notice or figure something out. But everyone is too distracted and in their own worlds. No one seems troubled by the way this is organized, so I settle and relax into Griffin's arms.

When the song ends, Dayne cuts in. Griffin goes to dance with Macy, and Cheryl dances with Soren.

Once again the song playing is another romantic love

song that could easily be a couple's first wedding dance. But it's a more upbeat song everybody knows: 500 Miles. Dayne and I didn't really have a song we thought of as "us", or a song that played on our first date that would be an appropriate first dance. And he came into this arrangement much later, so I didn't know him as well as Soren and Griffin when everything changed. I haven't had much time to ask why Dayne would commit to this, and to me in this permanent binding way when he dated me for a much shorter time. Why was he so willing to jump in?

And this song tells me so much about the things that lie under the surface with him. Plus it's probably the greatest song to ever come out of Scotland and Dayne's family comes from Scotland—he has a family tartan and a clan and everything—it fits him.

It isn't a slow song, so it doesn't have the opportunity for closeness that the other two dances allowed. But Dayne isn't troubled by this. The next song is a slow dance, and he pulls me closer, unwilling to relinquish me to anyone else.

"I haven't had as much time with you," he whispers, sending a shiver down my spine and echoing my own thoughts. I've tried to suppress it, but there is something very romantic to me about the speed of his certainty, how he was on board with so little time with me when Soren seemed so resistant and thought I was trying to trap him.

By this point I've stopped caring about what everyone else is doing and who is watching what. We're lost in the middle of a sea of people, surrounded by other couples who are caught up in their own love stories. I relax a moment too soon because Dayne takes the cover of the slow dance to speak low in my ear.

"Griffin and Soren may think they are above me in the pecking order, but just know this, silent background power is still power. It isn't loud like Griffin's, and it isn't outwardly demanding like Soren's, but you should *never* underestimate me."

I swallow around the lump forming in my throat as he holds me closer, tighter. I look around again self-conscious, wondering where Soren is, where Griffin is, if anybody is watching Dayne and I on the dance floor right now.

He leans in again, his voice guttural and commanding in my ear. "Tonight I'm going to put twins inside you. I haven't jerked off for a week, and I've abstained from listening in on Soren's nightly calls for that same time to avoid temptation. I am ready for you. I will win this race. Count on it. Mine will be the first born."

When he pulls back from me his dark gaze is fierce and knowing, filled with supreme confidence. And he's right. I'm at the right place in my cycle that I could get pregnant tonight. Dayne could definitely win this race. I wonder if he's been tracking my cycle just like he quietly watches and tracks everything else, waiting to make his move.

I remember what Soren said at the pre-nup about twins running in Dayne's family, and I shudder. He strokes my back, slowly, gently, as if to comfort me about the impending reality of twins growing inside me. When the song ends, he drifts back into the throng of guests without another word to me and pulls Cheryl into a dance.

Now Soren is back as if he never left my side.

"What's wrong?" he asks when he pulls me in close as another slow song starts.

I shake my head, "Nothing."

"We're cutting the cake after this song," he says.

Everyone seems to know the reception schedule but me.

EPILOGUE

SOREN, THE WEDDING DAY

Two weeks ago. Just before the wedding.

I'm standing at the front of the church with Griffin and Dayne at my side in front of two hundred and fifty of our closest friends, family members, and business associates. We're about to lie to all of these people. These decent, polite, pretty people think that Livia Fairchild is about to marry her prince. Her fantasy happily-ever-after is about to happen.

The maid of honor keeps looking over at Griffin. I'm not sure if he's noticed her schoolgirl crush or if he's intentionally ignoring it. I glance over to Dayne. He's holding the ring at the moment. I've noticed how he's rubbed his finger over the inside of her wedding band what must be a thousand times, as though imprinting the engraving of our three names on his sense memory permanently.

I never thought we'd all bind ourselves together in this

way. There's a part of me that's angry we can't just be open about it, that society is structured in such a prudish bullshit way. Why should only one of us get to call Livia our wife out in the open? Why should only one of us get to entangle ourselves and our relationship unnecessarily with the state and wear a shiny ring to tell the world of our love?

I'm not sure if we can call it love, not the way we did this. But I would do it again. Exactly. Like. This.

Livia is mine. She is ours. And I don't care what the fuck that says about me. No one says no to me, least of all, Livia Fairchild, our new toy, the girl who played with fire and lost.

Pachelbel's Canon in D begins. The guests stand, and Livia begins to walk down the aisle to lock herself formally into this unholy union with us. She looks like she might bolt at any moment, and I swear if she runs, I will chase her down like a fucking lion, pin her to the ground, and fuck her breathless in the open air in front of anyone who dares to follow us outside. She better hope she doesn't run from me.

The animal inside is close at the surface. Right now she is the most gorgeous creature I've ever seen, and I would move heaven and earth, break every law and rule of polite society to have her, to claim her, to sear her soul to mine in the most permanent and brutal way.

When she reaches me, I see the fear in her eyes and something dark inside me calms in response to it. Anyone else would think this is just wedding day nerves, but I know it's more. She glances over to Griffin and Dayne so briefly no one but me could have possibly noticed. I'm not even sure she realizes she did it.

I take her hand and help her up the two small steps. I

hold her gaze in mine, drinking in her fear and uncertainty, imagining all the ways I'm going to break her, ruin her, destroy her, remake her, rebuild her, cherish her, punish her, and worship her.

I stroke the back of her hand, reassuring myself that she is real, she's standing here, she's not going anywhere. Everything has gone exactly to my plan, and I am finally claiming my prize. We're all finally claiming her.

I don't hear a single word the priest says, though I somehow manage to hear Livia's soft voice as she promises to honor and obey me. I swear an audible gasp rises from the assembled witnesses, and I am filled with a visceral, male pride at these words I've somehow managed to get her to say in front of so many people.

There's an exhibitionism in these words, but I don't care. It was in the official traditional vows for hundreds of years, and I wanted it, and Livia submitted to it.

Despite being lost in her, I manage to say the words I'm supposed to say when I'm supposed to say them. We exchange rings. He pronounces us officially legally bound. I grip the back of her neck and pull her in for a possessive kiss, giving her a preview of what's coming in a few short hours. She shudders against me.

When I pull away and look into her eyes, I'm satisfied she's gotten the message that she is mine and there's no going back now.

Welcome to your fucked-up happily-ever-after Livia Fairchild. I hope it's everything you ever dreamed it could be.

The Sacrifice

Kitty Thomas

Burlesque Press

CHAPTER ONE: MACY

I've tried to deny it, but I've always known this was my fate. In certain families there are duties, and some of those duties are more unsavory than others. I've been kept pure for this, and tonight, I am their sacrifice.

I'm led blindfolded down a long hallway and through a door that creaks ominously as we pass through. My breath catches when I hear the men. I can't see them, but I've been prepared for this. I know what to expect.

They're young—ten of them, all close to my age. We went to private school together. The oldest is five years older than me. They are the future titans of industry, and they're here to fulfill their duty—to impregnate me and continue tradition. And may the strongest sperm win.

The blindfold comes off, but I keep my eyes cast down on the floor. My naked body is barely covered by a white cloak that ties at the neck and then a couple of places beneath that so my modesty is protected. My modesty.

Such a joke. No one will care about my modesty as soon as the initial formalities are over.

There's another man, this one older—one of the fathers: Mr. Kingston. We'll call him the Master of Ceremonies.

"Do you understand why you're here, Macy?"

"Y-yes, Sir."

"I'm glad you were prepared for this, though tradition requires me to explain it to you anyway."

Of course it does.

The coming narrative isn't for my benefit. It's for the benefit of the young men here, who will each get to touch me, taste me, claim me, bury their seed inside me in an attempt to be the victor. I will marry whoever is successful, whoever's heir I end up carrying, which will be determined by paternity test. I can't even begin to imagine how this was done before modern technology.

Maybe the ritual was different then.

"Each of these young men will please you. You are *required* to come for each of them. Do you understand, Macy?"

"Y-yes, Mr. Kingston."

"Sir was just fine," he says, his stern forest green eyes boring through me so that I find myself looking back down at the ground.

"Yes, Sir."

"Good girl. After that you'll be allowed a break. The entire ritual will take hours, you see, and we wouldn't want you to get light headed from hunger. Each of them will fuck you, and you are once again required to come for them. All of them. We'll know if you're faking. What happens if you fake or if you fail to come for them, Macy?"

"P-punishment, Sir." My face is hot, flaming, but the place between my legs flames more.

"That's right, Macy. Punishment. And we want this to all be about pleasure, don't we?"

"Yes, Sir."

Mysterious hands seem to come from nowhere to untie the cords that hold the cloak in place. Then the lush fabric is pushed from my shoulders to land in a pile at my feet. This entire speech is for the entertainment of the spoiled rich men who are about to enjoy their sacrifice. Though I will enjoy it, too. It was designed for my pleasure, after all.

Though I've been told it isn't really about my pleasure but about ensuring a pregnancy results from the ritual. Orgasms open the cervix. And I'm ovulating, so this is happening now. I'll be carrying the child of one of these men tonight. Fate will decide who I'll spend the rest of my life with, based only on the strongest swimmer.

I know every single moment of what's supposed to transpire. I know every move, every part of this ritual by heart. Mr. Kingston raises an eyebrow at me, his look expectant. In response, I take a deep breath and drop to my knees. I crawl slowly to him, and suddenly every eye in the room is on me. Previously the men had been scattered about, drinks in hands, low murmurs as they pretended to talk to each other, as they pretended I was beneath their notice. But they can't pretend anymore.

"Good girl."

A gasp escapes my throat as I feel his hand stroke through my hair and then move around to cup my breast. I thought only the guys my age would touch me.

Two of the men help me to my feet and guide me onto a table where I'll be examined by the doctor to ensure my purity is intact before it's destroyed in this one long orgy.

A phone rings, breaking my focus. Dammit. I was so close. The fantasy drifts away, and with it, any hope of an orgasm this morning. I roll over in bed to find Livia's name flashing on my cell phone screen.

"It's eight in the morning. You know that's my *me* time," I grumble when I answer. And she knows exactly what I mean by that. Other people have their morning coffee, I have my morning orgasm. This has been my go-to fantasy for months now. It hits all the buttons: exhibitionism. Multiple men. Lots of orgasms. The *demand* of orgasms. Helpless, vulnerable, arousal. And I'm working myself up again now just thinking of the elements of this perfect spank fantasy.

"Sorry," Livia says. But she doesn't sound that sorry. This daily appointment with pleasure isn't as sacred to her as it is to me, obviously.

She giggles in the background, and I hear rumbling male voices. Those would be her three... husbands? Is that what we're calling them? Only one is legally married to her in the sense that they went and got a marriage license and had a wedding. The other two have private business contracts that are basically the same as marriage without calling it marriage. Apparently as long as nobody calls it marriage it's not polygamy—at least not technically. I think. I don't know. I'm not a lawyer. Maybe it's still polygamy, or at the very least adultery. I need to research this because it's going to bug me.

"I thought we were going dress shopping today. It's your turn!" Livia sounds way more excited about this than I feel.

My best friend has been married for the past three months. Even though I caught the bouquet at her wedding, I didn't believe I'd be next because I wasn't even dating anyone. Then two months ago this guy I was friends with in college popped back into my life.

One night while drunk, we'd made this silly pact that if we weren't married by the time we were thirty, we'd marry each other. And when he called in this pact, I couldn't come up with a good reason why I shouldn't do it—aside from the fact that it's crazy, and drunken promises to marry someone you barely know if you happen to be single in a decade is hardly the kind of thing normal people expect you to follow through on.

William is nice. He's nice enough looking. He's got a stable job. And I really want kids. I've still got some time on the baby clock, but I don't see how the next ten years will be more fruitful for dating than the last ten were. I don't even know how to date in the land of the perpetual player. And I've got a bit of an awkward problem.

I'm almost thirty and still a virgin. Yeah, that part of the fantasy is real. I know I shouldn't be ashamed of it, but I am. It makes me feel like I'm some kind of loser who didn't have any opportunities—like no man wanted me. And I've walked through the local grocery store. I've seen pregnancies that defy all sexual attraction explanation.

But that isn't it. A lot of guys have tried to sleep with me. I just didn't because I wanted them to still be there the next day, and I could tell I was just a conquest—a curiosity. I've never been gifted with that ability to lie to myself that maybe this guy is *the one* when I know he isn't.

There's also that situation when you're in that zone where it's still totally normal to be a virgin, lots of other people your age are, and then suddenly everybody else has done the deed and you're still standing there, suddenly out of the loop. It felt like I went from *this is totally normal* to *it's getting kind of weird* almost overnight. Then I just stayed there. Like I'd somehow accidentally taken a vow in a convent, and that was that. Sorry, too late now, best to accept your spinsterhood. Here's your free starter cat!

Most good men are freaked out by my late-stage virginity as though it's a red flag all by itself. Or they don't want the responsibility of being my first. It's too much pressure. Only the bad men really like it.

And I'm just so shy and awkward.

I'm always researching everything and know weird facts about everything, and I mean, that's kind of strange for dating. Right? And I don't have that thing. You know that thing? The sexy airy breezy way some women have about them? That power over men. That *siren* thing. That certain *je ne sais qua*. I don't have it. Though I've googled how to get it, to little avail. Everybody makes it sound so easy, but it just isn't so easy for me. I'm not like that, and I just feel fake and awkward when I try. But I want to be that woman in my imagination so much I can barely stand it.

"Macy, did you just stroke out or something? You have to have a dress. You're getting married in six months."

I resist the urge to say *Don't remind me.*

"Do you think he's gay?" I blurt out.

"What?!?" Livia laughs out loud on her answer.

"I mean… why is he in such a rush to get married? And he hasn't tried to sleep with me. We are getting *married* and he hasn't pushed for sex once. That's weird, right? I want to call it off."

"I don't think he's gay," Livia says. "He's just shy. And he knows you haven't… Maybe he thinks you're religious, and he's trying to respect your boundaries."

"That pisses me off," I say.

"That he's respecting your boundaries?"

"No. That he might think it's because of religion. Also,

my skirts are a little short for fundamentalism. Don't you think?"

I'm about two seconds from launching into an extreme, likely thirty-minute rant about how the way I am is how almost *all* women used to be. I mean, not obsessively researching arcane random facts, but the chaste until marriage thing. That used to be normal. I don't want this one more thing to make me feel *abnormal*. I already feel abnormal enough.

Then I start crying. I don't know where this is coming from. I mean I do, but I was fine a minute ago. Fine-*ish*. And now I'm sobbing over the phone like I'm about to be thrown into a volcano instead of getting married to a nice enough, good looking enough, and financially secure enough man.

"Macy?" Livia sounds concerned.

"I don't want to marry him." The words come out in a rush, more blubbering than speech. And then I get into a pathetic hiccuping sob where I can't fully catch my breath, and I sound like a two year old having a meltdown over no ice cream for dinner.

We've booked the venue. We've got deposits down on everything. I'm sure this is why I don't have a dress yet, why the idea is giving me stress acne instead of making me feel excited. I don't want to marry this guy. I don't feel anything for him. And I just know he'll be missionary position lights out guy. I can't spend my *life* with missionary position lights out guy. I mean look at my fantasies!

This is probably another reason I'm still a virgin. I don't know how to ask for what I need or want. And even if I could say the words, even if I could let a man in on my twisted mind, there just aren't any men I can trust enough for that. How would I ever do the things I want to do with anyone? I've never even been naked with a man before. And I don't know how I'll ever be able to bring myself to do even that. I can't picture it in my mind at all—being naked with a guy. I can picture it when I'm fantasizing, but I mean... I can't see it as a possible real activity that I could ever actually engage in. It's all just so... impossible.

I should call off the wedding, get some cats, and just call it done.

And I feel so stupid even thinking these things. At least I'm not saying them out loud. That would be worse.

My mind, body, and experience are not at all in alignment. I don't think anybody would guess that behind my bookish nerdy glasses are some very dark and wrong thoughts.

I mean it is so me to be a virgin trying to figure out how to get super kinky sex when I haven't even done it the regular way yet. You have to crawl before you can walk after all. No kinky puns intended. The whole situation embarrasses me.

"If you don't want to marry him you should tell him now before this goes any further. You haven't even ordered the invitations."

"All those deposits are nonrefundable," I say, flopping back on the bed as though I've suddenly been transported to the Victorian era. I'm a millisecond away from dramatically putting my hand to my forehead in distress.

"So? Is it worth sacrificing your life over? I can give you the money back if you need it."

I know she's right. And anyway it's not like it would be that much embarrassment on my end—calling things off, I mean. What little family I have, I'm not in contact with. The only people I was planning to invite to the wedding are Livia, her guys, and her family. I don't even know who to put in my wedding besides Livia. This whole thing makes me feel like I'm living a lie. I'm planning a wedding for a woman who doesn't exist. I wish she existed, I want to be her, but I don't know how to get there from here.

"Just come pick me up," I say on a sigh. "We'll go look at the dresses. I can at least try some on." And fantasize about a dream wedding to a man I actually want to marry.

"Are you sure? It was just a stupid pact. Nobody follows that *if we aren't married by thirty we marry each other* shit. Nobody. It's just a thing you say. Macy, you don't have to marry him. You know that, right?"

Don't I though? He feels like the last boat—the only boat that's coming. And I'm afraid if I don't do this I'll die alone.

* * *

IT'S late in the afternoon when I collapse on the sofa, dropping my bags beside me. I got a dress. It's green. Not pale green. Dark green. And I'm not wearing a veil. I can't bring myself to wear a white dress because I'll feel like I have a flashing neon sign over my head announcing my purity to the world.

Anyway, the white dress isn't as traditional as people think. Queen Victoria started the tradition in 1840. Before that, nobody wore white. They just wore their nicest dress, whatever that was. I'm starting to wish I hadn't read every book I could find on weddings when we were planning Livia's. I can't escape these million stupid facts all swirling around in my brain as though they mean something—like they're important.

I jump at the sudden knock on my door.

"Who is it?" I call from the sofa. I'm not expecting

anybody, and if someone's delivering pizza to the wrong apartment, I'd rather not get up.

"Soren."

I bolt upright. Soren is Livia's husband. The legal one. What's he doing here?

"Livia isn't here," I call back, still not moving.

"Could you open the door, please? I'm here to talk to you."

I struggle to get off the sofa, stopping to look in a mirror near the door. As expected, my long dark auburn curls are disheveled, and I can see the blush already starting in my cheeks, edging out the freckles dotting over my nose. I hate those freckles. I already look too innocent. Freckles are just a bridge too far in adorableness.

When I open the door, Soren sweeps right in without an invitation, smelling of whiskey and cigar smoke. I don't think I've ever seen him smoke a cigar, but he still smells that way. It's like that's just his natural masculine scent.

I can barely stand upright in this man's presence. Soren has a strong effect on me. I spent the entire time around Livia's wedding trying to focus my attention on Griffin, so I wouldn't be lusting after my best friend's soon-to-be husband. I didn't know at the time that Griffin was hers too. So it was a pointless waste of effort on my part. I put absolutely everything into that Oscar-worthy performance and made every effort not to even *look* at Soren. His pull was far too strong.

Then when I walked in on her and Griffin kissing, thinking she was cheating on the man I'd wanted... I locked myself in my car and had a long pathetic cry about it.

Soren is tall with dark forest green eyes and a body sculpted by the gods. But it isn't his looks or even his money that I'm so attracted to. It's his presence. The sheer dominant overpowering and terrifying essence that is Soren Kingston. Yeah, he's the *Mr. Kingston* in my long-standing fantasy. I make it okay in my head by aging him a couple of decades and not letting him participate. Much. Don't judge me.

He's like a storm that you just know will blow through and rip you apart from the inside out, but you're so enthralled watching it coming your way, you can't make yourself move out of the path of devastation in time.

"Do you have anything to drink?" he asks.

I still don't know why he's here, and I'm sure I'm so turned on he can tell. I wish I could turn this feeling off. I would never betray Livia—not that Soren would be into someone like me. But even if he was, I'd never hurt her. I just can't shut off my body's reaction to this man.

"Y-yeah. I-I have some tea. D-do you want tea?" Oh god, why am I stuttering? And I'm sure he means like a *drink* drink, like an adult beverage, but I don't really keep liquor in the house. I'm not much of a drinker, and it's a small studio apartment so it's not like I do a lot of entertaining here.

"That'll be fine. Make some for yourself, too."

It's a command, and I swear if he were single I would strip off my clothes and kneel at his feet right now. I've never felt this way around a man before. I have no idea how Livia managed to go months without sleeping with him. Is it possible I feel a stronger attraction to her husband than she does? That would be tragic.

I wish he'd leave. What's he doing in my apartment? I take a deep breath and force my mind to stop racing as I heat the water in the kettle.

"Earl Grey or English Breakfast?" I hear myself say. It

doesn't even sound like my own voice. It sounds far too high pitched and squeaky to be me. Or maybe it's more breathy like Marilyn Monroe.

"Whatever you're making for yourself is fine."

We're both silent in the kitchen. He stands several feet away, but it's still too close. In moments like this I'm jealous of Livia. I love her like a sister, but why does she get everything? She didn't just get one hot, wealthy, kinky guy. She got three. How is that even possible? It's statistically very unlikely. It just isn't fair. Meanwhile I'm about to marry a probably gay guy where I might get to have vanilla sex one time for the sake of procreation.

Lucky me.

Am I really going to marry him? Even though I'm going through the motions I'm still not sure I'll be able to go through with it. Livia's right though, I need to end things before the invitations get ordered. But why the hell did I buy a dress if I don't plan to actually marry him?

And I really thought we were to a point where a man could be gay and just be open about it. Why hide behind me and pretend? But then I remember that not literally everyone in the world is up to date on this, so maybe there's a reason he needs to hide. And I can feel sympathy for that, but it's still not right to hide behind me.

When the teapot whistles, I pour the tea into two cups and place them on the table. I can't stop thinking about how bizarre it is that Soren is standing in my apartment. And he still hasn't told me why he's here.

"Do you take milk and sugar?" I ask, desperate to fill the silence with anything but the sound of my raging heartbeat.

"Just milk."

I go to the fridge for the milk, wondering if he's planning some kind of surprise for Livia and wants my help. I leave the milk on the table, then grab the sugar for myself and some tea cookies out of the pantry. When I return, Soren is seated at the table, milk in his tea, already drinking.

I put sugar and milk in mine and take a couple of sips.

"So, why are you here again?" I ask. I'm sure I sound rude. I don't mean to, but I need him out of here before he figures out how much I wish I could be with him. I mean I don't have a crush or anything. I'm not in love with him. I just… he makes me feel like I'm in heat, and I kind of want to climb him like a tree.

"Are you nervous about something, Macy?"

I take a big gulp of my tea and then another. It's barely cool enough to be chugging it back like this, but I need a distraction.

"What would I be nervous about?"

"Let's not play games. I've seen how you react to me. You think I don't notice how you blush when I'm near? I think there's something dark and a little dirty in you. You probably have needs you've never even admitted to yourself."

The heat that was concentrated in my cheeks spreads swiftly through the rest of my body. *Oh, I've admitted them to myself, but thank you for that psychoanalysis.*

"You're married," is all I can say. Is he propositioning me? If this bastard is propositioning me I will geld him.

Soren laughs. "You're so adorable."

I'm about to speak again but my tongue feels… weird. I can't make words work anymore. Soren's face blurs in front of me. Then the world tips to the side and goes black.

CHAPTER TWO: MACY

I wake in a darkened room with a pounding headache. I can tell it's still day outside because heavy drapes cover the windows with light peeking in around the edges. I struggle to sit up in the bed, trying to remember how I got here. What happened last? I feel like I'm reading a sequel to a book where it's been so long since the first one came out that I don't remember the original plot.

I was talking to Soren over tea. What was it he wanted to talk to me about? I don't think he ever said. This is when the pieces begin to click together in a lumbering fuzzy sort of way. He *drugged* me. Why would he drug me? I try to get up, and the rest of my brain finally comes online as I feel the resistance and discover one of my wrists is handcuffed to the headboard of the bed.

I frantically search in the dim room for bolts I can unscrew to take the headboard apart. I have this sudden sharp clarity and vision in my head of how I can dismantle the headboard, slip the handcuff out, and find a way to escape. Except that I can't. This isn't some bag of bolts from a big box store. It's a nice bed. It was made as one piece, not a million that can be easily taken apart by a couple of drunk college students.

And then another troubling reality makes its way into my awareness. I'm naked under the covers. He took my clothes off? What is going on? Did he… did he touch me? I squeeze my eyes shut trying to block out that possibility.

"Hey! Soren, let me out of here! You motherfucker!" I can't believe I was attracted to this piece of shit. And now I'm starting to really fear for Livia's safety with this guy.

There's a vase of fresh flowers on the nightstand just within my reach. I take it with my free hand and hurl it across the room. The shattering of the vase is loud and satisfying even as it hurts my ears.

A moment later the door opens and Soren bursts in.

"What the fuck is this?" I shout. Even though he drugged me and kidnapped me and undressed me, I know this guy. I've known him nearly a year so it's hard for me to conjure up the normal fear response that this situation might otherwise create. I mean I'm pretty sure my life isn't in peril. And my body's still reacting to him like he's Christmas, which makes me feel so ashamed I wish I could melt through the mattress to hide under the bed.

He raises an eyebrow at me. "That's a very naughty word to come out of such a sweet mouth."

He glances at the shattered vase nonchalantly, but I can see the storm brewing inside him, that dangerous thing I'm so inappropriately attracted to.

Soren crosses the room to me and sits in a chair near the bed. "I'm afraid we're in a bit of a situation, and you've become the sacrifice."

"Are you going to throw me into a volcano?" It's meant

to sound sarcastic and angry, but it comes out small and weak as though I think that might be what's really about to happen here. And honestly I'm not sure because who talks like this? *You've become the sacrifice?* What sacrifice? And suddenly I'm back inside my fantasy again, except this time it's a nightmare.

This feels like some kind of punishment for fantasizing about my best friend's husband.

He chuckles. "No, Macy. Though you'd be an appropriate candidate for a volcano god."

My eyes widen at this remark. Does he know I'm a virgin? How could he possibly know that? That's private. Would Livia have told him? She wouldn't. Or is it just that obvious how innocent I am? He's so perceptive he can probably smell the purity on me. I wonder what purity smells like. Gardenias? Crisp fresh sheets? A mountain spring?

Soren must read the betrayal on my face because he says, "Don't worry, Livia didn't tell me, but I know everything that happens in my home."

I wonder briefly if he's got the place wired up so he can spy on her, and once again I'm worried about my best friend's safety and once again wanting to disconnect this guy's balls from his body. Not only am I a sex fiend in my imaginary world, but quite violent as well.

I'm grateful the room is so dark because I don't want him to see me blushing again. I wish I had the kind of skin that could conceal embarrassment instead of blooming out in bright pink for all the world to see.

"Why am I here?" I rattle the handcuff impatiently. I want to add *and why am I naked?* But I don't want to draw attention to this vulnerability even though I know he knows about it because he's probably the one who took my clothes off.

I want to beg him to let me go, but I'm not quite there yet. I don't want to be so pathetic so quickly—especially since it's still hard for me to believe this has happened. And there's a part of me still convinced he wouldn't hurt me because of Livia even though I'm now not sure if he'd hurt Livia.

But wouldn't he? Maybe he's a secret serial killer. I saw a six-part series on TV about killers who lived normal lives and nobody suspected until they had a big body count and were in handcuffs in a courtroom with cold dead-eyed stares which nobody seemed to notice before that exact moment. Their wives all thought they were wonderful.

After that I went down an internet rabbit trail about it and couldn't sleep properly for a month. It also didn't do my dating life any favors. On the one hand I was afraid I might date a serial killer, and on the other I was afraid I might be the girl who gets serial-killed while the clueless wife sits at home thinking he's amazing. So maybe Soren is that kind of crazy.

He sighs. "As I said, you're unfortunately the sacrifice. You see, I have a… what do you girls call it? A frenemy? Apparently some things I said caused some problems for him, and he believes I owe him. He's threatened to tell the world the truth about my unconventional marriage. This would also spill out onto Dayne and Griffin. And of course it would affect Livia. So you are the sacrifice that stops all that unpleasantness and keeps all our stock prices up."

He keeps saying that word: *sacrifice*. And I don't quite know what it means, but I know it can't be good.

He's quiet for a long time.

"You need to let me go," I say. My voice is less strong

than I'd like. "Livia will never forgive you if you hurt me." Is he going to hurt me? I'm so confused about what's going on. My head still hurts and feels weird from the drugs so I hear the words he's saying but most of them make no sense to me at least not enough for any deep thinking or analyzing.

"You're going to stay here and be a good girl for Colin."

"W-who's Colin?"

Soren just smiles. "The man who now owns you."

Twin feelings of terror and arousal flood my system at these words because it's not like I can just dismantle my entire sexual circuitry just because I'm an actual captive now. My responses are completely involuntary.

"A-and if I don't?"

"You will."

I wonder suddenly if he'll blackmail me about what I now think of as The Incident. About ten years ago, Livia and I went to Panama City for Spring Break. She was almost raped but somehow managed to kill the guy. In her struggle, she grabbed a large piece of jagged broken glass and swiped out, severing the artery in his neck. He bled out in seconds.

She called me instead of the cops because she was afraid no one would believe her since a lot of people had seen her with him at a party earlier that night. He was very popular. Nobody ever believes the hot popular guy could be a rapist—or that any woman would ever need to kill him in self defense. Because of course no woman could really say no to him. We may have come a long way, but women still aren't assumed to have agency with a man if he's well-liked, looks amazing, and has money. And that power combo? The triple threat? Forget about it. You flirt with that guy and you fuck him because nobody will believe your accusations when he crosses the line later anyway.

I helped Livia get rid of the body that night. It's the leverage Soren used to get her to marry him, and part of me is afraid he'll use that same leverage now for whatever this is.

But I know he won't because Soren doesn't bluff. He won't let Livia go to prison now that he has her securely tied to him. It's probably why he drugged and kidnapped me. It's not like he needs blackmail to get his way this time. I'm already captured.

Soren stands and moves closer to the bed. He stares down at me and strokes the side of my cheek. He seems like he might say something else. But instead he turns and leaves, closing the door softly behind him. I feel suddenly a bit like a pet that's been sadly left at the pound because a family member is allergic.

"Soren! Don't leave me here! Please..." I'm crying now. He's really leaving me in this strange house with some man he's just *given me to* as if he has that right. I was never his to give. But laws and rules don't matter to Soren Kingston. He's his own law.

CHAPTER THREE: MACY

When I wake this time the room is completely dark, the sun having long set. I have no idea what time it is. I don't even remember falling asleep again, but I must have cried myself to sleep. And now I'm hungry. I'm hungry, I have to pee, and I'm tied naked to a bed, *the sacrifice* to someone I've never met. My overactive imagination visualizes a huge terrifying beast will come to devour me when some distant clock strikes midnight.

"Soren?" I call, because I need to believe Soren is still here, that he hasn't left me alone here with… what was the guy's name? I can't remember. I'm only just now feeling semi-normal from the earlier drugging. I don't know why I hope Soren is still here except that he's the devil I know. And now that I'm thinking more clearly I hope I can reason with him somehow. Surely he can give this man something besides me.

Even if Soren were still here, he wouldn't hear me. I didn't call out loudly enough. And yet, after a few short minutes, the bedroom door opens letting light spill in from the hallway. The light falls over me on the bed, and I squint against it. I scramble to sit up, hissing as the handcuff digs into my wrist. I use my free hand to secure the white sheet over my body, preserving my modesty as well as I can.

"S-Soren?"

"Soren went home." The voice is male, low, and dark. If possible, he sounds even more ruthless than Soren, and my body reacts immediately. I haven't even seen this guy. Just three small words, and my body is excited. It clearly has no sense of self-preservation. I had thought this reaction was exclusive to Soren, but no, it's just men *like* Soren. With my body obviously against my survival, it's a miracle I haven't already ended up dead in a ditch somewhere.

Like Soren, this man has an overpowering ruthless energy that I can feel heavy on the air around me. It makes every nerve ending light up in response with the desire to be consumed and ripped apart by this new storm.

I can feel it in the air. He is darkness. I am light. He is guilty. I am innocent. He is war. I am love.

I'm sick. There probably isn't even a diagnosis for what's wrong with me.

I wish I could control my body's reaction. There are just some things that set me off in this primal animal way. Intellectually I know this man may really hurt me. Or he may be gross. Or he may be any number of horrible things, but even so, I'm wet.

He's cast in too much shadow for me to see his face, which calls back my fantasy from this morning, something else I definitely don't need to be thinking about right now. I'm not an idiot. I know I'm in real trouble here, and that this isn't some fantasy that's come to life. But I feel pulled into him as though the storm can provide me shelter.

All I can see are his shiny expensive shoes and his suit. I can't tell what color it is, but it's dark. Black or Navy.

He steps fully into the room, leaving the door open, then slips further into the shadows so that he feels more like a ghostly presence than a real person. But even if I hadn't seen his silhouette pass through, I would feel him. That's how loud his presence is.

"Do you know why you're here?" he finally says.

"N-no."

But I think I do. I mean I'm given to some guy as payment for some debt, and I'm naked. It's not exactly an unsolvable riddle. And it makes my arousal right now so inappropriate. I don't even know if I'll fight him. I don't know if I can. Not because I'll lose—which I know I will—but because I've been starved of male touch well past a point that's normal, and I need... I can't let my mind finish that thought. I will *not* finish that thought. What I need is a straitjacket and a room with soft walls so I can't hurt myself.

It occurs to me that I never felt in a big hurry for Will to touch me. Not once did my body remind me how starved it was for the sexual act while Will was taking me out on dates as a prelude to our sham of a wedding. And here this man—whose face I haven't even seen—speaks three uninspiring words to me, and I have to fight to keep my legs closed.

The stranger sighs. "What did Soren tell you about your situation?"

"H-he said I was a sacrifice. S-so his stock prices don't fall." I've just remembered that last part, and it enrages me enough to quiet my body's insistent whining for a moment.

The man chuckles at this. "And do you know what that means? That you're a sacrifice?"

I shake my head. I perversely seem to need him to spell out every tiny detail of my situation as though it's just another fantasy I'll touch myself to later instead of my actual harrowing real life fate.

"It means you now exist at my pleasure and for my pleasure. It means I'm going to take your innocence and keep you as my toy."

"I-I'm supposed to be getting married," I blurt out inanely. This is what I mean about socially awkward. Who says that in this situation? Like he cares about my wedding plans.

"Oh really? And when will that be?"

"In six months. I-in March."

"Well maybe I'll be tired of you by then and I can give you back to him well broken in. I'm sure your new husband will thank me for all that I'll teach you."

I start crying then, my reality finally eclipsing my body's stupid response to this man. "Please, I-I need to use the bathroom." I meant to beg him to let me go home, but my physical need to pee far outranks the larger need to get out of this house and escape whatever this stranger has planned for me. I still can't remember his name.

I flinch when he moves closer. The darkness cloaks him as though he's the grim reaper himself. He unlocks the cuff then points to a door behind me. "The bathroom's there."

I hesitate, remembering my nudity and try to figure out how to navigate this situation. Finally I tug at the sheet to free it from the rest of the bed and wrap it completely around myself, careful not to reveal anything. He makes no comment about this. We both know it's a pointless delay.

I shut and lock the door behind me before turning the bathroom light on. It's much larger than I expected for a bathroom connected to what seemed to me to be a guest bedroom. It's definitely not his room. I don't know why I'm so sure about this, but I am. The bathroom is black and white, both simple and elegant and also kind of old-fashioned somehow. That's when I realize this is a very old house and these are the original faucets.

After using the facilities, I test the latch on the window. Locked. But I realize to my dismay that we're not on the first floor anyway. It doesn't even feel like the second, we're so high up. Does his house have three floors? Who has three floors?

I pace back and forth for several minutes trying to figure out what to do next. I contemplate just staying in here forever, but I'm sure he can get in if he really wants to. I fight with myself for several more minutes before slowly unlocking the door. I don't bother turning the bathroom light off, but he still manages to stay out of the path of light even with another strip of it now flooding the room.

I'm beginning to think he doesn't want me to see him at all. Does he have some sort of disfiguring scar or is it to protect his identity? If I see him will he not ever let me go? Does he really plan to let me go? He implied he might.

This has me wondering if I don't please him will he let me go sooner, or will he do something worse?

He sits in a chair in the far corner, legs spread, relaxed. At least he looks relaxed. He doesn't *feel* relaxed to me. And I'm not sure where I've gotten these extra senses from all of a sudden, but I can feel him even from across the room in a way I've never felt another person's presence.

"Drop the sheet. I want to look at Soren's offering, to make sure I approve and can clear his debt."

From the way Soren spoke the debt wasn't even monetary, not really. Soren just did something that inconvenienced this guy in some way. Somehow this feels even worse for me.

His order makes me clutch the sheet tighter. My gaze goes to the open bedroom door.

"Don't even think about it. I run five miles a day. I'm much faster than you, and I don't want to have to punish you your first night."

I let out a hysterical and inappropriate laugh. I have zero control of my weird emotional reactions right now. The laugh is because I can't believe he really thinks I'm going to just obediently drop the sheet. I haven't even seen this man's face yet, and he wants to see everything from me?

My gaze darts around the room, finally landing on a vase of flowers on the night table nearest to me. This is when I realize that while I was sleeping someone came in and changed out the flowers. Is this guy a florist? Where is he getting all these fresh flowers?

This new vase isn't glass. It's silver and looks very heavy. Before I can think it through or let him figure out what I'm planning, I pick it up and hurl it at him. Without waiting to see how it lands, I rush out the door and down the hallway, his snarled curses ringing in my ears. I go down two flights of stairs and out the front door, clutching the sheet to me.

As soon as the door to the outside world opens, an ear-splitting siren starts to blare. I have to stop a moment to gather the sheet so it doesn't drag and cause me to trip. Then I take off at a full run, my bare feet landing softly against the manicured lawn. I glance back once at the enormous foreboding estate, then continue on.

I'm grateful when the open space finally ends in a thickly wooded area. I have to go slower in the woods because there are so many trees, and the ground isn't as soft, but at least I have cover to hide in. Finally, out of breath and exhausted, I slow my pace to walking.

I don't think he's even chasing me. The sirens have stopped blaring, but he hasn't shouted after me. I haven't heard any footsteps running. Maybe he decided it wasn't worth it to chase me down. Maybe I knocked him out cold with the vase?

It's only now that I've slowed down that I realize my feet and legs and arms are covered in small cuts from branches, sticks, and rocks. And now that it doesn't seem like anyone is chasing me my fear shifts to the dark woods and what might be lurking out here. Snakes? Bears? Wolves? Hell, I don't know. I don't know how far out we are or what wildlife may be present.

It's the dark moon so I can barely even see my hand in front of my face. And it's unseasonably cold for a late September night. I'm cold, hungry, bleeding, lost. I don't know what to do or where to go. For all I know this is the actual forest and it could go on for miles and miles like this. I could starve out here or freeze to death.

I don't know what else to do but sit on the dirty ground and cry and hope for the sun to rise.

* * *

"MA'AM? I'm officer Duke. Are you all right?"

I squint up at a flashlight. I don't know how long I've been sitting out here, and I'm starting to worry about hypothermia.

"I-I need help. Please… someone kidnapped me." I realize suddenly that he's not alone. There are a couple other officers with him. They help me to stand, and then one of them picks me up to carry me back the way they came.

The one who spoke to me pulls out a cell phone and dials a number. "Colin, we've got her. We're bringing her back to the house."

Colin. That's his name.

"What? No! You can't take me back to him. He kidnapped me. He's holding me prisoner!" I struggle in the arms of the man carrying me, but his grip is firm. Why are the police taking me back to him?

Maybe I misunderstood. Maybe he didn't say he was a police officer. Maybe Colin has private security on the house and sent them after me. It doesn't take very long to get back, which makes me realize I must have been mostly going in circles when I was in the woods.

Once we reach light, I see two police squad cars in the driveway. So no, they aren't private security. The actual police are taking me back to my captor as if this is all normal and okay. I've stopped struggling because there's no point, and I'm so grateful to be back inside the warm house. The immediate problem of freezing at least has been solved.

The officer carrying me takes me down a long hallway on the main floor and into what looks like a library. The walls are dark rich mahogany, and there's a large fireplace with a healthy crackling fire. The heat coming off it feels like life itself. The officer puts me on the ground in front of the fire. From my vantage point I can only see Colin's black shoes and suit pants.

"Thank you for retrieving her. I'll wire you some money in the morning."

The police don't say anything. They just turn and leave, shutting the library doors behind them.

"I assume that's the last time you'll run from me now that you understand how pointless it is," Colin says.

I look up to find furious icy blue eyes on me as I'm confronted with the face of my captor for the first time. Aside from the rage coming off him, he's beautiful. Tall, maybe six foot three, well built, chiseled jaw, full lips, blonde, tan. He looks like he stepped out of a magazine spread for sailboat enthusiasts. I swallow hard when I realize he's not wearing a shirt. My gaze is drawn to a large angry bruise on his chest near his shoulder. It looks fresh. From the vase I threw? Oops.

He leaves the room without another word. A few minutes later the door opens again and it's another man, a bit older than Colin. I flinch and shrink back, but then I spot what he's carrying: a tray with soup on it.

The man places the tray on the ground beside me. "You need to eat something, ma'am." He has a crisp formal British accent.

This is the most I ever remember being called ma'am in my life. He leaves me alone, and I eat the soup. It's really more of a hearty beef stew than a soup, and it didn't come out of a can. I wonder if he started making it as soon as I ran out the front door or if they just happened to have it already made. Talk about anticipating people's needs. Is this guy the butler?

He's too good-looking to be a butler. And he doesn't look like a bodyguard, though he does seem stronger than your average butler—not that I would know—all I know about butlers comes from TV and movies. I'm mostly familiar with all the versions of Batman's butler. So that's probably not a huge window into reality I can count on.

When the food's gone, I move closer to the fire. My feet are finally warmer. I was afraid to look at them, for fear I'd see signs of frost bite, but they're normal color and the feeling is coming back. My cuts and scrapes are worse than I thought, but before I can start to worry about infection, the library door opens again.

I jump at the intrusion, but it's only the man who brought me food. "Ma'am, I've drawn you a bath."

I gawk at him for a moment before I can finally form words. "I-I need to get out of here. I need to go home. He's keeping me prisoner. Please, you have to help me."

Surely Colin doesn't own the entire police department. It's probably just the officers that came out tonight. I could still report him and get free and go back to my life. And planning my tragic wedding to a man I don't want? Suddenly that seems a lot better than this. Safe. Boring. I find I'm ready now to succumb to safe and boring.

He shakes his head. "You belong to Mr. Black now. Your life will be easier if you accept this."

I wonder briefly if I hit my head and I'm dreaming. Is everyone around my captor a brainwashed drone? How much is he paying them? Does he have blackmail on them all? I can't understand what would motivate police officers and butlers to cover for this guy's crimes and enable him in carrying them out so easily.

"H-has he done this before?"

"Done what, Ma'am?"

"Kidnapped a woman."

He laughs at this. "Oh no. Mr. Black didn't kidnap you. He accepted you as payment for a debt from Mr. Kingston." He says all this as if I don't know this story and as if it's not completely insane no matter how he phrases it or how many times I hear it.

"Okay, has he ever accepted... *payment* of this nature for anything before? And if so, what happened to those women?" They're probably buried somewhere on his vast property. I shudder at that thought.

"His previous toys came to him of their own volition. They were compensated well for their time."

I bet they were.

I want to throw the empty soup bowl at this man. I'm so close to going off on a tirade about how evil happens when people just follow orders, as clearly everyone in Colin's life does without question or complaint. If he thinks I'm going to be one of his little order followers, he's miscalculated.

I decide now that I don't care about his fucking money or his looks or whatever it is about him that makes my body want to open and welcome him inside. I'm not going to be one of these morons falling at his feet. I won't make this easy on him.

"Do you know both he and Soren referred to me as a *sacrifice*? Like some offering on an altar. How the hell do you sleep at night?"

Before the butler can answer my accusations, the door opens again and Colin strides into the room, his hard gaze locked on mine. I'm sure he heard me from out in the hallway and I wonder how much of the conversation he listened in on before he decided to interrupt.

"That'll be all, Jeffrey. I'll take it from here."

"Of course, Sir."

Then Colin's obedient mindless robot drone leaves me alone with him.

"You can't keep me here like this." It's probably the stupidest thing I could say in this moment. My indignance borders on cartoonish.

"Oh? All evidence points to the contrary." He sounds bored.

"C-can I call Livia?" I know this is a stupid question to ask but it still came right out of my mouth.

She'll be worried sick. And then there's Will. And my job. I'm a research librarian. I help academics at the university find the things they need for their various papers and studies. Professor McKracken and I have been on an art history research deep dive for the past three weeks, so I will be missed.

"It's after one in the morning," he says.

"Tomorrow then. She'll worry. Don't prisoners get one phone call?"

He laughs. "Oh, Macy, you're not a prisoner. You're a sacrifice, remember? A gift to appease my wrath."

This wrath still simmers in his gaze as he studies me, and I find myself shivering once again, though not from the cold.

I scramble backwards when he approaches, but he's too fast. He picks me up and carries me out of the room and up to the second floor. I'm trying hard not to marvel at the fact that he can carry me this far and up stairs without even getting winded.

We go down the long darkened hallway into an expansive masculine room which I'm sure is his, and then through to an equally impressive bathroom.

Steam still rises up off the water in the huge tub. Jeffrey must have run it on scalding hot. Colin sets me down on my feet, and I hiss in pain and grip the edge of the counter.

"Sit," he orders, pointing to the wide tile ledge of the tub.

I sit, relieved to not be standing on the cuts and bruises I suffered in the woods.

"Now, let's try again. Drop the sheet." The order comes out more insistent than it did earlier in the guest room.

I shake my head furiously, gripping the dirty ripped

sheet tight against my body. Tears begin moving down my cheeks again. "Please… N-no one's ever seen..."

His eyes widen as he realizes what I'm trying to convey to him, that no one… at least no one adult and male has ever seen me naked. He covers his shock quickly. "Soren saw. He's the one who undressed you and put you in bed."

My entire body flushes at this, even though I suspected it was probably Soren who took my clothing.

He watches me for another moment then says, "When I return you will be naked in that water or else."

I watch as he turns on his heel and leaves, slamming the door behind him.

CHAPTER FOUR: COLIN

As soon as I'm out of the bathroom, I lean against the door, my fists clenching and unclenching at my sides. It's involuntary. I'm not going to fucking hit her or anything—at least not with a fist. She isn't a man. Men get punched, women get spanked. Or paddled. Or cropped. Or caned. I'm not a complete monster.

I pick up the phone on my nightstand. It doesn't dial out. I've long given up my landline for the ease and convenience of my cell. The phone is wired up as an intercom system to dial downstairs now. Jeffrey picks up on the third ring.

"Yes, Sir?"

"I need some ointment and bandages to tend to the girl's injuries."

"I'll bring them up right away."

Jeffrey has been with me for the last ten years. He's a man of few words, no questions, and no judgment. He's seen the dirtiest of my dealings both in blood and in sex, and he hasn't once flinched. Frankly that makes me wonder about him, but there was nothing concerning in his background check.

Though if he knew what he was doing, that could have been scrubbed easily enough.

I run a Fortune 500 company, but on a certain level it's become more of a criminal enterprise. Half the business I do these days is off the books. I've somehow gotten into shit in the past five years that would shock the mob. And I've started behaving like a mob boss in how I deal with my problems. More than one person has conveniently disappeared after threatening me with multi-million dollar lawsuits. I just don't like threats. They bother me. Especially threats that involve me having less money.

It's definitely not how my father handled the business, but I've become addicted to the power of it all and the feeling of invincibility. I'm either a sociopath or an adrenaline junkie, possibly some combination of both. I've taken things many steps farther than my father ever did, both by dealing with my problems in unconventional and illegal ways, and by my sexual habits which run equally dark.

If Soren were any other person in the world, his decision to fuck with my business dealings—however inadvertent—would have cost him his life. Instead, I decided to be more petty and less lethal. Besides, I try not to shit where I eat, and Soren isn't far removed enough from me to keep suspicion at bay if he turned up missing. I'm not a crazed psychopath with no self-control after all.

If he disappeared and it came back on me, well, that would probably revoke my membership at the club in Costa Rica, not to mention the risk of prison. It's not Soren's club, but Soren shares his wife with the man who owns it. So killing him was never anything more than a passing fantasy.

I'd be lying if I said I wasn't concerned with my own thirst for other people's blood and the guilt that never materializes over that reality. I sometimes wonder if there is a *me* inside this hollow shell at all. I know I'm not normal inside, but maybe I just have the balls to do what other men only fantasize about.

Maybe the problem is that I think life is a game. I've always thought this way. There's a sort of unreal quality about everything in the world to me, and I often think of others as mere characters in a virtual world—characters in my own playground, as if they exist only to move my story forward—as if they don't have their own personalities or desires; it's mere window-dressing, the shallow backstory of extras.

But hey, maybe that's what happened. Maybe technology advanced to the point that I really am playing a game set inside an earlier timeline. Yes, I know how that sounds. I know what it says about me. Crazy? Narcissist? I don't know. But I'm not right inside. I know that much. And isn't admitting you have a problem the first step?

Shouldn't I get some sort of pin or ribbon for this?

And here I am, crossing yet another line. Initially I'd thought to get Soren to loan his blushing new bride to me, but he came up with something better… *something sweet, that I can keep forever... with conditions.*

That something sweet is of course the beautiful and innocent Macy Laine. The condition Soren gave me was that I had to secure her future. Legally. I had to marry her. From his twisted perspective this somehow protects her and alleviates his guilt because she'll be provided for in a lifestyle she could have only dreamed about before. From my perspective it just seals her doom. Not all money is good money. And I am most definitely *not* good money.

He and I negotiated because I have no interest in getting entangled in a marriage with the state, being beholden to their arbitrary whims and rules of how things will go in my relationship and how they will go should that relationship ever end—not that it would ever end without my say so.

I don't understand why anyone would make a marriage contract with someone that they can't even dictate the terms of. So I had my attorneys draw up a *private* business contract which Soren read and approved.

By this point I'd already mostly given up my personal vendetta against him, solely focused on claiming this new tempting prize and starting this new game, this new diversion. Besides, a wife looks good to the stockholders. If I'm going to have a body count, I need to look as normal and respectable on the outside as possible. And nobody will make me look more normal and respectable than Macy.

This girl is so innocent and sweet, she doesn't even have so much as a traffic ticket on her record. I couldn't resist the urge to taunt her, to suggest that I might deflower her, use her, train her to all my dark and twisted desires, then return her to the man she's meant to marry. Of course that was a lie. She's mine.

I'm still not entirely sure why I accepted Soren's conditions. I didn't have to. I'm the one with the power here. I could have done as I'd threatened and outed his poly relationship to the world. But when I saw her and found out just how untouched she is, I was too greedy to fight him on his terms. I was all too eager at the prospect of keeping her, of *creating her* from the very beginning.

I don't have an unnatural attraction to purity for the sake of it. It's just that she has no bad training to undo. She's had no shitty lovers. She's picked up no bad habits.

She's not jaded. She's not bored. Everything is new and exciting and terrifying, just the way I like it with a girl. And it gets tiresome to pay for the reactions that will all flow freely and naturally out of Macy.

When Soren brought her here, I wanted him to undress her and put her in the bed so I could take my time unveiling her. That didn't turn out quite as expected. I press my fingertips against the bruise where the vase hit me. Fucking redheads, man. Even the sweet ones are lethal. If she'd hit me a little higher up and to the left she could have knocked me unconscious. I do everything in my power to ignore the twinge of fear at what might have happened to her out in the woods if I'd been unconscious for any length of time. It's an uncomfortable and unfamiliar feeling, fear. I wasn't even sure I could feel such a thing, and I'm torn between whether or not I should punish her for introducing me to this new unsettling emotion.

There's a curt knock on my door.

"Come in."

Jeffrey enters the room with the bandages and ointment I requested. We keep all that stuff downstairs in the servant's quarters, but I should probably keep a supply in my bathroom as well.

He drops everything on the bed and leaves. I'm surprised he hasn't said anything about Macy and my plans for her. He knows how innocent the girl is.

When I re-enter the bathroom she's in the tub, crying quietly. The water has gone a very pale pink from her blood. It isn't that any one wound is particularly dangerous, it's that there are so many of them. Three or four marks on each of her legs and her arms. And I'm sure there are some on the bottoms of her feet.

I'm not sure if she's crying about the pain of the water on those cuts or the hopelessness of her fate with me. She should save her tears for me. The cuts will fade. I wish I was the kind of man who could say these tears move me, stir some kind of guilt in me, make me feel like a monster craving redemption. But they don't. They just make me want to take her until her tears turn to moans and she surrenders to the heights of pleasure I'll take her to.

She's so completely perfect.

"Tears only excite me, so you should probably find a way to stop them."

She glances up startled, and it takes all my self control not to lean forward and lick the tears off her cheeks like some wild animal.

CHAPTER FIVE: MACY

I glance up to find his erection pressing against his pants. I would say it's terrifyingly large but I don't have a lot to compare it with. I'm not sure what's normal. He's not kidding about the tears exciting him, though this man doesn't seem like the practical joker type.

I turn away and try to stop crying like he suggested, but I can't. I've managed to quiet the tears, but they continue to roll down my cheeks no matter how strongly I will them away. I think I've cried more in the past few hours than I have for my entire life up until this point.

In general I don't cry a lot. Today is the most I've cried in years between the crying on the phone with Livia this morning and now. That feels so far away. Was that really just this morning? And the dress shopping? Was that truly this afternoon?

If I'd thought I didn't have enough normal emotions, I'm strangely relieved to know that's untrue. I have plenty of emotions. I'd just never had much to cry about before now. I should feel grateful for that, but even though I'm not on speaking terms with my family, I'm realizing how otherwise sheltered I've been from the world and how little real loss I've suffered. And now to have everything stolen from me in a moment is just too much.

My safety, my freedom, my apartment, my job at the university, my best friend, my stupid wedding to an *enough* man that I don't love. Even that last part feels like a loss because I'm not sure Colin will ever let me go, then I'll never have *any* wedding. I may not even get a funeral.

I stare at the blood tinged water. "Are you really going to let me go... w-when you're finished with me?" I don't know how long that will be. A few nights? A few weeks? Months?

I jump when his mouth is suddenly at my ear. "Never," he growls. It's a possessive claiming sound that no man has ever directed toward me before. And as badly as I want to say it is, not all of my shiver is from fear.

I turn to him as he pulls away and straightens. "B-but I thought you said..."

"And what? You're shocked that a man who would keep you captive and train you to be his obedient toy would tell you a lie? Really, Macy? Surely you aren't that naive."

I take a deep shuddering breath. "A-are you going to kill me?" *Shut up, Macy. Why even ask this question? What good could possibly come of it?*

He chuckles at this like the ending of my life is a hilarious concept. "I think we've already established that I'm an unreliable narrator so even if I promise to spare you, do you think you should believe me?"

I can't bring myself to look at his face again, but I can't stop looking at the bruise on his shoulder.

He notices and says, "Don't worry, I won't punish you

tonight. You didn't leave me much canvas to play with, now did you?"

He gestures to my injuries, and the hiccuping sobs start again. I should have just kept moving in the woods. With each passing second the thought of being ripped apart by a wolf or a bear feels like a better ending than this sociopath and whatever cruelly creative torture he might devise.

I flinch when he sits on the edge of the tub, and then he's stroking the side of my throat, his intense gaze locked on mine. Inexplicably my tears stop. One second they're flowing down my cheeks in steady streams, and the next, they just… stop. I take a deep breath. Everything inside me goes still. It isn't prey stillness. It's not the fear I felt half a second ago and know I should still feel.

Against every rational instinct, I find his touch calming. This is somehow more shameful to me than my arousal, that I would be stupid enough to let down my guard with this monster, that I would allow the person who created this terror to soothe it away with a gentle touch.

It takes every ounce of concentration and self control not to lean into his large warm hand like a cat seeking affection. I won't let myself seek affection from this man. If I do I can kiss goodbye the thought that I could ever be normal in any way. The number of things wrong with my brain and my body only climb higher with each passing second in Colin's presence.

"Look at me," he says. His hand hasn't stopped stroking the side of my neck. It's a slow, gentle repetitive movement. Calming. Hypnotic.

I realize suddenly I've been zoning out, staring at the water. And somehow in the intensity of his presence I've forgotten my nudity. I look up to find cold blue eyes burning through me. That's what it seems like. He is cold, but somehow I still feel so warm. His touch, his gaze, they ignite something inside me that spreads out in a fluttery warmth, culminating in what I'm sure is wet heat between my legs, and I've never been more grateful to be shielded by the water.

He may be able to see me, but my other secrets are safe, at least for the moment. But he isn't assessing my body. His eyes don't leave mine. He's making decisions and calculations about my soul.

After a moment, a choice is made and he leans closer. My breathing stops as he licks the wetness off the side of my cheek. And this just makes me start crying again. This act somehow breaks the peace and strange calm. It feels too *serial killer* to me, and I'm once again worried at the possible new brevity of my life.

"I fucking love these tears," he growls against my cheek. He pulls one of my hands from the water and places my wet hand on his erection as if I needed proof.

"Please don't hurt me." It comes out a whisper, but I know he hears me.

He pulls back, and his eyes meet mine. I've never felt so many feelings in one moment before. I don't even have names for categories to put them all in, which disturbs me. I've always been so organized. I've always been able to know what everything is and where to put it. But I don't know where to put anything now because there's just too many feelings I don't understand. And too many fears I can't give voice to.

Fears I'm crazy. Fears he'll kill me. Fears he won't and I'll become something even more abnormal because everything about this moment and my reaction to it is so very wrong.

He stands abruptly, dumping my hand from his lap. He

doesn't look at me when he speaks. "Clean yourself up then come back out to the bedroom. No towel. Just come to me..." His heated hungry gaze sweeps over me. "... like this. You have fifteen minutes."

His shoes click decisively across the tile floor, and then I'm alone in the bathroom with his orders ringing in my ears. It may as well be fifteen minutes left to live from the way he said those words. I want to ask how the hell I'll know if I'm late, but then I notice a clock on the countertop sitting between the two sinks.

Now that the room is so quiet and he's left me alone again, I can hear the ticking. It's so loud I don't know how I could have blocked the sound out before. All I want right now is to feel safe. I want to go back to that insane moment where somehow his hand at the side of my throat gave me the feeling that everything was going to be okay, that he would *make* it okay.

I uselessly start crying again, but I do what he said and get cleaned up. I use every single second that clock affords me trying to live in the eternal now just to stretch it out as long as possible, to savor each second of pretend safety I've been afforded.

Finally I get out of the tub and dry off.

I notice a robe hanging on a hook on the wall. I want to put it on, but I'm afraid of what will happen if I disobey him. And I know modesty is a stupid thing to try to preserve or reclaim in these circumstances. I wish I had that siren thing. Seduction feels like the one way to reclaim power or at least possibly save my own life. When he realizes I don't have that siren thing, it's over. The novelty of my innocence won't hold his interest once he realizes just how boring I truly am.

"You're one minute late," he says when I step out into the bedroom.

"I-I'm sorry." I look at the ground because I can't meet his sharp gaze anymore, and I need to pretend he's not looking at me.

He prowls around me in a slow methodical way. "Not yet, but you will be."

"Please… I'm sorry. Please," I whimper. The promise that I *will be* sorry has stolen my ability to think clear thoughts or take oxygen from the air around me.

"Master," he says. "I own you. So you will call me Master."

"Master," I hear myself say like his obedient sex robot. This word is a trigger—like in those movies where someone has been programmed by the government to be a killing machine, but they don't know it. They're just going about their lives, then one day the phone rings, and the voice on the other side says the trigger word and they go into kill mode.

That's what the word *Master* does to me. Except instead of kill mode it sends me into extreme sexual excitement mode. It's just been a part of my sexual fantasies for too long. Too many orgasms have come along with that word. The trigger is too deep, too strong. I'll never be able to deactivate it.

And now this evil crazy guy is using the trigger, and just like that, my desire belongs to him. I'm not suddenly unafraid of who he might be and what he might do to me. It's just that my body is no longer capable of not reacting to this word. I kind of knew a part of me was already lost. He's too attractive. It's that, along with his ruthless chaotic storm energy and the undercurrents that were in the air long before this moment of full admission of exactly what he is to me.

But I'd held out a small hope that I could push through all that and *not* react like this to my captor—or at least regain control of myself with time. Now all I want to do is kneel. I just want to give in, let him take me down this dark road, surrender to it and let the fantasies be real even if just for a little while.

I flinch when he takes a step closer. He invades my personal space and then he's touching me again, stroking the side of my throat, and I melt into him just as I did the last time he touched me. I'm so fucked up. I have no idea how I've managed to go about life pretending to be normal. There's nothing normal about me. It would be different if this were someone I trusted, and we were playing a game. But we aren't, and I don't. I could never trust someone like this. A man with soulless ice where his eyes should be. A man who thinks you can own a person and is just fine with it.

"You're going to be a very good girl for me, aren't you, Macy?" he says as his hand moves up to stroke my cheek.

A fluttery wave moves through my stomach.

"Y-yes, Master."

I look away from the satisfied smirk on his face, back to the ground, the only safe thing to look at.

"Good girl. Go lie down on the bed."

I want to turn and run again, but I already know how futile that is. I wonder how many punishments are coming. I was late. I threw a vase at him. I ran away.

Is he going to take my virginity right here and now? I'm pretty sure it will hurt. I've been tempted to try to break the barrier myself with a sex toy, but I lost my nerve every time I thought about doing it because I really have next to no tolerance for pain, which makes my fantasies even more insane.

Maybe if I could have just done that, no one ever would have had to know I'd never had sex, and I could have maybe found someone by now. Because it wouldn't be weird; it wouldn't push the good men away. And if I'd done that and found someone, surely I wouldn't be here now.

I can't believe I've already spiraled to a point of madness where I've convinced myself if I'd had the nerve to masturbate with a dildo years ago I would somehow be safe from Colin.

"Now, Macy."

I jump at his hot breath in my ear. He presses a kiss against the side of my throat, and this horrifying sound of longing slips past my lips before I can stop it.

"On your stomach," he says as I go to the bed.

"But... why?" Is he going to take me from behind?

Why can't I just admit to myself I want this man to touch me? Who cares if he's evil and had me kidnapped? I need to be touched. I just want all the thoughts in my head to stop for once. Can't I stop analyzing for one second? Can't I stop morally judging myself? It's not like this is my fault. It's not like I self-kidnapped.

"Now," he repeats quietly.

I lie down on the bed not sure if I feel more or less exposed than I would if I were lying on my back. But he doesn't take off his clothes or touch me in any inappropriate way. And I'm just now realizing that when he was touching my throat and the side of my cheek just now, his hand only needed to slide down a few inches to touch my breasts, but he didn't. What does that mean?

Is it me? Is there something wrong with me? Why does every man show so much restraint with me?

I need him to do whatever he's going to do so I can decide how I feel about it. I can't take this anticipation anymore. And my brain is freaking out not being allowed to put things into categories.

Instead, he rubs a cool gel into the cuts on the backs of my legs. I'd forgotten I even had them. The pain had dulled to a vague sort of background throb. I lie still as he takes his time taping gauze down over the cuts. Then he takes care of the bottoms of my feet and the backs of my arms.

"Roll over," he says when he's finished.

I roll over to my back, and he repeats this process with the cuts on the front of my body. He's lost in concentration as he does this. His heated gaze occasionally travels slowly up my body, to my eyes, and then back down again. I feel like a tiny flying insect trapped in a spider's web, and he's taking his time wrapping me up for his later consumption.

Colin doesn't say anything else. When he's finished, he puts everything back inside the first aid kit, then stands and covers me with the blankets.

"Go to sleep."

He turns off the light and leaves the room, shutting the door behind him. I hear a key turn in the lock and realize he's locked me in for the night. I lay in the dark, feeling my heartbeat thudding against my chest as it tries to slow back down to a normal rhythm. I didn't realize how scared I was until he left me alone for the night.

And now I'm even more on edge because I can't understand why he's doing what he's doing. I don't mean the kidnapping and enslaving part. I don't need a special explanation for that. Some people are just bad. I mean the *not* touching me part. The not fucking me or hurting me part.

I mean, I threw a really heavy vase at him. He's got a dark purple bruise. I ran away. And he hasn't missed a beat, as if he expected all of these reactions and had already made allowances for them—like he'd already decided to forgive me for them.

He doesn't return, and I realize just how exhausted I am. I'm just going to close my eyes for a minute.

When I open my eyes again, sun streams through the windows. The digital clock on the nightstand says it's eleven thirty. I bolt up in bed as I remember where I am. I'm still alone in the bed. But where did Colin sleep?

I look at the empty space beside me. The other side of the bed is clearly slept in, and when I press my hand against the sheets, they're still warm from his body. Realization that he slept here—with me—brings with it a cold chill. He must have come back to bed after I'd fallen asleep.

How did I sleep through the night with him beside me? Why didn't I wake up? Did he touch me? I'm sure I would have woken if he had. But then I'm sure I *should* have woken if he'd come back into the room at all, which he clearly did.

Did he lie next to me and watch me sleep like some creepy weirdo? Did he pull me against his body? Was he naked, too?

Before I can go deeper down the rabbit hole of this sinister sleeping situation, the phone rings. I just stare at it. But it rings and rings. It's a landline. Who even has landlines anymore? And there apparently isn't a voice mailbox set up because it just *keeps* ringing.

Finally I pick up the receiver just to make the noise stop. "H-hello?"

"Come down for breakfast," Colin says. Then the line goes dead.

CHAPTER SIX: COLIN

I pace in the bright airy kitchen waiting for her. Jeffrey has prepared an elaborate brunch with more options than she's probably used to. I barely slept last night, yet somehow she slept soundly even though I'd pulled her against my body, my arm wrapped around her to prevent escape—like if I didn't keep touching her she'd disappear.

I have no idea how she slept through it except that it was late and she was exhausted from all the fear and running and being out in the cold woods. Maybe she's just one of those people who could sleep through a hurricane once she's worn out enough.

No woman has ever begged me not to hurt her—not seriously, anyway. In sex games, sure. But no woman has actually been afraid of me before. They've known I was dangerous, but that's part of the appeal right? Some women have particularly dangerous tastes in men. They like the wildness, that animal edge that so many men have lost. And I'd become accustomed to the jaded nature of these women who somehow trusted that I wouldn't turn my darkness against them—that somehow because they were hot and I was fucking them, that they were safe.

And to be fair, they were right. Women are in a different category for me from men. For all my violence, outside of sex games, none of that gets turned on women. And yet. Macy isn't like the others. She's actually afraid I will physically harm her. This is the part where I'm supposed to feel guilty, and where if I had an actual soul I would feel guilty. I feel *something*, but it's not guilt. It's more like the intoxicating feeling of power finding a new way to express itself.

And because of this, Macy may be as dangerous to me as I am to her.

I tell myself I didn't start her training last night because it was so late. She was tired. I was tired. And I have all the time in the world. But I'm not sure if that's the reason. I don't want to call it mercy because I don't think it was that. Maybe it was just a stay of execution. Or maybe I wanted to be well rested and fresh before starting.

I'm not sure if I'm going to hurt her, but the prognosis isn't good. Her tears make me hard. Her pleading whimpers fill me with a sense of power. But were she to stop crying and pleading, I might punish her for taking these small pleasures away from me. I'm fucked up. And she's just fucked.

Her entrance startles me mid-pacing. I turn and suck in a sharp breath as I take in the exquisite delicate loveliness that is Macy Laine. She's wearing the robe from from the bathroom and looks afraid I might rip it off her. And honestly, if she were one of the girls who'd come here to temporarily play the roll of toy, I might have done just that. I might have allowed her to blush and be horrified by

Jeffrey walking in and staying a bit longer than necessary to do whatever task he was there to pretend to complete, all so he could take long lingering looks at my newest nude on display.

Jeffrey likes to watch and sometimes touch. And I like audiences, so… it works out. And it's always gotten my playthings worked up, making them that much more warm and wet for me to slide inside.

Beneath my greed for Macy, I know that if I push her too far too soon, I could break this new toy. I could end up with another hollow shell. And then there would be two of us without souls wandering the world lost. I need her to still be something so I can exist inside the energy I don't have the power to create within myself. She makes me feel… things.

I don't know what those things are. They're too foreign and rare to put a label on, but it's something more than I've ever felt. I don't know if it's because I now own someone, or if it's something about her specifically. I just know that when I touched her throat last night, I felt the way she relaxed under my hand. And it did something to me that I'm not sure can be undone.

Of all the reactions she could have had, this one unnerves me because it's not what she should feel. I'd expected her to pull away, to beg, maybe even to scream. I expected to see disgust, fear, and revulsion in her eyes. But she just breathed until her breath flowed into mine and mine flowed into hers. And for the first time ever in my life I felt a connection to another living creature.

I felt like there was something alive and pulsing inside me after all.

Half of me wants to hurt her for making me feel this thing. And there's the fear my weakness may give her power. The other half of me just wants to experience it again.

I realize suddenly that I've been standing here lost in my thoughts about this girl while she's looking at the floor and shivering even though she's in a long-sleeved robe and the house is plenty warm. Jeffrey turned on the in-floor heating an hour ago so even her bare feet won't get cold.

But on taking a second look at her I realize why she must be cold. Her hair is wet, probably from the shower.

I go to the bar and make myself a plate and return to the table. Macy still stands, tense and uncertain. I know she's waiting for me to comment on the robe, to make some demand that she remove it. But I don't.

"You should get some food before it gets cold."

I watch as she notices the food for the first time. She's not used to a spread like this. She's impressed, and I'd be lying if I said I wasn't a little pleased by this. So many of the women who come here are so jaded by wealth. Nothing impresses them. They're jaded by money. They're jaded by kink. They're jaded by the entire spectrum of male sexuality. They may not offer every single service on their menu, but they've heard it all. And every reaction to every thing feels calculated to please the client.

Macy tries to hide her reaction to the china. I'm sure that to Macy this is what many people call "the good china", but in my world, it's just the plates I eat off of every day. There is no "good china" that just comes out for company. All the china is the good china because there's no reason to use or have low quality anything, which reminds me, someone's going to have to take her shopping for suitable clothes if she's going to be Mrs. Black. Or we could have all her clothes custom tailored.

Macy watches me like a spooked doe as she eats. Jeffrey

comes in and pours us some coffee, then he disappears again.

"I-I don't drink coffee," she says almost too quiet for me to hear, as though she's afraid I'll hurt her for not being a coffee drinker.

"Oh? What do you drink?"

"Tea."

Oh, Jeffrey will love her. He's been trying to get me to drink tea for years. "Jeffrey, Ms. Laine would like some tea."

On hearing this, he bounds into the kitchen like a puppy, as thrilled as I knew he'd be by this request.

"I have Earl Grey, English Breakfast, Irish Breakfast, Darjeeling..."

Before Jeffrey can rattle off the likely hundreds of teas he's been hoarding for god knows what reason, Macy says, "English breakfast, please."

Jeffrey takes away her coffee and goes to work on the tea. She continues to focus on her food, avoiding my gaze. Then she does the strangest thing. She picks up the saucer and turns it over to inspect the bottom of it.

Is she looking for a brand name? A price label? Could I have a gold digger hostage of all things?

"I knew it. Bone," she says as if satisfied by this knowledge.

"Excuse me?" I ask.

"Do you know the difference between fine china and bone china?"

I have no idea what to say to this so I just shake my head.

"Bone china has cow bone ash in it. It's what gives it the softer warmer color and translucence. But it's no stronger than fine china. That's a misnomer. It's just a way to alter the color."

"And how do you know this?" I still can't believe that the first non-terrified thing she's decided to say to me is about the difference in fine and bone china. I didn't know the difference—largely because I don't care—but I'm fascinated she just opened her mouth to tell me this. Maybe I seem less scary in the daylight.

"Livia didn't know when we were registering for her china for her wedding, and so I looked it up. I like bone better because it just looks more elegant to me. It's not as harsh."

Her face falls, and I know immediately what she's thinking. She's thinking she won't get to register for a china pattern for the wedding that won't be happening now. I don't know why, but this crestfallen look on her face bothers me.

Jeffrey brings her tea, then disappears again. She seems to suddenly realize she's been explaining the finer points of china content to her captor, and the discomfort and anxiety returns to her face as she distracts herself with her tea.

We finish eating in silence and Jeffrey takes the plates away. When the table has been cleared, she looks a bit awkward then starts to get up. I place my hand over hers, stopping her retreat.

"Sit. We have business to discuss."

"W-what kind of business?"

It hasn't escaped my notice that she hasn't called me what I told her to call me, but I decide to leave that for the moment. I take the stack of papers from the nearby island and place it on the table in front of her.

"This little arrangement protects Soren's stock prices

from falling, and it also helps me. I need a Mrs. Black to make me look more normal and family-oriented. You will fulfill that role."

Her eyes go wide. "I-is this a pre-nup?"

"No. I have no interest in getting into a threeway with the state. This is a private contract that is meant to protect you and provide for you should I at any point choose to discard you. It was Soren's condition for giving you to me. It goes without saying that you won't be initiating an end to our arrangement. And, as stipulated in the contract, you will of course be giving me heirs."

She slides the papers across the table and crosses her arms over her chest. "I'm not signing this."

I'm surprised by this rebellion but I don't let it show on my face. "Not today you aren't. It'll be several weeks before I can take you out in public, and then we'll sign them properly at the attorney's office. I'm just informing you."

"No. You can keep me captive, but you can't make me sign these papers pretending a relationship we don't have."

I can't stop my eye roll. "Don't be ridiculous. These papers protect you. And from what I hear from Soren, you don't love the man you were going to be marrying anyway. So what difference does it make? My offer is better than his."

"You can't absolve your guilt by giving me the security of marriage. We're not in the Victorian age."

I place my palms flat on the table and lean forward so that I'm towering over her. "I don't feel guilt. You are mine, and this is a gift. And I really do need a Mrs. Black."

She shakes her head. "I'm not signing them."

"You'll sign them if I have to break you into a shell of your former self. You *will* sign them." I don't know what's come over me. I don't threaten women this way. I thought it was my one redeeming quality, but maybe it's just that no one's been brazen enough to challenge me.

"No."

"What happened to the girl who begged me not to hurt her last night?"

"She got some sleep and some food."

She's actually glaring at me as she says this.

"Great. So I only need to starve and sleep deprive you, and you'll be ready to sign? It's not the best idea to reveal all your weaknesses to me. Don't think I won't use them to get what I want."

A flicker of last night's fear moves over her face, and I'm satisfied this is only a bluff and boundary testing. It's her *attempt* to fight back, so she can say she tried and feel good about it. Fine. I'll let her have it.

"When were you supposed to be marrying this other uninspiring joker?"

"M-March twenty-eighth."

"March twenty-eighth," I repeat. "We'll be legally bound long before that, but I've got nothing planned that day if you want to have a wedding. Though you'll have to break it off with the other guy first. It might be awkward if we both showed up."

She stares at me like she can't tell if I'm serious or fucking with her. I can't believe it, but I'm actually serious. I'm taking everything from this girl—the life she knew, her choices, even her choice in who to marry. If she wants a wedding, well it's already partly planned, why not just trade out the groom?

While she's still caught off guard, I pull her phone from my pocket and place it on the table. "You said you wanted to call your friend."

She stares at it then back up at me. "Are you crazy? You

know you're committing a felony right? And you're just letting me use a phone? Why not go ahead and mail your fingerprints to the FBI?"

I shrug. "You said she'd worry, and you're going to have to be able to be taken out in public eventually. It's an opportunity for you to start building trust with me. I suggest you take it. Do you need me to show you the dungeon to give you incentive not to screw me over?"

She shakes her head quickly.

"Good. Put it on speaker."

CHAPTER SEVEN: MACY

I stare at my phone as Colin slides it across the table like it's some kind of trick, like if I reach out for it I'll get an electric zap. Finally I do reach for it. Just as my hand closes over it, his hand closes over mine. I gasp like a school girl at the contact.

Why is his touch so warm and soothing? I shouldn't feel so safe when he touches me. If we were animals out in the wild, this would be a predator thing like *look it's pretty, oh it's poison!* And even though I'm smart enough to know this in the way you know things out of a book, a deeper part of me doesn't know it and can't be convinced.

How can something this attractive be bad, the stupid part of my brain says.

I keep having to remind myself we aren't on a date. I shouldn't have to remind myself this, but in your average kidnapping situation you don't get brunch on the fancy plates with a butler making you tea. Plus Colin, while just as intense as before is starting to feel Soren-storm intense —which is comforting because it's familiar. Also, he's neither in shadows nor looming over me and glaring right now so I'm feeling maybe one percent less scared and ten percent more turned on.

And I hate myself with every fiber of my being for thinking this thought but he is so much hotter than Will, which seems like one of those evil tricks the universe plays. Colin is obviously… financially comfortable would be the polite way to say it. And if he doesn't murder me, he might be into the things I *think* I'm into. How does one know what they're truly into if they haven't done anything yet?

I've also fantasized about sky-diving or being an international spy, and I can say for sure I don't want to do those things in real life. I think. Plus this isn't a game, something I keep having to remind myself of because he's so hot it's hard to remember someone so beautiful is actually a monster.

"Where are your manners?" he asks, interrupting what otherwise would be a never ending rambling monologue in my head. Trust me, I can make it go for days.

My bravado of *you can't make me do anything because I ate food and slept and now feel like a super hero* from only a few minutes ago has completely shattered under both his steady touch and gaze.

"I-I'm sorry?" I say.

"What do you say when someone does something nice for you?"

"Thank you?" I say it like it's a question on a test I didn't study for.

He raises an eyebrow at me, and I know what he's searching for. I know what he wants me to say, but if I say it I'm afraid of how my body will react. I'm barely holding myself together right now. And I'm not sure what falling apart would entail in this moment.

It could mean crying hysterically, or unrestrained lust. Either reaction creates danger for me. If I cry nonstop he might decide I'm too much trouble and throw me into a volcano for real. But if I allow myself to be drawn to the pretty poison, that's not much better.

He's still waiting, and I decide maybe I should try to buy a bit of grace instead of acting like a little idiot who can't remember a simple conversation.

"Thank you, Master," I finally say. It takes every bit of internal strength I have not to look down when I say this. I need to see his reaction to distract me from my own.

His eyes darken with lust as that all-important word falls from my mouth.

"Good girl." His voice is a low gravel rumble more effective than a vibrator.

He finally removes his hand from mine, and I can breathe again. I take the phone and call Livia, trying to control the tremble in my fingers as I scroll to her name on my contact list. As directed, I put the call on speaker.

"Oh my god, Macy. I've tried calling you sixteen thousand times today. It's after noon. Did you go for marathon masturbation this morning or just sleep in because you don't work on Monday?"

"Livia!" is all I can say. But I know my face is burning hot. I can't help glancing up again just in time to see Colin's eyebrow go up along with the smirk that slides across his face.

"Wait… am I on speaker?"

"Yes, you're on speaker."

"Oops, sorry. Who else is there?"

"No one," I say quickly. "I'm just getting ready, and it's easier."

"Okay, then answer the question… and if it was a

marathon, which of your dirty kinky fantasies got you there? Because all three of the guys are going on some trip to do some merger that somehow involves all of them, but I don't get to go, so I need to understand your methods to get me through this twenty-four hour drought."

Colin is actively having to fight laughter. The only good thing about this is it drops my fear by another ten percentage points. If he'd mentioned me being Mrs. Black right now instead of before, I might have been tempted. Or at least I wouldn't have outright refused. I mean, I *did* say yes to Will, and that was just as stupid. Apparently I'll marry anybody who can put those words together in a sentence.

"Why did you call so many times?" I ask, trying to get Livia off the topic of my masturbation habits.

"I wanted to know which dress you ended up getting for the wedding."

Livia had to leave before I decided and bought the dress because she had to meet Griffin and Dayne for dinner. The mystery of why Soren wasn't going to be there was solved by me, though I obviously can't tell her what her legal-on-paper husband was doing while Griffin and Dayne were distracting her. It makes me wonder if the other two guys are mixed up in this situation too.

"I got the dark green one," I say.

"Good choice. I think that'll look great with your hair and eyes. I always thought you'd go with the traditional white, though."

My awareness of Colin's scrutiny is the only thing that keeps me from launching into the Queen Victoria story about white wedding dresses. I really want to explain how short a time period white dresses have been traditional. This need to knowledge dump is like an itch I can't scratch.

But I already nerded out earlier when I for some reason felt it necessary to tell the man keeping me as his slave the difference in fine and bone china. I cannot let him see this is a real personality feature of mine and not just some nervous tick.

"So was that all you wanted?" I ask not sure what the hell else to say to her with an audience and too afraid of what else she may say to let her keep talking on speaker.

"Yeah, and hey, do you want to sleep over tonight? I'll be all alone in this big house."

I look up, already knowing what I'll find when I do. Colin is shaking his head, reminding me why I should hate him instead of feel attraction for him. He thinks he owns me. And technically, if I can't find a way to escape, I guess he does. But in the light of day I'm starting to feel more optimistic about figuring out an escape route.

"I can't," I say.

"Of course you can. You don't have to work tomorrow. Just come over. We'll order pizza. Also… if you're wearing green, what color am I wearing?"

I feel too flustered under Colin's gaze to discuss wedding plans for a wedding that isn't happening, and I don't know how to get out of this conversation.

"Someone's at the door, I have to call you back." I end the call before she can say anything else.

"No," Colin says, his arms crossed over his chest.

"No, what?" I assume he's going to explain to me why I can't see my friend, which really is pretty obvious to me since he's breaking the law to keep me locked away in his castle.

"No, you're not wearing a green dress. You're wearing white like a proper bride."

"There isn't going to be a wedding," I say. And somewhere in the back of my mind I always knew this was true. I think I just wanted to pretend for a little while longer and plan even though I knew I couldn't go through with it. It's probably the real reason I got a dark green dress.

I'm not a total rule follower but I'm not a big breaker of tradition either. The dress was non-refundable, but it just looks like a formal gown. Nothing about it screams wedding, so I knew I could always save it and wear it to some other function later—not that I typically attend fancy functions like that but you never know. These white lies allowed me do some wedding shopping while still planning my exit strategy.

But now, given my current situation, there really isn't going to be a wedding.

"Yes there is," Colin says. "I told you we'll have one."

At first I think he just read my mind but then remember I actually DID say that that out loud before I started overthinking again.

"How would that even work? I can't just trade out the groom!" I say, finally.

"Why not? You haven't sent out invitations have you? If I recall correctly from my sister's wedding, invitations don't go out until much closer to the date. Did you send out save the date cards?"

"No… but..."

He has a sister? How in the hell does that work? How does a man like this have a sister and still do what he's doing?

"Do you have anything on order with both of your names printed on it?" he prods.

"No… but..."

"But nothing. You're getting married on March twenty-eighth."

"To my captor," I say, probably with more sarcasm than is wise.

"Yes." There is no sense of irony or humor in his tone. He is dead serious. "I told you, I need a Mrs. Black. A wedding makes it look less like the business equivalent of a green card marriage."

"I have to keep my last name," I say as though I'm just going along with this. But what good will fighting him do? I need to be agreeable, earn his trust, and then escape when he lets me go out. He said he's going to let me leave the house at some point. So when he does, that's when I can escape.

"Since it's not a marriage license marriage, that's fine," he says, relieving me of having to explain my mental rabbit trail of why I can't be Macy Black. It would sound like I'm trying to be a pop star.

"You're going to have to come up with a reason to tell Livia that you won't be able to see her for a few weeks."

I open my mouth to speak but then close it again. Finally I say, "There's nothing I can say that she'll believe. I see her too frequently and she knows me too well."

"What about a business trip?" he suggests.

"I'm a research librarian. My business trips are to the locked reference floor where we keep the expensive old books."

"A vacation then."

I shake my head. "I don't really travel. And Livia would want to come too."

"Sick relative."

"Nope. I'm not on speaking terms with my family."

He doesn't ask why, and I'm glad. I don't like to talk about it. The short version is they're kind of scummy scam artists and I got tired of bailing them all out with money I don't have so I moved to the other side of the country and changed my number. The entire family has this get-rich-quick mentality, and they're all obsessed with money in the way that people who play the lottery every time they go to the gas station are obsessed with money.

I couldn't live like that anymore. I'm the only member of my family who is responsible with money. I don't even know how or where I got this personality trait. Maybe I was switched at birth. An evil part of me kind of wants to reconnect with them now that Colin is demanding I be Mrs. Black. I wonder how fast he'd let me go if my entire family started coming after him for money and investment advice.

"What are you smiling about?" he looks suspicious.

"Nothing."

"Friends?" he asks.

"Huh?"

"Do you have any friends you could say you were visiting or helping in some way?"

"I'm kind of an introvert. Most of the time I don't spend with Livia, I spend at work at the library."

Colin sighs. "So you're telling me the only people in the world who will miss you are your work and Livia?"

I nod slowly, not at all liking where this conversation is going.

"I know a lot of people," I interject. "University staff, all the library people, lots of regulars who come in, Professors, Visiting professors…"

I trail off at Colin's raised eyebrow. It's probably for the best because I was close to mentioning the people who work in the campus bookstore and the janitorial staff.

I look down at my empty plate and take one more sip of

the tea before it gets too cool to drink. Finally, Colin stands. I feel the heavy weight of his gaze on me.

"Come with me, Miss Laine."

I look up to find his hand outstretched, something which would be a gallant gesture in any other situation with any other person. I take a moment to really take in the suit porn in front of me, and I feel extremely underdressed.

"Where are we going?" I ask, and immediately wish I hadn't.

"I need to punish you."

CHAPTER EIGHT: COLIN

I don't know why I said I *needed* to punish her. Shouldn't I have said *want* instead? Or I could have simply stated I was *going* to punish her. But as I assess the situation I realize that yes, need was accurate. I need to punish her, and she needs to be punished.

My shoulder is still sore this morning from the vase she threw at me. She ran from me and damn near got herself killed. She was belligerent. She danced around the title I demanded, and she said she wasn't going to marry me. Like hell she isn't. I think that last thing is what pisses me off the most.

Scores of women have tried in vain to get to be Mrs. Black, and Macy—the one woman I wouldn't mind having in my space long term—turned me down. Not that her refusal means anything. She'll still sign the papers one way or another. We will be contractually bound, and she will be mine.

She already is mine.

And Soren will get to keep all his dirty little secrets tucked away for another day.

Macy's hand trembles as she places it in mine. Her breath hitches in her throat. I don't say anything else to her —no words of reassurance. Better to start her initiation into my world now before she gets too comfortable. Besides, didn't her friend mention kinky fantasies? What darkness lurks in the mind of my sweet little virgin?

I lead her out of the bright kitchen and down a few hallways, each darker than the last as we move further and further from the natural light of windows and into the artificial light of dim wall sconces. I input a code at a door at the end of the hall, and it slides open. I guide Macy down the stairs into my fully equipped sex dungeon.

I let go of her hand when we get down to the lower level. I expect her to bolt, but she just stands there, taking in the array of bondage furniture, whipping implements, and toys.

"Take off the robe."

But she only pulls it closed over her.

"Are we going to do this again, Macy? I've seen you naked." And she seemed very confused by why I haven't fucked her yet. She is mine, after all. A sacrifice all wrapped up for me to devour at my leisure.

She blushes in the way that only a redhead can do.

"Close your eyes," I say when she makes no move to obey my previous order. She's shy, and unbelievably I think this is less about what I might do to her down here and more uncertainty… about herself? Her desirability? I mean I *am* the monster here.

Obviously I want her. I'm doing crime to keep her. And it's too warm down here for her nipples poking through that robe to be anything but arousal. So I know her hesitance isn't repulsion at the idea of me looking at her.

After another moment's hesitation, she closes her eyes. I pull a blindfold from my pocket and secure it in place. I can be merciful. I can make this easier for her. I find my hand stroking the column of her throat. A tiny sigh escapes her mouth as she leans close to me.

I stare at that mouth. I want her on her knees and that mouth wrapped greedily around my cock. I shake that thought from my head. Not yet. I want to do this right. I'm keeping this one.

My hand trails across her collarbone and down until it closes over her hand, still clasping the robe. Her grip releases under my touch, and she lets me pull first one hand, then the other down by her sides. The robe falls open and I push it over her shoulders and let it fall to the floor.

My gaze moves downward, and I'm shocked to find her bare. Perhaps I should have noticed this before, but it wasn't clear in the bath. And when she came out, I kept the room mostly dark to ease her into my world.

"When did you get waxed?"

"T-the other day," she says after only a moment's pause.

"I thought you were a virgin."

She blushes harder at this.

"I am."

"Were you planning to do something to solve that little problem? Who were you planning on showing your pretty pussy to?"

"No. N-no one. That's not why I wax."

I swear my eyebrow is going to get stuck in its current position of surprise. "If you don't wax for a man, why do you wax?"

I'm sure if she wasn't able to hide behind the blindfold she wouldn't answer me.

But she takes a deep breath and says, "For me."

I think about that for a moment. Does she like the way it looks? The way it feels? Does she prefer to touch herself without any hair in the way? Or is she a masochist? Does she like the pain? Or the endorphin rush afterward? I once knew a girl who kept regular waxing appointments to keep panic attacks at bay. She said the endorphin rush after made her calmer than even a massage could do.

I don't ask Macy to elaborate. I let the mystery be as I take in her small perfectly proportioned breasts, pink nipples, the feminine flare of her hips. The gentle softness of her belly.

It takes me a moment to realize I'm holding my breath. I've lost track of the number of naked women I've seen. It shouldn't still have the power to stun me, but there's something different in Macy's beauty, something uncomplicated, untouched, and uninitiated. Something sweet and innocent and new.

I notice she removed the bandages. Her minor injuries from last night don't look nearly as bad in the day. The cuts have closed and they aren't as angry and red as I expected them to be this morning. Even with these marks though, there's space for me to leave my own.

I have a moment of weakness where I'm not sure if I can bring myself to leave marks on her. But this feeling passes as quickly as it came, leaving behind the hunger that demands to be sated.

"Macy?"

"Y-yes, Master?"

But I don't answer her. I just wanted to know if she would persist in resisting the title I demand. I take her hand and guide her to the center of the room. She doesn't say anything or fight me when I raise her arms over her head and bind them together with soft leather cuffs hanging from the ceiling. She's standing on her toes.

"What size shoes do you wear?" I can't have her standing like that for long.

"Ummm, six?"

"Is that a question?"

"No, Master. Six."

I keep black heels in multiple sizes for these situations and 3 inches should be perfect to keep her off her toes.

"M-Master?" she says, sounding panicked when she hears me walk away.

"I'm not leaving you," I reassure her. I retrieve a pair of heels in her size from a large leather trunk and help her into them.

I spread her legs and cuff her into a spreader bar so she can't close them, then I stand back to take in her beauty and subtle curves. How is it possible that I'm the first man here?

"Have you ever been punished? As an adult?" I want to make it clear I'm not asking about childhood spankings. Just because she's a virgin doesn't mean she can't have done other things, though that seems unlikely if Soren was the first man who's seen her naked. I find myself irrationally jealous of this, even though I made that call.

"No, Master," she says barely above a whisper.

I move into her space, pressing myself against her naked body. I snake an arm around her allowing my fingertips to dance up and down her spine. I brush away her still-damp fiery hair and leave a soft kiss where her neck meets her shoulder. She shudders at this.

I hold her around her lower back so her arms don't

have to support her full weight. I'm sure she feels my erection pressing against her belly through my suit.

"I'll give you nine if you cry pretty for me and ten if you try too hard to be brave."

Her lip is already quivering.

I should start her with the riding crop or a flogger, but I want to leave cane welts. I want to leave a strong first impression.

I stroke her soft ass, and a whispering moan escapes her. I'm surprised she hasn't begged or struggled or fought. There is a part of Macy that wants to find out what happens, and I'm more than happy to allow her this discovery.

I let go of her and go to the box to retrieve the cane.

"You will count them," I say when I return.

She shrieks on the first one. Definitely a kink virgin.

"O-One."

I use more restraint on two through five. She silently cries through all of them as she counts. She hasn't begged yet. I'm not sure if I'm pleased or disappointed by this… if I should reward her or punish her harder.

Six is harder.

"M-Master, Please!"

There it is. The air is electric between us. "What number, Macy?"

"S-six, Master."

"Good girl."

"Please, please, please…"

I have never in my life shown more mercy than I said up front I would offer, but her tears are doing things to me. Both good things and bad things, and I can't separate and detangle these feelings. I can't decide if I want to keep going or if I want to stop. But I don't do mercy. I don't do kindness. I don't do restraint.

"Three more," I growl.

She's sobbing now. Maybe it's relief that I'm stopping at nine instead of the ten I threatened if she didn't "cry pretty" for me.

I pull back a little for seven and eight, but nine is as hard as the first, bringing that shriek out of her again. She has counted each one. Such a good girl.

I put the cane down and stand back to admire the welts I left on her. I stroke her back and move closer to leave a hungry, biting kiss at her throat.

My lips brush against her ear as I whisper, "I'm going to make you feel so many things, Macy."

Her reply is a whimper.

I remove the blindfold and when I look into her pale green eyes, I know without any doubt this girl is mine. Not because Soren brought her to me. Not because of any sordid plan. No, she's mine in a far deeper way. There is a thrumming, a hum hidden below the frequency of civilization… a primal place that exists in the recesses of long-forgotten memory. That is where Macy and I live together and why she is mine.

My gaze drifts from hers, down to her lips. I consider claiming her mouth but I don't. I don't want to break the intimacy or the energy of what we just shared together with a romantic cherry on a sundae. It would soften things. It would break things.

Instead, I reach up and unbind her wrists, rubbing them. "Pins and needles?" I ask.

"No, Master." Her voice is so quiet.

She rests her hands on my shoulders as I bend to uncuff

her ankles from the spreader bar. I don't even think she realizes she's doing it.

Then I stand, pick her up, and carry her up the stairs. Maybe she can walk, but I want to carry her. She's so slight that it isn't a burden to take her up a couple flights of stairs to my bedroom. She burrows her head in my neck.

I carry her past staff, past Jeffrey whose eyes greedily drink their fill of her as we pass.

I lay her across my king-sized bed.

"Roll onto your stomach."

She obeys, and I go get something to put on her welts. When I return she's crying again. I don't ask why. I don't want to break this with words. I've whipped a lot of women. I've caned a lot of women. I've fucked a lot of women, and I've never experienced anything like what just happened in the dungeon. There are no words to convey it.

It was such a small slice of time, and yet a lifetime of experience was poured into it.

I'm not good with words. Or feelings. Or really anything civil or human. I can pretend. I can put on the mask as any other man might put on his suit and tie and go to the office. Do normal men still even wear suits and ties to the office? Or is it all Zoom calls and Every Day Casual Friday, now?

I'm sure Macy felt it, too. But I don't ask her. I let myself believe that we shared something deeper than I've ever shared with a sub in my dungeon before today. I want to tell myself it's just that it's new. I've merely fed off her energy like a vampire takes blood. But I'm not sure that's it. I don't think it's her lack of experience.

I think it's her.

I stroke the marks. They criss-cross over her ass and

thighs. I run my tongue over the grooves and welts. When I rub aloe gel into them, she can't hold back the moan.

Finally I can't take it anymore. I have to know. I move my hand between her legs to find her dripping for me.

I roll her onto her back and press my mouth to her bare pussy. She jumps, surprised. Her breathing deepens as she watches me. I take my time tasting her, spreading her open with my fingers, fingering her while I suck and lick and kiss her small bud.

I raise my gaze to hers. "Are you going to come for me like a good girl?"

She swallows hard, but only nods. I don't chastise her for the lack of title. I don't think her words work right now.

I return her nod and go back to work between her legs. She tastes as sweet as I knew she would. She lets out these soft desperate pants as I drive her closer and closer to the edge. My hands dig into her thighs, pulling her greedily toward me. I'm sure I'll leave hand marks, but I don't care.

Her hips buck against my mouth, and she comes apart as I devour her.

When it's over, I stand and straighten my tie. I hold her gaze as I wipe her remaining wetness away. A soft knock interrupts the moment, and Jeffrey steps inside. If I weren't holding Macy's gaze, I think she'd try to cover up, but she doesn't dare. I feel Jeffrey staring at her, but still, she doesn't dare.

"Soren is on the phone for you, Sir."

"Thank you."

Jeffrey excuses himself, and I follow him out into the hall, closing the door behind me.

CHAPTER NINE: MACY

I lay in Colin's bed, panting, trying to will my heartbeat back down to a normal cadence instead of the galloping horses seeking to break free of my chest. I feel ashamed at how easily I surrendered my pleasure to him. It took so very little for him to draw out my orgasm, to have me open and willing, spread out before him like a gift. Like a sacrifice. Just as he said.

No man has ever touched me like this. Aside from some kissing and awkward teenage fumbling, no man has ever touched me at all. Despite my fantasies, my very brief encounters left me wondering if sex was even that big of a deal at all. Even with Livia's gushing details, I wasn't entirely convinced. Now I am.

I'd walked into the room afraid he'd rape me, and within twenty minutes I was desperate for him to be inside me. But it didn't get that far. Colin was pulled away by a phone call. He took the call in the hallway and although I couldn't make out many words, his serious tone was clear.

I pull the sheet up over myself, suddenly very conscious

of my nudity. What am I doing? What's *wrong* with me? I'm lying here like a little idiot fantasizing about my captor. This man is dangerous. This psycho thinks I'm his property. I'm angry at myself for giving in so easily. It took so very little for me to spread my legs for him. Even after the punishment, I shouldn't have been this willing to give myself to him.

I reason with myself that it's an extreme situation. I've been through a lot in the past twenty-four hours. Of course I'd want to appease someone this powerful and dangerous. Of course I would rather have pleasure than pain.

Before all of this I used to read romance novels with heroines captured by the hero. They would always fight so hard and end up getting hurt or punished in some awful way. The stories were easier to brush off when it was fantastical creatures like vampires and werewolves, but it seemed even stupider to me then that the heroine would ever behave in this way as though she had some latent super power that would emerge at just the right moment to save the day.

Even so, when I talked about these books with other readers online, they would always be so annoyed the heroine didn't fight back harder, not shy to tell us all what they would do in her place. I never said what I really felt about all that.

I threw a vase at Colin and ran. I took the opportunity I had. But now I know how futile fighting and running is. Now I can see how complete my cage is, how large his power. There's nowhere to run. I've already seen that first hand when I almost froze to death in the woods last night. I'm lucky something didn't come along and eat me. I still have the scrapes to prove the stupidity of my brief bravery.

If I were a heroine in a novel, all my online friends

would be mad at me and calling me weak saying I didn't try hard enough, and there has to be a way out. I think they'd feel differently if they were really here in this position. Life isn't a novel or a movie. Their bravery would evaporate much more quickly than mine did. Most people just want to be safe, and hardly anyone is brave when it really counts.

It's so stupid for me to care what an online book club called Shameless Stockholm Syndrome Addicts would think of me. But maybe they're right. Maybe there is a way out. Maybe I *haven't* tried hard enough. Couldn't I find car keys and escape? There's a gate on the property. I don't know the code to get out. But… I could find the code, find some keys, get in the car and…

My nonsensical escape fantasies are interrupted by the sound of Colin speaking more loudly now.

"Pack my bags. I need to be in the air in two hours."

"And the girl?" Jeffrey asks.

I stop breathing in the long pause, waiting to hear my fate.

"I'll handle the girl."

"Yes, Sir," Jeffrey says.

Then there's silence for several long minutes. Finally, Colin enters the room and drops some clothes on the bed—my clothes.

"Did I tell you you could cover yourself?" he asks.

"N-no, Master."

I don't forget the title. I won't forget the title ever again. I can't even convince myself that I find it horrible to say these words when I've touched myself night after night to this very scenario. No matter how afraid I am, no matter how much I know I'm not truly safe, my body can't be convinced that this isn't everything I've ever wanted. Every nerve ending hums with the thrill of the final consummation of all my needs and desires. Well, maybe not all of them, not yet. But I know it's coming, and I know I'll open my legs to him just as easily when he's there to take instead of give.

He arches a brow at me, and I slowly pull back the sheet to let him see what he wants to see. I feel my entire body flush as his heated gaze scans each inch of my flesh, finally stopping to take in the exposed juncture between my thighs. I'm so wet I know he can easily still see it in the full bright light of day.

"It's a shame I don't have more time with you," he says finally on a sigh.

My heartbeat picks up speed. A low internal alarm starting to sound. What does that mean?

"A-are you letting me go?"

He shakes his head. "Macy, I told you I'm never letting you go."

It feels as though a heavy stone has settled in my stomach. It pins me in place, and I can't move. The tears stream down my cheeks as if on cue.

"M-master, please. Please, I don't want to die. Please, I… I won't say anything. I won't… "

I flinch as he moves forward, his finger presses against my lips. "Shhhh. I have business to take care of. I can't take you with me, and I'm not leaving you alone with Jeffrey. He only has so much self control. Don't let his formal British accent fool you."

Colin opens a drawer in the night stand and takes out a gleaming silver bracelet. It's solid and sturdy. Heavy looking. He locks it around my wrist with a small key.

"Listen to me very carefully. You're going back to your life for a little while. You will not utter a single word about me. The bracelet is waterproof. There's a microphone, a transmitter, and a tracker embedded inside. If you try to take it off, disable it in any way, or try to escape me, well… I'd be sorry to lose you. I will collect you when I'm ready for you. Get dressed and Jeffrey will drive you home."

Colin stands and drops my cell phone on the bed beside me. He watches me for several agonizing seconds as I allow what he's just said to sink in. The horror of the implied threat is eclipsed by the silver lining. I get to go home. I can see Livia! I've still got a job. I've only been gone for the weekend, after all. No one will even know I was missing.

Like this is the part to focus on. Whoo, I get to go back to work at the library! What a sad, sheltered life. Even after kidnapping and the best orgasm I've ever had, I'm still craving the dusty reference books. I even want to slap myself.

"Are you going to be a good girl for me while I'm gone, Macy?"

"Y-yes, Master."

But my mind is spinning. Is there really a microphone? I can see a small pinhole in the bracelet. Maybe? Or maybe it's all a lie. Maybe there's no microphone. No transmitter. No tracker. Maybe he's toying with me and just wants to see what I'll do. Maybe it amuses him to think he's put some completely powerless bracelet on me, and yet I'll be obeying and fearing and never touching it or trying to take it off for fear some spy of his will take me out with a sniper rifle.

Does he even have spies? I know he's bought at least part of the police force. Jeffrey doesn't care what he does. And Soren *gave* me to him. How many men does he have loyal to him?

Is he really going to just show up in a few days and take

me back? It seems unlikely. Maybe he's lost interest—maybe something about me turned out to be not what he wanted after all. Maybe he's done with me and wants to see how long I'll keep his secret.

I'm not stupid. I don't run around spilling my guts about criminals. People who tell the secrets of criminals, die. And I'm sure this man has blood on his hands. What's one more body to him? There's something in his energy that feels like he and death are closely acquainted, good friends in fact.

Even so I can't help thinking about escape. Real escape. As much as my body has already begun to sing for him, I know he's not my fantasy. He's my doom. How can I not attempt escape? How can he trust or believe I won't do something stupid after I already ran from him last night?

"W-what am I supposed to do?" I ask.

"Go back to your life and live it normally. Spend time with with your friend. Go to your job. Plan your wedding."

I'd momentarily forgotten about Will and the wedding.

"I need to cancel the wedding," I say.

"No. You need to keep your life the same and not do anything different or strange. I will collect you when I'm ready for you."

"B-but I was going to cancel the wedding anyway. I can't marry Will. I don't love him."

Colin shakes his head. "Keep your life the same or I will punish you when I come to collect you."

This asshole. Come to collect me. My gaze darts around the room for another vase to chuck at him.

"If I say something you might kill me but the information will still be out there." Why would he take such a huge risk? But maybe it's not such a risk. Colin Black may not even be his real name. Maybe he has contingency plans. I don't know where we are or how to get here. What could I possibly say that would endanger him anyway?

He stops and pins me with a hard stare that makes me squirm, then he turns on his heel and leaves the room. I'm left gaping after him like a fish. My body is confused. I'm terrified but attracted. My brain is trying to interrupt this insanity to remind me that I've been kidnapped and this isn't a rom com. But the space between my legs reacts like Pavlov's dog to his intensity and the way he touched me.

His touch brings me comfort and pleasure even as everything else about him warns of my impending death.

And while I'm scared he'll make good on his promise and come collect me when he's finished doing whatever he's got to go do that's so important, I'm almost equally afraid that he won't come collect me and I'll be standing at the altar with William, sealing my fate to a man who I know won't be able to make me feel a tenth of what this man just did. And he got interrupted. He wasn't even *done* with me yet.

I try to remind myself that isn't the part to focus on.

I can't marry Will. Not after what just happened with Colin—not after getting a taste of the passion that's possible. I mean… I don't want Colin. Colin is crazy and evil. I want someone who can make me feel the way Colin just made me feel but in a safe environment. I repeat these thoughts over and over in my mind until they almost start to sound true, until I can almost believe I mean them.

I struggle to pull myself out of bed and put on the clothes he left for me. A few minutes later there's a soft knock on the door.

"Miss Laine?" Jeffrey calls in his proper British accent. "May I come in?"

I find it hard to believe Colin is worried about this guy

touching me because his formal British butler routine doesn't exactly scream, *are you ready for me to take you to my secret sex dungeon?*

"Yes, come in."

The door opens. He looks me over and then hands me a black scrap of fabric.

"When we get in the car I'll need you to put the blindfold on. For security. You understand."

I follow him outside, my gaze scanning the house for my captor to no avail. *Do not look for him, Macy.* I chide myself. *Good riddance to the psycho. God only knows what he was going to do with you.* But something inside my chest already clenches at Colin's absence.

Jeffrey opens the back door of a vintage Rolls Royce for me and I slip inside, my hands pressing against the buttery leather seats.

"The blindfold, Ma'am," he says, reminding me of the scrap of fabric still tightly clenched in my hand.

I tie the blindfold around my eyes, then he gets into the driver's side and starts the car. I'm not even tempted to remove the blindfold. I assume Jeffrey is going to be watching me like a hawk through the rearview mirror. It's not worth it.

CHAPTER TEN: MACY

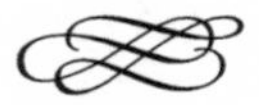

It's Saturday, the first week of October. It's been almost two weeks since Colin let me go. If it weren't for the reminder of the weight of the bracelet, I'd have long convinced myself it was all a dream or some psychotic break with reality. Though for the first week, I had the reminder of the cane marks. I ran my fingertips over them and looked at them in the mirror, willing them to stay with me, even as they faded a bit each day.

Then I berated myself for thinking something so unhinged. And now even his marks are gone.

I've returned to work in the library—it's busy with the fall semester in full swing. And I've gone back to planning the wedding I don't want to have with the help of Livia who is none the wiser that I was ever gone.

As a good best friend does, she noticed there was something off about me, and she commented about the bracelet but I just made up a story about it being a gift from a friend. Though simple, it is quite pretty. It looks like an actual piece of jewelry rather than what it really is.

Once I'd gotten out into the sunlight with it, I could see it was a gleaming silver metal with intricate etchings. It definitely doesn't make me look like a prisoner on house arrest. What if it *is* just a bracelet? I mean, yes, there's the tiny hole that could be the microphone, but what if it isn't? Or what if it's worse? What if it's a camera?

I know he said it's waterproof, but what does that mean, really? How are my daily showers not destroying it? Maybe it really is just a bracelet, and I'm living out my life waiting to be collected by a psychopath and afraid to speak or run because of an imaginary tether.

Is this his real game? Maybe there's no one watching me, no power in this bracelet at all but I'll end up wearing it for the rest of my days on the off chance that the moment I try to remove it a bullet will come sailing my way to end me. What a sociopath.

Despite all this, my daily masturbation schedule hasn't been thrown off even a little bit. If anything I'm doing it more. That one taste of pleasure with another living human ignited a fire in me. It's like getting a taste of a powerful drug and being unable to resist coming back for more. And more. And more. I'm afraid I'm hooked now.

If there's a microphone, who's listening? Is anyone listening? Do the blankets in my bed muffle the sounds of my moans? Does Colin listen? Does he hear me get off? Does he know that when I fantasize now, he's the one my mind can't forget?

With every passing day I wonder where he is and if he's coming back. I always expect my door to burst open, or to be taken off the street, even in broad daylight—such is the power I've convinced myself this man has.

I've taken to romanticizing my capture to a degree that frightens me. After all, what did he really do to me that was so terrible? He didn't personally kidnap me. Soren did that. He didn't throw me in a cell. He didn't beat or torture me. He didn't starve me. He didn't rape me. No everything he did on that score was fully desired—much to my shame.

When I tried to escape, he didn't hurt me. He got me warm, fed me, cleaned me up, and dressed my wounds. He gave me a warm bed instead of a cell or closet to sleep in. He fed me a nice brunch the next day in a sunlit kitchen where Jeffrey made me tea.

He *has* obliquely threatened to kill me or have me killed. So there's that. Obviously that douses the fantasy with a big bucket of frigid water. But I think that's just if I talk or try to get the bracelet off. *STOP rationalizing this.* Why haven't I gone to the police? Okay so maybe the police aren't safe but I could get help outside their jurisdiction. Surely they could trace the transmitter in the bracelet. They could find him.

But that's the problem. There is a terrible small sick part of me horrified by the idea of the police finding this man and taking him away. I should be committed to an institution, assuming there is such a place that would even know what to do with me.

But I can't forget the way his touch calmed me. I can't stop thinking about how it felt completely right to be touched by this man no matter how much he terrifies me or how wrong it is or how wrong he is. It doesn't matter how dangerous the flame is when its warmth keeps me from freezing.

It's too late to try to save myself because a part of me wants him to come back for me to save me from the horrible emptiness of a loveless and passionless marriage, my sentence which still looms over me. I want to cancel the wedding. I have far more fortitude to cancel it than I did before Colin took me, but he said no.

And I'm afraid to defy that order. I'm afraid to defy any order. I know that's not healthy. I know he's not my fairy tale prince. I spend every day just waiting for the monster to come out of the volcano and take his sacrifice. And that wait is just a little too eager. I want to talk to Livia about all this so badly. Maybe she'd understand. After all, didn't her relationship with her guys start out kind of the same? Or she could help me break the hold Colin seems to have over my mind and my libido.

But I can't say anything. What if his threats are real? And then I'd be dragging Livia into this, and she might be in danger too.

When I'm not worrying and obsessing about all this, I'm worried he hasn't come back because he can't come back. I'm worried something bad happened to him. What business did he have? Was it dangerous? Was it criminal? Was he killed or maybe arrested? Every day my anxiety climbs higher, equal parts fear he'll take me away from my boring safe life and fear that I'll never see him again. *I don't want to see him again.* But no matter how many times I force that thought through my mind, it never takes, it never feels real or true.

His cruel beauty haunts my dreams, and the memory of his touch sears my soul.

I was only with him for twenty-four hours. He can't have such a hold on me. Was I truly *that* lonely? And truly *that* stupid? Yes. I was that lonely—the perfect prey for a man like Colin Black. I try not to beat myself up about the stupid part. Loneliness can make you think and want stupid things.

The phone rings, jarring me out of my racing thoughts.

"Macy, where the fuck are you? We had an appointment to taste cake at three o'clock. It's five minutes after and Claudia is glaring daggers into me. If you're not here in fifteen minutes we'll lose the appointment. You know I had to pull strings to get it in the first place."

It's Livia. Shit.

"I'll be there in ten," I say. I hang up the phone, put my hair up in a loose top knot and throw on a sweater and some jeans. The sweater goes off the shoulder, revealing a red bra strap which makes it look like I'm trying hard to look like I'm not trying hard to be sexy. But I don't have time to care about that.

The baker is only three blocks away, so I throw on some tennis shoes and jog the whole way. I'm out of breath when the bell rings over the door as I push it open.

"Sorry," I say, panting. I might really need to do some cardio if I can't even run three blocks.

Despite not wanting the wedding I'm still very lucky to get this appointment. Claudia is in huge demand for wedding cakes. The little cakes are already sitting out on the table waiting for me to taste and select. I don't know why we're even doing this. I should have just chosen what Livia chose. Lemon cake for the wedding, chocolate for the groom's cake. But I don't want to copy her. She's already tried to talk me into canceling this wedding about thirty more times.

"Get the strawberry," Livia says. "Remember how much we loved it but Soren's stupid uncle was allergic? Now I can have my dream strawberry cake!"

She raises and lowers her eyebrows at me in quick succession, and I can't help laughing. In an ordinary situation this might make her the worst matron of honor in the world, trying to vicariously live through my cake, but we both know this wedding with Will is a sham. It may be legal, but there's nothing else real about it. What difference does it make what cake I pick?

Livia isn't the only one here to taste cake. Will is here, too. It's the first time I've seen him since before Colin took me, and I look uncomfortably away, worrying that Colin's touch is some visible brand Will can see.

He holds his hands out to me and grips them, pulling me toward him in the most awkward… I don't even know how to describe what he does so I'll just say it's awkward.

"Macy, finally! I told you the other day I could swing by and pick you up," he says.

I force a smile to my face and try not to shudder at his hands on mine. I want to cancel this wedding. I want to cancel this wedding. I want to cancel this wedding.

Then I start thinking maybe I could figure out a way to get Will to cancel the wedding instead. Would Colin punish me if Will was the one who canceled?

Will pulls out my chair and I sit, then the three of us start this bizarre rotation of cake tasting, passing the plates along in an assembly line of sugar gorging, and drinking black coffee in between bites.

"Oh, I do love the strawberry," Will says.

Truthfully I love it too, but I can't stand the idea of having this wonderful amazing cake with a man I don't love. Lately I can't even remember why we were friends in school. We have next to nothing in common but he seems oblivious to this as he guides the process along, cementing just another step in our ill-fated joining.

"Macy, what if we did alternating layers? We could have two layers of strawberry and then a layer of chocolate and yellow marble cake in the middle for guests to have an option.

It would be like Neapolitan ice cream, but with cake." He is far too into this. I know it's customary for the groom to attend the cake tasting, but his interest in selecting wedding cake just convinces me further he's using me as some sort of beard.

I wonder if his family is super conservative, and that's why. I haven't met his family yet, which I realize is very strange, but they all live out of town and Will has such a busy work schedule. He isn't even going home for the holidays this year. Is there a reason he doesn't want his family to meet me? Or me to meet them? Would they not approve of me? Would they see through all this and know it's not real? Why did he even ask me to marry him? Maybe he wants kids too, and this seems like the normal way. I don't know anymore what's going on.

"Macy? Is that all right with you?" Will asks, indicating the two cake flavors.

I find myself nodding and going along with this selection, barely cognizant of the fact that Will and Livia just chose the wedding cake without any real input from me.

"I'd like hazelnut for the groom's cake," Will says.

I watch as he thumbs through the groom's cake design book. Livia shoots me a look behind his back. The look screams *If you don't end this sham wedding, I will!*

I ignore her and go back to studying Will. He's an architect and recently got a job at a firm here in the city though I'm not sure which one. He's kind of quiet about his work. He's quiet about a lot of things. His work. His family. He's like a shell with no person behind it, or like a movie extra with no backstory. His dark hair falls into his face as he looks at the groom's cakes.

I glance up at the baker and the employees who brought the sample cakes out. Surely they have to see this man and

I are not in love. What must they think about this painfully awkward pairing before them?

My mind strays again for the millionth time to Colin's dark promises in my ear, his mouth on my neck, his hand between my legs, the way I came apart for him, the way he put me back together as quickly as he'd shattered me.

I force the thought from my mind and stop the tear before it slides down my cheek. I will not pine over a man who kidnapped me. Though am I more upset about the kidnapping or the abandonment... the fact that he set me free? I twist the bracelet around on my wrist. Not free. Electric fence. Unless it's a lie and it's just a bracelet. Unless I really am free except in my mind.

What if I'm the one who holds the key to my own cage? I push this thought away as quickly as it arises.

"I think this design for the groom's cake," Will says, pointing at a glossy photo. "What do you think, Macy?"

"Hmmm?"

"That was Soren's groom's cake," Livia says.

And she's right. The photo is a chocolate cake that looks like the art museum where Livia and Soren first met. But I can see why an architect would be drawn to it.

"I apologize," Will says formally. "I didn't realize."

"No, no, it's okay," Livia says. "You didn't know. If you want that cake, you should have it."

"Are you sure?"

Livia plasters on the fakest smile I've ever seen her face produce and nods like an overly happy robot.

"Well, okay, if you're sure." He nods to the baker to indicate that yes he will in fact have the exact same groom's cake that was featured at my best friend's wedding reception. I'm not sure this could be a bigger parody.

"Sorry," I mouth silently to her.

She just rolls her eyes and shrugs, though I know the eye roll isn't intended for me.

Then we look at the cake designs for the main wedding cake. I choose buttercream frosting and the first design I can find. I oooh and aaah over it and act like it's my dream cake just to make this confectionery nightmare end.

Will's chair scrapes out as he gets up and stretches his arms over his head. He's tall and despite his awkwardness he dresses sharply, like a man who understands clean lines and design. He has a kind face, kind eyes, a goofy sort of adorable smile.

"Macy, I'm afraid I've got to meet a client to do a walk-through of a building he wants redesigned."

He leans in and kisses me. It's just a brief peck on my lips, but I pull away as if burned. He smiles at me, seeming oblivious, and then leaves me with Livia.

I make the final arrangements with the baker and start to pay the deposit but she tells me she's already got Will's card details. I nod and Livia and I collect our things and go outside. I feel both grateful and guilty that Will seems to be picking up the tab for everything. His card mysteriously shows up to take care of each expense.

"Oh my god," Livia says as soon as we've gotten outside and she's checked to make sure Will isn't still within hearing distance. "I cannot deal with this bullshit wedding anymore. You can't marry him. You have to end it right the fuck now. Oh my god, that kiss. I need to bleach my eyeballs and take a shower from that kiss. He's so… cloying. Oh god."

Livia is beside herself. You'd think she was the one in this situation and not me.

"I want to do it," I say. I have to force these words out of my mouth because I one hundred percent do NOT want to do it, but I'm still holding out hope that Colin will show up and rescue-kidnap me before the wedding happens. And if he doesn't, I can still run on the wedding day. Because if he doesn't show up by then, he's not coming.

My mind screams at me for wanting a dangerous criminal to come kidnap me away from a wedding to a nice man who would give me a good life and be kind to me. Who the hell knows what awful things Colin would do to me?

A bolt of heat flares to life between my legs because my body knows exactly what kinds of things Colin would do to me.

"Why?" Livia laments. "Why do you want to marry him? You don't love him. You're not attracted to him. The way he touched you in there made my skin crawl. I cannot stand to watch this. I can't be a part of it! You deserve better than this. You deserve a man who will light you up inside. I don't understand why you're still doing this… why haven't you canceled already?"

"You know why. I want a baby, and I'm not getting any younger. I'm not going to find the right guy, Liv. If I was, I already would have found him."

Livia's hand moves over her belly almost imperceptibly. I stop for a moment to really observe her. I've been so wrapped up in my own dramas that I haven't *really* looked at my friend in a while. I notice her clothes aren't nearly as form fitting as they normally are. Her boobs look a little bigger…

"Liv…?"

She looks up with a guilty expression on her face, and I know she knows I've caught her. "Hmm?"

"Are you pregnant?"

She sighs. "I was waiting for the right time to tell

people. I didn't want to steal the thunder of your fake wedding."

I can't even laugh at that because it's too tragic. "Whose is it?" There are after all three potential fathers.

She shrugs. "Soren insists it's his, but I don't think so. He couldn't make it to one of the doctor's appointments and I haven't told him yet... there are two heartbeats."

"Twins?" I ask stupidly, because of course it's twins. It's not like she's got an alien baby growing inside her, though that would definitely be a plot twist.

Livia nods. "Twins run in Dayne's family."

Dayne has always seemed like the most mysterious of the three. He has a quiet kind of power that's more calming than it is unnerving.

Livia's eyes widen suddenly. "Oh no you don't! You aren't changing the subject. We were talking about the wedding and why you need to cancel it."

I've got to get her off this subject for good. I can't go through the next five months hearing this endless refrain, especially since we're ordering the invitations soon.

The only explanation I have for why I can't cancel the wedding, I can't tell her. Colin said not to. He said to keep doing everything just as I had done it. There's a twisted part of me that's afraid if I cancel the wedding he won't come for me. And that thought nearly breaks me because I shouldn't want him to come for me. Or maybe I'm afraid he'll punish me if I defy him. Is that a reasonable fear? I'm not sure. I'm not sure if it's reasonable to think the bracelet really is all he says it is either. I don't know what's reasonable anymore because all I have are my own crazed thoughts echoing around in my head and nobody to bounce them off of.

Maybe he got bored with me before he even got started.

Maybe he gets off on ruining people's lives in petty ways—like lying about the bracelet and tricking me into going through with the wedding I don't want.

I'm not crazy or stupid. Probably. I don't want to be Colin's captive, but holy fuck, the way this man made me feel... the long wait for any man to make me feel that way...

Finally my mind surrenders, and I admit the grotesque truth. I want Colin to take me away from all this. I want to take the terrifying risk with a man who isn't safe because I'd rather feel more of what he made me feel than go my whole life feeling nothing at all.

Even as I think this, I know if he showed up I'd beg him not to take me, the fear of the very real situation would quickly edge out all the fantasy and desire.

"Macy!" Livia shouts.

"What?"

"It's like you're on another planet. Did you hear what I said?"

I didn't, but I'm sure it was about why I shouldn't marry Will.

"It doesn't matter Liv. Look, people get divorced all the time. Will is a nice guy. He's got a stable situation. I'll marry him. I'll have a baby. I'll live a nice quiet safe life and if somehow the guy of my dreams shows up later, I'll get a divorce."

"Seriously?" Livia says, throwing her hands dramatically in the air.

It makes sense to me. I mean it's not like we live in a time in which I'm truly trapped in marriage once it happens. I'm not trapped. I can try it out, see how it goes, and if I'm miserable or find someone else later, I can leave. I feel like a terrible person even thinking this, but I don't think Will really wants me that much either. And anyway, how many people are resolutely serious when they say til death do us part?

The divorce rate would suggest not many. What people really mean is… being with my one true love for all of time is a really romantic notion but I deserve to be happy, so if I'm not in a few years we'll end it. Most people make the promise with good intentions, unable to see how unhappy they could become in just a few short years. The difference for me is I don't have that fairy tale mist hanging over me and my vows.

Livia finally sighs. "Fine. You know you can always stay in the guest wing at my place if things go south."

It's nearly five, and we still have an appointment with the florist. I've half convinced myself that it's actually reasonable to take Will's offer so I can shift myself into the next level of adulthood. He can be my starter husband if Colin doesn't come back. At this point I'm not sure which outcome would be worse.

CHAPTER ELEVEN: MACY

ive Months Later.

I PACE in the makeshift dressing room inside the church. Colin never came back. It seems like it was a lifetime ago when I belonged to a terrifying and beautiful stranger for one day, and he made me feel things I didn't know were possible.

I stare down at the bracelet, more convinced than ever that it's not what he claimed it to be, that he's somehow just fucked with my head and ruined my life because that's what men like him do. Still, it seems such a petty form of evil for a man so all-encompassing.

There still lingers that other part of me that says something happened to him. That he's dead. He got in over his head with something and that's why he didn't come back and now I'm only moments away from my ill-fated wedding.

I met Will's family finally at the rehearsal dinner last night. They seem like nice normal people who weren't overly concerned about the fact that they hadn't met me before because Will is quiet and keeps to himself. That's what they told me.

That statement of course has me worrying that maybe I got it all wrong. Maybe Will is a serial killer. Maybe that's why he needs a normal-looking life, so he can maintain a reasonable murder schedule. The more I think about that, the more I worry it's true. I need to run. Colin isn't coming. And it's crazy for me to want him to.

"Why aren't you dressed yet?"

I look up to find Livia wearing a light green dress. I ended up getting a few girls from the library to be bridesmaids. Their dresses are off-white. Livia's is light green, to go with my darker green. We've almost entirely reversed all color expectations for this wedding.

Liv is about to pop out of her dress with the pregnancy. I swear she could have the babies five minutes ago; she's that pregnant. Of course I didn't know she was pregnant when I set this date, and she probably didn't know either.

There are close to a hundred guests out there. Will invited his whole big extended family, everybody he works with and some college friends. I invited Livia and her family and her men and people I work with. I'm not sure how we ended up with a hundred people, but with all the plus ones and everybody's kids, it adds up fast. At least I can have a normal-sized wedding cake without too much left over.

I'm not dressed yet because I'm still contemplating running—like literally running and fleeing the scene of my own wedding. But I can't do that to Will. I know I've treated him like a stranger these past several months, but we were pretty good friends in college. I actually do like this man. Just not that way.

I think that's why I said yes originally because it somehow seemed less crazy in the moment. That is, until we went on several awkward dates and it became painfully clear to me what a mistake we were making. But we've both soldiered through, refusing to address the elephant in the room.

I finally unzip the garment bag holding my dress and have to fight back the gasp of surprise.

It's not my dark green dress. The dress in the bag is white.

"What is it?" Livia moves closer and she lets out the gasp I couldn't. "Oh my God. Where's your dress? How did this happen?"

I had last minute alterations and a final fitting last week. Maybe my dress got accidentally switched with someone else's. But even as I think it, I know that's not true.

It's Colin. It has to be Colin. He'd remarked on my dark green dress and how I should be married in white My heart thunders in my chest as I try to decide what to do.

"Macy?" Livia asks.

"I went back and got a white dress. I'm sorry. I lost my nerve with the dark green," I lie.

"Oh, honey. But you looked so great in that dress. I was so excited."

I shrug. "I know. But it's too late now. I have to wear the white."

"Did you want the dark green? Did you return it? Do you still have it? If you still have it I could go get it if you want. I mean they can't start the wedding without you."

"No, it's fine. I'll wear this. It's fine." But my hands are shaking as I run my fingers over the fine fabric.

"Do you need help getting dressed?"

I stare at her very pregnant belly knowing there isn't much she can do to help except maybe button some buttons. If there are buttons. I don't even know what the dress looks like.

"I think I've got it," I say, not at all convinced any more by any of my many lies.

Colin is here. It's the only thought that will penetrate my brain right now. Colin is here. He's here. Is he going to take me before the wedding? Is he going to dramatically interrupt the wedding and take Will's place? No, that would be insane. You have to get a marriage license. That kind of thing just happens on soap operas.

But maybe he'll object and drag me away to the horror and gasps of the assembled guests.

I should run. I should run from both of them. I think I'm having a panic attack.

"Are you okay?" Livia asks.

My entire life has become one surreal reality show. How is this my life? How is any of this happening? It's been one innocuous decision after another leading to my doom. Accept an old friend's marriage proposal, what could possibly go wrong? Leave Soren alone with my tea, what could possibly go wrong? Keep planning the wedding I don't want, what could possibly go wrong?

Everything.

I shoo Livia out of the room so I can think. After about five minutes alone, I finally unzip the bag the rest of the way and free the dress from its protective casing.

It's Colin. It's Colin. It's Colin. My mind shrieks like a hyper-active candy-coated toddler.

It's a stunning gown—one I didn't see when I bought my dress. But that's not unusual because I didn't even look in the side of the store with the bigger designers. I knew I couldn't afford it and didn't want to fall in love with a dress I couldn't have.

I stare at the dress as though it might attack me and then I continue to pace. I'm afraid to put the dress on and be taken by Colin, but I'm equally afraid to put the dress on and marry Will. Part of me doesn't want either fate.

I shake myself out of this craziness. There was a mix-up at the shop. Colin isn't coming. If he were coming he wouldn't wait until the very last second. He wouldn't wait until half an hour before I was getting married. Either he decided he didn't want me after all or something happened to him. And why do I care if something happened to him or if he doesn't want me? He's crazy and evil. He wanted to *own* me.

For God's sake, get a grip!

He talked about me like I was going to be presented on some altar to an angry volcano god.

I internally review my original stated plan. Marry the nice normal guy with the nice job and have a nice kid in a nice house. Life isn't a fairy tale. I know Livia got everything I wanted. I know there are men out there who could fulfill my fantasies if I had the courage to go out there and meet them, to try, to risk. But I don't have that kind of courage. My fantasies will remain safely tucked inside my head, and I will live the normal life fate dealt for me.

I take a few deep breaths and slip into the gown. It's silk and deceptively simple, a creamy soft white. The front hugs my curves as though it were made specially for me. The train is sort of bunched up or gathered in the back in a unique way that makes the gown look regal. And there is a veil. I said I wouldn't wear a veil. I said I wouldn't wear white, but I put it on anyway.

And now I am the antithesis of everything I said I would be.

I look down at the bracelet still on my wrist. How long am I going to wear it before I finally find some way to get it removed? Will hasn't asked about it. He probably hasn't even noticed it.

My dark red curls cascade around me as I pin the veil in place. The gown has a zipper so I don't need assistance. I stand in front of the mirror and just stare. Who is this woman? What is she about to do?

I should run. I should change out of this dress and run.

Before I can climb out a window, there's a knock on the door.

"Come in."

Livia's mouth drops open when she sees me. "Holy shit, Macy. You look beautiful."

I think I should be offended by her shock. But she's right. Normally I'm cute. Pretty maybe. But the glamorous woman in the mirror isn't Standard Macy by any stretch of the imagination.

I'm not wearing my glasses today, opting instead for contacts. My makeup is subtle but was professionally done along with my hair earlier in the day. My curls were relaxed around my face. I look like a glam 1940's Hollywood Starlet.

"Oh wow," Livia says again. "This is so much better than the green dress."

I hate to admit it, but it really is. It's the most beautiful dress I've ever seen in real life, and I'm wearing it.

Livia hands me my bouquet of soft white roses. Spring green shoots of filler flowers pop out around the edges.

They match the gown exactly which seems so strange when I didn't plan it that way, but then white roses only come in so many shades and with a green dress what other color flowers was I going to carry? Then she grips my arm and guides me out of the room.

"Come on, the music is starting."

Before I know what's happening, the bridesmaids and Livia are halfway down the aisle. Then the music changes to the wedding march and everyone stands. I had momentarily considered Pachelbel's canon in D but Liv used that, and I really don't want to copycat her entire wedding even though that's the only other completely standard walk-down-the-aisle song aside from the one I'm actually walking down to.

Will looks slightly nervous standing at the front waiting for me. It's the first time he's seemed nervous or unsure this entire time. Maybe he does have feelings for me? But why? We have literally nothing in common and not even zero chemistry. We have negative chemistry.

My gaze keeps darting around looking for Colin. It's not like he can kidnap me out of the middle of a crowded church. How exactly would that go? And I realize of course that he can't object during that part of the ceremony. I mean he could but… he can't. Still I look for him, and a part of me is surprised he isn't here.

But most disturbing is realizing that some part of me really expected him to stop my wedding and that same part wanted it to happen. I need so much more therapy than I can afford.

The minister starts the ceremony, and it finally sinks in that I'm standing in front of a hundred people, my hands inside Will's hands, saying vows and exchanging rings and pledging to be together until one of us dies. Suddenly the flippant thoughts of leaving if it doesn't work out seem much more difficult, as though wedding vows were some sort of magic binding me unwillingly to this man I don't love or even want to sleep with.

This is a great time for me to be realizing I don't want to sleep with the man I just randomly decided was going to father my children. And if I didn't have the strength of will to run away from this wedding to begin with or cancel it at any point, how will I find the will to leave and end it? By the time I've worked through all this the minister is to the point about objecting.

No voice rises to save me. I want to object, but of course I don't. I just stand there numbly allowing this nightmare to continue, making no move to save myself from this lackluster fate. I'm so angry at myself right now, for just allowing this to happen without stopping it. I should have stopped it before now. Fuck what Colin said. Who the fuck is he? I should have canceled the wedding.

Finally the minister pronounces us man and wife, and Will and I share a kiss as clumsy and painful to watch as the few others that have preceded it. We are announced as a couple, the music starts, and we go back up the aisle past smiling faces.

When we get outside in the bright sunlight, Will is smiling, too. He seems actually happy about this. "Well, we did it. We're married," he says.

"Yay," I say, and it's such a fake yay I don't know how the hell he doesn't hear it.

The rest of the day goes by in a blur. First it's about a million photos before the reception. By the time we get to the party, it's already in full swing. Then I'm confronted with every single person Will has ever met. I listen for a good two hours as person after person says Will and I are just perfect for each other and they knew he would find the right girl someday. Everyone is welcoming me to the family, and I feel like the worst person who ever existed.

Our first dance is a slow song without any fancy choreography. I eat at our table while Will is distracted talking to some people I think he works with.

"How do you feel?" Livia whispers, slipping into a chair next to me.

"Like I might vomit," I say.

She looks extremely worried, and I realize maybe I shouldn't have been so honest. After all I haven't bothered with honesty for months now. My best friend doesn't even know I was kidnapped. I glance over to the table Livia was sitting at. Soren's dark gaze is trained on me.

I wish I knew what he was thinking. I wonder if he knows something about Colin. But there's no way I'll ask him. How would that conversation even go? *Hey you know the guy you gave me to? Well he let me go temporarily and said he'd come back. Haven't heard from him and just wondered if maybe he died because I really don't want to be married to this other guy and I can't stop touching myself thinking about the man you gave me to.*

I look away from Soren, and finally, after several long minutes I feel his hard gaze leave me, and I can breathe freely again.

"Where are you two going on your honeymoon?" one of Will's cousins asks.

"I'm taking her all over Europe. To England, Ireland, Scotland, Spain, Italy..."

"How will you fit that all into a week?" she asks.

"It's not going to be a week. My firm is sending me on some work assignments overseas, so it's a working honeymoon. We'll be gone a month."

"Oh wow. Macy, what about your work?"

"Oh, I got a leave of absence," I say.

I've only known about this honeymoon plan for the past two months, but I'd convinced myself it would give us some time to get to know each other.

"Well that's lucky!" she says. "I'm so jealous. I'd love to go to Europe for a month."

I smile politely, biting back the urge to offer her my ticket and crawl under the table.

We cut the cake next, and I get to have some of that nearly magical strawberry cake. Will's family goads him to smash it on my face because that's what you do, but Will is a perfect gentleman.

I somehow survive the garter experience and more of Will's fumbling while everybody laughs and cheers, and then I toss the bouquet. The reception finally winds down and we leave through a tunnel of sparklers to a limousine that takes us to a nearby hotel.

"I can't wait to get to the room," Will says once we're alone in the limo.

I shrug away from his kiss. "I'm kind of tired after today," I say.

"Well, it is our wedding night. I was very patient with you."

Alarm bells start to go off but then he laughs and says, "I'm kidding. You should see your face. Yeah I'm tired too."

If anything this *joke* raises even more alarm bells because it doesn't feel like a joke. He seems very different all of a sudden from the person I thought he was.

My heart pounds against my chest as he leads me to the third floor and down the hallway to the honeymoon suite. What do I really know about this man? Aside from being casual friends in college, I mean. He slips his key card into the door. A silent beep and a flick to green. Then he opens the door, picks me up, and carries me over the threshold.

He sets me on my feet and shuts the door behind him. There's champagne and chocolate and strawberries on a tray on the bed which is covered in red rose petals. Candles are lit around the room. There's a fire roaring in the fireplace. And even though it's March, the fire is welcome because it's still very cold outside. The bathroom door opens, and a man in a suit steps out drying his hands on a towel.

I shriek, shocked that someone else would be here, but then I look into his face and my heart nearly stops.

Colin.

I expect Will to demand to know who this man is and what he's doing in our room. But instead he says, "Sir, your toy. You've got her free and clear with nobody missing her for the next month."

I gasp and spin to find Will blocking my exit.

"Will? What are you doing?"

He rolls his eyes. "Oh please. Anybody could see you didn't really want to marry me. Imagine if I'd wanted to marry you. You would have dragged me through a loveless marriage. Really, Macy, I kind of think you deserve this if we're being honest. You could have canceled the wedding at any time."

I turn back to find Colin smirking... "What? Why? I... what?" I really can't form coherent words or thoughts right now nor can I figure out how this is even happening.

How does Colin know Will? How is Will working for Colin? What is happening right now?

Colin just smiles. "William has been working for me."

"But, what if I'd canceled the wedding?"

Colin shrugs, seemingly unconcerned. "I had contingency plans, but you would have been punished for disobeying me."

"But... what about Will's family? Aren't they going to ask questions when I just never show up again? Holidays are a thing."

"Are you sure that was *really* his family?"

I'm gaping at him now. I mean the more explanation I get the less real it sounds. I'm trying desperately to make this make sense. But even if both Will and Colin said "Gotcha!" it still wouldn't make sense.

"Who the hell else would they be?" I ask. I feel the more I allow myself to be pulled along into this insane alternate reality the more pieces of my otherwise sound mind are drifting away from me.

"Actors. They think they're part of a sort of hidden camera reality show. And they all signed NDAs about it because of supposed rules with the studio. They think this is a pilot episode and may not make it onto TV. So when it doesn't, they'll just shrug and move on with their lives."

"You said you had me for a month free and clear. What happens after a month?"

"By then you'll belong to me so completely that you won't want to get away. Right now only your body is mine. But soon your soul and mind will belong to me as well."

He says this as though he's collecting baseball cards. As if all these pieces of me will at some point be put in a display case for guests to ooh and aah over.

I should be offended, but my body only has one setting with this man: turned on. Seriously how did I even survive on this planet this long? My libido obviously wants me dead.

"Here are the papers," Will says, pulling a manila folder

out of his tuxedo jacket. "I took them off the minister when he wasn't paying attention."

Colin takes the papers out, studies them, then tosses them in the fire. "Congratulations on your divorce, Macy. No legal filed paperwork, no legal marriage."

CHAPTER TWELVE: COLIN

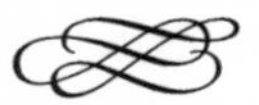

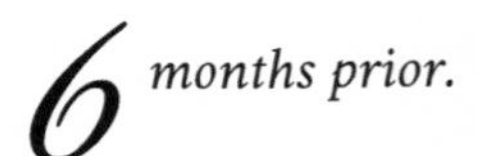

months prior.

I STAND OVER MACY, feeling quite satisfied with myself when Jeffrey interrupts with a phone call. Fucking Soren. I could strangle that motherfucker. He has the worst timing. I take the phone out into the hallway.

"What is it?" I growl.

"I spoke to Dayne about your request."

"And?"

"You can come back to the club, use his cottage, and have the collar under one condition."

"And that condition would be...?" Soren is the most infuriating person I know. What? Does he want me to beg him for information? Perform tricks like a circus monkey? He just doles information out like breadcrumbs in the forest that I'm supposed to happily scoop up and put in a basket like some frolicking Red Riding Hood.

He forgets I'm also a wolf.

"A sacrifice," is Soren's cryptic reply.

"What in the fuck does that mean?" He's twisting things around on me. Macy was payment.

"And there's one other condition. She has to remain untouched. We want a *virgin* sacrifice," he says.

"You couldn't have told me that before you brought her to me? I could have just kept her under surveillance with Will."

"We hadn't decided our terms yet. So you've already fucked her?"

Already? I've had her for nearly twenty-four hours. I *should* have already done it. And I'm still not quite sure why I held back.

"No. Went down on her," I say. What I really want to do is accuse Soren of knowing exactly what he's doing, setting me up so I can't meet the requirements of his offer.

"Anything else?" Soren asks, his tone deceptively calm.

"No." I want to kill him. Who the fuck is he to control what I do with the woman he *gave* me? Has he forgotten how this all started and who has the power? Who *had* the power. Now that it's something I want that he has, I'm no longer the one calling the shots. It's just like that miserable bastard to flip things around again so somehow he's the one in control of everything.

"Colin?" Soren says like I just hung up.

He knows what I'm thinking… the complicated calculus running through my head, trying to decide if it's a win or a lose for me. He'd be running the same calculations through his head if our positions were reversed. He probably ran them when he offered me Macy to begin with.

"You're getting something you want, too," Soren says. "Doesn't that make it a win-win. And nothing changes the fact that she's yours. Come to Costa Rica. We're all at The Cottage. Meet with us. You can pick who will be involved. We have a list of members for you to select from, but we can't discuss the details over the phone. You know where to meet. Tomorrow night, nine o'clock."

"I can't just leave Macy here alone with Jeffrey, you know how he is. I can't guarantee purity if I do."

"I'm sure you'll think of something." Soren disconnects the call.

Fuck. Fuck. Fuck.

I haven't wired Will's money yet. I could sweeten the deal and keep him on Macy for a bit longer. But I can't let her out of my sight without at least a tracker.

I had the bracelet made, knowing I'd need to monitor her when I first let her resume her life more-or-less. I can't keep my wife under lock and key, after all. So, I can test the leash.

I don't know. Maybe I should just let her go. She's already getting inside my head.

Jeffrey has been lurking within earshot since we got out into the hallway. I turn to him now. "Pack my bags. I need to be in the air in two hours."

"And the girl?"

"I'll handle the girl." Maybe this is for the best. Maybe with enough space and distance from her, I'll come to my senses. Maybe I won't return for her at all.

CHAPTER THIRTEEN: COLIN

he Present

MACY LOOKS like she may go into shock. As soon as Soren returned from his honeymoon, he gave me a dossier on her and told me his terms. I was intrigued but not quite ready to collect or commit. At the same time I was paranoid she'd meet someone while I was making up my mind. Ordinarily that wouldn't be a problem, I could arrange something. I could have her no matter who entered her life. But I got caught up in this virgin sacrifice idea. When Soren first used those words with me, something dark and primal kicked in.

Since that time, it has been brought to my attention that Macy is a kinky little thing. How one woman can be simultaneously so innocent and so filthy is anybody's guess.

I couldn't have anybody deflowering her before I was

ready for her. And so the deep dive into her past commenced as I tried to figure out who I could bring on board with my plans. Who could I get to babysit and guard her virtue?

As it turned out there was a man from her past who had a lot of debts which I could make go away. When I interviewed him and discovered he'd actually made one of these *if we're both single by thirty* pacts, I knew Macy was a gift from the universe—or more likely some particularly dark god who just liked my style. Synchronicity like that doesn't just happen. I couldn't have planned for it. But it was a perfect set-up.

"That will be all, William," I say, dismissing him finally. He's been standing here leering at my prize as though I'm going to let him in on the action. While I like to share, I wouldn't share her with this guy. I know she doesn't want him and sharing is as much about her pleasure as it is about my power to do so.

When he doesn't move, I say, "The money has been wired. Remember my terms."

He nods and leaves.

William won't talk. He knows what will happen if he does. Plus, he participated in the crime, and he knows I have evidence to that effect.

Macy backs away, fumbling for the doorknob.

"Do you like the dress?" I ask.

"W-what?"

This clearly isn't what she expected me to say. "The dress? Do you like it?"

She looks down as if she's forgotten what she's even wearing. Her hands skim over the smooth silk. This one dress costs more than Macy makes in a year. I saw it live on a runway. I'm not ordinarily the type of man who goes to a bridal couture runway show, but I had business with the designer. I happened to look up, saw the dress, and claimed it for Macy. It's one-of-a-kind. Just like her.

This girl was absolutely not going to wear a green wedding dress.

"It's beautiful." Then she looks up at me, and there are tears in her eyes. "I thought you were going to stop the wedding. Why didn't you?"

Now it's my turn to be shocked. She was waiting for me to come for her? I stand still for a full minute while my brain goes completely offline as I try to grasp the fact that she was waiting to be rescued from this wedding… by me of all people.

In truth, once I met her in person I'd meant what I said. I did want to trade Will out and marry her. I wanted to rewrite my entire carefully crafted plan. Not a legal marriage, of course… but I wanted to be the one standing at the front of the church reciting vows. The fact that I wanted this—even fleetingly—still disturbs me.

But then I remembered Livia was present when Soren first promised Macy to me, and she'd likely put two and two together. Then Soren called, demanding my presence at the club.

"I just wanted the dream wedding. Like Livia," she says, and the sadness in her voice is palpable.

"Wasn't it the dream? You got all the things you wanted."

She thinks much of her wedding was financed through Livia by Soren and that other things were favors and lucky breaks and discounts. But behind the scenes I was the one signing all the checks. Metaphorically, of course. Nobody still writes checks. I used my black card.

She just looks at me like I'm the stupidest human who

ever existed. "No! It's not the dream. It wasn't what I wanted. I wanted…" She trails off as though she's already said too much. And she has. Somehow I know what she was going to say. Maybe not in these words, but she didn't want the wedding. That's not the fairy tale. The fairy tale is the perfect wedding to the man she wants.

And somehow, she wanted me. *Who* is this creature? How does she exist in the world?

She holds up the bracelet. "Is this even real? Or is it just another trick?"

I capture and hold her gaze in mine. "I heard every. Single. Orgasm. Were you thinking about me while you had them?"

She blushes furiously and looks away. That's a yes.

I loosen my tie and take two strides toward her. She flinches as though I'm going to hit her.

"You got all the things you wanted, Macy. Just not all in one package."

She shakes her head stubbornly, the tears still moving down her face. "No. I wanted a man who loves me."

I freeze. It's like she knows this is the one thing I'm not sure I'm capable of giving someone. I can give her luxury, comfort, safety—from everyone but me at least—pleasure, kink. I can buy her anything she wants, but I don't even know if I have a heart to give. And I don't trust anyone, including myself.

I push her up against the door, my hand wrapped around her throat. Any other sane human would struggle at this point, but her body melts against mine as though my hands on her could never be bad in any context. And I find it still unnerves me. I don't know what to do with this level of trust aimed at me.

"No," I say, "That's not your fairy tale. You don't want

some boring sweet vanilla man like William to ride in on a horse and take you off to a normal happily ever after in the suburbs with a minivan. You want the fire that burns you, the storm that consumes you and sweeps you out to sea far from any hope of rescue. Wish. Granted."

Before she can respond, there's a knock on the door. "Mr. Black?"

Right on time. I stand back and level a hard look at Macy. "My attorney is as ruthless as I am and, much like me, he considers laws little more than options to consider. You *will* sign the papers."

CHAPTER FOURTEEN: MACY

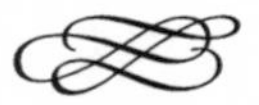

Colin's words about the fire and the storm and the sea ignite something in me. Am I this transparent? My dangerous desires are going to get me killed. He is not safe. He's made this explicitly clear, and yet even if it were real with William, I didn't want him or that boring safe life. That's the problem with safe… it's also boring.

I've been rescued from boredom and thrown into uncertainty with a man who lights me up even as I know I can never trust him. I jump as a knock reverberates against my back.

"Mr. Black?" a male voice says from the other side of the door.

Colin gives me some breathing room and the look he sends me has my heart fluttering in my chest. I'm not sure what this look is meant to convey. It could be some kind of warning, or a promise for what he has planned later after this interruption has gone away.

"My attorney is as ruthless as I am and, much like me,

he considers laws little more than options to consider. You *will* sign the papers."

I just stare blankly at Colin like a little idiot.

What papers? But then I remember breakfast the morning after I was given to him when he showed me the legal documents and how he needed a "Mrs. Black."

I'd been full of tea, flaky buttery croissants, and bravado. I can't seem to find any of that bravado right now. I mean there's still a tracking and surveillance bracelet around my wrist. And he's set up this entire insane scenario. I still can't wrap my mind around the fact that Will was working for him. This whole time. He never would have contacted me about that stupid pact otherwise.

And that kind of hurts my feelings a little bit. But I can't start crying about it now because that would be ridiculous with everything else going on.

Maybe Will and I weren't that great of friends in college. And we were sort of drunk that night when we made the pact. But still. How did Colin find out about that? How did he know he could get Will to turn on me for some money? How much did he pay him to go along with all of this?

It occurs to me suddenly that maybe Will had liked me back in college, that maybe he'd wanted more than friendship but either I didn't see it or didn't want to see it. So was this some kind of payback because I couldn't call forth those feelings from the romance aether?

I move out of the way as Colin opens the door to invite his attorney inside. The man gives me a long, slow once-over that gives me the creeps.

"She's off limits," Colin says.

So that wasn't my imagination. I'm reassured at least in

this moment that nothing seems to get past Colin, and he's veto'd whatever desires were in the attorney's gaze.

The attorney doesn't comment on this, but he does stop leering at me. Suddenly he's all professionalism. The three of us sit at a table in the living area part of the honeymoon suite. The papers are passed to Colin. He skims over them as if making sure everything is in order and signs them, then the papers are slid to me along with a blue ballpoint pen. Two expectant gazes land on me.

"Sign," Colin orders.

"I-I need to read them to know what I'm signing," I say.

"This isn't a negotiation. It doesn't matter what they say. You're signing them. They're for your benefit."

There's no reaction to Colin's coercion from the attorney. It's super nice to know we have such ethical people working in law.

"If they're for my benefit I should be able to read them." I fight not to flinch as I say these words. Sometimes I can be very stubborn, and my anger is about to edge out my fear. Maybe.

The attorney raises a brow. "You've got your work cut out for you training this one," he says. And the leer is back again.

"Oh, she will bend to me," Colin says, sounding supremely confident.

He's probably right. That growl in his voice just now? Oh, I felt that in places I shouldn't feel it.

I feel the blush rise to my face so I look down at the papers. I'm hoping the boring legalese will douse the flames of these feelings because I don't want Colin or his creep attorney to be able to figure out that I'm turned on right now. There are about a thousand ways that could go badly for me.

I know realistically I'm not getting out of this room until I've signed these papers and that Colin possibly is never letting me go anyway. And didn't I spend months fantasizing about him? Didn't I spend months hoping he'd rescue me from this farce of a wedding?

But still, I want to know what I'm signing, and unless he plans to murder me right here right now or punish me in front of the attorney, I'm not signing until I know. Oh my god... why did I just think that? His attorney is a slime ball, but still, somehow the idea of him watching Colin turn me over his knee and spank me in front of him excites me.

"Just sign," Colin says interrupting my crazy mental babbling.

It takes me a whole five seconds to work up the nerve to stop pretending to read and look up. I stare at Colin. "You waited months. You can wait fifteen minutes while I read."

He actually laughs at this. "By all means, Mrs. Black. Read, then."

And so I read. If I leave I get nothing. If I leave after children, he gets custody but I get very generous terms around seeing my own kids. How magnanimous. We both know he's not letting me go anywhere so that's just for show so no red flags get triggered when the paperwork gets filed. I'm not sure how this could be legally enforcible anyway. It seems so one-sided.

Except the children are referred to as heirs—heirs which I'm contractually obligated to deliver to him. Like a broodmare. This is what I imagine pre-nups for royal weddings look like. Yes, I've done all that background research too. There is this totally creepy level of fertility checking and demands of doing one's duty to produce royal babies. And while officially this offends all my modern sensibilities, on another secret level I don't like to think about, this idea turns me on. A lot. My spank bank fantasies could fill a library, and a lot of them are in the *breeding an heir* category. Don't judge me.

I'm not marrying into a royal family, but I may as well be. Colin has an enormous amount of money and power.

On paper he really is the dream. But I also get this distressing vibe that he's murdered people, so that takes the shine off things just a little.

If he leaves me, very generous terms provide for my safety and comfort. It is *lavish*. I mean there are specifications about properties I will be given and sums of money so big I can barely comprehend it. I even get staff, like people to drive me around and guard me, even personal shoppers for things like grocery shopping which apparently wealthy people never do for themselves… unless they like doing it, of course. If he can afford to give me all this if he leaves, then how much must he actually *have*?

There isn't even some no-cheating stipulation, just, if he leaves me, here is the long list of extravagant shit I get. You'd think he'd *want* me to read these papers, since it makes him almost look like a human being, instead of a man posing as a god, accepting me as tribute.

"Do they meet with your approval, Mrs. Black? Would you like a larger palace in the event I take your virtue, get bored, and toss you to the curb?"

I don't respond to his goading, I just sign. The reality is… I don't need his money. Sure, it might make certain aspects of my life more comfortable but if I had the freedom to leave and did so, the *you get nothing* threat, really just doesn't land with me. *We're not all gold diggers, asshole.*

The attorney puts the papers in a briefcase, gives Colin

a copy, and then leaves me alone with my generous captor. Colin slides the deadbolt into place, then turns to me.

I stand, totally still, a deer frozen in front of the oncoming car as he stalks me. He stops a couple of feet away.

"Take off the ring."

"W-what?"

"The ring. Remove it."

I glance down at my shaking hand, already having forgotten the shiny gold wedding band.

"But... I signed those papers and... don't you want me to wear a ring?" Maybe he wants me to wear a ring he picked, instead of William's ring. But if Will was working for him this whole time, wouldn't the ring really be Colin's? He no doubt paid for it.

I take the ring off and offer it to Colin.

He shakes his head. "No, read the inscription."

It never occurred to me that the ring would have something engraved inside the band. It's not the kind of thing Will and I talked about. I cross the room to a floor lamp and hold the ring under the light as I examine the engraved inscription.

In harsh block font, the words read: "Mrs. Colin Black."

An involuntary shiver runs down my spine, as goosebumps pebble out across my exposed arms. I thought I was saying vows to Will, but the ring slipped on my finger shows me belonging to another man entirely. It feels as though some kind of dark magic swirled around as I was tricked, sealing my fate to Colin, even as I thought I was marrying someone else.

I'm not sure what to say to this or how to react, so I start to put the ring back on.

"Give it to me," he says, holding his hand out.

So the ring was just him making a point about how foolish I am? How easily he can move me across his game board into whatever strategic position he wants me in?

But I don't argue. I can't bring myself to argue to wear his ring, a ring that brands me as his and basically has a "property of" sticker on it, in case anybody gets confused about ownership rights. I pass the gleaming ring to him, and he slips it into his pocket.

"Don't worry, Mrs. Black. You'll get it back at the appropriate time, but I should be the one to put it on you. I want the moment to have… gravity."

My mouth is dry as I stare at him. I feel so awkward. What now? I'm caught off guard by his next words because they're so normal.

"You picked over your food at the reception. Would you like me to order you something?"

I don't know what I expected to happen when we were alone again, but it wasn't for him to order me room service.

"Um… yes?" And suddenly I find I can't meet his gaze. I don't know why I'm like this. One minute I'm all bravado and defiance and staring people down, and the next I am so unbelievably shy that it's painful to even have his gaze on me.

"Yes, what?"

I stare at the upholstery of the sofa. I know what he wants. It's been a while since I was alone with him. But I played and replayed that day over and over in my mind for months. I touched myself thinking about it so many times I lost count… all while going along with the engagement to William. But the shyness comes over me again and… I just can't say the word.

There's a long silence—a silence that stretches before me like an infinite dark forest.

I yelp when his hand is suddenly wrapped around my arm and he drags me back to the chair I'd sat in to sign the papers.

"Don't move," he says.

I watch as he crosses the room and pulls out a black case. He removes something—I can't determine what—and strides back across the floor to me. I shrink back. There is resolute purpose in his gaze, and I want to blurt out "Master", but I can't force the word out.

Because I'm me, and I like to make things harder than they need to be. It's clear to me when I'm using the intelligence I supposedly have that this man will not be denied. He has seemingly infinite resources and just managed to set up a situation where I won't be missed for a month. I don't want to think about the implications of that.

He ties my wrists behind my back with black rope and gags me. It's a ball gag which I can tell came from some super high-end kink store because the leather straps are soft. The ball isn't too big. The way it fits is actually... comfortable? I know that sounds weird, but it's not a distressing feeling. At least not physically. I'm a little bit distressed mentally over the fact that I'm not screaming or fighting him.

He bends so he's eye level with me. "You won't speak again until you're ready to say it."

Then he crosses to the phone and orders us some food like all of this is just a normal day for him. When he gets off the phone he sits on the sofa and pulls out some papers and a laptop and starts doing some work. I have no idea what kind of work because I don't know what he does, but he's very engrossed in it, whatever it is.

I have time while we wait for the food to think about my predicament. I still don't fully understand why this man is doing all of this. I mean surely he could get any woman he wanted. Even if his social skills are lacking, he's rich and hot and commanding, and that opens the legs of probably eighty percent of the female population all by itself. Maybe he's already fucked all of those women.

And if he doesn't want to be bothered with relationships, he could pay for sex. Hell, he could pay for this *stockholder-pleasing Mrs. Black* he claims to need. It could be a business arrangement instead of a felony. I think about the papers I signed. Did Soren read these papers and approve them? Are these the terms Soren secured for me?

Am I supposed to feel grateful about this?

CHAPTER FIFTEEN: COLIN

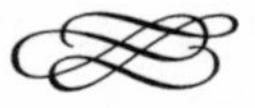

I'm pretending to work because I'm suddenly a teenage boy with a raging hard on and a crush. This is so fucking ridiculous. I need to punish this girl for all the things she makes me feel. She watches me, and I watch her. Predator and prey. But I swear a fucked-up part of me thinks I may be the prey. I just don't buy Macy's innocent act.

I know she's a virgin, so there is a sense in which she's innocent, but I can't make any sense out of her reactions to anything. That first night when Soren delivered her to me… all that made sense. And on some level her coming apart under my attentions made sense. But right now she isn't making sense. She's not fighting or struggling or crying or whimpering. Is she in some kind of shock?

I have no idea.

Within a month I'm sure I won't have to worry about letting her off the leash. I'm half not worried about it now, considering what a good girl she was while she was away from me. She didn't try to run. She didn't try to remove the bracelet. And those sweet moans almost-but-not-quite cloaked by the shower spray… then the moans later when she was in bed each night and every morning… yes… my Macy is a very good girl.

I'm the one acting like the virgin. Hundreds of women have been in my bed. They've knelt for me, crawled for me, sucked my cock, swallowed, bared their asses for their spankings… all of it. Most of it was an act. But they did these things. And I'm about to be taken down by this… freckle-faced, red-haired… virgin with impossibly innocent green eyes along with that unexpected fire that intrigues me.

My internal insanity is interrupted by a knock on the door. Room service. I ordered for Macy since she was in no position to tell me what she wanted. Maybe she should have followed my rules.

Macy's eyes widen as I cross to the door. I'm curious about what she'll do. I could inform her that I could have the person delivering the food killed or that I could kill him myself. Both things are true. But I don't want to influence her reaction. I want to see what she'll do without any input from me.

I open the door to allow the food to be rolled in. The man—really kid… he's about twenty—stops cold when he sees Macy. She sits there, bound and gagged in her wedding dress at the table. Her pale green eyes are wide, and her face is flushed. I'm just now noticing the way her wrists are tied back combined with the dress she's wearing, pushes her breasts up in the most inviting way.

It's a testament to how much she's messing with my mind that I'm only now noticing this.

The guy stares at her tits, and I know he can't decide if he's walked in on a hostage situation or a sex game. The hard on he's sporting suggests he thinks probably the latter. It's a reasonable deduction. She is, after all, wearing a wedding dress in the honeymoon suite, and I'm not behaving in the sneaky way of a kidnapper.

"You can put the food on the table," I say, still watching them both with interest.

I am fascinated. Macy has this small golden opportunity to struggle or cry or make any sort of distressed sound to alert this guy to the fact that she's in trouble. But she's smart.

And she seems to understand implicitly that remaining calm will keep the kid alive.

"Y-yes, Sir," he says.

I arch an eyebrow at the title and look at Macy. I'm sure she understands that look… like… See? He can give me a title. Why not you? I admit Master is a different thing than Sir, though both indicate that someone is above you in some sort of power hierarchy. Still, Master is the more objectifying title. For her, not me.

He puts the food on the table, barely able to tear his gaze from Macy's tits.

"Would you like to stay and watch me deflower her?" I ask. She won't be deflowered until Costa Rica, so this kid isn't seeing shit, but I'm enjoying this show.

He flushes brighter red than Macy if that's even possible. "N-no, Sir. I… I have work."

I laugh at this and turn my attention back to my sort-of bride. Wait… is she turned on right now? Her pupils are dilated, and her breathing is coming out in a way that in any other circumstance would suggest to me a woman ready to come.

I pull out a roll of hundreds and press them into his hand. "Nobody likes a gossip," I say.

"N-No Sir."

He scurries out of the room like he's on fire. As soon as I shut the door I pick up my cell phone and dial my guard at the end of the hallway. "Follow and stay on that guy. Let me know if he talks to anyone."

I hear the obligatory *Yes, Sir* before the call disconnects, and I turn my attention back to Macy.

I'm not too worried about the kid. I'm registered under an alias. Someone else signed in for me. I kept to back entrances. No cameras have caught me. This whole suite was swept for electronic bugging and cameras before I entered. And no fingerprints will be left behind. It's all very… clean.

I sit at the table across from my captive and remove the silver lid from my steak and baked potato. I leave Macy's covered for now.

"Are you ready to give me a title?" I ask conversationally as I cut into the steak.

She watches me for a minute as if weighing her options.

"I'll feed you either way," I say. I may be a bastard but I'm not going to starve her. She needs to know she's more-or-less safe with me, and I won't withhold any basic needs. That doesn't mean there won't be punishments for all of these infractions. I'm keeping a list.

And of course she tests me by shaking her head no.

I sigh and take a bite. It's medium rare and perfect. The guys in the kitchen know how to make a steak.

"Why not?"

She can't give me a real answer, she's still gagged. And I love the way she looks now. Gags aren't a big fetish for me, but I realized it might be necessary with her. I didn't know if she'd start screaming and make a scene. I could have had her delivered directly to the jet, but I wanted to sleep on the ground tonight. Although the jet has a large and very comfortable bed, I'm not the biggest fan of air sleep. I'm not great with flying, though I mask my anxiety well. After all, I would hardly inspire terror in people if they knew I was a nervous flyer.

She just shrugs.

I finish my dinner and drink down the glass of cold water that came with it. Ordinarily I'd have something a bit stiffer than water, but I want to maintain a level head.

I motion her forward, and she looks confused at first but finally figures out what I want and bends forward so I can remove the gag. When it's gone I press a glass of water to her lips and allow her to drink.

"Are you going to untie me?" she asks.

"Are you going to address me?" I counter.

"I can't. It's weird."

But the blush on her face tells a different story.

"It gets weirder the longer you resist it."

She seems to consider the truth of this. I take the lid off her food and cut her steak.

"Are you fucking kidding me?" she asks.

"Language," I say, as if I'm chastising a toddler. I hold a piece of the meat up to her mouth.

She considers me. "Am I going to survive you?"

"Most likely."

I prod at her lips with the steak, and finally she relents to let me feed her.

CHAPTER SIXTEEN: MACY

I can't believe I'm letting this man feed me like a small child. This steak is amazing though. It's taking everything in me not to rattle on about Angus beef and inform Colin about all the random weird facts I happen to know about it. Also, this meat was pasture-raised. I can tell. Factory farmed meat is the worst. Even aside from the animal cruelty, it just tastes bad. If you're going to eat meat, it's important that your food eats good food, too.

Letting him feed me is probably strong terminology. It's not like I have a lot of choices here. But he's not starving me or beating me. And I know that's in him. That potential. I didn't just imagine it the first time when Soren took me to his estate. This man is dangerous. He has a wicked looking scar above his left eye that seems to underline this point. It doesn't detract from his beauty… but it does give one pause.

Did he get into a knife fight? Did someone try to assassinate him? Is he in a position where his death would be called assassination?

I honestly don't know why I'm resisting calling him what he wants to be called. I don't know why I'm pushing him. There is this deeply fucked-up part of me that desperately wants to be his good girl and do whatever pleases him. But there is another part of me that wants to find out what happens when I say no. How will he react? How safe am I ultimately with this man?

You don't know how safe you are with a man until you tell him no.

And I know that's stupid, because if I'm not safe—and why would I be safe?—goading him into… punishing me... It could put me in a lot of danger. But he's being very calm about all this.

As he's feeding me the baked potato I also have to really fight to not tell him why restaurant baked potatoes are so different from how people normally make them at home.

What they do is they drizzle them with olive oil and salt and pepper the skins before wrapping them in the foil to bake. Some of the oil bakes into the potato which is what makes them fall apart and taste so great. But I don't say this. I'm still mortified I rambled about the difference in fine and bone china the last time he had me. Like he cares.

And part of me is afraid if I let too much of my Encyclopedic weirdness out that he'll get tired of it, and me, and that it won't be safe for me. I'm not sure I believe in that contract I signed, that he'd just let me go and give me the fairy tale without the prince. Like a Barbie Dream House… Ken not included.

He doesn't push me again about the title. I don't think he's given up this battle, he's just choosing not to do anything about it right now. Maybe because we're in a hotel—not tucked away at his private compound—and if I scream, someone might hear.

I'm not sure why I haven't screamed.

He unties me and guides me into the bedroom part of the suite. Okay, this is happening. This is happening right now. I'm about to be deflowered on my fake wedding night by a man who basically somehow owns me, and I want him even though I shouldn't but… I can't just…

"C-Colin?" My voice comes out small, but he heard me.

He comes up behind me, pulling me flush against him. I feel his hard erection press against my lower back through the silk of my dress. His hand wraps around my throat as he pulls me closer.

"What did you call me?" he whispers in my ear.

And suddenly I'm so overloaded with so many feelings and sensations. Terror, arousal… safety. I know that last one doesn't make sense at all, but when his hands are on me… it's how I feel. I don't understand it but when he touches me like this I know he would protect me from anything. And I don't know how I know it or why I know it. But it comes from my *knower*. You know, that part of you that just knows things? It's not logical. I can't break it down with charts. It's not even my feelings… it's not emotional. It's just… I know.

A breathy sigh leaves my throat as my body melts and surrenders against his.

"I'm sorry, Master." The resistance has left me now because when he touches me like this, I feel too much his to call him anything else. The word that before felt silly and out of context and embarrassing, seems like the most normal thing in the world to call him when he unleashes this side of himself. That ruthless storm. Like Soren. I can't resist that energy. I feel the same things with Colin as I felt around Soren, which both relieves me and repulses me.

It relieves me because these feelings aren't directed at my best friend's husband. And it repulses me because Colin isn't playing a kinky game. I am *actually* his property. I'm trying hard to hold on to rage and indignance and offense about this but I just want him to take me and finally rip away this barrier to all the desires that have been kept locked within me for far longer than is normal.

He spins me to face him.

"Good girl," he says. Then his hand is around the back of my neck, his fingers threading into my hair as he pulls me in for one of those kisses only he can make real. I know I have practically no experience, but I've kissed men, and the way Colin kisses is… it's like he literally needs his mouth on mine for survival.

These desperate mewling whimpers are coming out of me. He turns me away from him again and unzips the dress. I don't want to take it off. I want to wear it forever because there will never be another day in my life when I can wear this perfect dress. It's the softest, smoothest silk. So much stronger than it looks. It should be delicate and breakable, but it's strong.

I will not start talking about all the properties of silk right now. I won't. I might need him to gag me again before I ruin this moment. Wait, shouldn't I *want* this moment ruined? This psycho who I'm sure has killed people is ripping my clothes off—metaphorically because remember silk is strong—and I'm worried about ruining the moment rambling about fabric.

"Take it off," he growls in my ear, his warm breath causing goosebumps to erupt all over me.

My hands shake as I push the gown down my body. Colin helps me step out of it. I'm still in a strapless bra and a thong, but I flush under his gaze anyway. I try to remind myself that he's seen me naked before so I shouldn't feel like this, but the way he looks at me is so intense. It's exactly like all the fantasies that ran on repeat for years, even before I met Colin.

I know it's not a fantasy or a game. I really do know this. But it's still all the things I want. A beautiful, powerful, wealthy man, and kink. But weren't those fantasies about… captivity and enslavement? Did I somehow invite this?

No. That's blaming the victim. And I don't blame the victim, especially when the victim is me. But the thing is… when he looks at me like this… making me feel all the things I didn't know I could feel with a man… I don't feel like his victim. I feel like I'm writing this story *with* him.

"Something blue?" he asks, arching a brow.

"I-I'm sorry, what?" I glance down and remember my bra and panties are a pale blue. The garter that Will tossed at the reception, matched.

I blush because suddenly I'm thinking about the fact that Livia was at my wedding. She watched that horribly awkward garter toss. She thinks I'm losing my virginity in awful fumbling sex with Will right now.

"Take off the rest," he growls, not bothering to wait for a response about the *something blue*. I'm pretty sure the question was rhetorical anyway. And I really really don't want to say something stupid right now.

So I don't say anything, I just take off the bra and panties. I'm not wearing anything like pantyhose. At this point I think only old people wear pantyhose. And my shoes actually didn't even make it up to the room. I've been so nervous I forgot about that. They got left in the back of the limo. My feet were hurting and so I slipped them off, and the limo drove off with them.

First I was nervous about the fact that I married Will and might be about to have awful sex—like for the rest of my life. So I got halfway to the elevator before I even realized my feet were bare. Then soon after that we were walking on carpet. Then we got to the room, and I forgot again because suddenly I was worried about… Colin.

"Get in bed," he says.

I do, and then he goes to the bathroom and turns on the shower. He's in there a *long* time. Like way too long for a shower. I start to worry about what he's doing in there or if he had a freak accident. I'm about to get out of the bed to check, when the shower finally turns off.

A few minutes later he comes out wrapped in a towel. He turns the lights off and gets in bed with me.

"Go to sleep. We have to fly out early in the morning."

I should be more alarmed that he's taking me to an unknown destination on an airplane, but I can't get past the fact that it's my wedding night and I'm a virgin and he's telling me to go to sleep. I didn't imagine the way he looked at me, like I was something to be devoured. So why do I feel so… rejected and not up to his standards? And why do I want so badly to be up to his standards?

"But I thought you were going to…" I can't get the words out because… this man has basically kidnapped me. I mean yes I wanted him to come for me and stop me from having to spend my life with Will, but this is still illegal in about a thousand ways. I might have Stockholm Syndrome.

His hand snakes around my waist and he pulls me against his warm body. "Don't worry. I will deflower you, my little virgin. In Costa Rica."

Costa. Rica. There is this stupid part of me that wants to say: Why Costa Rica? What's in Costa Rica? But I know all about Costa Rica. Livia told me about Dayne's underground—secret, not literally under the ground—kink club. And I know that's where Colin is taking me. It's too big of a coincidence, and I don't believe in coincidences.

Colin strokes my hair. And I just can't help it. I say the stupid words out loud because maybe it is a coincidence and there's no connection whatsoever to where Livia went on her honeymoon. "Why Costa Rica?"

He chuckles. "Didn't Livia tell you about Costa Rica?"

We've hit that point where a word starts to sound like nonsense because it's been said so many times. Costa Rica. Costa Rica. Costa Rica. It sounds like one word, like it could be someone's name. Meet my friend, Costarica. It also sounds like maybe it could be a spice. Like paprika. If I ever decide to to write a poem, I now know what rhymes with Costa Rica. Any gods in the universe? Please stop me now before I find a way to rhyme every spice in the average kitchen pantry.

"Didn't Livia tell you about the club?" he asks, when I don't reply. "I'm taking you to Costa Rica to train you. I told you... you're a sacrifice."

What the fuck does this mean? I tense, beginning to really worry he has intentions to kill me. Do people still do human sacrifice? Surely if that exists it's just tribes out in the middle of nowhere—like places where someone has to eat a virgin's heart every so often so the sun will keep rising.

I don't think Costa Rica is one of those places. I know the kink club isn't.

Then I remember he said most likely I would survive

him. But this just worries me more. Is there a chance I won't survive him? And if so, why am I still not screaming and running from this man?

CHAPTER SEVENTEEN: MACY

I think I got maybe three hours of sleep. Despite everything that has led up to this moment, this morning has felt normal and domestic. Colin ordered us some breakfast. He didn't tie me up and feed it to me. We took showers—separately—and got ready, now we're on his private jet coasting down the runway. I'm strapped into my seat, and Colin is strapped into the seat across from me, doing some work on his laptop.

Jeffrey is in a seat across the aisle from us. I tried to cover my shock when I got on the plane and Jeffrey was here. Why is the butler coming with us on our honeymoon? All at once Colin's voice is in my mind telling me not to let that posh British accent fool me, and that Colin doesn't trust Jeffrey alone with me. At least not for long periods of time.

Why even have a butler if he can't trust him? And if he can't trust him in that way then why the hell is he coming with us to Costa Rica for a month? Will we be in Costa Rica for a month? I'm not sure about that part.

I know in the fake set-up I was supposed to be gallivanting across Europe for a month, the cover story that lets Colin do whatever the hell he wants to me for four weeks without a single soul missing me. I shudder at this thought, even as I feel the familiar throbbing ache between my legs. I know my reactions to this man are not normal.

What he's doing is not okay. This isn't the 1500s. You can't just force a woman to marry you and then train her to be your obedient sex toy. Though I'm not sure that happened in the 1500s. I think it was more forced breeding, and the man would find a separate whore back then. They were all about this idea of the chaste and innocent wife, which you know isn't true once the babies come out, but whatever. Those times were bad and weird.

And now I feel jealous. Is he going to have other women on the side? But even the pang of inappropriate jealousy can't suppress the obedient sex toy thing, and yeah, that thought is not helping. It only makes me more excited. I can feel the blush coming to my cheeks. I look down at my hands, willing this reaction to settle down. This is not normal. This is not normal. *This* is not normal.

I distract myself with thoughts of Colin's jet. Let's not downplay the jet. This is actually the most lush and biggest jet I've ever seen. Okay, so I've never really seen any private jets in person but… I've seen rich people movies. I mean, movies with rich people in them, not movies *for* rich people. I don't think there are special movies made just for rich people.

My mind goes down another one of those random bizarre dirty thought loops as I think about illicit super exclusive privately made porn for the wealthy. And now I'm wondering if custom made-to-order porn exists. What would it be like to have that job?

I close my eyes and take a deep breath while I try to shift my mind to my original distraction that was supposed to get me off the filthy train. Colin's jet is huge. I didn't even know they made jets this large for private use. I can't even imagine how much it costs to fuel it and keep it in the air. And the maintenance costs. Wow.

I find myself running imaginary calculations in my head for things I can't even begin to understand the cost of —like not even theoretically.

Before we got strapped in and started down the runway, I was given a tour. There's this sitting area, of course. It's right next to the cockpit at the front of the plane.

A large curtain separates us from another area. I thought maybe it was a bathroom or something, but no, it's a complete freaking living room. There's a super elegant white leather couch with an S-shaped design. It's one of those arty couches. Like what you find in a design or architecture magazine but don't imagine anybody actually owns or sits on. I swear rich people always seem to have expensive white couches… it's like… who cares if I spill wine on this fifty thousand dollar sofa, I'll just get another one!

There's a full bar in this area and the ability to cook light meals because doesn't everyone get the urge to cook at thirty thousand feet?

There's a giant flat screen TV opposite from the couch. Do we even really call them flat screens anymore? Or is this just the default TV now?

Then… another curtain. Surely the bathroom. Right? Nope. It's a bedroom with a king-sized bed and a closet much larger than one would expect to find on even the most luxurious of private planes. There's a door at the back of the bedroom right next to the bed and yes, that is the bathroom.

Finally.

It's huge. It's got a luxurious shower and all the amenities, and I can't quite understand how it's possible to have this stuff while flying through the air. I'm sure the technology behind this would fascinate me, and I plan to Google it if I'm ever allowed to be on the Internet again.

I'm not sure about that part, because even though I did want him to rescue me from a loveless marriage to Will, I was forced to sign myself over to him, and he has no intention of ever releasing me.

I can't imagine he'd allow me such easy access to the outside world without supervision, and if he DID supervise me, that would just be awkward. I can't Google the tech behind private jet amenities right in front of him. That's private Googling time—on the same level as porn for me.

"Where does the pilot or co-pilot pee if they have to go during a flight?" I just blurt these words out. I have no filter sometimes. I really can't help being this way. And my nerves over this entire situation aren't helping anything. I'm surprised my mind is capable right now of forming semi-coherent thoughts between the oscillating fears that he'll get tired of me and kill me, and the anticipation of what he's going to do to me sexually. And that's swiftly overridden by the guilt and shame for feeling anticipation over that rather than fear or revulsion, which I'm sure is what would be in the official "Acceptable human emotions for various scenarios" handbook, if such a book existed.

"What?" Colin asks, momentarily stunned by my weirdness. I think this is the first time he's looked up from his laptop since the plane got in the air.

I feel suddenly very self-conscious, but I plow on anyway. "Well, I mean… the bathroom is at the very back of the plane, behind the bedroom. You literally have to go past the bed. So… what if you're sleeping or having sex and the pilot or co-pilot has to pee? What then?" I wonder if they pee into a bottle or something at the front of the plane.

Colin chuckles and I'm sure I go bright red. I feel the heat in my cheeks, and do I want to call his attention to the bedroom right now? I was surprised and maybe just a little bit offended that my sex fiend captor hasn't already thrown me down on the bed, since there is one on the plane. I mean didn't he already make it clear that I basically exist now to serve his every whim and perversion?

"There's a second smaller bathroom, like what normal planes have, in the living area just behind the bar," he says.

"Oh." I vaguely recall seeing a few doors in the big living space that looked like they were possibly storage for food and bar stuff. Like a pantry or cabinets or something.

"Go explore the jet on your own if you like," he says, waving a hand in that direction as though there's some grand benevolence in this gesture. There has been no title on my part this morning, and I'm surprised he hasn't yet demanded it. Though for all I know, what he's typing on the laptop is a list of punishments for all my minor infractions.

I glance over to find Jeffrey clearly amused with me and my question. There's something else in his eyes I'm not sure I like. And I'm also not sure I don't like it, and that's more confusing and upsetting than the first thought. So I roll with the first thought. It's one thing to be turned on by Colin, it's another thing to be ready to go for any semi decently attractive male who decides he wants to lay claim to me. Also he's the butler and older. He's hot, but still, that feels so… I don't even have words for how it feels.

I notice Colin and Jeffrey aren't wearing their seat belts, I still am, which shows how unfamiliar I am with flying. I mean obviously we can take our seat belts off. What else would be the point of the different rooms and amenities on the plane?

I unlock the buckle and get up to stretch my legs, making my way back to the deeper interior of the plane and getting some much needed breathing room from the men.

Just as Colin said, there's a little bathroom behind the bar area much like what I'm used to from normal planes.

I make my way to the back of the jet to get a better look at the bedroom and especially the bathroom setup. The bed has a thick, downy white duvet on the top. I pull it back curiously and run my hand over the cool silver-grey silk sheets. I sigh and suddenly want a nap even though I haven't been awake long enough for a nap. I don't know how long one needs to be awake before a nap is appropriate but I feel like there's a protocol. Also, I am not a girl who naps. I'm a girl who works in the real world. Naps are for rich people.

I blush, as I realize that technically I'm now a rich person. I mean, I read that pre-nup. I get an allowance. And if he ever lets me go I get a very generous… severance package? That somehow feels like the right term because I'm here to fulfill a role. This isn't about hearts and flowers and kittens and long walks on a moonlit beach. Either way, I live with him in all this luxury now. I wonder if he'll even let me work at the library anymore.

I mean maybe I wouldn't need to do it full time, but I actually like my job. I like the people. I find the research interesting. And there are at least six professors who consider me completely invaluable and swear they'd be lost without me because nobody else at the library knows how to find a damn thing. I know we have the Internet now, and you'd think that would be enough. But there are many old and obscure texts that aren't online yet. And even those that are, are behind expensive paywalls, which the library has membership to but not every professor can afford on their own often meager salary.

I make my way through the door to the bathroom at the back. It's massive, so much bigger than you'd expect on a private jet. Marble floors and counters. Fixtures that I'm sure cost more than my apartment rent. The towels. Oh my god the towels. Thick, and plush, and so soft. I didn't even know fabric this soft existed. And he's got those tiny hand soaps.

Obviously he has a person who handles this sort of thing. There's no way a man—let along a man like Colin Black—would ever think about or desire to have fancy little soaps. They smell like lavender and peppermint, and I can tell they were made with essential oils. The smell is authentic, not artificial. And I imagine these were hand milled in some artisan boutique in France somewhere.

I'm not saying that's how they came to be... we're just in Macy's Brain now, and I attach a story to everything. I wonder if other people's internal monologues are like this. I blame all the time I spend alone. It's like when fairy tale heroines make friends with all the birds and squirrels... or household mice. It's an occupational hazard of introversion.

I gawk for a few minutes at the shower and the whirlpool tub—two things I still can't believe I'm finding on a plane—before making my way back to the living area.

I poke around in the bar for a bit and find a small refrigerator with some sandwiches. I barely ate anything at breakfast. A nice spread from room service was delivered to the Honeymoon suite which I picked over like one of those tiny bird women out on a date who pretend they don't eat food. But I wasn't trying to impress my new husband with the idea that I subsist entirely on oxygen. I was just too nervous. Will Colin be mad if I start eating his sandwich stash?

I don't know, but I'm suddenly ravenous.

These are really nicely made sandwiches—not like what some kid carries to school in their lunchbox. Thinly sliced rotisserie chicken with tomatoes and high quality cheeses. I can smell the vinegar. I love sub sandwiches with vinegar. There's fresh romaine and pickles on it. To be honest I've never had fresh romaine lettuce on a sub sandwich. It's normally that pre-shredded iceberg lettuce, the kind with zero nutritional content. It's basically like eating shredder paper. No taste, no vitamins, just filler.

The sandwiches are wrapped in the paper like you get at a sub shop. But this paper has no brand label on it, just an embossed gold foil seal, so I bet Jeffrey or an outside personal chef made them before the flight. Either that or it's such a high-end sandwich boutique that they consider visible branding gauche.

During my long time away from Colin while I was wedding planning, I found myself looking at a lot of fashion magazines and browsing all the clothes I would wear if I were Mrs. Black. And it became somehow very important to me in this imaginary world that I wouldn't wear visible designer labels. Because that screams middle class pretending to be rich. I mean I am middle class pretending to be rich, but there's no reason for the whole world to know it.

I find some ginger ale in the fridge and sit at the bar, swiveling the stool so I can view the television. It's set up for in-flight movies.

I jump when the curtain is ripped back and Colin walks in.

He arches a brow and strides into the room, pulling the curtain closed behind him. He wears a suit so well-tailored it's clearly bespoke, and shoes that must be the same—too completely unique to be a common designer, even a high end luxury designer. And of course in the short time of our acquaintance I've never seen an obvious label on anything. The most obvious label was the snowcap star on the top of his Montblanc pen.

Colin is the kind of man who has nearly everything custom-tailored to him and his exacting desires and demands.

His tie is very pale gray, only a single shade darker than the crisp white linen of his shirt. My gaze drifts to his hands. He's got the sexiest hands.

I have this thing about men's hands. Large. Veined. Strong. He's well-groomed, and I can tell someone somewhere attends to his hands and nails—not in some girly feminine way—but because that level of impeccable detail speaks of one thing: Power. Someone so competent and in command that no detail escapes his notice. Nothing about him is unkempt or disheveled. Ever, most likely.

Meanwhile I feel like a hot mess just standing nearby and looking directly at him. I drop my gaze to my sandwich. Technically *his* sandwich.

"You know, there was a time when hands were chopped

off for stealing food. But I'll need your hands later, so I'll let you keep them for now."

He says this so calmly I'm not even sure if he's kidding or not. I mean obviously yes, this is a historical fact about the penalty in some places for theft, but I doubt he'd chop off my hands. As he said, he'll need them, and I can only imagine the purposes he might need them for.

"I was hungry," I say around a giant mouthful of food. I almost choke when the vinegar in the sandwich hits the back of my throat wrong. It's like I'm a novice eater who hasn't yet figured out… swallow your food, then talk. I file this dining tip away for later.

He moves closer into my space, now a mere few feet away, glaring down at me as I pop the last bite of sandwich into my mouth and take a sip of ginger ale, once again with my mouth full. This man is never going to be able to take me anywhere upscale without me embarrassing him. I'm sure of it.

"You've gotten a little too casual with me," he observes.

I flush under his gaze, swallow the last of the sandwich, and inelegantly wipe my mouth with the back of my hand, paranoid I've got crumbs on my face. I wonder if, now that he's seen my truck driver table manners if he still finds me an appropriate wife to make him look good to the board.

Surely I'm not the kind of woman he should be parading on his arm for fundraising galas. I can't even remember how to properly hold a champagne flute. I know I'm supposed to hold it by the stem but I can't actually remember to do it on the rare occasions I have champagne.

I push my glasses up. It's this nervous tic adjustment I sometimes do. I usually don't even notice I'm doing it, but I'm so tense right now that I'm noticing everything: my breathing going in and out, the way the ambient air temperature in the plane's cabin feels against my skin, every fidget I make under the hard penetrating gaze of Colin Black.

Yesterday was so weird without my glasses. I swear, I tried to push them up a hundred times only to find they weren't there. Of course I'd packed them into my bags that had been delivered for me to the honeymoon suite.

"Macy, you try my patience. You know what I want from you."

I do know what he wants. The formality. The title. This piece of my surrender and obedience wrapped up like a tiny gift in shiny paper.

"I'm sorry, Master." I say it quietly. Jeffrey is just on the other side of this curtain, after all.

Colin winds a strand of my curly auburn hair around his fingers. For a moment I think he'll tug me down to my knees right here, the thought sending a sharp wave of arousal straight to my core. But instead he lets his hand drop and picks up the remote before going to the couch. He takes up so much space, sitting in the middle, his legs splayed out wide, his hands resting on the back. He looks like he's posing for a magazine cover… the picture of the illicit wealthy playboy.

He pushes a few buttons on the remote and soon my movie selection is a distant memory, replaced by panting, moaning, and begging, interspersed every few moments with threats and a cracking whip. The harsh crack against flesh is answered by sobs of "Please, Master, please, I'll be a good girl." I don't have to look to know he's got kinky porn playing.

"Take your clothes off, Macy. Let me see what now belongs to me."

My breath hitches in my throat. I know he's seen it all

before, as recently as last night even, but the room was semi-darkened, and it was night. The last time before that was months ago. Also, he didn't have porn in the background at the time. I worry he's got the porn on to compare me to the girl on the screen, and it makes me so self-conscious.

"Turn away from me, watch the screen, and remove your clothes," Colin says. His voice has gone dark and guttural. I won't even be able to watch him to see if he's looking at me or the actress on the screen. Is this better or worse? To not know? I don't know why I should care. This isn't a real relationship. We aren't a couple. I'm just his... sacrifice... Even so, I'm so wet right now.

There is something severely wrong with the way my brain is wired. On the one hand, it's so awkwardly nerdy and full of trivial facts about nonsense nobody really cares about, and on the other hand, it's so darkly sexually twisted.

"Now, Macy. Or I'll call Jeffrey in here to watch you get your ass spanked."

"Yes, Master." I whisper the words but his answering, "Good girl," tells me he heard them just fine, even over the mewling whimpers of the girl on the screen.

I remove my top and jeans. I don't know if this is supposed to be a strip tease. I've never done that before. I wouldn't know where to start. The dominant on the screen lubes a toy and presses it into the girl's ass as she squirms and thanks him, arching back, trying to force the toy in deeper and faster. It's hard to know which of them is the more aggressive, the physically powerful male, or the tied-up woman.

My clothes are on the floor now, and I stand, the

arousal flooding me as I watch the people on the screen, transfixed.

I hear the curtain open then and a posh British accent. "Finally unwrapping her?" Jeffrey says. "May I?"

"Help yourself."

I stand perfectly still while the sex sounds play in the background, and the crisp scent of the butler moves closer to me.

You don't think of butlers as sexy guys. I really only think about Batman's butler but that's probably a Macy quirk. Jeffrey is more like an older Batman than an Alfred. Except, you know, the accent.

I hold my breath as he prowls closer to me, assessing me more intensely than I've ever been assessed. It's just now I notice a whiskey glass in his hand. Brandy? Bourbon? Scotch? I don't know a lot about alcohol. But it's a strong-scented amber liquid he swirls around the glass. He takes a sip, his eyes never leaving me. There's stubble growing on his face. I've never seen him anything but perfectly clean-shaven.

This seems extremely odd to me. I mean from the start I thought maybe Jeffrey was some sort of bodyguard/butler combo but this seems outside of any parameters of employment—drinking on the job, I mean. My brain can't even process the rest. Is he on the job right now? Maybe he's using vacation time. Would he go with his employer on vacation? Maybe they're also friends. Though Colin doesn't seem like the kind of guy who has a lot of friends. This whole thing is so weird.

As if reading my mind, Jeffrey says, "Mr. Black, has a very generous employee benefits package. I get certain, *perks*, unavailable to other members of staff."

The *perks* part of that statement has goosebumps popping out over my skin.

He's done a full walk around me as he's talked, but now he's standing in front of me again, giving me a slow once-over. He ignores the porn that still rages on in the background, the intensity of the anal play ramping up.

I take in a sharp breath as his warm hand reaches out to cup first one breast, and then the other, as if testing their weight. It's like I'm some piece of livestock he's deciding whether or not he wants to purchase. I should be offended, but I'm too turned on for that.

"Will you be sharing her? Fully?" Jeffrey asks.

"Once she's been bred," comes the answer from the couch.

I can't believe those words just came out of Colin's mouth. And yet at the same time I can. I knew *heirs* were part of the contract I signed. It wasn't as though I had much choice in signing it, but I was going to be Colin's with or without the contract, not only because he'd clearly decided to keep me, but because I can't tamp down my foolish desire for him. The only thing signing the contract did was protect me. It left a legal paper trail. It would be hard for me to disappear now and for Colin to claim he'd never met me. At least I think that's true.

Also, being his *Mrs. Black* for the board members means people will see me. In public. He's not going to be able to keep me locked away in a basement somewhere, or keep me as some *Jane Eyre* style attic wife. I hope.

And anyway, he already let me roam on a long electronic leash for six months. So if I'm honest, I'm not even afraid he'll abuse me in any standard way. After all, he isn't going to want a *Mrs. Black* that looks like a hostage. He has a plan and an image to maintain. So I do have some amount of power in this arrangement, even though his mere presence often makes me forget this fact.

I jolt, surprised to feel Jeffrey's hand move between my legs. He holds me in place with one hand on my ass as the other explores my body.

"She's so wet," he murmurs, and I'm sure I blush hotter than I've ever blushed before. Damn my red hair.

"Is she?" Colin asks. I hear the thread of amusement in his voice. "Mrs. Black, is this true? Are you wet for him?"

"Y-Yes, Master."

I've realized since the contract signing why he wasn't bothered that I wasn't going to legally take his name. He doesn't care. Given our private contract, I don't have the automatic legal right to take his last name anyway—a realization which feels very odd to me. But Colin doesn't care what my name says on any piece of paper. He intends to refer to me as Mrs. Black. He intends to introduce me as Mrs. Black, and he intends for other people to think of me as and call me Mrs. Black. So my little rebellion of *not changing my name* means nothing.

Like anyone running in his social circle is going to ask to see my driver's license.

He will call me whatever he will call me. And the more I hear it, the more I like it, because it's him claiming me and showcasing that claim. It's him enfolding me into his family—not just some side piece or whore or toy or pet. Not even just his property or slave, but his wife. Mrs. Black. I'm not easily disposable. If we split it will be in the financial pages of the papers. It will be a scandal. It will hurt his stock prices. Maybe. Depending on what kind of business he runs. When there are heirs it'll be even messier. No, he needs to keep me, and he needs to keep me reasonably happy if he doesn't want questions. How would it look to the shareholders, after all, if Mrs. Black appeared to the world abused and mistreated?

"Mrs. Black," Colin says, jarring me out of my mental rambling. Jeffrey helpfully turns me to face my new husband. The way Colin looks at me is even more intense than Jeffrey's assessment. But his eyes never leave me. He never strays even for a second to the screen behind us where the moaning has gotten louder.

Colin crooks a finger at me. He points at the floor, and like some well-trained dog I drop to my knees before him. He strokes my hair and the side of my face.

"Good girl. Spread your legs."

I do, and that's when I feel Jeffrey's suit against me as he sits with his chest against my back. His hands move around to stroke my breasts and between my legs as Colin unzips his pants and frees his cock.

He doesn't say a word. He doesn't make any demands or orders. He doesn't instruct me. When really, maybe he should. I don't have the slightest clue what I'm doing here, but I lean closer. Tentatively I run my fingertips over him and then my hand. He's uncut.

I'm strangely excited by this. I've only really seen dicks on film and in images, and yet, a dick in it's natural state is somehow exciting. So many in porn are cut that it's kind of like finding a unicorn in the wild, this totally new and unexpectedly magical thing.

"Just how innocent are you, Macy?"

There's no judgment in his tone, just curiosity.

I look up at him and shrug, the shyness overtaking me again.

His hand continues to stroke through my hair. "I don't care what any stupid boy has told you. There's no wrong way to do this."

The way he's being with me right now is completely unexpected though I'm not sure what I expected. My only experience with him was a punishment and him going down on me. I guess I just assumed this experience would be like what I'd seen in porn, that he'd push me down and shove his cock down my throat and just not care how I felt about it.

A part of me finds that idea exciting, but I know the reality wouldn't evoke the same feelings. I grip his cock and slide his foreskin up over the tip and back down again. Then I experimentally lick, and taste him. He shudders when the wet tip of my tongue begins to explore him, and this alone gives me confidence to continue.

CHAPTER EIGHTEEN: COLIN

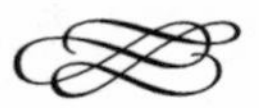

This girl is going to kill me. I never thought I was into the innocent ones—the ones who don't know what the hell they're doing, who need to be told every little thing. I do enjoy giving orders, but there was a certain kind of woman I thought I was into. And I find now that Macy's here, I was a complete idiot.

The reason none of the other women did it for me for very long was because they were being paid to be there. They'd been trained in the porn school of sex, which, as it turns out, isn't very accurate. Not because sex isn't as good in real life as it is in porn, but because artificial sex isn't any good, period—sex that's scripted and acted and performative.

Something can look good without feeling good, and something can look ridiculous and feel amazing. This is never more true than when it comes to sex. I don't think I realized just how tired I'd grown of all the performance and artificial fakery until this moment. The overly collagen-injected lips that made them too puffy and pouty to be real. The fake tits. The fillers and Botox. The overly made up faces. The overly sexy outfits. The choreographed and calculated movements. The cat-like walking or crawling across the floor. The demure glances that were never really honest. The way they'd look up at me from the ground as they sucked my cock as though they didn't know if they were doing it right when we both knew they did, that they'd done it thousands of times. All part of the act. All part of the show I was paying for.

Even though ultimately they weren't that amazing. What they thought they knew, they didn't know at all.

Deep throating really doesn't do much for me. I guess for the men who like it, it's a power thing—this idea that some woman is willing to choke herself on your cock, that she's willing to give up oxygen just to pleasure you. But really, my cock ramming down the back of a woman's throat just physically does nothing much for me. Nerve endings aren't being hit in any special way after all. It only takes a moment of thought for anyone to realize this. But few take that moment.

A talented tongue though? Kissing, sucking the tip, swirling her tongue around, worshiping me, the vibration of her moan against my dick...now that? That is magic, and it's what Macy in all her innocence is actually doing right now.

She has no idea what she's doing, that much I know. But… the effect is still the best blow job I've ever received because it's not performance art. It's real. Just like Macy and this entire fucked-up situation.

She's not competing with other women who were well-trained to give me the sexual experiences they *thought* I wanted. A lot of men complain about innocence because it's inexperienced, but it's also without bad training, hang-ups, bad experiences. It's without artifice. It's without assumption. It's teachable and willing to learn.

If Macy is as innocent as I think she is, no man has been a fucking tool and choked her with his dick because he saw it on porn once. And I'm eternally grateful for this. I may like to share my toys but my dick is the only one that goes in her mouth, ever. I never want her to have that experience with oral. I want it to always be like this—almost painfully sweet and genuinely eager. Not fake eager. I want her to like doing it.

She hesitates.

"Good girl," I murmur, as I stroke her hair, encouraging her. "Keep doing exactly what you're doing."

I take her hand and guide her to wrap it around my cock and show her what I want. With the combination of her pumping me with her hand, and her sweet mouth licking and sucking and kissing, her tongue dancing around the head of my cock, it doesn't take long for me to come.

When I do, I do the first thing I've done in this exchange that could be considered in any way aggressive, the one movement that reminds her she's not with a dog that's been housebroken. I wrap my hand possessively around the back of her neck and hold her in place as I come down her throat.

"Swallow." I say the word quietly, but I know she heard me. Jeffrey continues to pet her like the good girl she is as her throat works to swallow every last drop of the mess she created with her sweet mouth.

I pull out of her and zip up. "Good girl." I lean back and watch Jeffrey. He's teased her this entire time, his hands moving from her perfect tits to her dripping cunt. His hand drifts between her legs again, and this time he's done teasing.

I'm not sure what it says about me, but I love watching another man touch what's mine. Maybe that's not normal, but fuck what's normal. There's something so primal about the whole thing, that I will pass her around and watch her come and lose herself to any man I point to, and that she'll love every second of it. That she'll give herself to me in such a complete way, that she will surrender this fully. That her lines are my lines, and I have almost no lines.

What can I say? I like to watch. And the *American Psycho staring at yourself in the mirror while fucking* thing just doesn't do it for me.

Macy looks at the ground, distracting herself staring at my shoes.

"Mrs. Black. Look at me. I want you to look at me while you come for Jeffrey. You were such a good girl; it's time for your treat."

Her large pale green eyes rise to mine. Those glasses, man. I can't get over them. This is the first women with glasses I've ever fucked—such a strange thing to realize. I think there was a librarian role play once, but this girl is an *actual* librarian. A virgin librarian with nerd glasses. Could I be any more of a cliché right now?

"Jeffrey!" I bark, realizing what he's about to do.

"Yes, Sir?"

He's still so formal, even now. "Don't penetrate her. That's for me."

"Oh, right."

He sounds ridiculously proper when he says those words, so proper in fact I'm sure he'll finish it off with a

Cheerio and then just exit the plane in midair to go on a fox hunt.

He forgot Macy was a virgin. I doubt he could accidentally pop her cherry with his fingers, but still, that territory is mine to explore the first time. He'll get his turn later.

Macy's eyes start to stray again, so I place my hand under her chin and raise it so her gaze is forced to mine.

"If you don't hold my gaze, there will be punishment. Do you understand?"

"Y-yes, Master."

I nod, pleased that she's not pretending not to know what I want. Macy's too smart for that shit. She probably thinks she has a punishment coming for eating the sandwich but those sandwiches were prepared for both of us, and I'm not such a control freak that she has to ask me every time she needs to pee or eat. I'd find that level of micro-management completely exhausting. And I don't need it to own every corner of her soul. By the time we get done in Costa Rica, she's going to know exactly what the word Master means.

She finally let's herself go, jerking against Jeffrey's hand, unable to hold back the sweet whimpers as my thumb caresses her jawline.

"Yes, just like that… give us your pleasure."

She shudders a final time and her eyes drift closed. Jeffrey presses his finger to her mouth, the finger she made wet. Without instruction or struggle, she opens and allows that finger to penetrate her mouth as she moans around it. I need to take this girl in a way I've never needed to take anyone. This unsettles me more than I'd like.

"Leave us," I say to Jeffrey, and like the good little house servant he ultimately is, he quietly gets up and leaves. I pick her up and carry her to the bedroom, tucking her in to the silk bedding.

"Get some rest."

She opens her eyes. "Aren't you going to stay?"

I shake my head. "No, from this point on there are things you have to earn, and sharing my bed, is one of them."

CHAPTER NINETEEN: MACY

I don't wake until the plane lands. And even then, I don't wake until I'm being literally carried off it. I don't have to open my eyes to know it's Colin carrying me, and I'm glad it isn't a paid member of his staff. I can sense him in this almost supernatural way. There's a way he moves and a solidness to him that other people don't have.

Underneath all of that is his scent, a combination of the barest hint of cologne, and him. There are women who spend a long time putting on makeup in such a way to make it seem as though they aren't wearing any at all, like they're just naturally that beautiful. That's the illusion. And most men who say they don't like makeup on a woman, that's what they mean. They love makeup, but they love makeup where the illusion is so painstaking and complete that they can't tell it's there. They can't smell it. They can't see it. They can't taste it.

It's completely silent and invisible like servants under the stairs.

This is the way Colin wears cologne. It's so barely there, that for a moment I might be able to fool myself that he just naturally smells this way.

I'm still naked, but at least he's wrapped me in the sheet from the bed. It feels decadent being carried from the jet wrapped in silk. He deposits me into the back seat of whatever luxury car will be driving us to our location and gets in the other side with me. Despite all the random fun facts I know about absolutely everything, luxury cars is not on that list. I couldn't tell you the difference in a Bentley, a Bugatti, and a Lamborghini. Though at least I know those words, so that's something, I guess.

When the car starts to move, Colin speaks. "I know you're awake. I felt your breathing change."

I think he means he noticed that big obvious sniff I took of him like I was a dog engaged in social bonding when he was carrying me a few minutes ago.

"Why didn't you wake me to get dressed?" I ask.

"Because I don't want you dressed right now, Mrs. Black. If I want you naked, you'll be naked. Be grateful for the sheet."

This is the point at which a normal woman would start yelling or cursing or throwing things or at least be internally offended. Or maybe even cry, scream, or beg. There's a huge range of the emotional experience I could be having and expressing right now—if I had more sense.

Given some of my circumstances, I could almost be forgiven if I were too afraid to fight back. But this isn't a fear thing, it's a… I desperately want to ride his cock, thing.

I don't want to fight him, not because I'm truly afraid he'd harm me, but because he might let it slide and do nothing. There's something between us that I don't want to break. I don't care how archaic it sounds or how wrong it is, but I like his control. I like the ruthless power that rolls off him. I've always been this way.

I was barely able to be in Soren's presence without spontaneously kneeling. Being in his energy made me want to be owned and dominated in ways which aren't polite to admit to and which definitely are not feminist.

Then there are the general twisted fantasies which I've had way longer than feels normal or appropriate to me. I don't know exactly why I'm like this or if there's something wrong with me. But I know I respond to Colin's power, and after the blow job on the plane, there's a part of me that—sick and wrong or not—trusts him to keep me safe.

He didn't hurt me, or push me, or force anything on me. He was gentle and let me handle it my way. And it made me want to. Though I won't lie and pretend I haven't had rough fantasies. This is the big fight within me, the reality that being a real captive isn't a fantasy, and yet… here's Colin the kidnapper who feeds me brunch on the fancy plates.

With every piece of this situation that locks into place, I am more ensnared, but feel somehow more safe which I know is crazy because Colin is dangerous. This isn't a role he's playing. I don't know why I'm so sure about this, but I really think he's killed people. I feel unhinged thinking that, like maybe it's just my wild imagination, but there's this dark coiled thing inside him that I'm just happy isn't aimed in my direction. I still worry maybe someday it could be.

As if sensing my thoughts, Colin pulls me against his chest, his fingers stroking through my hair.

"Master? Where are you taking me?"

"To the dungeon," he says. And I'm not sure if he's

kidding or not. But he doesn't say anything else so I don't ask any more questions.

About half an hour later, we end up at a huge isolated resort. Small gold lettering inset into the brick beside an iron gate reads: "The Dungeon."

As soon as he mentioned Costa Rica, I knew we'd be coming to Dayne's club. I just didn't realize it was actually called *The Dungeon*. I'm pretty sure Livia doesn't know either. After all, there isn't some giant tacky glowing neon sign announcing this name. And as Colin gives his access code and we pull through the large iron gate and around to the main building, there's no obvious sign. Nothing on the grounds, nothing on the door.

The only indication this place even has a name was that small, tasteful gold engraving on the brick outside the gate which I'm sure nobody really ever reads, except me, but I google literally everything, so I'm probably a statistical anomaly.

Colin leaves me in the car to go inside. He's in there for a few minutes, and I'm glad the window is up between me and the driver. I'm feeling more naked now and being completely covered by a giant piece of silk for some reason isn't helping much.

It's funny how our brains work that way. I'm more covered up right now than most of the clothes I wear, but a sheet isn't clothing. And my knowledge of that makes me somehow still naked, even fully covered. I'm still pondering this when Colin returns to the car and the driver takes us down several winding paths away from the main building to a very large house with it's own iron gate. The engraving outside of this one is "The Cottage". I would never put the person who named these buildings in charge of nail polish naming. Could you imagine? Instead of colors like "Salacious Gossip" we'd have "Red" and "Pink". Half the reason I choose any nail polish color is the name.

There's a live guard here. The driver stops to speak to him, then the gate opens and we pull in.

"This is Dayne's cottage. Soren arranged for us to use it during our stay," Colin says.

Cottage is the most wrong description I can think of for this place. It's really more like a mini-mansion. There's a pool and a hot tub, and three ridiculously large bedrooms —like individual loft apartments, all with their own bathrooms. There's a full kitchen and dining room and living room and game room. These are just the parts I see as Colin leads me to one of the bedrooms on the second floor.

"This will be your room," he says taking me inside one of apartment-sized rooms. And I'm being literal here, this room is actually bigger than my apartment. I could probably fit my apartment inside this room twice and still have a little space left over for a medium-sized dog.

"I get my own room?" Suddenly I'm wondering if we're going to be one of those married couples with separate bedrooms who never have sex. Or maybe couples with separate bedrooms have *more* sex? There's a theoretical way in which that works. If you can have it all the time, any time, just inches away from you, do you really want it anymore? Isn't that why most marriages grow stale and the sex goes away? Or is it because of kids banging on the door and puking in the middle of the night? I'm not sure. Maybe it's a bit of both.

Now part of me worries Colin has some virgin fetish to the point that he plans keep me a virgin forever while maybe enjoying my mouth. God what the fuck is wrong with me? This thought really turns me on. I mean I don't want to be an eternal virgin or anything, that's kind of depressing. But the *idea* of this gets me going. The fantasy.

And then I remember the *heirs* part of the contract I signed. Of course I'm not going to be a virgin forever. Unless he just turkey bastes me into pregnancy. Then he could have the best of all worlds, I guess.

I stand in the hallway outside the room just zoning out thinking about this as Jeffrey brings my bags in and deposits them on my bed. I guess he's back to being the butler again and we're going to pretend that sort-of devil's threeway on the plane didn't happen.

"Get dressed," Colin says.

"For what? Where are we going?" I stand in the hallway, still wrapped in the sheet from the plane. By now a part of me wants to just cut this fabric up and sew it into an evening gown, we've gotten to that level of coziness—me and the sheet.

"It's our honeymoon, Macy. We're going to the Sloth Sanctuary." He says this as though this should be the most obvious thing in the world, as though it's impossible to come to Costa Rica on your honeymoon and not visit the sloths. It's just not done, apparently.

I nod and go back to my room to pick out an appropriate outfit for a day of honeymoon tourist attractions. But inside I'm giddy.

Livia told me all about the Sloth Sanctuary in Costa Rica, and I was so jealous. First she had these three hot men, her own man harem, all engaging in her dark dirty fantasies—and let's be honest, *my* dark dirty fantasies, and they took her on an amazing honeymoon where she got a private tour of sloths. And I wanted a private tour of sloths, too. It's not that I need to copy everything Livia does, like some robot person without their own independent personality, but there's a reason we're friends. We like a lot of the same stuff.

Though, really, who doesn't like sloths?

We don't bother to eat, I mean I had that giant sandwich on the plane. I'm still good, and Colin probably ate while I was having my post-orgasmic nap.

I've kind of been shoving a lot of that to the back of my mind. The butler gave me an orgasm while Colin smugly watched on. How am I supposed to feel about that? I mean I know how I'm *supposed* to feel about it. I'm supposed to feel horrified, used, abused, dirty, ashamed. I'm supposed to be scared of what's coming next. But that's not what I really feel.

My experience with Colin that first day... with the punishment and then in his bedroom, and my experience with him last night where he didn't even do anything, and my experience with him on the plane... where he was so surprisingly gentle and encouraging... all these things add up to me feeling safe with him. I don't feel judged by him. I don't feel afraid of him even though I know I should. If there's any man a smart woman should feel afraid of, it's Colin Black. But the way he's been with me, the way I feel when I'm with him... it just doesn't add up to all the things I'm *supposed* to feel.

Instead, I want to pinch myself to see if I'm dreaming. My mind goes back to Colin's "Wish, granted", and I shiver. Be careful what you wish for?

Maybe I am a little afraid, afraid of getting everything I've ever wanted, and afraid maybe there's another shoe that will drop, or it'll become too much and I'll fall out of the fantasy before I've had the chance to completely surrender to it. But I can't help but be so grateful that I'm not in Europe right now with Will, having repulsive missionary sex with a man and a life I don't want.

Despite everything society and people I know might think about it, Colin might be the life I *do* want.

CHAPTER TWENTY: COLIN

By the time we return from the sloth sanctuary, Macy is relaxed. She must have squealed in delight at the sloths twenty times or more while we were there. Normally, if a woman did that I'd be done with her. I'm not into these giggly silly girls, but it's different with Macy. I felt this odd warmth at her happiness. It was as if my Grinch heart grew two sizes today.

I arranged for the private behind-the-scenes tour, which isn't as easy to get as one might think—even with my money. Soren got me the details on it from when he was on his honeymoon with Macy's friend. I stood back and watched her cuddle and feed baby sloths most of the afternoon. I didn't participate. My inner sense of self is already taking a beating from my happiness over Macy's happiness, me holding a baby sloth and feeding it like a proud new father was out of the question.

This isn't how it was supposed to be. Soren was giving me a fucking virgin sacrifice that I could train and use according to all my twisted dark desires. I was going to breed an heir—probably several—and keep Macy as my pet, and her feelings weren't going to play into any of it. But I wasn't prepared for this girl.

I wasn't prepared for this bizarre mix of nerdiness and sexiness. I've never experienced a woman like this before. She may be innocent, but she's eager. She wants me. I told myself I didn't care if the woman Soren gave me wanted me or not. I didn't care because she was mine. Mere property. Payment for Soren's fuck-up.

I thought I wanted a woman who was afraid of me. Genuinely afraid. Not pretend afraid. I thought I wanted genuine begging. Genuine desperation. Because I'm fucked up. I've always been fucked up. In a different set of circumstances I would be the serial killer living with a lot of stuffed animals—taxidermy, not toys. But the only genuine thing I want from Macy is her surrender, and that doesn't have to be dramatic or traumatic.

The longer I'm around her, the more I want this to be mutual. I still want a toy, a pet, a plaything. And I fully intend to share her. But I don't want her to be a traumatized victim huddling in a basement with tears streaking down her face while she begs me not to hurt her. Even the idea causes a sick feeling to form in my stomach.

When you have my kind of money, it isn't logistically difficult to kidnap a woman, keep her under lock and key, and do whatever the hell you want with her, including sharing her with your equally rich and amoral friends. But my new desires—her happily going along with this, her desire for everything, including being liberally shared—require finesse.

I've long held this perfect image in my mind of mascara streaks on a woman's face, her wide scared eyes staring up at me, and the rush of power. I don't know what's wrong with me. I should probably be in prison... if not for my desires, at least for the people I've made disappear. Macy is lucky, I've at least never killed nor wanted to kill a woman. So she's always been safe on that score, no matter how hard I sold the bluff—even to myself. If she'd tried to remove that tracking bracelet or told anyone the truth I could have just moved up my timeline.

I thought I wanted something real and not a game. I thought I wanted a woman who belonged to me, one who wasn't acting. But I find I have no true taste for this woman's suffering. I need her in this with me, fully committed, and the only way to do that is to have her trust, her willing surrender to my twisted games.

Is that even possible? I've gotten a glimmer that despite her innocence she has at least a bit of a kink streak. The phone call with her friend months ago at breakfast, intrigued me forever. I at least knew from her masturbation schedule that Macy has a strong healthy interest in sex, which made it even more puzzling how such a beautiful woman could be nearly thirty and still untouched. And I knew from her response to me both that first too-brief morning, and this morning on the plane, that she's definitely more than meets the eye.

She didn't react in a prudish way to the porn on the screen. And she didn't pull away when Jeffrey started to touch her. I'd expected her to get shy or uncomfortable or upset or beg, and I wasn't sure what I'd do about it.

Macy and I sit together in the back of the car. We've just returned to The Cottage. There's a private, fully outfitted dungeon in the basement which she hasn't seen yet, but she's about to. I want to start her training before I unveil her to others. Screw Soren's rules. He'll get his virgin sacrifice, but she's mine, and I refuse to be managed by that asshole.

I don't know what to do with the feelings Macy creates inside me—the loss of control I feel around her. That tiny sense of fear that I've never experienced before... *What if something happens to her?* Before Macy I'd never thought that thought before in my life. The first night when she ran from me, it gripped me in a kind of terror I didn't know I could feel at all. About anything. I didn't think I was capable of feeling it. Every moment with this woman has been like this.

It wasn't rational. There was no reason for me to give any kind of shit if she died out in the cold woods. It was stupid for her to run. That's just natural selection at work. That's what I would have told myself with any other woman. But this girl was different.

And then everything after that... from her bizarre trust under my touch when no part of her should trust me, to her weird facts, to the way she came apart and surrendered under my tongue. I needed six months just to get my head sorted. I seriously considered not coming back for her.

I picked up the phone at least a dozen times to call Soren, call it off, and get him to find me someone else or extract the payment from him in a different way. Macy is too dangerous to my sanity. Let her wear that bracelet forever, I told myself. What do I care? Maybe she'll never take it off. Maybe one day she'll realize she can. Who the fuck cares? Let her stay in a cage of her own making until she decides to step out of it. What difference does it make to me? As long as I was free of the redheaded witch and her strange spell, I could go back to the way my life was before.

I could give up the desire and need for this thing to be

real. Paying the whores was safer. It was cleaner. Ironic though that is.

I wonder what Will would have done if, after marrying her, he'd come up to the honeymoon suite to deliver her to me but I hadn't been there to collect. I was so close to letting that happen. Would he have consummated the marriage? Would he have kept the ruse going and tried to contact me? Would he have kept her for himself? In five years would these two be living lives of quiet desperation because I was too afraid to take what I wanted? I've never been afraid of anything. And now I feel like I'm afraid of everything, at least where Macy is concerned.

I realize now, while we're sitting in the car together, the driver pulling us through the gate, that I don't want her trust. I have it. Even if she doesn't know it, I have it. As stupid and wrong as it is, on some deeper level she senses I'm not going to harm her—at least on purpose. She new it well before I did. There are a million ways I could hurt her from fear and sheer stupidity but I try not to think about that.

No, I have her trust. Now I just need to not lose it. And the biggest question rattling through my brain is… how do I get all my needs and darkest desires met, and bring her along for the ride as my *willing* toy? How do I guide her and myself through this experience I think, inexplicably, we both want?

CHAPTER TWENTY-ONE: MACY

Colin has been quiet the entire ride back to the cottage. I have no idea what he's thinking. He seems tense and on edge. This isn't the reaction you'd expect from someone who's just been to a sloth sanctuary. I felt self-conscious at first because he wasn't participating, but eventually I gave in to the overload of cuteness.

We had access to everything. And this wasn't the official behind-the-scenes tour. I know this because when Livia told me about everything, I scoured the internet to learn all about the sloth sanctuary's behind-the-scenes tours. They are a little exclusive, but they aren't *super crazy wealthy people* level exclusive. And what Livia described to me was above and beyond what the website offered.

No, this was... much more "I know a guy", than that. I'm pretty sure we got the same ultra-exclusive tour that Livia and her guys got. Colin and I were there for hours and were even served a meal in a private fancy dining room in a building hidden from view of the public. Colin just watched me during the meal. I won't lie, I felt a bit like a bug kept in a jar for observation.

Even so, there's something peaceful in his stoic demeanor. He's like a human version of the library, and I'm comfortable in libraries. My mind is so loud that I need the quiet.

He guides me into the house, his hand on my upper arm like he's guiding a captive to the dungeon. And then we go down a set of stairs and it actually *is* a dungeon.

I never thought you could call a dungeon "swanky" but, this is about the most luxurious and elegant room I've ever seen that's intended for tying people up and whipping them.

"Master?"

"I'm glad you haven't forgotten my name," he says as I take it all in.

"Only in private, though, right? In public I'm supposed to be your wife. What do I call you in public?"

"You *are* my wife." He sounds annoyed.

Colin does that one-handed tie-loosening thing that drives me crazy. I don't know what it is about the way a man jerks his tie loose like that that sends me into a frenzy, but it's not just me. It's pretty much a meme in romance novels so… I feel like I'm in good company with this. One of my few *weird things* that doesn't feel quite so lonely.

"It depends on what you mean by in public," he says, his eyes never leaving mine.

I lick my lips. I keep waiting for him to take off his shirt, or his jacket at least, but he remains dressed.

"I-I'm sorry Master, what?" Did he just say something?

He chuckles. "Distracted, Mrs. Black? I said there will be plenty of times in public when you'll call me master, but you'll know by the venue. It'll be obvious what those places are. In most public places, I don't care what you call me. Just play the role of the respectable wife. You can pick your own pet name."

I can't even imagine coming up with a normal couply pet name for Colin. Just the idea of it almost makes me burst out in laughter. I wonder idly if I could get away with calling him my little marshmallow.

"A-and what will you call me… in public, I mean?"

"Depends on where we are… in some venues, whore, slut, pet. In normal places… I haven't decided…" he gives me a long slow once over, as though he's a computer running a program to determine an appropriate name.

My heart is fluttering so fast. If there are times in public I'll call him master and he'll call me… those other things... it means we're going to the resort's public dungeon… and maybe more places or situations like that. The things we do won't just be behind closed doors. Is he going to share me with more than just Jeffrey? A thrill slides through me which I know probably shouldn't be there.

This would all be different if I'd met him on a kinky dating app. It would be different if I'd agreed to be his sub, but that's not the case. Still, the way he's been with me isn't anything like what one would expect in a situation like this. Maybe my body isn't crazy for trusting him. The most harmful thing he did to me was let me go, to believe I'd have to spend my life with a man I didn't love.

But I don't love Colin either. I don't really know him. I'm attracted, sure, but however this goes, at least I didn't choose him. I'm just along for the ride.

But *could* I love him? I turn this thought over in my head. I don't want to love Colin. I can't think of anything more dangerous than falling for this man. I have to keep it about sex and remember that I didn't volunteer to be with him. I was coerced into signing that contract. I'm obligated to produce heirs!

If I think these thoughts enough, I might be able to actually remember them, instead of getting sucked into this kinky Barbie Dream House fantasy. No matter what happens, I can never, ever let myself fall in love with this man. Even as I think it, I know it's already a lost cause. I'm so screwed.

Women and men don't have sex the same. I know, I know, I'm still a virgin, but… I'm well read. The point is, we can pretend to be like a man. Drink like a man, do business like a man, fuck like a man. But we can't really do any of that. Most of us can't drink a man under the table because we have smaller bodies on average so most of us biologically can't handle the same amount of alcohol. Some women can do business like a man, so I'm not taking it back to the 1950's here or anything, but still, we have to be "go getters" and never relax, and for most it's unnatural and wears you down hormonally after a while. Again, go girl power and all that, these are just biological realities for most. Don't shoot the messenger. And then… there's sex, the biggest issue of all. And our prime enemy? Oxytocin, the cuddle hormone.

Women with a lot of experience can learn to just ignore this hormone, but it's a kind of hormonal bonding, like out of some werewolf book. And it's the primary reason why men can emotionally separate sex and love in ways that most women can't. And that's the danger here, that no matter what my mind wants or what's smart, the more he touches me and makes my body feel good, the more I'm going to bond to him and mistake that big stew of swirling hormones for love.

I've been casually glancing around the room while my

mind went on this obsessive fact spewing holiday, but now when I look at Colin, he ensnares my gaze, and I can't bring myself to look away again.

"Undress, Macy. I'm ready to start teaching you how to be a good and obedient wife."

And... this pair of panties is ruined. Seriously what is wrong with me? These kinds of things shouldn't excite me. On the up side, I've finally managed to completely ditch my inappropriate crush on Soren. Soren, who? A part of me thinks I just feel guilty for my kinks full out, because I always find some kind of shame or guilt to attach them to. With the way Soren made me feel, it was guilt that he was Livia's husband, even though we never did anything, and I would never betray her. So that was easy to justify. Of course I should feel a little guilty for that. I was lusting over her man—one of them anyway.

Now with Colin it's the way I came to be in his care. But is there any situation in which I wouldn't have these guilt and shame feelings? I feel wrong that I'm still technically a virgin—like there's something broken in me, or else surely I wouldn't still be... untouched. Though that's a stupid way to think of it, I have most definitely been touched.

I feel wrong for my desires—another thing that feels broken. I just feel perpetually... wrong. And I'm not sure what the solution to that is. All I know is that my mind is a constant hamster wheel of noise. Normal people might take up meditation, but am I crazy to think Colin can help me be quiet inside? That day he punished me wasn't at all what I expected. I can fantasize and touch myself and bring myself to orgasm, but you can't self-spank. I'd always fantasized about it, but in the end, it still felt nothing like what I thought it would feel like when it finally happened.

Part of me thought it would never happen. I couldn't imagine myself telling a guy I'd like him to tie me up and spank me. I already felt so out of step with the rest of the world and everybody in it that I didn't want to call attention to yet another thing.

But when Colin had me in his dungeon... when it was actually happening, it felt... peaceful and quiet. Like standing under a waterfall out in the forest. The warmth on my skin was like lying by the pool in the sunlight. I could be quiet inside my own mind, if only for a few moments, and more than the pleasure and fantasy, I want to keep having that. And I didn't feel judged by him. He'd initiated it, and it was out of my power and control, and so I didn't have to feel the awkwardness and shame I might have otherwise felt.

I mean yes, I know... it's not the fifties. I'm allowed to have desires. Kinks are okay. I know all this stuff intellectually, but you can't just change your wiring on command. Though maybe I could do it if Colin commanded it.

"Well?" Colin says. His arms are crossed over his chest as he watches me and waits for me to comply with his demands while I'm busy spacing out.

"A-aren't you going to undress?" I ask when he just stands there, watching and assessing like he does.

A slow head shake. "No. Like sharing my bed, that's another thing you'll have to earn."

I've seen him without a shirt one time, the night I ran away, but it seems that was just meant as a preview to torture me... *All this can be yours with absolute obedience...*

My hands shake as they move to unbutton my jeans. He's seen me naked multiple times. I repeat this mantra in my head over and over. Why should I feel nervous? And things were brightly lit on the plane. The lighting is dim down here. Why should I feel self conscious when he's already seen me naked so many times?

I'm going to give myself a panic attack. I take a deep breath and slowly start to peel the clothes from my body as Colin's hungry gaze takes in every movement.

"Get on your knees and spread your legs, like you did on the plane."

My breath flows slowly in and out of me as I follow his order and wait. The quiet is upon me now, inside the peace of his commands. All the inane mind chatter and random facts that otherwise swirl around my head fall away as I stare at his shoes and the part of his suit I can see from the ground. I'm barely aware of my fingers digging into the carpet.

I jump when his hand is suddenly in my hair, petting me.

"Good girl."

He begins to slowly circle me.

"M-Master... when are you going to..." I can't say the word deflower, it's too old-fashioned even for me. I mean I've thought the word, and sometimes it shows up in my morning *me time*, but I don't ever say the word *out loud*.

He chuckles as if he can read my mind, and I'm sure he probably can. My facial expressions practically have closed-captioning. "Deflower you?" he asks, just shamelessly putting that word out there.

Okay, I do like that word. I like all the dirty, politically incorrect, wrong things it implies.

I nod, blushing.

"At the ritual. I told you, you're the sacrifice." He says this as if it's an item on a to-do list he's mentioned to me a hundred times. There is no emotion or added significance. It's more like *I told you, I'll pick up the milk after I get off work.*

It's only now that I realize all of Soren and Colin's talk about me being a sacrifice wasn't some kind of metaphor or inside joke. It wasn't just that I was being given to Colin to pay some debt.

No, he's being somehow literal. There's a plan, and it's been in place since Soren gave me to him.

"When is this happening?" My voice comes out way calmer than I feel.

"Tomorrow night."

CHAPTER TWENTY-TWO: COLIN

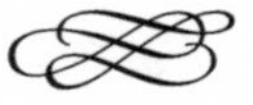

"You trust me, don't you?" I ask the question not expecting a reply, at least not expecting an *honest* reply. I've never done this particular dance with a woman because it's never been real, not even in the vanilla relationship version. But I've watched women deny men many times—not their bodies, but their truth.

In my world, few women deny the men in my social circles their bodies, but they all guard secrets. They won't confess their love unless they believe it will get them something of value like a ring or a house in the Hamptons. And they never confess their trust. Too many women have been burned by trusting men in my world.

It's too easy for a man with money and power to destroy any woman who trusts him. If she doesn't have her own empire he can destroy her financially simply by removing his presence from her life, especially if he was very smart about the pre-nup, or if he only kept her as a concubine on the side, constantly promising her more, but never delivering.

Getting used to a certain type of lifestyle is like a drug, and he can pull it away at any moment. Once tasting the luxe life, most of these women aren't willing to give it up. They make endless concessions and guard their emotions. If Cinderella's story had continued, I sometimes wonder if the prince would have had another woman on the side while she pretended everything was perfect in her fairly tale just so she could stay in the castle a little while longer.

For many women, it's not a fairy tale. There's a dark side. He can cheat. He can trade her in on a newer, younger, fresher model when she becomes too *last season*. As a result, many women in my world simply do not trust. They put on the fake smile, they do the performance art blow jobs, they dress pretty like our little dolls and get all the Botox and injectibles and other treatments and surgeries, the butt lifts, the breast enhancements—all in the hopes of keeping our eyes from straying to the next pretty young thing constantly on the prowl for our attentions.

They don't make waves, hoping against hope that all this work they're putting in will at least buy them a little loyalty and security, even if he's flying to the south of France with his secretary on the side. At least she'll have the ring. The title of Mrs. And some of those last names are currency all on their own. There are names everyone knows and those names open doors.

She believes she can trade a bit of her soul. She may not really be *The One,* but she'll be the one on his arm at all the formal events, the one with the respect, the one all his friends know, even if she can't always be the woman who holds him spellbound in the bedroom. She won't be the one he loves above all things, including his own hedonistic pleasure and the newness of getting his dick wet in a new supermodel every weekend, but at least she won't be his dirty little secret.

It's only a bit different if the woman has money of her own, an empire of her own. But even so, money can't solve a broken heart. To let a man in who can have anyone is dangerous ground to walk upon. And we know it… the men. We know it and we play upon that weakness. We play up our dominance and show that we know we have all the cards, but it's only because we could, theoretically, lose all of our power under the thrall of the right woman. We can never let them know how much power they could hold.

Each side must play their role. She must resist falling for the man who can't fall under her spell, and he must resist her spell.

Because of these all too harsh realities in my world, I expect a fight or denial from Macy when I ask if she trusts me.

"Yes, Master, I trust you."

I wonder if she's the most foolish woman in the world. Definitely she's the most naive. Yes, I realize I kidnapped her, forced her to sign documents legally binding herself to me… promising me heirs for fuck's sake, but… to just gift wrap her trust and lay it at my feet like this? To not even pretend to deny or refuse me her honesty? To not hold even the tiniest thing back from me?

If this were anyone but Macy, this sweet and naive admission would be her downfall. Macy will still fall, but she'll fall *with me,* not beneath me. I won't abandon her when she hits the ground. She holds an ace she doesn't even know she has. I've had plenty of women—an endless fucking parade of them. All flavors. Exotic types. Worldly women. Women most men couldn't dream of having on their arm even for a night. And yet… every single one of them left me cold.

Except Macy. I can only assume that whatever thing inside me is dead, somehow is allowed to breathe when she's near. And that to me, is worth everything. Even the potential loss of power.

"You feel safe when my hands are on you," I say, as though I need to clarify this. There's something pathological inside me that needs to know exactly what she means when she confesses trust in a man little better than a rabid dog. She's not a stupid woman. At least she's not book stupid. Maybe she's street stupid, but she doesn't strike me as that either. Her response to me seems to have nothing to do with what her mind tells her. No, she's following a different lure altogether, a different way of knowing and sensing that I can't begin to guess the finer points of.

"Yes, Master." Her voice catches when she says it, and I stroke my fingers across her downturned face, to feel the tear that escapes.

"Do you know how foolish it is to trust me or feel safe in my presence?"

Her shoulders are shaking now. This wasn't what I was planning to do with her down here. And yet, here we are.

"Y-yes, Master."

I swallow past the lump in my throat and say something I've known to be true since the moment I first saw her. "It's foolish, but in your case, it's true. You are safe with me. But this doesn't mean I won't push you or ask things of you which may seem… unconventional."

This is quite possibly the mildest way to describe what I plan to do to her and with her, but I don't want to break her delicate trust. I need to find some way to prepare her for what's coming, without breaking my contract with The

Dungeon. I need her *with* me. She seems to me like a butterfly, pushing it's way out of its cocoon. But if I try to help her break free, she might not make it. Her wings are still far too fragile for the bumbling of a human's touch.

She's silent as I continue to use a low and soothing voice, as though I were trying to gentle a wild cat. There is nothing wild in her in this moment. She's so far removed from the woman who threw a vase at me and ran away, risking the dark forest over me. Now she seems willing to risk kneeling at my feet and waiting for my commands—a whole other kind of forest with a whole other set of creatures which may devour her, body, mind, and soul.

"Deep down, we both know that while you may somehow be pure on the surface... underneath it all, in the depths, you are as dark as I am. You are a filthy wanton whore."

She flinches at this description. And who can blame her? What woman wants to be called a whore? Particularly one who hasn't even parted her thighs for the first man yet. It's as though I'm proclaiming her fortune rather than referencing her past. I'm declaring her destiny—or maybe telling her without telling her what I plan to do and pretending it's somehow just in her DNA to do it.

"I didn't say it was a bad thing. What if that word didn't carry the judgment? What if it was just a statement of the facts? What if it was no more consequential than preferring one type of chocolate over another? Tell, me, Macy... in the dark recesses of your mind, in your fantasies when you touch yourself... how many men are you with? If you lie to me, I'll know."

She blushes furiously, as only a redhead can do. "I-I can't..." is all she says.

I grip her by the hair and angle her face up to mine so

she'll stop using these submissive gestures to hide from me. "You *can*."

She may have fantasies that mirror my own but she is not weak, so these demure gestures of obedience don't fool me. In fact, they're starting to grate on me. They make me want to punish her for this pretense. I haven't done a single thing to have her in such a state of submission. Not once, outside of that one day in the dungeon—which she liked—have I physically raised a hand to her.

She shakes her head, her jaw set. There it is—the evidence that she isn't so agreeable. My fierce little librarian.

"Tell me," I demand.

CHAPTER TWENTY-THREE: MACY

My heart flutters so fast in my chest. I can't tell him this. I'm not sure why exactly I can't tell him. Am I afraid he'll judge me? Punish me? Am I afraid it'll make him feel he has permission to pass me around just because of what I fantasize about? Fantasies aren't consent.

I know full well that my fantasies don't mean I literally want to do all these things in real life or be treated this way. And yet Colin's very existence and the situation I've somehow fallen into, excite me in ways I didn't think possible. It's so far above the fantasy that I can't bring myself to fantasize anymore. The fantasy is too pale of a comparison to everything Colin is in reality. The way he makes me feel, what his mere presence does to my body. I've never felt things like this before, not even around Soren.

The big question that looms before me now is am I really that woman from my imagination? Or is she only a mirage? I'm terrified to admit to these things only to discover the reality isn't my fantasy, but my nightmare. And then I'm stuck, and I'll blame myself forever. My body trusts Colin implicitly, like some scraggly little tail-wagging puppy who will happily follow his master off a cliff.

My mind rebels at this, but when he puts his hands on me, I'm powerless. I find myself sinking into the soft peace of his touch, the way his fingertips brush lightly against my skin, the way he touches my hair, the pleasure I remember his tongue bringing me between my legs. That moment feels like a lifetime ago.

"Mrs. Black?" His tone is like a prosecutor in a courtroom, and I feel incapable of perjury—as if there might be a legal punishment for lying to Colin.

"I don't remember exactly," I hedge.

"Estimate."

"Sometimes five, sometimes ten. I don't know, sometimes it's all blurry." This is so far from the truth. There is no blurry. There is no *random, faceless, I can't keep track of them* fantasy men. They are clear, and explicit. I can see the fabric of their crisp shirts, the sheen of the silk on their ties. But Colin doesn't question me further on it. He seems to accept my answer.

I let out a long, spiraling breath as I feel him move away from me. My gaze tracks him across the room to the exposed brick wall and the red leather sofa that sits against it. Colin sits in much the same way as he did on the plane. He crooks a finger, and I swallow hard.

I don't bother standing up, instead I crawl across the plush carpet. When I get to him, he reaches down between my legs, and I blush as he discovers just how wet I am.

He smirks. I move my hands to the zipper of his suit pants, assuming this is what he wants, a repeat performance of the plane, this time with more privacy. But he takes both of my hands in his and holds my gaze for a long moment.

"Straddle me."

I move to sit on his lap with one leg on either side of his body, but he shifts me so that I'm straddling just one of his legs. Somehow this makes me blush harder than everything else so far today because I know what's coming.

He leans in and whispers, "Ride my leg until you come, little whore."

"I-I can't… I'll mess up your suit." A suit that no doubt cost multiple thousands of dollars.

"So, you'll mess up my suit," Colin says. "I have a closet full of them." He holds my gaze for a long moment. "Of course… you'll have to be punished for messing up my suit."

If I were smart I'd be scared of him, but maybe I'm just not all that smart. All the facts swirling around my head could never protect me from a man like Colin Black. There isn't a piece of knowledge I could possibly access that would help me right now. No library, no internet search could provide me with 'that one crazy trick…' that could help me now.

Colin doesn't hide his wealth. He doesn't try to play the Billionaire next door game, living in a middle class house, carrying a green card instead of black. But at the same time his wealth isn't loud or showy. It whispers. I adjust myself so that I'm straddling only one of his legs like he demanded, and I begin to grind against him.

He grips me by the shoulders, his mouth next to my ear. "That's a bad girl."

"Only because you want me to be," I retort.

He actually laughs out loud at this. I wonder if amusing him will reduce my punishment.

It takes a shockingly short amount of time for me to come, rutting against his leg like an animal in heat. He puts a hand over my mouth as I scream to muffle the sound. I'm not sure why. I already know he likes an audience, and we're underground anyway. No one can hear me scream. That thought should terrify me, but it only drives me.

He urges me onward until the last bits of pleasure have been wrung from me, then he pushes me back to the floor on my knees. Now I'm eye level with the mess I made.

He shakes his head in fake disappointment. "Clean it up."

I look at him blankly for a moment. Like does he want me to go get a wash cloth? I don't know the first thing about how to clean a suit… I feel like this is something I should have Googled at some point in my life but I can't even begin to imagine what the search phrase for this particular situation would be.

He holds my gaze and smirks. "I meant, with your tongue, Mrs. Black."

I blush.

Oh. Wow, I really am a virgin. Let us never speak of it.

I do as he asks, this humiliating, fucked-up thing which we both know is not improving the state of his suit. He strokes through my hair as I taste the evidence of my own pleasure.

After several minutes, his hand at the back of my neck stills me. "It's time for your punishment."

CHAPTER TWENTY-FOUR: MACY

I wake to the first full day of my honeymoon, alone. I knew this was how it would be, but still. I'm married, sort of. I'm on my honeymoon, and... I'm still a virgin. I must be cursed.

I trail a finger over the fresh cane welts Colin left on me in the dungeon last night. I'm not sure if the punishment was for messing up his suit or for the million tiny infractions he's probably been keeping track of in his head. Or maybe he just likes me marked like this. I can't honestly say that I hate it. There's a dark intimacy in these marks of possession that warm my flesh.

And afterward he dragged his tongue slowly over each one then made me come again with that same talented tongue. Then he put me to bed. I'd offered to return the favor, but he said... "I'll get what I need tomorrow night."

The sacrifice. My stomach flutters with nerves. Whatever the sacrifice is, it's happening tonight.

I'm still very aware of the fact that Livia thinks I'm on my honeymoon with William. I can't believe it was just two days ago that I stood in a church and promised to love and cherish Will through sickness and health, til death do us part. Or until the unfiled paperwork gets thrown in the honeymoon suite fire. Whichever.

I can't think which thing would be worse: For Livia to know that I'm actually with Colin—his more-or-less kidnapped bride—or to labor under the delusion that I'm closing my eyes and thinking of England with Will.

I know Colin has used a lot of restraint with me. I can see in his eyes that there's so much he wants to do with me, and yet he holds himself back. I could pretend I don't know why but I do know why. Haven't I had this same fantasy about a thousand times? Whatever is planned, he wants me as untouched as possible. I'm starting to think this may be the true reason he stayed away so long, because he knew he wouldn't have the self control otherwise. I know that sounds somewhat arrogant but virgin or not, I'm not stupid. I can see the lust burning in his eyes. No way does a man like Colin want a woman that much and not take what he wants unless there's a larger plan in place.

I just don't fully understand the purpose for that plan.

If Colin were another man, I could assume it was honor that restrained him. But after kidnapping and surveillance, those character traits are pretty much off the table.

It's ten in the morning and I haven't heard from him. Would he leave me alone in Dayne's cottage on our honeymoon? I take a quick shower and put on a pair of jeans and a T-shirt, then work to tame my dark red curls so I can get my hair into a ponytail.

I've tried using a straightening iron but when I put my hair in a ponytail after that I look like I'm time traveling and going to the disco.

When I get downstairs, I'm surprised to find Colin

sitting at the table, reading a paper, and drinking coffee. There's a big spread of brunch food that was clearly delivered from the main kitchen at the resort.

"Did you sleep well?" he asks, not looking up from his paper.

"Yes."

I pour a cup of coffee and sit down.

"I thought you didn't drink coffee," he says looking at me like he's caught me in a gigantic lie.

"I don't, but..." I trail off because I'm not about to tell him I need something stronger than tea to cope with my jangled nerves and figure out what the hell I feel about anything, if I should be trying to escape or not, what the possible consequences of *that* might be, along with about a hundred thoughts I haven't properly filed and categorized yet, and whiskey is way too big of a leap for me right now. So coffee, it is.

The heated way he looks at me, I swear any moment he'll just take me over the kitchen counter, but he doesn't.

Will things feel normal between us after whatever he has planned for me tonight? Is there a way anything can be normal between us given the nature of our relationship and how it started? *Do* we have a relationship?

Colin stands abruptly. My gaze goes to his pants to see the tell-tale signs of his erection. Yes, he definitely wants me, but he makes no move to touch me, nor does he make any request for me to take care of his needs.

"I have some business to take care of. The kitchen is fully stocked. I'll see you tonight."

And then he's gone. Something in my chest tightens, worried the business he has to take care of is his raging erection and that he doesn't plan to just use his hand.

I spend most of the day pacing around the house like a

caged animal. I can leave and wander the grounds but it should be no mystery why I'm not too excited to wander unescorted around a place called The Dungeon.

Jeffrey is staying at the main resort, and it's too quiet. Once again I think about escaping. Is Colin giving me that out? But no, he never removed the tracking bracelet. He could still find me and drag me back. Is this some sort of bizarre loyalty test?

I think about running but I'm too curious about tonight. I know it's stupid. What if whatever's happening will be horrible? What if it traumatizes me? What if it's painful or... but I'm just too curious. I just need to know. And so I waffle on whether or not to run or stay.

I pace the house. I eat the food set aside in the kitchen, and I wait for the sun to make it's journey across the sky and bring us to night.

It's almost sunset when I go upstairs to my bathroom. I find a note on the counter with bathing instructions. He's left a small bottle of champagne for me, along with candles and rose petals and fragrant vanilla oil. So I follow his instructions, and take a bath with candles and champagne in the bath oil.

A white dress is waiting for me on the bed when I get out, and Colin stands there, dressed in a suit. He doesn't speak a word to me as I drop the towel. His dark eyes drink me in, but still he doesn't take what's his to devour.

"Get dressed."

There's no bra and panties, only the dress. It's long and flowy, like a much simpler wedding gown, but no veil or flowers. No train at the back. I put on the dress and the gold heels. He pulls a key from his pocket and unlocks and removes the bracelet from my wrist.

"Just for tonight," he says. Then he guides me downstairs.

While I was in the bath, room service was delivered to the cottage. The table is set with a white linen table cloth. A light honey scent wafts from the beeswax candles. Dinner is a chicken and vegetable dish over noodles in some sort of white sauce and white wine—all things relatively safe to eat while wearing a white dress.

He doesn't say a single word to me, and I can't bring myself to say anything either. I want to ask what's going to happen. I want to ask him anything, but I can't find any words to speak. That's a Macy Miracle. I can always find something to talk about, but even my nervous chatter doesn't make an appearance right now. Everything feels too heavy for words.

Does he *want* to do whatever's about to happen?

Finally I do find words. "Master? Will I be safe?"

His dark gaze holds mine for nearly a full minute, and he nods.

I let out the breath I didn't know I'd been holding. For some reason I believe him. Maybe I shouldn't. Why should I believe a man with probably no internal compass?

We finish dinner. He stands, snuffs out the candles, and offers me his hand. I take it like the absolute fool I am, and allow him to lead me to whatever fate is planned.

CHAPTER TWENTY-FIVE: MACY

I'm inside the fantasy now. No longer am I separate from the visions and images that drifted by each morning for years on rotation… the private porn library of my mind. Now I *am* her. I am that woman, about to be taken for the first time in a room full of strangers.

In a bizarre way, this feels like our wedding, the thing that actually binds us. A contract isn't a ceremony, and we didn't get the ceremony. I think the only thing Colin is capable of promising me is that he'll never let me go. And now like some queen of the dark ages, I have an audience for the consummation of an arranged marriage to a powerful man whose word is law.

Colin stands beside me, his hand in mine, near the entrance. No one has noticed us yet. For the moment we blend into the rest of the group. His hand feels warm and solid wrapped around mine. It doesn't escape me, especially given the environment that we're in and the ways various couples are engaging, that he could hold me by the arm like a prisoner, or by the scruff of the neck like some dog. But instead, his fingers are laced with mine. It's somehow reassuring.

My heart hammers in my chest, and all I know is that somehow tonight I'm the main event. I take a slow breath to steady myself and calm my nerves. I don't know why I haven't run from him, why I haven't struggled. It seems obvious to me that these people are here willingly. I've been made aware of the contracts that get signed before people come into this space. They aren't a thousand pages, they are a single page with very clearly spelled out rules in a readable big font. Nothing can be mistaken. There's no fine print here. So if I screamed and begged for help, I'm pretty sure, someone would help me. I think. Okay I'm not completely sure, but it seems like everyone's agreement is really important here, so it's hard to imagine they'd all be okay with me being here against my will.

And, I didn't sign anything. Colin signed something, but some understanding or awareness passed between him and the people at the door with the contracts, and I didn't sign anything. What does that mean? Does it mean my desires and consent don't matter? Or is it protecting me from being bound by some rules I might not want to be bound to?

I'm really not sure. Colin's touch still inspires the same stupid trust it has from the first time his hand rested against my throat. Against all reason I trust he'll keep me safe. I don't want to scream or fight because I'm so close to getting to have my fantasy come to life, and I want to let it play out. I don't know how or why I'm sure, but I'm *sure* if I were in true distress, Colin would protect me. He'd do whatever it took.

I turn my attention back to our surroundings. There's a

stage off to the side with musicians; it's large, but it isn't the focal point of the room. I hear slow deep drumbeats along with other percussive noises... a tap tap tap tap, lighter than the drum beat, like an animal bone being struck against another animal bone. It's like we've traveled back to a time where everything is life and death and nature cycling and spiraling endlessly around us with no other complications.

It's mostly dark with no electric light—only candlelight. All the flames are contained and protected. There are maybe a hundred people in this room, and we wouldn't want to create a fire hazard. There's a large semi-circle multi-level elevated platform set up like an amphitheater, so everyone can watch the same activity in the middle of the room without having their view obstructed. Some people are already milling around on the different levels, choosing the vantage point from which they'll watch.

Along the wall, near the stage with the musicians is another elevated platform, a second, smaller stage. There are three regal-looking chairs up there and I see Dayne, Soren, and Griffin. Livia's men. Dayne stands in the middle, the other two sit in the outermost chairs.

My face flames. I don't know what I expected but I didn't expect to see Dayne, Soren, and Griffin here. I thought they'd be back home. After all, they were at the wedding. It never occurred to me they might get on their own jet to come to Costa Rica. Did Soren know this was happening when he first delivered me to Colin? Is *this* what he meant by me being a sacrifice? But no, this can't be the thing keeping his stock prices up.

Before I can ask myself further questions, the music stops for a moment and a spotlight lands on Dayne. Silence falls over the room. Finally, when the tension and anticipation reaches its zenith, he speaks.

"As you all know, when you enter this space with a toy, you must share with everyone. Consent to step into this space is consent to play or be played with by anyone here. The one exception has always been the gold collar. My collar. In the past this collar has been reserved only for myself with my own toys, the women I didn't wish to share here because it *is* my club."

The room fills with polite chuckles.

Dayne continues. "Now that collar is worn exclusively by my wife, Livia."

I look around, but I don't see my best friend, something I'm ridiculously grateful for. Whatever's about to happen, I think I could stand for her men to watch it—after all, Soren has featured in my fantasies about a million times in just that capacity. But Livia? Yeah, no, I'm not there yet. Maybe never. Dayne continues.

"Starting tonight, there will be a new exclusive level of membership in the dungeon called The Silver Circle. Silver Circle membership will be by invitation only, so don't ask. Griffin, Soren, and myself will decide who we wish to include. The steep annual membership includes private events only for members and the right to control who gets to play with your pet inside the dungeon whenever you're here. Initiates must participate in a public ritual and present a virgin sacrifice."

A gasp rises from the crowd, and this time Dayne chuckles.

"I know, it's so rare to find a virgin anything. The sacrifice must be at least 21 years old and here of her own free will." I feel like Dayne looks directly at me when he says this. Colin's hand squeezes mine tighter as though he fears I might run away.

I hear murmurs as people make quips like "Good luck with that." I imagine the numbers of women who've reached twenty-one without deflowering are a pretty small group, something which makes me feel like an even greater freak at almost thirty. No one here seems too troubled by the term sacrifice. So either they all understand this is somehow symbolic or they're all closet serial killers. I'm hoping it's the former. I'm 99.999% sure that Colin isn't planning to murder me just to be part of this stupid Silver Circle thing, and Dayne did mention free will. Nobody is volunteering for that kind of sacrifice.

Dayne clears his throat, and the crowd settles down. "The Silver Circle gives members in this exclusive level the right to use of a silver collar in the dungeon which entitles them to share the woman wearing it only with those of his choosing and no one else. It carries the same weight and authority as my gold collar. Anyone who doesn't respect the rights of the silver collar, will be blacklisted from the dungeon for life."

Dayne keeps talking, but I don't hear the rest because Colin has bent to speak low in my ear. "Do you understand why you're here now?"

His nearness and rumbling voice against my skin has such a strong effect on me. I've gone to great pains to not make it obvious how strongly I want this man, even though there are a million reasons why that's probably the stupidest desire I could entertain.

Colin's mouth remains next to my ear as he continues. "I like sharing my toys, but I want to call the shots. I plan to bring you to the dungeon often, and I don't intend to be held to the rules of sharing."

It's kind of... sweet, in a Colin way. And it occurs to me that the entire Silver Circle was probably created to accommodate his desire to control who he shares me with. Though maybe Dayne, Soren, and Griffin don't like the idea of me being shared indiscriminately either, given that they know exactly how I came to belong to Mr. Black.

Colin leans close to me again and whispers, "I selected the men who will be involved tonight."

"What's going to happen?" I finally have the nerve to ask this. I've wanted to ask it since the moment I knew *something* would be happening. But I was afraid to know.

"I can't tell you. You'll be given the option to go forward or say no."

"And if I say no?" I turn again to face him. His expression is unreadable.

Finally he says: "As my wife, you'll be accompanying me here. So unless you want to have to sleep with anyone who happens to be in the room at the time, it's in your interest to be the sacrifice. No one will fuck you but me tonight, that's the one thing I can promise."

My breath catches as it comes into sharper focus that very soon I'll lose my virginity in front of a live audience. I always knew this, but it's only now really hitting me. If feels somehow as though everything in my life has been culminating to this moment of consummation.

The response I should have to his proclamation of what's to come is horror, shame, terror. I should want to escape. I run through my options now. What happens if I say no? Yes, he says he'll bring me here again and then my options will be gone, but... no because I'd have to sign the contract to get into this room.

Could he make me do that? It seems there are strong rules here to keep everybody and everything above boards legally. Dayne wouldn't want his club to get shut down. I'm not sure what the laws are in Costa Rica, but it still seems important that everyone involved has given consent, and coercion isn't consent. Would he just play with someone else if I refused? That bothers me more.

As I stand here I'm angry. I live in a constant war with myself—the battle between how I'm supposed to feel and react to things, versus how I actually do feel. The things I'm supposed to want and not want, versus the things I actually desire. The fight over the rightness and wrongness of things. The politics of things. The free will or lack thereof. The possible coercion. What society thinks, what other people think. It all rolls over me in an attempt to steal my true will and desire, to subjugate me into a family-friendly version of myself, something appropriate for mass consumption.

I've played this up with my bookish ways, weird facts, and nerd glasses. And of course these freckles. God, the freckles. People see freckles and assume innocence. There is no known seductress in the history of the world with curly auburn hair, and freckles. And so I've played into this image, this character that people feel most comfortable with, this girl everyone else wants me to be.

It's not that I'm not those things, but somewhere inside me I know I'm more, if only I could set her free.

Is there a single choice in life we get to make that is one hundred percent free of coercion, manipulation, or someone else's viewpoint shoehorned into our minds when we're too young to fight back? How much of me is a separate complete thing, and how much is a collection of experiences and other people's ideas? I just want to be free and be the version of me that's locked tightly inside my mind, never able to fully express herself because of other people's oppressive opinions about what is and isn't okay to feel, do, or be in this world.

And how the fuck do they know? Who died and made them god? Who gave them authority over my life or internal processing? When did it occur that anyone but me had the right to live my life? I'm the one who faces the consequences of my life. It's no one's business but my own.

And yet...

I feel stuck in an endless limbo where the only other person on the battlefield is another version of myself. There is the me I want to be lined up against what's socially acceptable, politically correct, expected, normal, nice. That polite unoffensive me is the one loaded down with all the weapons, handed to her via *other people's opinions and moral judgments,* other people's busybodying. Aren't they kept busy enough with their own lives? If only they spent half so much energy on themselves.

I'm not supposed to want to do this with Colin. I'm not supposed to want to lose my virginity in this way. My mind fights and rails and screams, but my body says yes. Of the two me's on the battlefield, the real me is what my body wants. My simple, primal desires beneath the lie of everyone else's story, even beneath the lie of my own story.

Suddenly there's a shift in the crowd as attention is pulled to me and Colin. People start to notice us, and I feel Colin's hand on my back as he leads me forward. A soft spotlight shines down on the center of the room, and I'm back in the fantasy only this time it's real. And instead of imagining and pretending, I am finally doing and to hell with a world that tells me I can't.

My mind flashes to my dark book group... "I would never do that..." "She barely tried to escape..." "It's so unbelievable..." "If it were me I would..."

I squeeze my eyes shut for a moment to block out all that fucking stupidity. Who the fuck cares what they would do? This is MY story.

I feel the change come over me, as though I'm a shapeshifter in the forest, and I have the realization that this actually *is* the full moon. I caught a glimpse of it when we were walking from the cottage to the main building earlier, but I didn't allow myself to process it, to give it too much weight. Desire prickles over my senses. It feels like a wave of fire licking over me, burning away the parts of me that hid behind the other parts of me society would find acceptable and normal.

I spent months jealous of Livia, that she got these three hot kinky men, that she got to surrender in this way and have pleasure without the shame and without the guilt. And here I am, in this room. Somehow I have brought this fantasy to myself. I'm not the victim here so don't you dare frame me that way.

I manifested this. I called this up from the aether. I added magic to it every single morning in the ritual of my orgasm, and now I'm claiming what I sent out into the universe because it's mine, and no one has to understand that but me. I don't know what I think about the reality of Colin, but I know what I feel about this moment. I'm not a sacrifice. A sacrifice is something demanded. It's an obligation. It's forced or coerced. It's something done to you. But I am not a sacrifice. I'm a willing participant. The real sacrifice was all the time I've lied and run from myself. All the time I've wasted standing in somebody else's truth.

I stand in the middle of the room under the spotlight. There's a large round table with white leather upholstery.

Dayne speaks again, and this time it's to Colin. "Is this your offering?" he asks, indicating me.

"It is."

Dayne turns to me then. "Take your opportunity to leave this place, Macy."

It's jarring to hear him speak my name in a place that feels like I should be anonymous. Colin's hand squeezes mine again. I don't think he realizes he's doing it.

"No. I'm staying," I say.

Is Dayne trying to save me? Is he trying to go against the agreement between Soren and Colin? The agreement he had to have signed off on? Or was he going along, and now he's having second thoughts? A guilty conscience? Was he watching me? Did he witness my internal war just now? Is he, like so many others, trying to save me from a struggle that wouldn't exist without their judgment?

I note an angry expression on Soren's face and am sure if I had the nerve to look at Colin I'd see the same anger. Yes, Dayne is going off script.

"Macy, do you understand what's going to happen here tonight? Multiple men will touch you. You'll be laid out like a sacrifice, and your virginity will be taken in front of a crowd of strangers. You should leave. I will protect you."

Does he not understand that Colin won't release me either way? Dayne's protection only extends to his club. Maybe he could demand Colin release me if Colin wants use of the club, but I have a feeling he'd choose to keep me over his membership.

I feel the fury surge through me like a wave of electricity. If my hair were literally on fire right now, I wouldn't be surprised. Of all people, someone who owns a place like this judging me and what I can handle and deciding what's best for me and what I should want...

"NO! I know what I'm doing."

Dayne looks shocked. He actually reels back, as though

I've slapped him, or as though the power of that definitive no, actually caused his head to snap back.

Indistinct murmurs rise up around us, and I know the people here also realize Dayne isn't following whatever script was laid out. Or perhaps it's the shock of someone yelling at Dayne when all anyone seems to show him is the greatest deference. Oh, the intrigue.

His expression is inscrutable as he stares down at me. It's so strange to me that it's Dayne and not Soren holding this role. Though Soren never would have tried to save me —something I strangely respect. A part of me may hate the man Soren is, but I respect that he hasn't treated me like a helpless child in need of shielding. Finally, Dayne sighs and nods.

The drumbeats start again from the stage.

Then it's Colin who speaks. "I offer, my wife, Macy Black, as a sacrifice to the dungeon in exchange for founding membership in The Silver Circle."

There's a unified gasp from the room, and I'm pretty sure it's the *wife* part that's throwing them. I feel strangely giddy he presented me in this way as his wife. Not his slut, pet, whore, toy, concubine... his wife.

He guides me to the table and helps me onto it. The zipper for the dress is on the side, he pulls it down, and I think he's about to undress me in front of the curious crowd, but instead someone passes him a white sheet. He unfolds it and drapes it over me before helping me out of the dress. The sheet continues to keep me veiled from hungry eyes who have forgotten how all this started and are now interested in watching the scene unfold before them like any of a million twisted kinky games played out in this room before tonight.

Colin fades back into the shadows and several men all

dressed formally as though they should be at a fundraising gala step into the light. With the tribal drum beats going deeper and louder, I'd expect something dramatic like black cloaks or raw nudity, but the suit thing is a Colin thing and I can't help but feel this is his vision as much as Soren's.

I count nine men, and they each take a place around this large table. My body laid out before them only covers a very small part of the space. You could lay eight other women out on this table all spaced apart like numbers on a clock.

They aren't wearing masks. If any of them were convicted criminals I could probably pick them out of a lineup or a book of mugshots, but none of them seems worried about this possibility, which tells me they're all squeaky clean officially and that even with their faces uncovered, they remain truly anonymous to me.

They're all attractive, and it occurs to me that Colin picked men who any sane woman would *want* to have touch them. No one creepy or gross or slovenly. Any one of these men is the kind of man women would viciously compete for the attentions of; and tonight, all their attention is on me.

No one speaks. Aside from the initial talk, there doesn't seem to be planned narration for this ritual. The first man approaches. He holds two black boxes, the smaller stacked on top. He places these boxes without comment on the table.

The drumming intensifies.

Then the first stranger's hands are on me. He skims gently over my body, touching me through the sheet, but never directly touching my skin. He strokes and fondles my breasts. My nipples grow erect in response to this attention, poking through the sheet, clearly visible. He leans over me and kisses me on the mouth.

I moan into him, my inhibitions scattering away. He rises and stretches my hands over my head, enclosing them in gleaming silver cuffs attached to the table. He strokes my hair and the side of my throat. My hips arch up to meet his hands as they move farther down, between my legs, stroking my warming core.

He massages and strokes but he never goes beneath the sheet. His hands never stray to my bare flesh. I understand implicitly, that's for Colin. The stranger continues until I realize he isn't going to stop until I come. This isn't just some symbolic gesture.

And then I blush as I realize that I'm expected to come for all of them with all these onlookers even before anyone sees an inch of my nudity or any actual sex occurs.

I close my eyes and a moment later I hear Colin's voice in my ear, urging me on. "Come for him."

Was I waiting for this permission?

I let go, accepting the pleasure on offer, my body writhing under the sheet as I grind against the stranger's hand. When the first man has finished, taking nothing for himself, the table is rotated to the next. This process happens nine times. Each man claims my mouth, demanding I open to his kiss. The only part of his body allowed to plunge inside any part of mine is his tongue, and only my mouth. They each stroke my hair, and my throat, my breasts over the sheet, and between my legs. I give them each my pleasure as Colin demanded, as the drumming goes on, and the voyeurs watching this display seem to disappear into the background with each orgasm until I feel alone in the spotlight with these men.

By the time they're all finished, the sheet is soaked with

a giant wet spot, visible to all who watched. It's clear I didn't fake my pleasure. It wasn't just a show. And still, I'm so turned on because Colin is next.

I open my eyes when he approaches. I'd expected the men to move back into the crowd but they've just shifted to make space for Colin at the table. He uncuffs my wrists. The first guy takes the two boxes from the center of the table and holds them as Colin spreads the sheet out over the center of the table.

He guides me to lay back on it, spreading my legs wide. Nothing shields me now from the men who touched me or our larger audience. I swallow hard as Colin loosens and removes his tie, his gaze never leaving mine. I expect him to take something else off, but he doesn't, not for this show because it's not about him.

He takes the smallest of the black boxes and opens it, revealing my wedding ring. He holds out a hand, demanding mine. I offer him my left hand, and he slides the ring on my finger. And somehow, this twisted fucked-up moment feels like my real wedding. Not the moment in the church with Will, not the signing of the contract, but this moment.

He unzips his pants, freeing his cock as he leans over me. "And now, Mrs. Black, I'm finally taking what's mine."

He shoves into me so fast I don't have time to process the pain, and somehow I know that was for my benefit. The *rip the band-aid off fast* approach. Once he's broken through my barrier, he goes still, waiting for me to adjust to him. I arch my hips up in invitation, and he begins to move, slowly rocking into me, as he cradles my body against him. More shocking than the public way this is unfolding, is his unexpected tenderness.

The drumbeats and light and people all seem to go

away, and it feels like we're alone in the dark. I've never thought it was realistic to expect a virgin to have an orgasm from her first time, but my body has been so primed from nine other orgasms, that I'm on the edge again as he drives into me harder. I claw at his shoulders, trying to hold on as I buck wildly beneath him.

I'm not sure who is fucking who, but finally my pleasure crests over me in a wave, and then Colin is spilling his seed into me. He holds me tight against him as he thrusts until the act is complete. As he withdraws, my awareness slowly returns to the room. The audience, the men standing around the table, the drumming, and finally Colin's possessive gaze like an animal who just marked his territory.

He picks up the second black box and opens it to reveal the silver collar.

I distantly hear Dayne speak again. "Colin Black, The Dungeon welcomes you to The Silver Circle."

The engraving on the outside of the collar reads: "Property of Colin Black. Touch only with permission." He unlocks it and slips it around my throat.

Polite applause breaks out into the space as though we just performed a symphony instead of a sex act.

As Colin helps me up, I glance back at the table. The white sheet has my blood on it, evidence that Colin has indeed produced a virgin for this event. It's taking all my willpower not to mentally ramble about the fact that you can be a virgin and not bleed, but I guess it doesn't matter now. I bled, and now Colin's in the inner circle.

He wraps the sheet around me, picks me up, and carries me out of the ballroom.

CHAPTER TWENTY-SIX: MACY

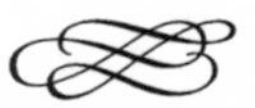

I wake and glance over at the alarm clock. The red numbers read 2:33. I'm in Colin's bed, but I'm alone again. The house feels empty. I push back the blankets and get out of bed, grabbing the silk robe off a nearby chair. After he took my virginity in the hottest, most fucked-up expression of my own twisted fantasies, he brought me back to the cottage.

He fed me champagne and strawberries and put me in a bubble bath with candles to relax. When I got out of the tub he gave me an ornately wrapped gift. Black paper, white satin ribbon. Inside the box was lingerie. Not just any lingerie. It wasn't kinky or dirty. It wasn't revealing. It was classy and the most expensive lingerie that has ever been on my body.

I knew it was expensive, not because it was silk, but because it was La Perla. The long white silk gown with pale gold frastaglio embroidery, and the matching robe with the same detailing at the sleeves and hem. It was several thousand dollars… for sleepwear. I only know this because

Livia has some of their lingerie and was looking through their website the last time I was at her house. My eyes nearly bugged out at the prices.

So now, I'm wandering through this giant misnamed cottage, wearing lingerie several times more expensive than my first car, looking for my husband. There is a pang of unfamiliar fear low in my belly. For the first time I'm worried… what if he's cheating on me? On our honeymoon.

I didn't sit and worry about this before, but now that he's taken what he wants from me… and the mystery is gone, there's a part of me that fears this is when it starts, the sneaking around.

Maybe Colin is sharing some woman with Jeffrey at the main resort. If he's sharing me, doesn't he expect me to share him? I know it's not fair, but I don't care. I don't want to share him with other women. I shouldn't want to be with him at all, but now that I am, I want him to be mine, not just for me to be his.

I stare down at the gold band on my finger as I make my way through the dimly lit hallway. It's quieter than a tomb. The main level is much the same, but darker. A few lights from the pool outside shine in through the windows, along with light from the full moon.

It's a sort of funny coincidence. Don't sacrifices happen on the full moon? In stories? What are the odds that my wedding would just happen to coincide with the growing moon and that the night of this ritual deflowering would occur when it officially reached fullness? Maybe it was planned this way, though I chose the wedding date. Maybe it was fate.

I run my hand over my abdomen. I can't believe I didn't realize when it was. I'm one of those women with an obnoxiously regular cycle and almost no symptoms of any kind. And, I'm in sync with the moon. The only symptom I get is a low warm twinge when I'm ovulating. I feel that low twinge now and I realize what this means. Leave it to me to get pregnant the first time I have sex. I'm at the peak of my fertility standing in the moonlight, feeling the evidence of this truth, possibly carrying my captor husband's child, and he's what? Already bored with me? Already fucking another woman somewhere?

I swipe at the tears. No, this isn't my fairy tale. Or maybe it's how all the fairy tales go. After all, they all seem to end at the wedding, don't they? We don't know that the princess is really happy forever, or how short this *forever* might actually be.

Every Disney princess that I watched as a little girl now feels like a lie as I imagine all the princes slinking around with a parade of women behind the princesses' back, while she sits alone in the castle getting fat with his child.

Part of me wants to go back upstairs and just pretend I didn't wake up to an empty bed. When I fell asleep he had me pressed against his body. He didn't even try to fuck me again. He put me in the lingerie and put me to bed. It felt sweet at the time. But now it feels like boredom, his boredom.

I'm about to go back upstairs when I notice a small sliver of light coming from the dungeon. Does he have a woman down there? I don't know why it should bother me that he might tie another woman up, that he might spank her, that he might demand a title from her—Master or Sir. Of all things to be jealous and upset about, this seems the most ridiculous.

I'm suddenly filled with rage. I can almost feel my hair glow with it, as though I carry some arcane power of fury in my red hair. I feel like I could eviscerate this man with my glare alone. Who does he think he is? Fuck him. I'm going to go down there and I'm going to scream at this motherfucker. What's he going to do? Kill me? He went to far too much trouble for me for that. Right?

There's a ninety-nine percent chance that he set off a chain of events tonight that will result in me carrying his child. Is he going to risk that? My contract *did* explicitly call for heirs after all. So I know he wants kids. What's the motherfucker going to do?

I fling the door open and fly down the stairs like a banshee about to start shrieking, when I hear a voice and stop short. I'm in a bricked-in stairwell. He hasn't seen me, and I don't think he's heard me yet. I'm two steps from the bottom. If I'd taken one more step, I'm sure in my flurrying rush that the silk gown would have flashed around the edges of the brick wall, revealing my presence if he happened to glance that way.

The voice I heard wasn't Colin's, and it wasn't a woman. I hold my breath wondering if I can ease back up the stairs even as I feel compelled to stay and eavesdrop.

"P-please. Please Mr. Black. I'm sorry. I'm so sorry."

"Are you?" Colin's voice comes out darker and more terrifying than I've ever heard it. He sounds like the angel of death, and I know with striking clarity that this man isn't getting out of this basement.

"I'm on the board!" he says.

"We'll vote on a new member when you don't show up for the next meeting."

"B-but… they'll ask questions."

"Will they? Costa Rica is a dangerous place. When they finally find your body it will no doubt be mauled beyond recognition. You were known to go off on dangerous adventures alone without a guide."

I can't explain his voice right now. It's dark and terrifying but so deceptively calm. It's like he's still, peaceful inside as the storm and terror rages around him, as it emits from him to destroy everyone and everything in his path. But he remains untouched by all of it.

Colin continues. "Anyway, I think the board will be distracted at our next meeting. I plan for Mrs. Black to be carrying my child by then, and you know what that means."

I don't even know what that means, but my hand goes to my stomach protectively wondering which is worse, a boy or a girl? Which gender is safest from whatever Colin is? How could I ever protect my child from this man? I've known deep down that he's a killer, and somewhere in my head I fluffed it off as though I were watching a movie and not living my actual life—as though there were no actual consequences for the truth of what he is.

The reality sinks in now that there may be a third person to worry about. Not just me.

"I-I didn't think you knew."

"You don't think I know when people betray me? Are you trying to insult me, Jack?"

"If you knew why would you let me touch her tonight?"

This man, Jack, was at the sacrifice. He was one of the men that touched me before Colin… I squeeze my eyes shut trying to block the memories out because I know how my body will react to them, and not in any kind of appropriate way considering the even darker turn the night is taking.

"What better way to get you alone? Over a hundred people witnessed you touch Mrs. Black tonight. They know I chose everyone. Why would I let a man I intended to kill touch my wife? You think you're the only person who discounted that possibility? And you knew you were guilty of betraying me. Nobody else does. Nobody betrays me, and you knew that. You're off the radar in the middle of nowhere. Everyone is distracted by alcohol, drugs, and sex. I think it's perfect. Don't you, Mrs. Black?"

I freeze in the stairwell. Oh god. He knows I'm here. Oh god. Oh god. Oh god. I'm no longer as cavalier and brave as I was two seconds ago. I'm no longer convinced he won't just kill me, too. Can't anyone be his breeding stock? Am I more dangerous than I am valuable to him alive?

"Macy, I know you're there. I have ears like a wolf. You think you can run down those stairs, and I won't hear it?"

Why didn't the other guy hear it? But I know why. He's focused on whatever weapon Colin has. His entire life is narrowed down to the power wielded over him. I know that feeling very well, except I knew it wasn't going to end in my untimely death. Except now I'm not so sure.

"Macy. Come. Here."

I breathe deeply and take the last two steps down into the dungeon. I'm surprised by all the plastic lining the walls and the floor underneath them. It stretches so far, I'm standing on it, the plastic crinkling under my bare feet.

Of course he can't get blood on the carpet. Seriously, who carpets a dungeon? In all my innocence, even I have enough sense to see that.

In spite of this fucked-up situation, I blush as I see one of the men who touched me tonight—the first one to touch me. He's so handsome and about Colin's age. He's tied to a chair under a spotlight in the middle of the room. It's all very cinematic. Colin stands over him holding a large knife, looking crazed like a horror movie monster.

He stares at me, daring me to run from him right now.

"C-Colin..."

He raises a brow... "You really think this is the time to be on a first name basis? You know what I want from you, especially when you know you've been a very bad girl."

"M-Master," I breathe.

How the fuck can he play a sex game at a time like this? Though I think I've always known, it was never just a sex game with Colin. He genuinely and truly sees me as his property. Something clenches inside me at this. I have fantasies, yes. I'm attracted, yes. He can provide all sorts of things for me, but I want to be loved. I want to be seen. I want someone who is truly *with* me. I want someone I'm safe with.

"Please don't do this. Don't hurt him," I say.

"I think you're *really* scared I'll hurt *you*. You don't know this man. What is he to you?"

"He's a human being!" I want to add: *you psycho*, but that might be a little much, and I don't want to taunt the psycho with the knife. The psycho that is my husband and may be the father of my child.

The concept of a human being doesn't seem to register with Colin. It's as though no one but him is really real. Everyone is a means to an end. Or a prop. Or a plot point in his story. Or a scripted character in his game. There is no light of recognition that killing this man affects his world in any meaningful way.

The tears stream down my cheeks. "Please don't do this."

"If you knew what he did, you'd support me."

"Don't listen to him," Jack says. "He's a liar. He's a sociopath. Can't you see?"

"Yes, him standing over you with a giant knife was a big clue, Jack."

I can't believe I just said those words out loud, but I'm so stressed out right now. The adrenaline floods me. There's a ringing in my ears, and it's true, my biggest fear is that Colin gets a taste of blood, and I'm next. But if I can somehow stop him, then nothing really happened tonight, and he won't feel compelled to kill me too, to erase the witness because I'm not stupid enough to think he's attached enough to me to spare me if I've become a threat.

After all, he just let me go and stayed away for months while I planned my sham wedding. He likes things to follow his script. And this is not following his script.

"Please, I'm sorry," I say, echoing Jack.

"What do you have to be sorry for?" Colin asks. He seems genuinely perplexed. Didn't he just tell me I was a bad girl? Did he mean for trying to stop him? Does he not care that I saw this? My mind races trying to figure out what any of it means.

"I should have stayed in my room." I back toward the stairs.

"I didn't say you could leave. Stay right there."

I stop, trying to assess my options, trying to figure out how each plays out. "Don't kill him."

"I can't let him go now. He'll talk. He'll destroy me. Or kill me. He might even hurt you."

"I won't! You can let me go!" Jack shouts, struggling to no avail in his ropes.

"Why would he hurt me? You're the one with the knife."

"He hurt my sister." Colin's words come out a growl.

Jack's eyes widen, and it's clear that he wasn't aware of something. "I thought this was because I fucked you on the

Connors' account and voted against you on that thing at the board meeting last month..."

Colin leans down until he's an inch from his face. "My. Sister." He enunciates each word.

"She wanted it."

Colin backhands him hard enough the chair tilts back and he has to catch it before Jack falls.

"If you knew that, why the fuck would you let me touch her?" Jack says, his head tilting toward me. "Why would you let me be the *first*?"

I'm frozen to the spot. I don't know the exact details of what Jack did to Colin's sister, but I have ideas. And it doesn't exactly enshrine me as a woman Colin cares anything about. If this man is a monster, why would Colin let him touch me? I shake that thought from my head. Colin's a monster, and I've been A-okay with *him* touching me this whole time.

Jack's chair faces toward me, he's reasoning with me with his eyes, willing me to see what I can already see. Colin let this monster touch me so as soon as he takes out the trash, I'm next. Colin stands behinds Jack, his eyes also on mine. Two men trying to communicate with me non-verbally and one of them is holding a knife.

Finally, Colin speaks. He's speaking to Jack, but he's still looking at me.

"When you turn up missing and then turn up dead, do you think anyone from this club would ever think I would know what you did to my sister and still let you touch my wife? Do you think that's even a thought a normal person could imagine? I closed, every. Fucking. Loophole. Motherfucker."

And with this final pronouncement, Colin swipes the knife clean across Jack's throat. There's a horrible gurgling sound, as way more blood than I could ever imagine comes bubbling out of this throat. I'm going to be sick.

Finally I come unfrozen from the spot, I turn and run up the stairs. As soon as I'm on the main floor, I rip the robe off and fling it away from me, I hike up the silk nightgown and flee into the night across manicured rolling lawn. Rich people and their fucking manicured lawns.

Do they get a manual or something the second they come into money? *Welcome to the Rich People club. All lawns forevermore that you possess shall be no taller than an inch and a half and perfectly plush, soft, and green. Any violation of this law shall be severely frowned upon and no more white parties for you.*

I can see better running this time, in the bright full moon. It's like everything has come full circle. The first time I ran into the night away from Colin, the moon was new and dark, now it's full and all has been illuminated. And if I don't escape him this time…

I can't think about that. I just keep running. Thunder cracks in the distance, but the storm feels far away.

"MACY!" Colin roars from the house. He sounds feral, like a wild animal. It's so loud and surreal, I'm sure he'll wake the entire resort, even though the main building is off in the distance. There's a lot of privacy and trees and rolling hills between the cottage and where all the people are, where safety is.

CHAPTER TWENTY-SEVEN: COLIN

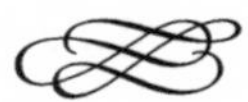

I'm covered in blood as I run after her, but I don't care. I can't let her get away with this knowledge inside her. My mind tries to intrude with thoughts about what I may have touched in the house chasing her. What trail of DNA or blood I may have left behind. What do I have to clean? Besides the body, what do I have to do to get things back on track?

I usually feel calm when I remove a problem, but right now I feel anything but calm. I don't know what I'll do when I catch her, but I have to catch her. I'm dimly aware that calling out to her in that insanely loud roar might not be the wisest thing to do. The resort is far away, it's the middle of the night, but still. I'm not following all my carefully crafted plans. I'm coloring outside the lines and it makes me feel… wrong.

It makes me feel unsure and unsafe, and I just have to get to her. She left her robe in the house, I nearly tripped over it lying in the middle of the floor as she fled out into the night. I wonder if she's ripped off the gown so she can run better. The thought of her running out here in the night naked, the thought that someone else could reach her and pin her down before me sends my adrenaline surging.

I resist the need to call her name again. The more I scream her name the more she knows how close I am. She knows I'm chasing, and I need some element of surprise. I didn't chase her the first night she ran. I don't know why. I knew there was nowhere she could go and I didn't have to get my hands dirty running her down, but this is different. She has a golden moment to escape.

And what will she say? Will she turn me in? Will she say I killed a man right in front of her? Will she tell them what I've done to her? Thunder rolls in the distance but it's getting closer, it's coming this way. I feel like the storm and I are one thing, and the more erratic I become, the faster and closer the storm moves. Could my own storm consume me? I have never once had this thought. I've always felt invincible. Before Macy.

So she's the problem. She's the one making me weak. *Eliminate the problem*. My mind screams it at me. It's the only way to put all the pieces back together again. It's the only way to stop myself from being consumed by my own storm. Everything was neat and orderly before her.

This whole time while my mind is out of control, I'm running with so much focus it's as if that chatter and panic isn't even happening. I finally reach her at the opening of a wooded area, and I tackle her to the ground. I wonder if she would have hid from me if she'd made it into the woods or if she would have kept running to the club.

I flip her over onto her back and straddle her. I'm destroying the lingerie I gave her. The silk is streaked with dirt. I destroy everything I touch.

This is why we can't have nice things, my mind taunts. And Macy is such a nice thing—far nicer than I could ever deserve.

"I'll scream. They'll hear me," she pants, her terrified gaze holding mine.

Another roll of thunder. Closer. It's closer. It's coming for me. It's coming to consume us. Maybe I won't have to do anything at all. Maybe the storm will just take us both.

"At a BDSM club? Do you think they'll come rescue you? Do you think they'll even register a scream as actual duress?"

I can see the lights from the main resort. In between the distant rumbles I almost think I hear laughter carrying on the wind. I don't know if I'm finally going completely mad—if the laughter is my own inner demons—or if we're closer to the main club than I thought. *Could* she scream? Would they hear her? Would they recognize it as true duress and not a power game some couple is playing on the grounds?

But I just glare down at her, willing her to buy into the confidence I don't feel right now. She wilts under me, and something inside me cracks open. I don't want things to be this way with her. I don't want her afraid of me. I like Weird Facts Macy, the girl who tells me the difference in fine and bone china. The one who knows arcane trivia about crown molding, which I'm sure she does.

I want her sharp mind and determination mixed with her sweetness. I want her to give herself to me, to surrender like she did earlier in the night. But that moment feels so far away from this one and impossible to reclaim now.

My gaze drifts down her body, and I notice her hand covering her belly as though she's protecting something.

It's a fragile place on the body, but my attention up until now has been on her face. My eyes go to hers and back to where her hand shields her stomach.

Her eyes widen and I'm sure mine comically mirror hers. Her face is so expressive. I can read her like one of the books in her library. The words flit across her face as I look at her. Could she already be carrying my child?

How would she know this soon? But wouldn't it be a natural thing to fear? I took her virginity tonight in the most dramatic way with no protection and no birth control. Of course she'd fear she might be pregnant.

Don't read too much into it. I can't allow myself to be clouded by this possibility, I already feel too out of control. There are already too many variables and too many things broken beyond repair.

"Please," she whispers, tears streak down her face as lightning lights up the sky. I can see now that I've gotten Jack's blood all over her, all over that perfect pure white gown. I taint everything I touch. I destroy everything I touch.

Is she afraid I'll kill her? The woman who might be carrying my child? Isn't she right to fear that when even I don't know for sure?

Is she afraid I'll rape her? After killing Jack for the same crime? I don't want to ask these questions. I can't stand to hear her say just how big of a monster she thinks I am.

I'm breathing hard as I stare down at her, trying to find the words to erase all of this. I know I don't deserve her. I could never deserve her. She'll never look at me with anything but fear.

A dark thing inside me whispers to kill her. It's too late for us. She will always look at me with fear and revulsion.

She will always try to get away from me. We can never be normal. She can't be the Mrs. Black I need to show the world, the image I want them to see. This was a stupid way to do this. I could just hire a woman to be Mrs. Black. I could find a gold digger and give her what she wants.

What's one more lie? But I wanted Macy. I wanted her. I let myself believe that we shared some desire together and that we could be somehow on the same team. Why did I let myself believe something so fucking stupid? It would be mercy to kill her now, to spare her the constant terror of my presence.

But what if she is carrying my child? She can't know this soon. That's impossible. She doesn't know. She's not pregnant. It takes more than a few hours. Even if she would become pregnant from tonight if left to nature, she's not pregnant now, in this exact moment. It's only potential. It's not real yet. It can still be undone. She can be undone. We can be undone.

I look down at her as time freezes between us, and I feel how cool it is for the first time as the winds pick up and the storm relentlessly rolls in. The thunder and lightning are coming closer together like something about to be born, and I feel the energy crackle the air. Goosebumps pop out over Macy's arms and I both want to kill her and protect her in this moment. I want to wrap her in a blanket to keep her warm. And then I want to kill her again because it feels too unsafe to feel anything so soft or kind.

A sharp, ragged breath leaves me as I say the only words that come to me. They are desperate, urgent words. They come out harsh and crazed, but I say them as our gazes lock.

"Tell me you see me. Tell me you're *with* me."

I don't know where that came from. Of all the things to say. No "let me explain", which might have sounded reasonable. No threats, which would be normal for me. *Tell me you see me. Tell me you're with me.*

What the fuck? These are impossible things to ask for, like asking Santa for world peace.

Something in her expression changes. And then a miracle happens. Somehow those stupid words have shifted things. She doesn't struggle. She doesn't scream. She doesn't pull away. She raises up with the small range of motion I've allowed her, and then her mouth is on mine.

It's not some *appease your captor* kiss. It's not a kiss of seduction. It's raw and electric. I respond to her, my hands taking her face into mine, my fingers moving through her hair as I deepen the kiss.

I shove the silk up her thigh, stroking her skin until her legs fall open for me, and a small shuddering moan escapes her. "Please," she breathes. But she's no longer begging for her life, and taking it is the farthest thing from my mind.

I struggle with my pants. This is all so fucking wrong. I'm covered in Jack's blood. She's covered in Jack's blood. There are streaks of dirt all over her, all over me, and we're about to what? Rut like a couple of animals outside?

The rain starts to fall on us as I slide inside her. "Macy," I say the word like a prayer. I don't know what just happened between us, but something has changed. And I have no idea how or why. What could have been so special about those words? They were only words. And I just killed a man. Something I remind her of with the blood we both now wear.

If she gets pregnant tonight, will it be from the big public display earlier, or this private moment between us? I drive into her wildly, like something possessed. I'm completely out of control in this moment, but she's with me. She's *with* me.

What does this mean? What do I want it to mean? I can't think. All I can do is feel her velvet softness, the sweet wetness that tells me she is absolutely with me in this moment. The whimpers and murmurs, the way she clutches at my shirt, as though just trying to hold on for the ride.

The storm swirls in full force around us. The harder I fuck her, the harder the rain comes down, the louder the thunder, the closer the lightning. It doesn't escape me that this storm could actually kill us because we're too stupid to move this indoors. But it's too late. Both of us are too close. We're too on the edge of an ending and a beginning, a death and a birth, and the hope that there's something happening now that will change everything for the better.

She shrieks into the night, but it's not for help. And even if it were, everyone has gone inside to escape the raging storm. I follow quickly behind her, letting out a long shuddering breath as I cover my body with hers, trying to protect her from the elements.

She continues to grip me as our breathing returns to normal. I pull her destroyed gown back down over her, my hand shaking. It clings to her in the rain. I zip up and then I rise and pick her up and carry her back to the house. I know she doesn't have the energy right now to run. I don't have the energy to run with her in my arms.

A lightning bolt comes down and strikes a tree not thirty feet from where we are. I hurry to get us to the safety of shelter. The odds lightning will strike again so nearby are slim, but I feel the adrenaline buzzing through me from the close call. Macy doesn't know just how close. Her head is burrowed against my neck to escape the unrelenting rain.

I'm breathing hard when I get us both inside. I strip the wet gown off her and start a fire in the fireplace. I've never been more grateful for a quick start log already in the grate. It's one that actually does quick start. A single match has the fire roaring to life. I leave her sitting in front of it, wet and shivering, trying to get warm and go get her a towel from the nearest bathroom.

I'm sure I'm cold, too, but I don't feel it. "Are you going to run from me again?"

She looks up. "N-no, Master." I think the stutter is more from cold than fear. At least that's what I tell myself.

I get down next to her, so that we're eye level. "Colin. I'm Colin to you."

We've shared an intimacy deeper than sex tonight. She's on my team now. No one has ever really been on my team before. I have staff. I have people who fear me, people who obey me, but I don't have anyone who is truly *with* me.

Only now, maybe I do. I don't understand what changed out there, and maybe I don't need to.

I can no longer see her as some piece of property. As appealing as the idea of owning Macy was, the idea of having her as a true partner, someone who has seen my worst and chooses me anyway, that's far greater. To have a confidante.

Macy's face falls a little. What the…? Does she want…? But then I understand. She thinks I'm going to become some romance hero on her. That we'll have sweet tender sex with candlelight and rose petals. That those darker fantasies she harbors and can't show anyone but me will go back to being unexpressed fantasies.

This woman. I feel the smirk edge up. "The rain didn't wash the kink off me.

But when we aren't playing, I'm Colin."

She nods. I wish I knew what she was thinking.

I turn to go to the dungeon so I can deal with Jack's body. I had a plan, and my mind goes back to the plan... leaving him in the middle of the rainforest, to be discovered or not discovered after the animals have gotten to him.

Macy's voice stops me. "So... I'm not a sacrifice anymore?"

I turn back to her. "You're just... mine." If she thinks I'm going to let her go... I'm not that man, but I don't want her to be my prisoner. "Traditionally a sacrifice dies, and you're still here."

I don't know why I felt the need to add those words at the end. If anyone is a sacrifice tonight, it's Jack. But he's a sacrifice, not to some god, but to my own fury which has been only moderately appeased. I wish I'd had more time with him. But I couldn't do all the things I wanted to do with Macy there. Jack got mercy, and it pisses me off that the piece of shit who touched my sister, who hurt her, would get such an easy death in the end.

Macy watches me, and I can practically read her thoughts again. We both know she almost died tonight. I was so close to convincing myself it would be good for her to die, a kindness somehow. But then she saw me.

I look away. What is this awful feeling eating away at my gut? Is that guilt? Fucking guilt? I didn't know I could feel guilt for anything. Is it shame? Again, not something I thought I could feel.

"I'm going to take care of the body. Once you get warmed up you should take a hot shower and go to bed. Leave the gown. I'll get rid of it. It's evidence."

She nods. “Colin? I wanted someone to see me, too.”

“I do see you, Macy.” It’s the only thing that saved her life tonight. And then I leave her because I can’t spend another minute in this uncomfortable moment with all these feelings I don’t know how to feel.

CHAPTER TWENTY-EIGHT: MACY

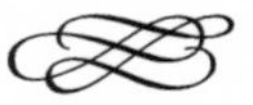

I watch him go down the stairs and I sit staring at the fire trying to process everything that's happened since I woke. I find I can't sit still. I can't stand to just sit here while he… what? Chops up a body? And with what? IS he going to chop it up?

I hear a lot of sounds I can't fully decipher coming up from the dungeon. He left the door open. I keep waiting to hear a chainsaw, but I don't. Instead I hear a strange sliding sound. It sounds heavy. When I see him again, he's pulled Jack's plastic-wrapped body on some sort of wheeled thing, like a gurney but lower to the ground. The body is strapped on and the wheels can be folded in, which I imagine they were as he dragged him up the stairs. Now that he's on a level flat plane, the wheels are out, making it easy to move the body.

"W-what if you get caught?" This feels like such a stupid thing to say. How many people has he killed? This certainly looks like he knows what he's doing.

"I won't," Colin says, sounding far more confident than I feel about this.

"Colin...?"

He looks up. "Yeah?"

"When will you be back?" The storm has settled down to just heavy rain, but I'm still worried.

"By sunrise. Get cleaned up and go back to sleep."

We both know I could escape while he's gone. He could choose to chain me up in the dungeon to prevent that, but he doesn't. He either doesn't care or is absolutely confident that what happened outside earlier changes everything somehow.

And doesn't it?

I just nod, and he leaves. I can't help going back downstairs. He's already done a lot of the cleanup. All the plastic wrap is gone, rolled up neatly and duct taped closed. Where is he disposing that? How is he disposing it? I close my eyes and take a deep breath. He's not going to share this kind of information with me. I know he knows what he's doing and deep down I know Jack isn't the first. And I know they weren't all men who did things as bad as what I think Jack may have done to his sister. Can I really be the woman who looks the other way while her husband does these terrible things?

It didn't escape me that Jack thought he was being killed for a business betrayal and not something far more personal. I go upstairs and carefully pick up the silk robe and take it to the second floor with me. I don't even look at the gown. I know it's ruined beyond repair, but the robe at least, is still perfect.

The robe still feels like "Before Macy". It's me before what happened outside. Before everything changed completely and forever. It's telling that I feel like there was still a "Before Macy" when I watched him kill Jack and ran up the stairs, and the thing that splits time for me is what happened outside. I go upstairs and lay the robe on the bed and go into the bathroom.

I stare at my reflection for a long time. I look wild. Jack's blood was all over the gown, so I know it was on me, too. But the rain washed all of that clean. And any mud that might have been on me, Colin dried off with the towel. I look and feel too clean for everything that's happened tonight.

Am I being stupid for not running? I'm no longer wearing the tracking bracelet, and Colin's distracted covering up a crime. I make excuses for myself like where would I go? Where is my passport? I have no money to travel by myself. I can't just hide out in Costa Rica, I have to go home. Is Colin not concerned I'll run? Or did he just forget he removed the bracelet?

I could turn him in and get a free trip home. I could run to the main resort, tell the truth about everything, and get to some imagined safety. But it feels like too deep a betrayal, not only of him, but of myself.

I'm not sure if I love Colin or if I can love him. It's too soon to know something like that. I'm not sure if he can love me, but I can't deny whatever thing flowed between us outside in the rain.

Tell me you see me. Tell me you're with me.

When he echoed my own thoughts of less than an hour before right back at me, I could no longer deny what I felt. It doesn't matter if it's right or wrong. He's the only man who can ever truly get me. I feel like the only woman who could ever truly get him. And so that's the way it is.

For better or worse.

BEHIND THE SCENES WITH KITTY

Hello my little Godiva chocolates with white chocolate drizzle,

If you're new to me, that might be a bit much for a reader endearment, but it is what it is. Before I get into this author's note, I do want to reassure you that there is more Macy and Colin coming, and I'll get more into that a little further into the note.

I didn't know when I started writing The Proposal that I was writing a duet. It wasn't until I got to the end, the scene at the kink club where Colin and Soren are speaking and Soren offers him something innocent that he can keep forever with conditions that I realize Macy is going to get all her dark twisted fantasies fulfilled after all.

I love the idea of Colin and Macy because they are both the exact same amount of wrong. Colin may come from the darker side of the spectrum and Macy may come from the lighter side, but they meet in the middle.

I'm also not inordinately into "virgin stories". That's not

necessarily my kink… the innocent virginal lamb meets the big bad wolf. It's just how it happened. With The Proposal, Livia isn't actually a literal virgin, but because of the set-up of the book, it ends up having that same sort of energy. And in many ways she is a virgin because she certainly has never been with three men at once. And waiting for the wedding night to consummate continues the theme and keeps the tension high.

The whole idea of virginity, while it comes with it's own issues, at its root, it's really about being initiated into a new experience either as the initiate or as the initiator. It's about a rite of passage with a defining act that moves you from one state of being into another. And I think this is why when we have two virgins getting together it doesn't have the same energy as someone experienced and a virgin because with two virgins, no one is the initiator, and we don't get that polarity. It's just two nervous people awkwardly fumbling.

Even though Livia wasn't a virgin in The Proposal, all the men being in on the situation and all of them having a lot of experience and planning to consummate with her all at once on the wedding night, sets up this initator/initated dynamic.

So since we sort of got on the virgin kick with The Proposal, the energy if not the literal thing itself, I decided to continue that pattern into The Sacrifice with Macy. I loved the idea of Macy as this woman who has such a filthy mind but just hasn't had the opportunity to test it out yet.

We've all had a point in our lives where someone who supposedly was older or wiser than us or more experienced thought they knew us better than we did or thought we didn't know what we wanted or what we liked because how can you know if you haven't done it? Sometimes we do know.

This comes up a lot with whether or not women want children as well as our sexual likes and dislikes, as though we're complete blank slates and have to try absolutely everything out first to know whether we'd be into it or not. I like that Macy is into it before she's even tried it and that Colin finds the person who isn't pretending.

All these other women he's been with are so experienced. But they aren't into it. By contrast, she's so inexperienced, but she is.

The story started to build around The Sacrifice as a metaphor, and then into an actual ritual event that ended up in many ways mirroring the opening scene where she's fantasizing.

I love the way the book opens because if you've read me, it's not hard for you to imagine that yep, this is actually what's somehow happening right now. If you'd read The Proposal first you might have tiny little twinges that something is off or doesn't logistically add up in that scene from what you already know. But for the most part you're buying it.

And then the phone rings.

I hate the "it was all a dream" plot device, but I think you'll forgive me if it's the opening scene. It's a small surprise that doesn't feel like a betrayal because we're just getting started... especially as we build toward creating a version of this very scene for the end of the book. Because if you've read me much you know I love the story mirror.

I got really blocked on this book for a long time. It took me over a year to write it, during which time I took a break to write Berserker because I was so stalled out. And part of the issue was that I realized this is two books, not one. I was so married (no pun intended, ok maybe a little bit) to the idea that this was a duet, that I didn't realize that Colin and Macy require more than one book.

This book is literally "The Sacrifice". That's what it is. It's how Macy came to be with Colin. It's their origin story. But there's more. I could have put it all in one book but it would have been an unnaturally long book with weird pacing issues.

I could have tried to cram 60,000 more words worth of fiction into 10,000 and rushed the ending. But I decided instead to just finish the duet and then write another book or novella that isn't exactly part of the duet, but continues Macy and Colin's story. I will likely link all three together. Or, I may put it into a new series revolving around The Silver Circle.

For this reason I wasn't able to have the "Livia finds out about things" scene because that's part of a much larger plot and story. I hate cliffhangers, and I don't feel I've written one. Yes there's more story and there's a subplot I didn't wrap up because I can't in this book. You'll understand when we get there.

I'm not sure when this next book is coming out, but I try to write all my books as stand alones even when part of a larger world so you aren't "tied to" a long series or a big book commitment and having to remember everything or being frustrated by cliffhangers. Did I mention I hate cliffhangers? That was one reason I was blocked so long because I hated the idea that I'd have to do another book to do this right and how do I do that without making readers feel they've been set up with a cliffhanger? The solution to me was to focus on wrapping up the main point of the book, indicated by the title, then start fresh into a new story with them.

Anyway I think that's about all the rambling I can do about this one.

Thank you so much for reading/listening to and supporting my work! Be sure to subscribe to my newsletter at Kittythomas.com to know about all the things and for a free book.

Kitty out.

ACKNOWLEDGMENTS:

Thank you to the following people for their help with THE DARK WEDDING DUET:

Charisse Lyn beta reading. Thank you for your eagle eye on this book when I needed it!

Robin Ludwig Design Inc. Cover design. Beautiful cover as always. This may be my favorite one, but I say that about every book.

Lori Jackson for teaser graphics.

And special thanks to my Silver Circle Angel Patron, Lilith Teaspirit for supporting the work.

Made in the USA
Columbia, SC
22 November 2023